COWBOYS AT COCONUTS

Coconuts Series Book 4

BETH CARTER

SOUL MATE PUBLISHING

New York

COWBOYS AT COCONUTS

Copyright©2019

BETH CARTER

Cover Design by Wren Taylor

This book is a work of fiction. The names, characters, places, and incidents are the products of the author's imagination or are used fictitiously. Any resemblance to actual events, business establishments, locales, or persons, living or dead, is entirely coincidental.

All rights reserved. No part of this publication may be reproduced, stored in a retrieval system, or transmitted in any form or by any means (electronic, mechanical, photocopying, recording, or otherwise) without the prior written permission of both the copyright owner and the publisher. The only exception is brief quotations in printed reviews.

The scanning, uploading, and distribution of this book via the Internet or via any other means without the permission of the publisher is illegal and punishable by law. Please purchase only authorized electronic editions, and do not participate in or encourage electronic piracy of copyrighted materials.

Your support of the author's rights is appreciated.

Published in the United States of America by
Soul Mate Publishing
P.O. Box 24
Macedon, New York, 14502

ISBN: 978-1-64716-035-7

ebook ISBN: 978-1-64716-023-4

www.SoulMatePublishing.com

The publisher does not have any control over and does not assume any responsibility for author or third-party websites or their content.

Books by Beth Carter

Sleeping with Elvis

~ ~ ~

Coconuts Series

Thursdays at Coconuts
Chaos at Coconuts
Babies at Coconuts
Cowboys at Coconuts

~ ~ ~

"Santa Baby" in the anthology

Sizzle in the Snow

To cowboys and city girls.

And especially to my dad, Jay Holmes,

who instilled a love for life's simple pleasures

including the history of the Ozarks.

He taught me how to skip rocks across ponds,

search for arrowheads, throw a softball, ride a bike,

sled, pitch a tent, camp, and so much more.

Thank you for enriching my novel and my life.

I love you, Dad.

Acknowledgments

To my loving husband who puts up with my laptop and random notes gracing our breakfast table on most days. Thank you, honey, for ignoring the mess and for your ongoing, tremendous support. You're better than the yummy cop! (Inside joke, people.) I love you.

As always, a huge thanks to both of my parents for their love, support, and for providing a wonderful, rewarding childhood. I couldn't have a better Mom and Dad.

Thank you to Charlie and Rosa Robbins for making dandelion wine years ago. That was my first sip of moonshine (and likely my last!) I'll never forget the taste and enjoyed writing this funny scene.

A huge thanks to my amazing Beta readers, Shirley Hales, Carol Holmes, and Amanda Brown. I appreciate your quick response, incredible feedback, and stellar proofing abilities. You're the best!

Thank you to former classmate Melody Teegardin who posted a photo of a crazy hillbilly swimming pool. I knew I'd find a use for it someday and saved the picture for inspiration. I used it for a unique scene in this novel.

To classmate Dale Fisher Milan and several Facebook friends who helped me with the pool lingo since I'm probably the world's worst pool player.

As always, a huge thanks to Beth's Book Babes, my reader group, for your enduring support, motivation, and loyalty. You're the reason I keep writing! Many of you have stuck with me for years and encouraged the initial book, THURSDAYS AT COCONUTS, to become a series. Thanks to you, it'll be a six-book series!

A huge thanks to Soul Mate Publishing's senior editor and founder, Debby Gilbert, who believed in me from the start. You'll never know how much that meant.

Also, a special thanks to my cover artist, Wren Taylor, who always creates stunning artwork.

Finally, a big shout out to the entire writing community. Writing is a solitary endeavor. Author friends and readers make it an exciting process.

Chapter 1

Cheri's stomach plummeted when she spotted her almost-forgotten, happily ignored engagement ring shoved to the back of her armoire. She had pushed the engagement to the furthest recesses of her mind hoping the ring would somehow disappear, yet here sat the enormous diamond, almost taunting her. *Why didn't I end my engagement when I had the chance?* Mouth dry, she felt extreme guilt as she considered her betrayal to her workaholic fiancé, her parents, and her girlfriends.

Sebastian didn't have any idea the magnificent five-carat diamond he had purchased over a year ago sat cloistered inside a Tiffany's box deep within Cheri's jewelry armoire rather than on her ring finger. But Cheri didn't have remorse. She didn't feel anything except freedom. No tears. No second thoughts. *He's such a workhorse he won't even miss me. I've wasted over a year of my life worrying about this. I'll explain it to Sebastian when he returns from Dubai.*

Considering what would likely be an unspeakable shock to her fiancé and her parents, Cheri rubbed her temples. *God, they'll be furious.* A tiny twinge of guilt tugged at her but the weight that had been lifted far outweighed her brooding thoughts.

At the sight of the flashy ring, Cheri swallowed hard. With her Nana's death, her move to Branson, and her busy catering business, she had tried to forget about the ring—and Sebastian—which was no small feat. Their families knew one another. They were often in the society pages. It was messy. It was embarrassing. It was o-v-e-r.

Sometimes she wondered why she had accepted the ring to begin with. She and Sebastian had never had chemistry, nor an iota of the romance she witnessed in most couples. Staring at the dazzling diamond, she realized she had accepted his ring because it was expected by their peers and especially by their high-society, uber wealthy parents. Cheri's parents thought Sebastian was marriage material. His parents thought she'd make the perfect wife because she had an impeccable pedigree. Constantly worried about keeping the broken engagement from her parents—especially her mother—Cheri didn't want to add stress while they were jet-setting in Europe, plus Sebastian was an architect who had built and renovated several of her dad's corporate buildings. The last thing she wanted was to confuse business with her love life.

Still, she didn't love him. And, honestly, the fact that she rarely received any contact from him—a quick text once a month, if that—made Cheri think he felt the same. *Maybe I'm doing us both a favor. Maybe he'll be relieved too.*

Timidly she placed the ring on her manicured finger for the first time in over a year. The diamond was flawless. The enormous ring overpowered her small hands. She yanked it off, placed it back inside the signature blue Tiffany's box, and shoved it to the back of her armoire.

The engagement was a secret, dreadful noose around her neck, albeit tucked safely in her closet in Manhattan. Ending the relationship should be simple, but with the family expectations, society pages, paparazzi, it was all too much right now. Plus, she couldn't bring herself to tell her former—although he didn't know it—fiancé via email or the phone. She had to end the relationship properly—in person. The fact that he had been working in the Middle East for over a year made an in-person breakup an impossibility. Unable to resist Googling him months ago, she read an online article which included a photo of Sebastian standing on a concrete slab wearing a spotless hardhat while overseeing construction sites for two new modern hotels. Naturally, he'd never get his own hands dirty. *At least I don't have to worry about running into him on Fifth Avenue or at a Starbucks. And he'd never find me at Coconuts.* She laughed to herself. *I hope he meets someone else.* She blew her bangs out of her eyes. *I've got to finish packing.*

Zipping her leopard print bags closed, Cheri plunked them near the front door and called the doorman to remind him to arrange a car service.

She grimaced while pacing across the plush, white carpet. *I wish I hadn't seen the damn ring. At least Suzy, Alex, and Hope will never know. They'd be upset I hid it from them and wonder why I went on those ridiculous Internet dates. Hell, I wonder why I went on them. I guess I was trying to make darn sure. Or feel normal. Or both.*

Crystal City awaits. Cheri took a few deep cleansing breaths in an effort to calm herself. Glancing at her gold Rolex, she said to no one, "Coconuts, here I come."

Chapter 2

The next morning while her driver made his way through heavy traffic to LaGuardia, Cheri answered emails to her head chef at Fifth Avenue Catering who was already complaining about Julio "getting into his business." Rolling her eyes, Cheri knew she never should have hired Julio, her former childhood chef. After reassuring Chef Liam O'Leary that he was the one in charge and pleading with him to work it out with Julio chef to chef, she emailed menu options to three celebrity clients, turned off her phone, and tried to relax. But images of her fiery redheaded Irish chef in his almost daily kilt and chef's jacket filled her mind. *I can't lose him. He may have a temper, but he's the best. He knows our clients' likes and dislikes, allergies, plus the staff actually like him. What have I done?*

~ ~ ~

After the plane landed, Cheri pushed negative thoughts out of her mind, gathered her leopard print carry-on from the overhead compartment, and accidentally banged a man in the head with her bag.

"I'm sorry. Are you okay?" She opened her shiny black designer bag and reached for her hot-pink wallet. "I can pay for the doctor."

Waving his hand in the air, the man said, "I'm fine. I don't need no doctor, pretty lady, but if you want to have a drink later, I wouldn't mind that—"

Gulping, Cheri said, "Thanks, but my, er, husband is waiting."

The man glanced at her ring finger. "I don't see no ring."

With her brightest smile, she said, "We don't need material things. We decided not to buy rings. They're expensive."

Guffawing way too loudly, the portly guy said, "From the looks of your fancy clothes and shoes, you like material things just fine." He shifted in his seat and unlocked the tight seatbelt across his bulging belly.

Cheri decided to ignore the rude comment. Stiffening in the aisle, she half turned toward him and said, "Again, I'm sorry. Have a nice evening."

"Let me walk you out. Help you with your bags."

This guy is a real piece of work. "No need. My husband will help." Willing the passenger in front of her to move forward she locked eyes with the flight attendant who was merrily talking to another stewardess and oblivious to her plight.

Determined to outpace the annoying passenger, Cheri edged closer and closer toward the door, bumping a couple of passengers with her bag. After several "sorrys," she sprinted through the airport like a long-distance runner. After stepping past a female security guard perched in a chair, she spotted them. *The enemy. Paparazzi. Dammit. How could they have known?*

Chapter 3

Wearing a hat, Cheri did her best to blend in with other passengers as she made her way toward the baggage carousel. But it was no use. Three paparazzi with giant camera lenses pointed toward her face took photo after photo, seemingly hundreds within seconds. Placing her arm over her eyes as protection against the blinding flashes, she glanced from side to side but Gage, her limo driver, was nowhere to be found. *He's never late. He sure picked the wrong day. Crap.*

Onlookers inside the Crystal City Airport gawked at the unusual Midwestern chaotic scene and began taking their own photos, likely assuming she was someone important. Cheri noticed a TSA guy even snuck a photo with his Smartphone.

As Cheri covered her face, she overheard several comments. "Who is she?" "Must be famous." "Is this a Branson entertainer?" and "Maybe I can sell this to *The National Enquirer*."

Desperate to escape the maddening intrusion, Cheri spotted a tall, lanky, hat-wearing cowboy who appeared nonplussed by the commotion. Gathering every ounce of courage she'd ever had, she rushed across the room to where he stood, grinned her brightest smile, and flung both arms around his neck. Nuzzling his neck, she whispered, "Kiss me. I'll explain later."

"Yes, ma'am." The handsome cowboy's eyes crinkled as he wrapped an arm around her waist and leaned in for a deep, passionate kiss, which she returned. *Twice.*

With his arm still around the socialite, the cowboy leaned in, lips still close. "Are they chasin' you?"

Weak and confused by her body's reaction to the cowboy's kiss, Cheri stumbled.

"Whoa. You okay?"

His arms still on her shoulders, Cheri attempted to gather herself. *I don't know this guy. I can't tell him the truth.* Straightening her sunglasses, she asked, "Who? Me? Why would anyone chase me? I'm a simple girl."

The rugged stranger eyed her. "You don't look like a simple girl to me but whatever you say, Ma'am."

"Ma'am? Are you serious?"

Chuckling, he said, "I was raised to respect women and my elders. You're definitely not the latter."

He held up his hand as the flashes nearly blinded both of them. "Looks to me like they're houndin' *you*." Chuckling, he said, "They're definitely not here for me."

"Mistaken identity, I guess. You know what they say, "everyone has a twin somewhere."

"I've never heard that." He kept his arm across her shoulder.

Glancing toward the photographers, Cheri decided to hug the cowboy again. She lingered and stared into his sapphire eyes, hoping the paparazzi would leave. It worked. Lowering her voice, she said, "They're gone."

"Nice job throwin' them off the scent." He winked. "Does that mean we should stop huggin' and kissin'?"

She grinned. "Um, yeah. Thanks, cowboy."

He tipped his hat. "I should be thankin' you. I haven't been kissed like that in a long time." Tipping his hat, he reached for a small, worn bag and headed toward the parking lot. "See ya around, I hope."

Studying his lean, taut backside a little too closely, Cheri stepped across the room to get her luggage. *That was interesting. Wait until Alex, Suzy, and Hope hear about this.*

Chapter 4

As she gathered her bags still rotating on the carousel, Cheri realized her phone was turned off from the plane ride. After powering it on, her cell vibrated with several texts from Gage, her limo driver. She frowned at the multiple messages, assuming something was wrong, and sighed when she read:

Sorry, Cheri, I'm sick. I've had bronchitis for three days. I'm in bed and on antibiotics. I'll be well in a day or two but I'm not taking any chances. Trust me, you don't want this. You've probably landed by now. Can you take a cab home? I'll make it up to you. Again, my apologies. Gage

Great. Cheri piled her smaller bag on top of the largest piece of luggage while slinging her huge purse over her shoulder. Bags fell to either side as she struggled toward the front door. Peering from side to side, she didn't see a cab. Not. One. *I've never heard of an airport without taxi drivers.*

Steadying her luggage, she reached into her purse for her cell phone. As she studied the desolate parking lot sprinkled with cars, trucks, and a few passengers coming and going, she scrolled through her contact list to find her friend Alex's phone number.

Before she pressed the button to call Alex, the slow rumble of an engine caught her attention. Glancing up, she spotted the cowboy who'd just made her knees weak. He sat behind the wheel of an ancient light-blue pickup. Slowing to a stop in front of her, the cowboy reached across and hand-rolled the window down. Grinning, he asked, "Lost?"

"What gave me away?"

Shrugging, the cowboy said, "I don't think you're from around here."

"What makes you think that?"

He gestured with his hand. "Does anyone else look like you? Most people are pretty casual in the Ozarks."

Cheri stared at her four-inch hot-pink stiletto heels, short, white denim skirt, and silky, pink blouse. A gold cuff bracelet circled her tiny wrist. Diamond hoop earrings completed her outfit. She chuckled. "This *is* my casual outfit."

"Gotcha." He chuckled. "I'm not complainin'. Need a ride?"

Quickly weighing her options, she said, "My dri—" Stopping herself before she showed her rich hand, she added, "The guy who was going to pick me up is sick." She thought the cowboy's face fell a bit.

He recovered. "If your boyfriend is sick, I'd be happy to take you home, if he doesn't mind."

"He's not my boyfriend. He's my li—" She caught herself again. "He's just a friend."

The cowboy reached over and opened the passenger door. "Hop in. I'll get your luggage."

Chapter 5

Cheri hesitated half a second before deciding the country guy was surely trustworthy. Climbing inside, she noticed he easily—and gently—tossed her luggage into the back of the truck and couldn't help but notice as his muscles flexed.

"Nice bags. Sorry, my truck's a little dirty." He threw a rope and chain in the back and wiped the seat off with his hand. "It's a workin' truck."

Cheri immediately loved his honesty and hard work ethic. She could only imagine what he'd think if he knew she normally arrived in a shiny stretch limo. *I don't think I can ever tell him I'm a Van Buren.*

As he climbed back inside the truck, she studied his rough, calloused hands. He leaned close and turned on a country music station. Her previous boyfriends always had delicate hands almost as soft as hers. The cowboy's ruggedness was as sexy as hell. Stomach fluttering, she surprised herself. *Why am I getting excited about a total stranger? And a country one at that?*

Tamping down her excitement, she waved her hand. "Don't worry about the truck. And thank you. I appreciate the ride."

The cowboy extended his hand. "The name's Cole, by the way."

Cheri smiled. "Nice to meet you. I'm Cheri."

Placing his hand over his eyes, he chuckled. "Those are some white teeth. You could do toothpaste commercials."

"Too white? I could tell my dentist to tone down the—" She paused. "Never mind. Thanks." Cheri studied his face. He had a day's worth of light-brown stubble, clear aquamarine eyes, short wavy dirty-blond hair, and slight sideburns. His playful smile could melt a car bumper. He smelled like the outdoors—clean and fresh.

Glancing at his tight jeans and well-worn, brown cowboy boots, Cheri realized she had never, ever been in a truck with a cowboy. And she liked it. Her mind raced. "It's nice of you to do this. I could have called a car service or Uber."

He cackled. "I don't know if we have Uber, but we definitely don't have car services here. Heck, we barely have any taxis." Cole straightened a stack of mail on the seat. "Sorry about the mess and muddy tires. We've had a lot of rain lately."

"No worries. I hadn't even noticed. This is much better than standing on the curb, trust me." Cheri rummaged in her purse to see if she had any ones left for a tip. *Should I tip the guy or would that insult him?* She quickly decided against it.

Cole broke the awkward silence. "Hungry?"

"A little. The flight was bumpy so they didn't serve food—" She caught herself again, realizing he likely didn't fly first class. "How far is it to the restaurant?"

"Fifteen minutes. Most everything is fifteen minutes in any given direction."

She liked the easy nature of this cowboy. Cheri retrieved her phone to text her mom that she had landed but decided against it. There would be far too many questions about Gage, and if she mentioned Cole, a total stranger who was giving her a ride, her mother might charter a plane from Europe.

"Welcome to Crystal City, by the way. Where are you from?" Cole said.

"New York City."

He nodded and gave her a once over. "Figures. Never been there but my guess is you fit right in."

Unsure of what to make of his comment, she settled for, "Thanks."

"Guess we always want what we can't have. I always wanted to be rich." He slapped the steering wheel. "That ain't never gonna happen."

Cheri gulped. If this were a cue or a sign, she wasn't taking it. She didn't want to scare him off. "There's always the lottery."

He nodded. "Yeah, I 'spose." He shrugged. "I have everything I need. It may not be fancy but it's mine. What about you? Do you have a house in New York?"

"An apartment. It's small. Tasteful but not very big."

"I couldn't live in an apartment. I need land. Space. Big skies and acres of green grass."

She turned toward him. "It sounds peaceful. I'd love to see it."

"Peaceful is the right word. You can hear the crickets and birds. Heck, you can almost hear the flies. Owls hoot at night and coyotes howl. I couldn't live anywhere else."

Her eyes widened. "Coyotes?"

Cole laughed. "They won't bother you. We have to watch our newborn calves and other small animals. We also have snakes and the occasional mountain lion. Black bears are moving into the area, too."

She nodded and shivered. "Wild animals? That sounds dangerous."

"Not any crazier than New York, I imagine."

"Touché."

Glancing at her Rolex, she adjusted the setting to Central Standard Time, and slid the watch face underneath her wrist, far out of his sight. Her belly growled. "Guess I am hungry."

"You don't look like you eat much. We can fatten you up here in Missouri. "Do you like Cracker Barrel?"

"Cracker what?"

"You'll love it. Let's go."

Chapter 6

As they reached the restaurant, Cheri noticed the parking lot was packed. "Doesn't anyone drive cars in this town?" she asked, amazed at the number of pickups.

Cole laughed. "We do like our trucks. They come in handy."

"For what?" she asked.

"Haulin' stuff."

Cheri wondered what he hauled but didn't ask. Once inside, she marveled at the old-time artifacts and photos on the walls. Cole explained how some of the antiques were used on farms for pulling horses and buggies, branding cattle, or churning butter. Cheri felt as though she had landed on another planet in another time. A much earlier, simpler time.

She studied the menu and frowned. "Everything is fried."

"They probably have salad but a little fried food won't kill you." He rubbed his belly. "It's delicious."

"But not exactly healthy."

Cole shrugged and ordered fried chicken, mashed potatoes, gravy, green beans, and corn bread.

Cheri's eyes widened. "That's over a day's worth of calories."

"Who's counting?"

She giggled, decided to splurge, and ordered a vegetable plate with pinto beans, a baked sweet potato, green salad, and cornbread. "Look, they have a kale salad."

"Kale?" He winked. "Don't they line salad bars with that stuff?"

Cheri giggled. "This one has too many calories anyway."

As she continued to study the menu, a waitress appeared to take their orders. With her pen poised over a pad, she glanced at Cheri. "You get a fourth item."

Cheri studied the menu. "What do you recommend?"

The waitress pointed toward the sides. "Okra."

"What's that?" Cheri asked.

Cole leaned across the table. "You've never heard of okra? What do you eat in New York?"

"Not okra."

"Then what?" he asked.

"Pasta, salads, seafood, sushi, and vegetarian dishes."

"Try the okra," Cole said.

Her brows knitted. "It's fried, isn't it?"

"Just try it."

As they waited for the food, Cheri's curiosity got the best of her. "What do you do in the country? I mean for entertainment."

His eyes twinkled. "Let's see. Besides farmin', calvin', and hayin'?" He ticked off his fingers. "There's county fairs, hoedowns, pool parties, go-cart rides, ATV races, truck pulls, muddin', fishin', skippin' rocks, findin' arrowheads, drive-in movies, and picnics." Cole chuckled. "It's a pretty hectic lifestyle."

Grinning, Cheri said, "I don't have any idea what some of that is but it sounds fun."

He raised his eyebrows. "I figured a big city girl would think country life was boring."

"Nope. I can't say I've done any of it, but I'd like to try."

After the heaping plates arrived, they ate mostly in silence. After devouring every bite, Cheri patted her round belly. "I can't believe I ate that much. Look at my stomach. It's sticking out. This is all your fault."

Cole winked. "You need some meat on your bones. You could gain fifteen pounds and still be the skinniest girl in town."

While Cole insisting on paying the bill, Cheri browsed in the country chic gift shop. Standing behind a tower of costume jewelry, she stole a glance in his direction and downright stared as he sauntered toward the restroom. Unable to take her eyes off his slow, sexy gait, her eyes fell to his tight jeans and even tighter white tee. Tingling like a hormonal teen, she spotted a cowboy boot candle, rushed to the cashier to buy it, and hid the candle in her purse.

When Cole returned, they stepped into the fresh air. Cheri commented on the row of rocking chairs on the elongated sidewalk and noticed a giant game of checkers on a wooden table.

Grinning, Cole said, "It's pretty excitin' around these parts." Strolling toward his truck, Cole opened her door. Cheri smiled to herself. She wasn't used to having men open doors for her unless it was her limo driver and decided she could get used to the cowboy's sweet manners.

After he swung her door open wide, she thanked him and grabbed the handle above her seat. Climbing in, she leaned back against the headrest. "I've been in Crystal City several times but realize I haven't been in this part of town." Glancing out the window, she said, "Missouri is so different from New York."

Cole nodded. "Never been to the Big Apple but I can only imagine."

Thoughts of Manhattan flooded her mind. On many occasions, she had jumped into one of the thousands of yellow cabs to avoid paparazzi. Horns honked incessantly, cars drove literally inches apart along several lanes deep on roads that snaked Manhattan. Millions of pedestrians flooded the sidewalks below towering skyscrapers and provocative billboards. She loved the city but hated being chased by eager photographers. She would often close her eyes behind dark, shaded oversized sunglasses as cameras clicked and flashes practically blinded her. Photographers were always trying to get a glimpse of a Van Buren for some rag magazine. Occasionally, she'd smile at the camera or wave if she knew the photographer since he or she would make a tidy sum on the photo. But, usually, she wasn't in the mood for their antics.

Normally only racing to Coconuts to meet her friends or to the grocery store in Branson to buy food for new recipes, Cheri realized she had never taken the time to revel in the lush green, peaceful scenery. She marveled at the fact there wasn't one photographer. There were no yellow honking cabs and no one rushed to an unknown destination on city sidewalks. There were no smells of salty pretzels or hotdogs from street vendors. Just Cole and Cheri riding along in his truck. In fact, it was so quiet that if she heard a sound, she jumped. She wondered if she could get used to this unobtrusive, Midwestern life full time. *I doubt it. I think I'd be bored. What do they call Missouri? A flyover state. So why am I enjoying it so much?*

"Someone's in deep thought over there," Cole said.

"I'm just relishing the peacefulness. It's extremely quiet here."

"I suppose I take it for granted. Ready for some fun?" Cole asked.

"Like what?" Cheri asked.

"I think you need an official Missouri welcome from my friends. What do you say?"

She glanced at her watch. It was almost eight—actually nine to her—since she was still on East Coast time but she was wide-awake now. "Sure."

Chapter 7

Cole reached for the radio dial. "Chicken Fried" by the Zac Brown Band blared. "Too loud?"

She shook her head. "I like it."

He kept beat by tapping the steering wheel.

"Nice song. I don't hear a lot of country music in New York."

"That's all I listen to." As Cole approached the town square, Cheri noticed pickups were parked side by side like dominoes. The storefronts were dark. She threw her head back and laughed.

"What's so funny?" Cole asked.

"Like I said before, doesn't anyone drive a car in this town?"

"Never noticed that before. Let's get out."

Eyebrows raised, Cheri asked, "And do what? Shop?"

Cole howled. "Stores around here are closed. We roll up the sidewalks at six. How late are shops and restaurants open in New York?"

"Seriously? Something's always open 24/7."

"Guess they don't have cows to milk or roosters crowing at five in the morning."

"No, thank goodness." Cheri winked, opened her door, and stepped down. Her stiletto caught on the running board. Reaching for the handle, she yelped as she sprawled into an embarrassingly ungraceful position, half splayed on the ground with one foot still partially in the truck.

In seconds, Cole ran over to help her. Once he steadied her, he asked, "Are you okay?"

Cheri brushed off her skirt and inspected the four-inch heel on her designer shoes. "I'm fine. Looks like I need to buy some new heels."

"Nice entrance. If you wanted to get noticed, you just did." He steadied her. "Sure you're alright?"

"I'm fine except for my ego." Cheri noticed his biceps bulged when he reached for her.

Keeping his arm around her, he said, "You took quite a fall."

Cheri felt her cheeks redden. "I know how to make a grand entrance, don't I?"

His eyes twinkled. "That you do."

Cheri dusted off her clothes as another, tall, lanky cowboy with long, dark hair appeared. "I see Cole has a new friend."

She stared from Cole to the stranger. Patting the man on his back, Cole asked, "How's it goin', Wyatt?"

Grinning a sideways smile, the man extended his hand. "Wyatt."

She took his hand. "I'm Cheri."

"You're not from around here, are you?" Wyatt asked.

"How can you tell?"

He laughed. "You don't have a Midwestern drawl. Or a southern drawl, for that matter." He shrugged. "Don't matter none. Want a beer? I've got a cooler in my truck."

Cole's sky-blue eyes twinkled. "A beer sounds good to me."

As the threesome popped the beer tabs, they stood on the quiet square and stared at the stars until a loud motorcycle roared. Turning in the direction of the sound as the motorcyclist ripped around the square, Cheri watched as the biker drove in a big circle twice, kicked up gravel, and eventually braked barely a foot away from their feet.

Frowning, Cheri turned in the biker's direction. The driver wore a black leather fringe jacket over a low-cut white tee, black boots, and skin-tight jeans with holes at the knees. As she put the kickstand down, the woman glared at the trio.

Removing her helmet with a flourish, jet-black, flowing hair cascaded past her shoulders. She was well built and tan like everyone else. Cheri noticed the woman had an air about her that commanded attention. All eyes were on the gorgeous motorcyclist. *And it's obvious she enjoys having all eyes on her.* Cheri sized her up quickly. Her height was average but her confidence made her seem six feet tall.

Without saying a word, the woman strapped her helmet to the handlebars and bent over, giving the guys full view of her nice, round bottom. She stayed in the same position for far too long and eventually retrieved a small leather purse from the back compartment.

Amused, Cheri watched as the woman eyed her, opened a compact, and applied lipstick. Red lipstick just like Cheri's. The motorcycle mama took her time applying the lipstick to her full lips. The men never took their eyes off her. Cheri wasn't sure the guys even swallowed or blinked.

When she finally spun around to face them, Cheri noticed a small tattoo beneath her short tank top. It peeked out the bottom of her exposed belly but Cheri couldn't determine what it was. The woman glanced briefly in Cheri's direction, and then swiveled toward Wyatt and Cole.

"Hiya, boys. Who's the pretty lady?"

Cheri hated being dismissed as though she weren't there. She extended her hand. "Hi. I'm Cheri."

"Cheri? Quaint." The woman stared at Cheri from her head to her toes but didn't offer her own name. Instead, she asked, "Do you like to play pool, *Cheri*?"

Cheri glanced at Cole who was regarding the motorcyclist suspiciously. "I've only played pool twice, but sure, I'm game."

The woman smiled a wicked smile. "Good. Let's see what you've got."

Cole lowered his voice and leaned toward Cheri. "This might not be the best idea. Are you sure you want to do this?"

The woman raised her eyebrows. "Are you with Wyatt or Cole?"

Cheri decided to keep her guessing. She had a guy vying for her attention, plus a female enemy, all in the matter of a couple of hours. Challenging the woman's black, flashing eyes, she said, "Let's go." She loved a challenge and would enjoy nothing more than beating this gutsy woman at a game of pool. She peered at Cole and Wyatt. "Are you coming?"

"I wouldn't miss this," Cole said.

"Wish I could but I've got a hundred dairy cows to milk. Rain check." Wyatt tipped his black cowboy hat toward Cheri. "Nice meeting you. Maybe I'll see you around."

"Same here." She grinned at the second cowboy. "I hope so." *What's wrong with me? I just met these people. My wealthy mother would think I've lost it.*

The woman in black put both hands on her hips. "When you're done fawning over the newcomer, hop in your truck. Last one to Lefty's is a rotten egg." She unhooked her helmet from her handlebars and slowly strapped it on while never taking her eyes off Cheri.

As he opened her door, Cole said, "Looks like someone feels threatened."

Once they were inside Cole's truck, Cheri said, "I take it you used to date Harley girl."

"What gives you that idea?"

"Women know these things."

He snorted. "Calling it dating might be a stretch. I suppose you could say we dated. Off and on. More off. Everything was all about her. Jade's got a fiery temper. I got sick of it."

"Is that her name? Quaint."

Cole howled. "You're quick. You'll be able to handle Jade."

"I hope so." Fidgeting in her seat, Cheri continued, "So that's all the info I'm going to get about you two?"

"Pretty much." He winked. "I hope you're a good pool player. She's a shark."

"Oh. Not really." Cheri's face fell, wondering what she had gotten herself into.

As he steadied the stack of mail between them, Cole's shirt brushed against Cheri's bare leg. She shivered.

"Are you cold?"

"No." Peering at Cole sideways, she studied his chiseled profile. His sandy blond hair touched the back of his collar and was short on the top and sides. It wasn't a mullet by a long shot but rather a sexy, longer hairstyle. Just enough to hold on to. *What's wrong with me? I just met the guy.*

Chapter 8

Leaning against the headrest, Cheri tried to relax. *I need to calm myself before the pool match.* As she freshened her lipstick, she asked, "How far away is Lefty's?"

Before Cole could answer, she examined her clothes. Glad she had worn hot-pink stilettos, even if the heel was a bit wobbly after half-falling, she pulled her silky pink blouse out of her white denim skirt, unbuttoned the bottom buttons, and tied the shirt at her waist.

Hearing the commotion, Cole glanced at her and raised his eyebrows. "What are you doing?"

Cheri grinned and said, "Getting ready."

"For what?"

"Battle." Cheri flashed a knowing smile. He winked before turning back to the road. "Ready for battle, huh? With Jade? That's my kind of girl." Stammering, he said, "Not that you're my girl or anything. We barely met. Darn it. You know what I mean."

Relaxing, she said, "I can think of worse things than being your girl."

It was nearly dark but she thought she noticed a pink hue creep up his neck. They listened in silence to "Shotgun Rider" by Tim McGraw. Cole hummed along.

"You have a nice voice."

He gave her an 'aw shucks' look.

"All I've heard is country music since arriving today."

"Is there another kind?" Cole laughed.

Giggling, she said, "New York City isn't exactly the country music capital."

"Nah, that would be Nashville or even Branson. Country music tells a story. That's why I like it," he said.

She listened to the words of the song. "You're right. The song does tell a story."

He laughed. "Usually about exes, dogs, drinkin', and trucks."

Studying her handsome driver, she asked, "Do you like being a cowboy?"

Cole placed his tan hat between the seats. "Do you assume I'm a cowboy because I wear a hat?"

"Don't forget the boots and oval belt buckle," Cheri said.

"You must be a detective." He drove onto a tiny gravel driveway. "We're here."

Peeking out the window, she laughed. "More pickups." Tensing as she heard the familiar roar of the motorcycle, she bristled as Jade parked next to them, did her sultry routine with the helmet, and tousled her hair as if she were in a commercial with a wind machine.

Cheri studied the tiny building made from what looked like aluminum on all sides, even the roof. The bar appeared to be about the size of two large RVs. A dark green awning welcomed them with faded letters declaring LEFTY'S except the "S" was missing. The minute they stepped inside, thick smoke enveloped her. Wrinkling her nose, Cheri waved her hands in front of her face. "I'm not used to this. They banned smoking in New York years ago."

Cole waved his hat in the air to clear a path. "I hate it too. That's one reason I don't come here often. But the drinks are good, plus I enjoy pool and dancing."

"Dancing?" Cheri brightened. "I'm intrigued. Let's get a drink. I have a feeling I'm going to need it."

"What do you like? Wine or a fancy drink?" Cole asked.

"Surprise me." She set her purse down, glanced at the blue jean, boot-wearing patrons, and women in short skirts. Several men wore cowboy hats and everyone chatted excitedly, most while holding a beer. Cheri glanced up as Cole stepped toward her with a pink martini and a foamy beer.

"I figured a classy lady like you would like Cosmopolitans." Cole held it toward her.

Cheri noticed Jade rolling her eyes. "I'll take the beer."

Chuckling, Cole said, "That was for me but you can have it." He handed her both drinks. "Be right back with one more beer."

Jade stared at Cheri. "Pink suits you." As she strode past, she elbowed Cheri so hard some of the Budweiser spilled onto her expensive shoes. "Damn it. These are new."

Jade grabbed the beer out of her hand. "So sorry. Thanks for this." She raised her glass. "Here's to the victor."

Cheri cupped her hands around her mouth and shouted over the music. "Cole told me your name is Jade. Quaint."

Jade spun around, took a step toward Cheri, and narrowed her eyes.

Cheri glared back, determined not to show weakness, even though her heart hammered. *God. What a witch—and what a way to meet Cole and his friends. Or girlfriend. Whoever she is. I wish I had played pool more than a handful of times. Jade will probably defeat me in record time.*

Likely assuming she had already unnerved Cheri, Jade sashayed toward one of two pool tables, nodded toward a couple of handsome country boys, and grabbed a cue stick. Cheri watched as she rubbed chalk on the end for far too long, obviously enjoying the guys' attention.

Cole returned with his own beer, stood by Cheri, and caught Jade's eye.

She continued bending over the table and straddling the cue stick as if she were seducing Cole in front of everyone.

Cheri grimaced inwardly. *Why do I care? I don't even know this guy.*

Jade locked her dark, flashing eyes on Cheri's. "Hey, New York, you gonna play pool or are you just here to let Cole buy your drinks?"

Stiffening, she said, "As I said earlier, my name's Cheri." She stepped toward the pool table.

"Yeah, New York. Got it." Jade eyed the pool table. "Let me know when you're ready."

Cheri stared at the pool cues and wished she had had a few pool lessons but it was too late now. She had a newfound energy and purpose to beat this woman at her own game. Since Jade had taken her beer, Cheri took a big swig of the Cosmo. Then another. Eventually, she set it behind her purse in the corner and stalled as she rubbed chalk on the end of the cue.

Jade leaned against the table with her arms crossed. "Are you going to massage that thing until it's a Kobe beef or are we going to play?"

Cheri muttered, "I'm surprised you know what Kobe beef is." Raising her voice, she said, "Rack them up."

Jade bent over yet again giving every bar patron a good, long look at her backside before she placed the balls inside the triangle.

"Visitors first. That is, I assume you're visiting. I'm sure you'd never move to this dink town, New York."

"You never know." Cheri decided to let her wonder.

"Whatever." Jade stared at Cheri from head to toe. "Too bad there aren't any pink balls to match your stupid, girly pink shoes."

Chapter 9

Cheri let the second snide remark pass. She had to concentrate. Angling around the table on all sides, she studied the balls in comparison to the six pockets. Once she decided on the easiest shot, she placed the pool stick between her thumb and index finger and aimed at a green striped ball. Surprisingly, it went in.

Jade shrugged. "Beginner's luck."

"Nice shot," Cole added.

Cheri then took aim at an orange striped ball. It also landed in a side pocket.

"That's nothin'," Jade said.

Cole winked at Cheri. "Nice."

She leaned across the table and poised the cue between her finger and thumb. Moving around several times before she made contact with the ball, she took her time. She wanted to win this game. She had to win. Eventually taking aim at a yellow striped ball, it bounced against a solid red ball and missed going into the corner pocket.

"That all you got, New York?" Jade bent down and took aim at a red ball, then a solid blue one. One after another, she put four balls away, first in the right pocket, then the left, and side pockets. The balls zigzagged across the worn green table. She examined the table with great scrutiny, before each successful, catlike move.

Cheri frowned as she guzzled the rest of her Cosmo.

"When you're finished with that girly drink, it's your turn, New York."

This time, Cheri took her time rechalking her cue stick. She stepped around the table, heard a couple of guys mumbling about the fancy "newcomer," and forced herself to concentrate. Leaning across the table, she focused on the striped balls and surprised herself by easily putting two more into corner pockets.

Jade raised her eyebrows. "Not bad, New York."

Cole stood a foot away with one hand in his pocket. Grinning, he said, "I gotta admit. Two beautiful women playing pool is a huge turn on."

Cheri didn't dare make eye contact with the cowboy. She had to concentrate. After surveying the table trying to figure out her next move and realizing she and Jade each had the same number of balls left, she knew she had a real chance of winning. That is, as long as she didn't accidentally put the eight ball in. Maybe it really didn't matter if she won. She had already proven she could play and possibly earned Jade's respect, though doubtful. Relaxing slightly, she studied the table. She'd have to knock one ball against the side and hope it would bounce back hard enough to knock a second ball into the pocket. She walked around the table twice studying every angle.

Her strategy worked. In fact, she easily knocked two more striped balls into corner pockets. She only had one ball left. Cheri glanced at a seething Jade.

"Think you're something don't you, New York? Playing pool in stupid high heels."

"And winning." Cheri stared at Jade defiantly.

"Be nice, Jade," Cole said as he polished off his beer.

Jade leaned against her pool cue. "Do you know anything about New York, Cole?"

"She's very nice as far as I can tell," Cole said.

"I'm right here," Cheri said as she studied the remaining balls. Glancing up just in time to see Jade roll her eyes, Cheri decided beating this woman at her own game would be the best revenge. Pacing back and forth beside the table, she walked around it once more before determining the best angle. Noticing a small crowd had gathered, she did her best to block out everything but the game. She only had one ball left and Jade had two. She leaned over, guided her pool cue between her fingers to take her last shot, as someone heavy fell on top of her.

"Hey, watch it." But it was too late. Her stick hit the black 8 ball. As if in slow motion, she winced as the ball eventually landed in the side pocket.

A drunken guy reached for the table to steady himself. "Sorry." He tipped his big, black Stetson. "Hope I didn't mess up your game, pretty lady."

Chapter 10

Leaning against the pool table, Cheri couldn't believe her bad luck. *What are the odds that a drunk guy would fall on me and ruin my game?* Her stomach sank as Jade cheered.

Cackling, Jade pumped both fists in the air. "Game's over. I win."

Frowning, Cheri said, "That guy fell on me. It wasn't my fault." She crossed her arms. "I was ahead."

Cole put his arm around her shoulders and led her away. "Let's get a table. You're a really good player. You proved yourself. Don't worry about it." He had already picked up her purse as he attempted to lead Cheri away.

"But I would have won. I know I would have," she protested.

"We could all see that. Especially Jade. She's not used to women standing up to her. She was ready to spit nails. Want another drink or do you need to go home?"

"Are you kidding? I need a victory drink," Cheri said.

"Another Cosmo?" Cole asked.

Cheri glanced at Jade who was on her second foamy beer. "I'll take a beer."

"You surprise me every minute. Be right back." Cole returned with two beers and straddled a seat across from her. "Tell me more about you."

Cheri didn't know how much to tell him. Cole seemed like a nice guy. A real gentleman. But he was a cowboy. He'd never understand her jet-setting life, her parents' wealth, nor her massive trust fund. She never divulged much, especially to strangers. Usually, she was recognized everywhere but enjoyed the fact that people in these small towns didn't know who she was and wanted to keep it that way.

It was hard to believe that last week she was at an invitation-only, red-carpet event for A-list celebrities in New York, and now she was at a remote, smoke-filled honky-tonk playing pool with a Harley-riding, tattooed woman and having drinks with a cowboy. *And I love it. What a difference a day makes.*

"Earth to New York," Cole teased.

"Sorry. Just thinking about everything."

"Want to dance? I know you've had a long day. If you're too tired, that's okay." The band played "Aw Naw" by Chris Young and Cole swayed to the music.

Cheri sipped her beer. "I'm not the greatest dancer."

"You also said that about pool, so I don't believe you."

She shrugged.

"Want to warm up with a slow dance?" Cole asked.

Cheri raised her eyebrows. "I'm afraid Harley girl will hit me with a pool cue."

As the band played "Heartache on the Dance Floor" by Jon Pardi, Cole said, "Let's try it." Reaching for Cheri's hand, he led her onto the tiny, wooden dance floor. Already crowded with cowboys and cute girls, they made their way to the middle of the partiers. As Cole swayed his hips, Cheri could see he had rhythm and did her best not to stare. *Country boys are so different from the sleek businessmen in New York. And completely different from my former fiancé who would never step foot in this dusty bar.*

Pulling her close, Cole's shirt brushed against her skin while his big belt buckle pressed against her belly. Cheri allowed him to hold her close and wondered what his story was. *It doesn't matter. I like him. A lot. Who am I?*

Wondering what her parents would think, Cole whispered in her ear, "Relax. You think too much. Have some fun."

He turned his megawatt smile toward Cheri. She could only imagine how many hearts Cole had melted with that Crest grin.

Before the song was half over, she felt a tap on her shoulder. "My turn," Jade said.

Cheri and Cole stopped dancing. Cheri felt surprisingly annoyed as she observed Jade clasp her hands behind Cole's neck. Thankfully, the slower song changed to "Redneck Woman" by Gretchen Wilson. Breaking away, Cole thrust his hips to the music. Cheri giggled at the title and couldn't take her eyes off him. Likewise, Cole seemed entranced by Cheri, which obviously annoyed Jade who sneered at her. Before the song was over, he left Jade standing in the middle of the dance floor and joined Cheri.

Yelling something that Cheri couldn't hear over the music, she nodded anyway. Once the song ended, Cole said, "Let's get out of here." They left without saying goodbye to Jade. With every step, Cheri could feel Jade's eyes boring into her back. When they reached the dark parking lot, she shivered since the temperature had dropped. Cole removed a denim jacket from his truck and placed it around Cheri's shoulders.

"You're such a gentleman. Thanks."

"Guess I was raised right." He glanced at his watch. "I'm sure you're tired from travelin'. Besides, I have an early day tomorrow. Where are you stayin'?"

"Branson. Sorry. I know it's not around the corner."

Cole didn't flinch. "That's fine."

He gripped the wheel with his rough hands. It took him three tries to start the engine but the truck finally chugged to life.

"Where to in Branson?"

"To my late grandmother's house on Bee Creek Road." Out of nowhere, Cheri began to cry. Between sniffles, she said, "She's only been gone a year. This is awkward."

Cole reached into his pocket and retrieved a handkerchief. He extended it to Cheri. "Tell me about her. I understand. I was close to my granny, too."

As he drove, they spent the next thirty minutes discussing their late grandmothers. Cheri had never had soulful talks with Sebastian nor with her parents, for that matter.

When she finished, she let out a long breath. "Thanks for listening. I guess I haven't allowed myself to grieve."

"You're human. It's normal. She sounds like she was a wonderful woman. I see where you get your good genes."

If he only knew about my absent parents who are always in Europe. My mom who wears silky pajamas that would make Hugh Hefner jealous, and my father, the wheeler-dealer workaholic. "Thanks."

Chapter 11

As she studied Cole's profile, Cheri's mind did double time. *Never in my wildest dreams did I think I'd be in an archaic truck with a very handsome, sweet cowboy. If my New York friends and family could see me now.* She chuckled.

"What's so funny?"

"I'm just thinking about how different life is here than in Manhattan. In New York, there's an energy unlike anywhere you've ever seen—not that there wasn't plenty of energy on that dance floor."

He grinned. "Tell me about Manhattan."

Smoothing her skirt, she said, "There are millions of people on any given day, swarms of honking yellow cabs, and an eclectic mix of people, every nationality imaginable. It's an amazing city. I love New York, but the paparazzi drove me—"

"Paparazzi? Are you famous?" Cole visibly stiffened.

Dammit. I didn't want him to know. Not so soon at least. "No, I'm not famous if you mean a movie star or anything. Nothing like that." Forcing a laugh, she said, "Not even a reality television celebrity." She hated to lie but said, "It was probably a case of mistaken identity at the airport."

He glanced at her sideways. "Somethin' tells me you're not tellin' me the full story." Eyes back on the road, he said, "But I won't pry. You'll tell me when you tell me."

Cheri noticed Cole absentmindedly chewed on his bottom lip, likely trying to figure out who she really is. *He'll hate me if he finds out I'm filthy rich.*

~ ~ ~

As they continued south on Highway 65, Cole asked, "Are we gettin' close?"

"Yep. In about five miles, take the exit to Bee Creek Road."

"Will do." Cole took the exit and rounded a bend. A picturesque, winding road and wooded lots greeted them.

"Nice neighborhood. I've never been back here."

"I hadn't visited since I was a kid." She sighed. "I wish I had come sooner when Nana was still alive."

"We all have regrets."

As they approached a gray house with a sloping drive and overgrown landscaping, Cheri pointed. "We're here." A bright red door welcomed them.

Cole threw the truck into park and walked around to open her door.

"Always a gentleman, aren't you?"

Shrugging, he said, "I like treatin' a lady like a lady. Thanks for dancin' with me. Great pool game, by the way."

"This was a fun welcome to Crystal City. Much more interesting than if my lim—" Scolding herself for almost giving away her secret again, she wondered how this evening would end.

"I can't stay long. I've got to bale hay in the mornin' if it doesn't rain."

Relieved to hear Cole say he had to leave, since Cheri wasn't about to jump into bed with the cowboy. He was a looker but they just met. Besides, she had a lot of baggage to clear up in New York.

Feeling unsure about how to end the evening, she asked, "Want a nightcap or some coffee?"

Cole shook his head. "No, thanks. I have a long drive. I wouldn't mind seein' the house, though."

"Sure. Come in."

Chapter 12

Cole followed Cheri toward the expansive kitchen. Spreading her arms wide, she asked, "Isn't it beautiful? I oversaw some remodeling from afar." Giggling, she said, "Nana had a heck of a time figuring out how to send me pictures from her Smartphone. Apparently, some kind soul at a Starbucks helped her."

She ran her hand along the smooth brown and tan speckled granite. Six bar stools were covered in a rustic, southwestern fabric surrounding the curved countertop. On the opposite end was a large stone wall separating the kitchen from the living room.

Cole touched the plush material of the bar stools as he scanned the kitchen and spotless stainless-steel appliances. He raised his eyebrows. "This is really nice." Staring at his boots, he said, "It's a thousand times nicer than my house."

"I'm sure you have a lovely home." Stepping behind a rectangular wooden dining table, Cheri threw the curtains back. Pointing, she said, "The house overlooks Crystal Lake. Too bad it's dark outside. The view is stunning."

Cole nodded. "Yes, ma'am. I'm sure it's pretty."

"Ma'am? You've got to stop saying that."

He tipped his hat. "Habit. We're probably close to the same age. I hope I get to see the view in the daylight sometime soon."

Cheri folded her arms and grinned. "We'll see, cowboy. We'll see."

"Playing hard to get, New York?" Cole leaned forward and kissed her on the cheek, very close to her mouth. She wanted to turn her head and kiss him full on the mouth but held back. She liked this country boy but it was too soon for a relationship. Besides, she was officially still in one, plus the small matter that they were from two different worlds. They would never, ever work as a couple. Still, he was intriguing.

"I almost forgot. Wait a minute." Cheri fished in her purse until she found the cowboy boot candle she had bought at Cracker Barrel. She handed the candle to Cole. "A little something for your trouble."

"When did you buy this?" Holding the boot in the air, he said, "I'm not used to gettin' gifts. Thanks. I've got just the spot above my kitchen sink." Kissing the top of her head, Cole said, "I thought New Yorkers were supposed to be rude. You're as sweet as a peach."

Cheri's eyes twinkled. "I've never been called a peach before."

He winked, crossed the living room and kitchen, and stepped toward the front door. As he reached for the handle, Cole said, "I'm gonna be busy all week hayin.' As long as it doesn't rain, hayin' could go into the weekend. Hopefully, we can go out soon, though." Pausing, he added, "If you want to."

Cheri didn't know anything about hay and rain but knew she wanted to see him again. "No problem about the hay. I need to get settled here and take care of some business." She didn't want him to know she was the proud owner of Fifth Avenue Catering in New York City. "I'd like to see you again. Thanks again for a great evening. It was fun."

"Nite, pool shark." Grinning, he patted the gift. "Thanks again for the boot candle." As he stepped onto the porch, he said, "Hold on. Your luggage is in my truck." Cole insisted on bringing the heavy bags inside, placed them in the hallway and left.

She watched him drive away through the peephole. *What is it about this cowboy?* Searching the pantry, she found a bottle of Smart water and retreated to the guest bedroom. Cheri still didn't have the heart to sleep in her late grandmother's bed. After flinging her purse on the bed, she opened a bag containing toiletry items. *I should have brought more casual clothes. I'll have to shop at Target in Branson and pick out some type of cowgirl attire.*

Grinning to herself like a schoolgirl, she stared at her phone and noticed a text from Gage: *Sorry again about the airport. How did you get home?*

Glad he couldn't see her silly smile, she texted: *I'm resourceful. I hope you feel better. Take a few days off. Nite.*

No one else had called. Cheri groaned when she realized she and Cole didn't exchange numbers. *I didn't give Cole my number nor my last name. And I don't have his. It never would have worked anyway. We're too different. He might as well live on another planet.*

Suddenly exhausted, Cheri stretched and yawned. *I need to see my girlfriends.* As she powered on her laptop, her favorite Internet dating site popped up. Internet dating had become a bad habit—almost an addiction—since becoming unhappy with Sebastian, plus it was an easy way to feel normal in her not-so-normal socialite world.

Having difficulty breaking her ridiculous online behavior, Cheri scanned a few new images, but her thoughts turned immediately to Cole. *Why do I feel guilty trolling this site now? I barely know the cowboy. It never bothered me when I was with Sebastian.* Before she turned the computer off, she noticed the image of a handsome man with dark hair and prominent eyebrows. He had a nice smile and wore a pinstripe suit but Cheri immediately imagined him wearing a cowboy hat. *How is this country guy already under my skin?* With a heavy sigh, she vowed to stop her Internet dating compulsion once and for all. Probably. Maybe. *At least until I hear from a certain cowboy . . .*

Chapter 13

Best friends Alex and Hope gathered at Coconuts, their favorite Happy Hour oasis. Seated at their favorite high-top table, Alex studied the growing crowd, practically shouting above the racket. "It seems like the whole town has discovered Coconuts." Groaning, she said, "I hate it. It's good for business, but hell, I miss the old days and regulars." Crawling with singles, couples, golfers, college students, and suit-wearing conference goers, nearly every table and bar stool were taken.

Nodding, Hope said, "I guess they like the relaxed island theme too. Have you noticed everyone who comes here seems so, I don't know, routine. Ever wonder if their lives are as crazy as ours."

"They should make movies about our lives." Alex giggled as she sipped her chardonnay. "I'm so ready for boring and normalcy. I've forgotten what it is."

Plunking a lime in her margarita, Hope said, "Actually, my life is a study in boredom."

"Silly girl." Glancing around the crowd, Alex denied a patron their third bar stool. Grabbing it, she said, "Taken." She turned to Hope. "Where's Suzy Q?"

As if on cue, Suzy appeared. Clutching the table in an obvious attempt to steady herself, she placed a hand over her mouth. "Damn morning sickness."

"Actually, it's late afternoon," Alex said.

"Okay, damn all-day sickness." Suzy eased herself onto a bar stool. "I feel like a queasy green Martian. I can't shake the nausea."

Wrinkling her nose, Hope said, "That sounds dreadful."

"Yuck." Alex winced. "Sorry, Suzy Q. Can your doctor give you something for nausea?"

Reaching into her purse, Suzy unwrapped a piece of ginger candy. "This helps a little. The doctor told me to put dry saltine crackers by my bed and eat them before my feet touch the ground every morning, but it doesn't help much. The nurse also suggested popsicles." Sighing, she said, "They don't work either."

Shaking her head, Alex said, "Make that reason 101 why I'm not having kids." Brightening, she said, "The good news is you don't even look pregnant." Patting her best friend's belly, she said, "It's as if you had a big burrito for lunch."

"*Alex,*" Hope said.

"What?" Shrugging, she said, "That's a compliment."

Absentmindedly rubbing her belly, Suzy chuckled. "Thanks, I think. With twins, it's only a matter of time before I'm bigger than this table."

"Better you than me." Hooting, Alex said, "Can you imagine me with a baby, and twins at that? Nada. No way in hell. I like my single life too much."

Suzy tapped her watch and raised her eyebrows. "You do have a biological clock, you know, honey. No pressure but it's ticking while you're trying to figure out your relationship with the cop. Do you think you'll ever want kids?"

Alex sat silent, staring into her wineglass.

Hope raised her hand. "I can answer that. I have plenty of kids at school. I don't want any of my own."

Mouth open, Suzy swiveled toward Hope. "That shocks me. You're so caring. You treat that student, Britney, like she's your own daughter."

Hope shrugged. "Brit's close enough to my own kid for me. I can't manage caring for an animal right now. I'm always at school." She laughed. "Or at Coconuts with you guys. A man would be nice but . . . kids? Nope."

Alex leaned forward. "Hey, is this about Hope or about me?"

"It's *always* about you, Alex." Suzy winked at Hope.

Alex made a pretend-hurt face. "Very funny. As to your kid question, some days I notice every baby in another mother's arms. Other days when they're screaming out of control, I'm eternally grateful I don't have one. And—" She paused. "—there's the uncomfortable situation with little Joey, so I honestly don't know if I'd want to add to the mix. That is, if the cop and I work out." Tapping her almost-empty wineglass, she said, "But I do know I need another drink." Waving, she got Gus's attention.

The tank top, flip-flop-wearing server appeared, all smiles as always. "Evening, ladies. Refills?"

"Something new. Surprise me." Alex gave Gus her best come-hither look.

Hope rolled her eyes. "Oh, to be like you, Alex." Fluffing her frizzy hair, she grinned. "One more margarita for me."

"You know what I'm having. Something boring and non-alcoholic." Suzy fiddled with her purse strap.

Alex eyed Suzy over her wineglass. "That sucks. Add that to the top of my list why I never want kids."

Shaking her head, Suzy said, "It's only temporary and my doctor said I could have a glass of wine on occasion."

"In that case," Alex yelled at Gus, "bring Suzy a merlot."

"Thanks but I don't want any alcohol. I can do without it for nine months. I might be considered high risk due to my age."

Alex frowned. "You are almost forty."

Hope and Suzy turned toward Alex and said in unison, "So are you."

"Ouch." Alex sipped her fresh chardonnay. "Forty is the new twenty, right? We need to plan a big bash when we turn forty, ladies."

While waiting for their cocktails, Hope regaled them with stories about her latest students and had everyone in stitches about boyfriend drama and the horror of teenage zits. Making air quotes, she continued, "And totally unfair pop quizzes."

Alex shuddered. "I loved high school but I don't miss pop quizzes whatsoever."

"Nor the boyfriend drama," Hope added. "I tell the girls it'll pass but does it ever? I mean, what's a boyfriend?"

Suzy patted her arm. "You'll meet someone."

"Unless I meet them at my house, school, or Coconuts, I'm doomed. I never go anywhere."

Alex glanced around the darkened bar. "You never know who'll walk in that door."

Gus placed drinks on the table. Winking at Alex, he said, "Thought I'd surprise you with a Cosmo. Tonight you seem like a Cosmo girl." He set a Shirley Temple in front of Suzy, gave Hope a margarita, and disappeared behind the bar.

"Why didn't I think of a non-alcoholic cocktail? This is better than hot tea." Suzy examined the drink. "At least it's festive." Reaching inside her purse, she said, "Maybe a Tums will settle my tummy."

"You poor thing." Alex sipped the pink martini and called after Gus's back. "This is good. I might switch from chardonnay on occasion." She took another drink. "Nah. It's too sweet. I'm sweet enough. I can't stay late, girls. Early bank meeting tomorrow." Swirling the wine stem, she said, "As soon as I finish this, I'm outta here."

"Same here. I have a mountain of paperwork for some transfer students," Hope said. "I wonder what the New Yorker is up to."

Alex snorted. "Cheri? She's probably hanging out with celebrities."

Chapter 14

Racing to work the following morning, Alex cursed herself for never allowing even five minutes for delays. Sitting in traffic at what had to be the longest light in Crystal City, she muttered under her breath. *I hate starting the week out like this.*

Once inside the bank, she did an internal fist pump when she noticed her boss, the bank president, and the executive vice presidents, were behind closed doors. Slinking into her corner office, she sat her purse down, flipped the light on, and raced upstairs to grab a cup of coffee.

When she returned, her least favorite person—sans her boyfriend's ex, Nikki, was as perky and busty as ever. "Morning, boss," Hannah said.

Alex settled behind her desk. "Morning."

"What's on tap this fine Monday?" Hannah asked.

"Are you always this cheerful in the morning?" Alex didn't bother to meet her intern's eyes as she flipped through her old-school weekly calendar in an effort to plan her week.

The bank had barely opened, lenders were seated behind their desks, and tellers filled their cash drawers. Hearing Paula, the New Accounts rep, welcome a customer, Alex glanced up to see the first early bird customer of the day. Nearly spewing her coffee, her eyes widened when she realized it was her boyfriend's inconsiderate, rude cop brother. "Why the fresh hell is that jerk in here?"

"Who?" Hannah followed Alex's gaze.

Alex watched his every move. "That's Sean Montgomery. Sean Asshole Montgomery."

"*Sean?*" Hannah's perk had disappeared.

Alex noticed a pinkish red hue had crept up Hannah's chest while she focused on the lobby. Her intern's voice came out weak and garbled with an unconvincing, "Sean who?"

Studying her intern, Alex's mind skittered to the time she was almost positive Hannah dared to enter her haven, Coconuts, with a man no less. That man had looked strikingly like Sean. Happy Hour patrons and the server kept getting in her way, plus the bar was dark, so Alex wasn't one hundred percent certain her intern was with Tony's cop brother, but her stomach recoiled at the thought. To make matters worse, whoever Hannah's date was had had the audacity to send a drink to Alex. Shuddering in an attempt to erase the memory, she said, "Surely you've heard me discuss Tony's brother."

Chewing on her bottom lip, Hannah said, "I don't think so."

Alex eyed her intern who had transformed into Dolly Parton during her last vacation. "Stay away from him. You don't want any part of that shit show. Besides, he's married."

Her eyes got as big as doughnuts. "He is?"

"Yep. In fact, that horrible specimen of a man is married to Tony's ex, Nikki. Don't get me started on that bitch. She screwed around with Sean while married to Tony. Now his poor kid, Joey, is his freaking nephew. The kid is understandably confused, Tony remains in a funk over the situation, and Joey won't have anything to do with me." Alex leaned forward while keeping an eye on Sean. "Trust me. You don't want any part of that shit show. He's bad news and—"

"Well, well. The two prettiest ladies are in the same room and right here at Show-Me Bank. Who'd athunk it?" Leaning against the door jamb to Alex's office, he challenged her with his eyes, while simultaneously staring Hannah up and down like a hungry wolf.

"We're busy." Alex turned toward her computer and tapped on the keyboard.

He laughed. "It might help if you turned it on."

Hannah giggled; Sean winked at her.

Alex caught their interaction and stood, maintaining her best authoritative pose. Squaring her shoulders, she took a step toward him. "If you'll excuse me, we have a board presentation to prepare."

"Sounds fascinating as hell." Sean scoffed. "And hello to you too." Patting the doorframe, he said, "Is this any way to treat a new customer?"

Hannah avoided eye contact but muttered, "Thanks for your business."

"Seems like you could teach your boss a thing or two about customer service." Pausing, Sean said, "I assume she's your boss since she's behind the desk and you're not."

With a clenched jaw, Alex said, "I'm Hannah's boss. Now, if you'll excuse us."

Beaming, Hannah stood and extended her hand. "I'm the bank president's daughter. Hannah. Hannah Hooban."

Alex observed the exchange and noticed Sean held her hand for far too long, the corners of his mouth twitching the entire time. *They're playing me. I know it.*

"How about a bank tour, Han-nah." He drew out her name as he focused on her recent twin peaks.

Hannah jumped up, sending her breasts bouncing. Alex was surprised they didn't give her intern a black eye in the process. "Okay with you, boss? He, Sean—Lt. Montgomery—is a new customer, after all."

Alex smirked. "How do you know his rank?"

Adjusting her tight, plunging black sweater, Hannah shrugged. "Wild guess. He looks like a lieutenant, plus you said he was your boyfriend's brother. With my master's degree mind, I practically have a photographic memory."

"Is that so? A photographic memory is part of the curriculum, huh? Splendid. That'll come in handy when I make my report to the board." Alex waved them off. "Go. Give him a tour. Be back in fifteen minutes."

Chapter 15

After checking in at the front desk, Suzy settled into a chair at her OB/GYN's office. Glancing at a young woman who looked like she was providing housing for a watermelon or two, Suzy observed the tattooed, very pregnant girl. *She's so different from me.* The young mother-to-be wore earbuds, high-top sneakers with red laces, and torn-on-purpose jeans. Peering at her own mom-like brown wedge heels and knit tan sheath dress, Suzy chuckled as she made notes in her leather wedding planner. *What a generational difference. I could be her mother. Geeze. But moms are moms. We're all excited and nervous about our little bundles . . .*

"Excuse me," a young, pregnant mother pushing an enormous stroller addressed Suzy. "Is this seat taken or are you waiting for someone?"

Confused, Suzy said, "Uh, no. I'm here for my prenatal appointment." She paused and rubbed her pregnant belly.

A pink hue crept across the young mother's cheeks. "Sorry. I thought you were the grand—" She pushed the stroller toward another empty seat. "Never mind."

Suzy waved her hand in the air. "No problem. I am a new grandma—a *young* grandma," she clarified. "Plus, I'm going to be a mom. Again. My son is grown." Suzy wondered why she was telling her life story to this pimply faced, pregnant woman.

The young woman's eyebrows shot up. "Oh. Congratulations."

Across the room, a baby wailed with a high-pitched

squeal that could shatter glass. Flinching, Suzy said, "I hope I'm ready for this times two."

Why doesn't my husband have to deal with this? Crossing her arms, Suzy felt shame. *Why do I care what anyone thinks? I'm going to love these babies. Besides, I'm not old. I'm not even forty. Everyone here is ridiculously young.*

Studying the youthful women in the waiting room, for a nanosecond Suzy considered getting a weird piercing or a tattoo. *No, I'm going to be myself, a successful wedding planner who has a grown son and a new granddaughter.*

The nurse called Suzanne Jacobs. Channeling the confidence of a strutting show dog, Suzy stepped through the door to the patient rooms.

After an examination, Dr. Camejo gave her prenatal vitamins and declared her high risk due to her age and having twins. Putting her head in her hands, Suzy bawled. "I want healthy babies. What can I do?"

Assuring Suzy she'd be fine and that he'd take every precaution and order the proper prenatal testing, Dr. Camejo mentioned he had delivered hundreds of babies and added many of the moms were well into their forties. "A few were even fifty," he said. Smiling, he pointed to a wall filled with photos of newborns swaddled in blankets or sporting bows on their bald heads.

"Did you deliver all of those newborns?" Suzy eyed the adorable photos with thank-yous and notes of appreciation inscribed on many pictures.

Nodding, he smiled. "Every single one—and mostly in the middle of the night." Laughing, the middle-aged, kind doctor asked, "Do you have any questions?"

Unable to form coherent thoughts after hearing "high risk," Suzy shook her head. Dr. Camejo gave her a genuine smile, shook her hand, and told her not to worry. Standing beside her in a long white coat, he patted her on the shoulder.

"Call or email anytime you have questions." Suzy forced a smile as the paper-thin sheet crinkled when she shifted on the table.

After she dressed, Dr. Camejo stood on the other side of the door. As he walked her toward the exit, he grinned. "Please don't worry. Follow my instructions, take your prenatal vitamins, eat well, get plenty of rest, and this will be a breeze."

Nodding, Suzy thanked him, paid, and crossed the parking lot in a blur as if she were trudging through a blizzard. After she climbed into her SUV, she could only think about were those two scary words: *High risk. Ken will be on full alert if I tell him. He'll probably never let me out of his sight.*

Deciding to get her mind off the visit, Suzy pulled into a drive-thru and ordered the biggest chocolate shake she had ever seen. After slurping half while sitting in her car, she had brain freeze. As she scrolled through her Weddings by Suzanne Facebook page to get her mind on something—anything—else, her stomach churned. Feeling bile rise in her throat, she opened the car door and vomited in the parking lot. *I was never sick with Jon. This is not going to be an easy pregnancy.*

Chapter 16

Before school began, Hope watched students as they parked their mostly shabby cars with bad paint jobs or bald tires in the Hilltop High School lot. Several kids chatted on the sidewalk or beside their cars. By their body language, Hope could tell the girls were flirting with the boys and vice versa. She grinned. *I love my job.*

A few minutes before first hour, students ran inside the building, heavy backpacks bouncing and sneakers squeaking on the freshly waxed floors. Scrolling through her appointment list, Hope noticed, as usual, she had appointments with either star students academically or at-risk students. There was rarely anything in between. Realizing she had an hour before her first appointment, she reached for the phone, but a knock on her door made her jump. Glancing up, she was surprised to see Willow, the art teacher.

"Morning," Hope said.

"It's the best morning ever, an absolutely perfect morning, in fact." Willow spoke much faster than usual, sounding like a giddy schoolgirl.

Cocking her head, Hope said, "Someone's in a good mood."

Willow waved a piece of paper in the air. "I have good reason to be."

Eyes settling on the piece of paper, Hope asked, "What's that?"

"Just a marriage certificate." Doing an uncharacteristic twirl, Willow punctuated her glee with a fist pump. Other than her many bangle bracelets clanging together, there was an uncomfortable beat of silence. "Mac and I went to Eureka Springs and got married over the weekend. We even went on a ghost hunt. I love the paranormal. Mac doesn't believe in ghosts but puts up with it." Flicking the paper, she said, "Any-hoo! Can you believe it?" Willow waved her miniscule diamond and matching silver band in front of Hope's face.

Hope's eyebrows shot up and stayed there. Clapping her hand over her mouth, she gawked at the document dangling from Willow's hand. After an uncomfortable silence, she found words. "Talk to me like I'm a second grader. You did *what?*" Running her fingers through her unruly hair, she blew out her breath. "How could you?"

Willow huffed. "What do you mean? I thought you were my friend. I thought you'd be excited for me—for us." Turning on her heel, she stormed out of Hope's office.

Rolling her chair over a dingy plastic mat, Hope yelled, "Come back." She ran to the door before Willow was out of sight. "Please come back. Let me explain."

Hesitating in the hallway, Willow took her sweet time before sitting in a hard chair across from Hope's desk. "I'm all ears about why you think this is a bad thing. I don't know why you aren't happy for Mac and me."

Hope sat in her ratty office chair, wondering where to begin. "Did you forget about the newspaper article a few months ago featuring the woman in a nursing home? The one who makes macramé plant hangers for the residents?" Hope threw her hands up in the air. "I knew I should have taken Larry to Nashville the minute I read about Montana's being alive. This is all my fault."

Willow's voice broke. "I thought you were more than my Hilltop colleague, Hope. I thought you were my friend." Her eyes welled with tears. "Honestly, I don't expect a wedding shower or anything, but a genuine smile would be nice. I've never been married before. Mac and I are so hap—"

"He's still married to Montana." Crossing the room, Hope forced herself to embrace Willow in a stiff, awkward hug. "I'm sorry, but he is."

Willow wept on Hope's shoulder. "Mac and I are in love. Why are you ruining this for us?" She sniffled. "He doesn't remember being called Larry. He doesn't remember a Montana. Period. End of story."

After Willow wiped her nose, Hope put both hands on Willow's shoulders. "It's not the end of the story. Don't you remember I told you I thought the woman in the photo a few months ago was the same woman who raised me? Both she and Larry were thought killed in a tragic train crash. If that's her in the Nashville nursing home, she's married to Larry." Pacing, Hope said, "I never thought you two would move this fast."

The art teacher glared at Hope. "Mac doesn't remember her. He says his real name is Mac. I believe him." Willow's face hardened. "Maybe you're wrong. Did you ever consider that? We all supposedly have doppelgangers."

Hope's pulse skyrocketed. *I think I'd know who raised me. Mac's damn name is Larry. He and Montana were married. They adopted and raised me. I screwed everything up by not insisting we go immediately to see her when I saw that article. My adopted father not only doesn't remember me, his wife, nor his name now, he's also a freaking polygamist.*

"Earth to Hope," Willow said.

Hope glanced out the window as latecomers ran into the building. Weighing her words as lockers clanged in the hallway, she reached for the document. "Let me see that."

Hope examined the page, noting the date, time, and signature by two witnesses she didn't recognize. Suddenly wishing she knew when her adopted parents, Larry and Montana, had gotten married. She couldn't remember the day but it must have been over forty years ago. They had never been lovey-dovey, nor sentimental about anniversaries. She wasn't sure if she was a baby or toddler when they adopted her. Making a mental note to ask her biological dad, Paul, if he knew when they married, she stalled. *What does the date even matter? This union isn't legal.*

Both women turned toward an insistent knock on the door.

"Miss Truman, sorry to interrupt but will you let me know when you can chat about stuff." Hope's favorite student, Britney, stared at her dirty tennis shoes. "I need help getting my GPA up, so I can try to get those college scholarships we talked about. You know my mom and I can't afford—"

Willow turned to Hope. "We'll finish this discussion later." Glancing at the clock on the wall, she said, "I'm off to my art class. Miss Truman's all yours, Britney."

"Um, congratulations, I guess," Hope muttered. Reaching for her desk, she felt wobbly.

"Are you okay, Miss Truman?" Britney asked.

"I'm fine." Hope made herself switch gears and put on her counseling hat. "Now about your grade point average. Which classes do you need help with?" Opening her top drawer, she said, "I have a list of tutors for every subject. They'll help you get your grades up, Brit."

Wriggling into a chair, Britney said, "Does tutoring cost anything because you know I don't have—"

"It won't cost a dime. Seniors tutor students for free. They receive extra credit and other perks. Don't worry." Hope glanced at the list of students broken down by subject matter. "Which class do you need help with?"

Britney sighed. "Math, English, history, and science." Shrugging, the student grinned. "Apparently the only thing I'm good at is art."

Hope chuckled. "You're very good at that. I see that gorgeous peacock you painted on the back of Willow's van every day." Scanning the list of names, she said, "You're going to be a busy girl. Better clear four afternoons after school to study each subject."

"I will, Miss Truman. I promise. You know how much I need the scholarships."

"I'll research art scholarships as well, but you'll still need to get your GPA up to even be considered into college."

Britney's shoulders slumped. "Even a community college?"

"Yes. You can do it, Brit. I know you can. What's your GPA now?"

Frowning, Britney said, "I think it's 2.1. Maybe 2.0."

"You're a bright girl. I'm sure with training, you can get that up, maybe to a 3.0 or higher."

Britney's eyes bulged. "I'm not that smart."

"Yes, you are." Hope noticed a new zit had formed on the tip of Britney's nose, which she wasn't about to point out. The poor kid couldn't catch a break, even when it came to her complexion.

The instant Hope gave the students' phone numbers to Britney for the respective subjects, she made a beeline to find the janitor. *I've got to talk Larry-Mac into going to Nashville pronto before the entire school and community find out he's married. Again.*

Chapter 17

After another heated phone conversation with her main chef at Fifth Avenue Catering in New York City, Cheri wished she hadn't Skyped with Chef O'Leary. Trying to maintain a nondescript demeanor as she stared at his twisted, red face, she knew she had to let her hot-tempered Irish chef get his frustration about Julio off his chest.

I knew I shouldn't have hired Julio, my childhood chef, to work at Fifth Avenue Catering. Both chefs have dominant personalities and totally different styles. After Julio had surprised her with a trip to Paris to see her mom last spring and then confided he was dead broke, she didn't have the heart to turn him down when he asked for a job. After all, she had grown up practically drooling over the guy while a tween atop a chair in her family's kitchen.

Talking nonstop and so fast she could barely make out the words, she feared Chef O'Leary would have a heart attack. Attempting to portray calm, Cheri said, "Give it time. I'm sure you two will work it out."

"Time. Time? This is *my* kitchen." His voice rose. "You and I had the perfect partnership, Miss Cheri. Why did you hire another chef? I don't understand." Sneering, he said, "Julio struts around like he's the boss. He acts like he owns the place. The kitchen is my domain, not his."

Projecting more experience than she felt at age thirty, Cheri said, "Yes, it's your domain, Chef O'Leary. You do a phenomenal job. What exactly does Julio do that upsets you?"

Throwing up both hands, the fifty-something chef said, "What doesn't he do? Julio expects preferential treatment. He acts like he's in charge. And . . . he's trying to change the menu." Leaning so close to the phone she could see up his nose, he said, "And you say?"

"I say he's not in charge. You are."

Throwing up both hands, Chef O'Leary said, "So why did you hire him? We don't need two main chefs. Aren't you happy with me, Miss Cheri, because if you're not—?"

Sighing, Cheri said, "You know I am. I gave you a hefty raise last month. We've been together since I founded Fifth Avenue Catering." She knew she couldn't tell him about Julio's financial difficulties and the fact that she somehow felt obligated to employ him. "Why don't you two try and work it out? In the meantime, I'll talk to him."

Chef O'Leary's mouth formed a straight line. "I hope you talk to Julio sooner rather than later. I'm going to quit if this guy has equal say. I hate the omnipotent SOB. It's *my* kitchen."

Heart hammering, Cheri realized chefs were often volatile and she couldn't afford to lose Chef O'Leary. She relied on him for all of their mega celebrity clients. He knew her clients' favorite menus by heart, remembered who had food allergies, which ones expected lavish events and who wanted more casual affairs. Besides, most, if not everyone in the kitchen, loved him. Liam kept the business afloat while she was away. They made a great team. *I knew hiring Julio would be a disaster. I should have trusted my gut. So much for the relaxed time with the cowboy.*

Chapter 18

The next morning, Hope was greeted with a ridiculous scuffle in the hallway—all before her morning coffee.

"What's going on?" Standing with her hands on her hips, she said, "Break it up."

The four students argued over who had played first string, who was benched at last night's game, and who would likely play first string in the next game.

"Into my office. All of you." Leaning back in her chair totally drained, Hope fixated on the leak-stained, tiled ceiling. She didn't particularly enjoy sports but it came with the territory of being a high school counselor.

After hearing the male students' respective stories, which, not surprisingly, varied wildly, Hope weighed her decisions and eventually got the student athletes' attention by threatening to call the coach and have them all benched for the next two games. She doubted if she had the power to do that, but the students didn't know the difference.

Finally getting immediate results, plus apologies, she watched as the kids heaved sighs, eyed one another cagily, and eventually shook hands. Leaving her office, she watched as two playfully shoved one another.

One shouted over his shoulder, "Thanks, Miss Truman."

Another student said, "Sorry 'bout this. Don't tell Coach. 'kay?"

Hope grinned. "Behave and I won't." Attempting her best forceful glare, she added, "But don't let me catch you fighting again."

"Yes, ma'am," the third and fourth students echoed.

After her door closed, Hope did a fist bump. *Another small victory. I'll take it.*

Pettiness wore her out. Normally, Dr. Holmes handled disciplinary matters but the principal was at a week-long conference. Checking her voice mail for the first time that day, Hope listened to a message from her always-busy, biological father, Paul.

Smiling, she dialed his number. "Hi. Your timing is perfect. I've had a rough day. Want to meet for dinner at Rosa's Mexican Restaurant?"

"You read my mind, but if you've had a bad day, this might not be—" Paul's tone changed.

"Might not be what?" Hope asked.

He paused. "I have a newspaper article I want to show you. It's probably nothing."

Hope stared at a stack of phone messages before answering. "I've got some work to do, but I want to see you." She avoided discussing the article. "See you at six."

After they hung up, she stared at the macramé plant hanger in the corner. *I bet it's the article I've already read about a woman who appears to be Montana and is alive and well in a Nashville nursing home.*

Chapter 19

Swiveling in her office chair, Alex did a double take when she saw Gage standing in the teller line. Forgetting how cute he was, her heart raced. Smoothing her skirt, she strode across the lobby and extended her hand. "Hey, Gage. This is quite a surprise."

"Hi yourself." Grinning, he stuffed his hands in his pockets.

Her stomach did strange flip flops. "Fancy seeing you here."

"Yup." Shrugging, he said, "I needed some cash before I go back to New York."

Alex's eyebrows shot up. "You're leaving already? I didn't even know you were here."

Shrugging, he said, "Cheri has some business she wants me to handle in Manhattan. I'm her limo driver, remember?"

"Of course I remember, silly." Alex observed him as he spoke. *He seems different. Annoyed maybe. Likely because of the incident nearly a year ago with my possessive boyfriend at Coconuts.* Her mind raced. She didn't want him to get his money and leave. Not yet. "When you're done, will you step into my office?"

He grinned. "Said the spider to the fly."

Feeling her face redden, she said, "If you put it that way-"

"I'm kidding. I'll be there as soon as I get through the line."

Crossing the lobby toward her corner office, Alex felt his gaze on her back. She sat behind her desk and wondered what to say. She also wondered why it mattered. Thankfully,

Hannah had called in sick the past two days. She almost felt guilty for hoping the girl had the plague but needed a break from her master's degree marketing nemesis.

Gage knocked on her door while simultaneously walking inside. Winking, he asked, "No intern today?"

Alex grinned. "She's sick. Poor thing. I really miss Hannah."

"Uh-huh. I can tell." Gage nodded while standing beside her desk. His gaze undid Alex as she studied him. *Why does he have to look so damn good? Dark sunglasses were perched atop his head and the sleeves were rolled up on his crisp, white shirt. Limo drivers know how to dress.*

Pulse quickening for some weird reason, Alex motioned for Gage to sit in a chair. "It's good to see you. I guess this means Cheri's back in town."

"Yeah, I haven't seen her, though. I've been really sick with bronchitis." He coughed as if to punctuate the fact.

Grimacing, Alex said, "Are you sure you're over it?" Eyeing her can of Lysol, she made a mental note to spray it once he left. "How long will you be in New York?"

He shrugged. "I have to be flexible and work when I can since Cheri doesn't need a driver here. I got some calls to pick up several celebrities for an annual event. You know the kind where everyone wants to be seen entering or leaving a limo." Winking, he said, "It's a fru-fru red carpet affair. I can't pass this up. They're big celebrities and trust me implicitly. Some of them invite me to their homes." Grinning, he said, "They're big tippers, and there's always amazing food." Studying Alex's face, Gage added, "But I'll miss Crystal City, Coconuts, and mainly you."

Alex felt like a teen. "You will? Really?" She decided not to mince words. "I'll miss you too. By the way, Tony snatched your business card out of my hand that night in the Coconuts parking lot."

"You mean the night we were like two bulls fighting over you?" He chuckled.

She nodded. "That's the one."

"I wondered why you never called." Rubbing his chin, Gage said, "He's a real charmer, that guy. I'm not sure what you see in him, but hey, it's your life."

Alex knew her cop boyfriend could be a real asshole. Hell, that described him most of the time, and his ex-wife was even worse. Something drew her to the cop but she was finding it harder and harder to remember exactly what it was. Not sure how to answer Gage about her disastrous relationship, she avoided his gaze.

Gage met her eyes. "Want to try for lunch again?" Glancing at his watch, he asked, "Like today?"

"I'd love to, but I can't." Alex's face fell. "I've got a lunch meeting with a rep from the *Crystal City Business Journal*. It's been scheduled for a month." Sighing, she said, "Sorry. Rain check?"

"Lots of rain checks around here. I'm wondering if I should take a hint." Gage's disappointment was palpable. "Sure. Rain check. Probably. Maybe."

Alex stiffened. "*Maybe?* I hope I'll see you. I *want* to see you."

He stood and awkwardly shook her hand. "Bye, Alex."

She stared at Gage's back as he stepped through the lobby and out the bank's front door. *I hope I didn't make a big mistake. I should have canceled my damn lunch meeting.*

Chapter 20

At Rosa's Mexican Restaurant, a server placed chips and salsa on the table as Hope and her biological dad chatted about their respective days. Hope mentioned her favorite student Britney and her recent meeting with the macho, quibbling student athletes. Paul discussed his seemingly never-ending court case that had ended in a hung jury. Shaking his head, he added, "It's been all over the news so I'm not discussing anything confidential."

"As if you would." Hope dunked a chip in the salsa. "By the way, I like your purple tie. It's a nice change."

Paul glanced at his chest. "Better than my favorite yellow one I wear almost daily?" Fingering his new tie, he said, "The court reporter noticed it too. I guess I need to branch out more."

"Nah. I love your yellow tie. It's like sunshine." Eating another chip with a healthy scoop of salsa, Hope said, "So, mystery man, what's the news?"

"Want to order margaritas first?" Paul didn't wait for her response and waved the server over. "I think you'll want to have a drink."

"You're scaring me."

After their drinks arrived, Paul slid a newspaper across the table. "Read this." He pointed toward a photo with a feature story.

Hope studied the photo of a sixtyish-looking blond woman propped up in what looked like a hospital bed. The woman had balls of yarn spread across the sheet and was knitting. The headline read: PATIENT CREATES PLANT HOLDERS FOR RESIDENTS.

Hope's heartbeat did double time, even though she had already read the article in the teachers' lounge with Willow and had a copy tucked in her drawer. She had tried to suppress the irrational, shocking news and pretend it didn't exist like the weird dream after that ridiculous season of Dallas decades ago. But seeing her attorney father's serious face as he held the newspaper confirmed her worst fears. "I've already seen this."

His eyebrows shot up. "You have? Why didn't you tell me?"

"At first I was in denial. I thought I had buried Montana and couldn't deal with this roller coaster of emotions again." Hope set her half-eaten chip down. Staring at the table as feelings from jubilation to disbelief overcame her, she lowered her voice to an almost-whisper. "How is this possible? How can Montana be alive?"

Paul shook his head. "If this is her, it's unbelievable." He pointed to the article. "It looks like Montana based on her courthouse wedding photo I uncovered. She has aged but really hasn't changed that much over the years." Scratching his bald head, he said, "Beats me how she survived. No one thought either could have made it out alive after the train accident, but apparently they both did. You know what they say. Truth is stranger than fiction." Clearing his throat, he said, "I hope you don't mind but I hired a private detective to look into this case."

Hope took a huge sip of her margarita. Peering at him from above her frosted glass, she said, "No, I don't mind. In fact, I'm glad you did if it'll bring us answers. Have you learned anything?"

Paul reached into his pocket. Unfolding a piece of paper which contained two blurry photos taken in front of a convenience store. He slid them across the table. "The quality is bad, but even though the photos are grainy, you'll get the gist."

Hope stared at the pictures in disbelief. Wearing his usual worn, faded jeans, Larry appeared to have dark stains—likely from blood—and several tears on both legs. He sat along a curb propped up against the convenience store. Squinting at the photo, Hope noticed her adopted dad's stringy hair appeared to be blood-soaked as well. His favorite KISS tee was nearly shorn in half.

Wearing her customary short, fringed, denim shorts, Montana appeared to have something—a rag, maybe—wrapped around her knee. Hope studied the blurry photo. "Is a trucker lifting her into a big rig?" Brows furrowed, she asked, "Why would she leave Larry behind?"

"It's strange, isn't it?" Paul slid another photo across the table. "Here's another angle."

The other picture showed the back end of the truck as it drove out of the parking lot. Barely visible in the corner of the photo, sat Larry on the curb. He tipped a bottle of something wrapped in a brown paper bag, likely liquor, up to his lips.

Hope clapped her hand over her mouth. "I don't understand. Why would they separate?"

Shrugging, Paul said, "Who knows why? Maybe they didn't want to be found and thought if they separated they'd have a better chance of escaping authorities. Maybe they had pot in the van they were driving and didn't want to be charged."

Bobbing her head, Hope said, "I hadn't thought about that. I'm sure they had pot with them. They always did, so that's a likely scenario." She swallowed past a huge lump in her throat as tears filled her eyes. "Maybe they were escaping me after I threw them out of my house. I screamed at them." Between sobs, she continued. "I told them they were hippie losers and I was sick of paying their bills." Voice cracking, she buried her face in her hands. "I made them leave my house until they could stand on their own two feet. I'm the reason they—"

Paul got up and sat beside Hope. Stroking her hair as she leaned against him, he said, "There, there. I'm sure that's not the reason. I'm positive they love you. Everyone does." Looking into Hope's big, brown doe eyes, just like his own, he kissed her cheek. "Maybe Larry can explain everything to you."

Sniffing, Hope wiped her nose with a napkin. "Unfortunately, Larry still doesn't remember a darn thing." She took a big gulp of margarita for fortitude, blew her nose, and straightened her shoulders. "Do you think I should go see Montana? She may not have been a good mother but she's the only mother I ever knew."

Wincing, Paul said, "I wish you had known your biological mom. You would have had a very different life." Shaking his head, he said, "I still can't believe she died right after giving birth." This time, his eyes welled with tears. "But she gave me you."

Hope squeezed her dad's hand. "I love you and wish I had known her too. What do you think? Should I go see Montana?"

"She's in another state." Paul pointed toward the article in the paper. "Tennessee, I believe, near Nashville.

"Nashville is drivable in a day. Do you suppose she has any memory?"

Paul grinned. "There's only one way to find out."

Chapter 21

At home enjoying a Diet Coke with lime, Cheri curled up in a chair, munched on almonds, and stared at her laptop. *Even with the fiasco between my chefs fighting, I can't stop thinking about Cole. He knows where I live. Why hasn't he been by? Maybe this house scared him off. Maybe he didn't like me.*

Depressed, she reverted back to her old Internet dating addiction. *This is absolutely the last time.* She noticed a guy who seemed to have it all—great job, charming personality—online at least—was well traveled, and his photo was gorgeous, to boot.

According to their profiles, Dave and Cheri seemed to be a perfect match. Dave had been urging her to meet him since before she left New York. Since the cowboy hadn't contacted her, she finally agreed to a meeting at The Coffee Drip.

After perfecting new dessert recipes all day for a new hotel grand opening in Crystal City's renovated downtown area, Cheri was more than ready to get out of the house and meet this guy once and for all. Knowing her friends would disapprove, especially Alex, Cheri saw this as a challenge to show them good guys could be found via the Internet.

After taking a deep breath, Cheri called Suzy first, then Alex. She wasn't able to reach Hope. After telling them she was back in town, she asked her friends to go to The Coffee Drip and sit at another table, in spy mode. After scolding her a bit—or a lot—the two women curiously agreed to lurk on the sidelines.

After changing into black leggings, a long red and white geometric tunic, red hoop earrings, and black stilettos, Cheri decided to go for a casual chic look. Thoughts of the cowboy invaded her concentration, but she pushed them away. *I may never hear from him again. He could be dating Jade again for all I know.*

Driving to Crystal City in record time, she pulled up to The Coffee Drip and waved after spotting Alex and Suzy in a corner booth. After a quick glance around the coffee shop, she realized she had arrived before Dave. Since he wasn't there, she approached her friends.

"Hi, girls. Thanks for coming on such short notice." Alex groaned. "How the hell do you look so good in leggings? And . . . welcome back, stranger." Glancing toward the door, Alex asked, "What does he look like?"

Cheri bent toward them. In a low voice she said, "He's over six feet tall, muscular, and has dark, curly hair. He's *very* good looking. He has a great job and we seem to have a lot in common. For once, I think this one might work out." She peered at the door again. "Now, shush or the gig's up. I'm going to sit near the door and wait. Remember, don't act like you know me."

"We'll be perfect secret agents. I'm glad you're back in town," Suzy said. "Now, go away." She and Alex giggled as they walked to the counter to place an order. After dealing with morning sickness and crazy cravings, Suzy was more than ready for a fun distraction. She added cinnamon to her decaf coffee. "Where's Hope?"

"She said something about meeting with her dad." Alex ordered a lemon poppy seed muffin and they sat at a booth with full view of the restaurant.

Fidgeting in her seat and staring at her phone, Cheri stared at the front door every two minutes.

Soon a short, fat, balding guy walked in and studied the room. After he spotted Cheri, he grinned a mile wide, and headed toward her. She ignored him and went back to her phone. Short Guy approached her table and started to pull out a chair.

Cheri cut him off before he sat down. "I'm waiting for someone."

"Would that someone be Dave?"

Assuming this was one of his friends, Cheri twisted her hair in her finger. *Funny, he asked a friend to join him too. We do have a lot in common.* "Yes, as a matter of fact."

Short, bald guy extended his meaty hand. "Hi, I'm Dave."

Knitting her eyebrows, Cheri didn't shake his sweaty-looking palm. "You're Dave? But-But I've seen your picture. You have dark hair—a lot of it—and you said you were over six feet tall."

"Guess the joke's on you." He laughed. "I knew a gorgeous woman like you would never agree to meet a man like me."

The door opened and in walked Tall, Gorgeous Guy. Cheri recognized him from the picture on "Dave's" profile. Crossing her arms as the two guys high-fived each other, laughing at their big joke, she shook her head. Tall Guy was even more gorgeous in person but also sported a wedding band. She couldn't believe she'd been had by these jerks.

The guys laughed so hard snot came out of Short Guy's nose. Hands on hips, Cheri stood up. "Which one of you actually emailed me? Don't answer. I don't care. Bastards, both of you." Yanking her purse off the back of the chair, Cheri stormed off.

"Can I at least take a selfie with you to show my buddies?" Short Guy poised his phone in mid-air. "They'll never believe I had a date with you."

"Don't even think about it." Cheri put her hand in front of her face. "And we didn't have a date. We had a two-minute exchange, if you can call it that. You're an ass and so is your body-builder friend." Cheri peered at Tall Guy. "Does your wife know you're playing these stupid games? You're jerks. Both of you."

Huffing over to Suzy and Alex, a red-faced Cheri said, "Come on. Let's get out of here. I need a drink."

Chapter 22

Alex and Suzy drove to Coconuts wondering what had transpired. They couldn't hear the conversation but discerned something had gone badly wrong.

Cheri arrived first and ordered Angry Balls all around. Stat. Gus sat amber drinks containing maraschino cherries on the table.

Suzy and Alex rushed inside. "What happened?" Suzy asked breathlessly. Cheri relayed the story about how Short Guy had used Tall Guy's photo on his profile.

Alex and Suzy exchanged glances. Alex bit her lip to keep from laughing.

"That's not right," Suzy said, using her napkin to stifle a giggle.

Cheri made a face. "Glad I could entertain you. No charge." Letting out a groan, she gulped her cocktail. "Go ahead and laugh. I was had. Big time. I drove thirty minutes so these jokesters could pull one over on me." Shaking her head in disgust, she said, "I wish I smoked. I could use a cigarette right now."

"I think these strong drinks will do the trick." Alex giggled. "We told you to cut out this silliness a year ago."

"She's right. If I remember correctly, you promised you'd stop going on dates with strangers." Suzy pushed her amber cocktail toward Cheri and instead sipped a non-alcoholic Shirley Temple. Eying the New Yorker, she said, "Cheri, I'm sure I speak for Alex that we're thrilled you're back in town, but listen to me. I'm a mom."

"And a grandma," Alex offered.

Suzy continued, "You must get off the stupid Internet to find men. Have you met *any* good guys online?"

Cheri hated to admit it but she had had a string of online dating disasters. "You're right. This is the last one. I promise."

Peering over her drink, Alex said, "Good. In that case, tell us about some of your escapades."

"Let's see there was the adorable thirty-year-old stockbroker who's a virgin. He wanted me to show him the way."

"Adorable stockbroker who's a virgin?" Alex leaned forward. "And you didn't bed him? Why the hell not?"

"Too much pressure. He would have fallen in love with me, wanted to get married, have babies, the whole nine yards." Cheri shrugged. "I'm not ready for that." Grinning, she said, "I have more war stories. I met a surgeon with a huge ego and horse teeth to match."

"Handy for corn on the cob." Alex covered her mouth. "That was mean. Sorry. Not sorry."

The socialite put her finger to her temple. "And there was the thirty-something loser who still lives with his parents. Another guy was so cheap he didn't even offer to buy my coffee on the first date." She shook her head. "He actually had a *coupon* for coffee. I had to hold myself back from telling him I could buy the entire coffee shop." Glancing at her friends, she said, "I've met a lot of losers, haven't I?"

"At least you can laugh about it now," Suzy said. Alex rubbed her belly from laughing so hard. "I've missed you."

"Sure, go ahead, laugh at my expense. I know I haven't had much luck, but—" Cheri smiled a mile wide. "I met a guy the day I flew back. He's cute, sweet, charming, and handsome.

"Oh," both Suzy and Alex said in unison. After a brief hesitation, Alex said, "Don't keep us in suspense. Spill."

Leaning back, Cheri crossed her arms, for dramatic effect. "He's a cowboy."

Liquor spewed from Alex's mouth. "A cowboy? You're kidding, right?"

Suzy maintained her composure. "And where did you meet a cowboy?"

"At the airport. We've already kissed and—"

Alex held both arms straight out like an umpire. "Rewind, please. We've missed an important step here. You've got my attention." She waved to Gus. "Another round, please, and remember, no booze for Suzy."

After the drinks were served, both Suzy and Alex leaned toward Cheri. "Tell us everything," Suzy said.

"From the beginning," Alex added.

Cheri mentioned being shocked to see paparazzi at the airport and said she planted a kiss on the cowboy to distract the photographers.

"Oh, my God," Alex interrupted. "How did he react?"

"He kissed me back. Twice." Cheri wiggled her eyebrows. "It was amazing."

Shaking her head, Alex asked, "Then, why in the hell did you go on that stupid date at the coffee shop?"

Shrugging, Cheri said. "Simple. He hasn't called. I don't even know his last name. His first name is Cole." She stared at the table. "I may never see him again. All I can think about is that kiss."

Chapter 23

As the server refilled their chips and salsa, another realization hit Hope. Holding a chip in mid-air, she said, "We have a huge problem. Larry and Willow are married."

Paul furrowed his brows. "That name sounds familiar. Who's Willow again?"

"She's an art teacher at Hilltop and now an awkward friend." Managing a small laugh, Hope said, "She's a hippie too. No wonder Larry is attracted to her."

While the server freshened their chips, Paul sipped his margarita while studying his daughter. "I'm sure you realize the difficulties ahead." He paused. "Even though Larry and Montana were presumed dead, they're still legally married."

Hope ran her fingers through her frizzy hair. "This is too much. This is something for Alex to handle—not me. I'm the weak one."

"You're not weak. You're a strong, beautiful woman." He reached for her hand. "Want me to go with you to Nashville?"

"Maybe. I don't know. I can't decide what to do." Leaning back, she stared at the unknowing, happy patrons munching on Mexican food and realized they hadn't placed an order beyond chips and salsa. After several seconds, Hope made a decision. "Thanks for the offer but I think Larry should go. He needs to see her and vice versa. In fact, seeing Montana might bring his memory back."

Nodding, Paul said, "That's actually a good idea. Are you okay alone with him? I mean, I know he raised you but he doesn't remember you." Reaching for his phone, he placed it on the table and scrolled his jam-packed calendar. Paul made a face. "I can clear my client meetings but not the court cases."

Hope gave a half smile. "Thanks anyway. Maybe a road trip is what Larry and I need. Nashville is about six hours away. We can leave early on a Saturday morning—if I can convince him to go."

"You're taking this well," Paul said.

"I'm still in a fog, but nothing surprises me anymore. May I have those photos?"

"Of course." Paul peeked at his watch and grimaced. "I hate to eat and run especially after this bombshell, but I have a lot of work to do tonight before depositions early tomorrow."

"All we ate were chips and salsa." She laughed, then paused. "I can't eat now anyway. Thank you for doing the undercover work, Dad. Maybe we'll get to the bottom of this yet."

Paul hugged Hope. "Thanks isn't necessary. You're the best thing to come into my life. I think you know what to do, but it's your decision." He patted the article. "If you decide you want me to tag along, I'll find the time."

"I love you, Dad." After she got into her gray Honda in the parking lot, Hope leaned against the headrest. *How will I convince Larry-Mac to go to Nashville with me?*

Chapter 24

Practically dancing around the kitchen, Suzy said, "I'm so glad the boys invited us over for an impromptu barbecue. I can't wait to hold baby Violet."

Her husband, Ken, reached for the heaviest casserole dishes. "Let me carry that. You're pregnant, remember?" He loaded the car with every potluck side dish imaginable, plus Jon's favorite Sock-It-To-Me Bundt cake.

Examining the food to make sure she hadn't forgotten anything, Suzy said, "I can't wait to see all of them."

Nodding, Ken said, "It'll be a nice day. I wish Izzy had joined us."

"She's a teen. Teens like to be with their friends." Suzy secured the food, and they drove toward Vanessa's late parents' house. "I'm still amazed how well the boys' new marriage has worked out with Jon's former high school girlfriend and their baby. Who would have guessed Vanessa would become pregnant at their prom, Jon would come out a year later and find the love of his life with Fernando?" Suzy grinned, "Thankfully, Vanessa and baby Violet seem to delight in their modern relationship."

"It's a unique arrangement but seems to work." Ken stared at the road. "I wonder why they invited us over today."

"We're family. That's why. It's not a holiday nor birthday, so it'll be relaxed and enjoyable." Suzy winked at her husband. "I made your favorite pasta salad. I think you could eat pasta every day." Laughing, she said, "You could never survive on the Keto diet."

"Nope, I couldn't." He glanced at Suzy sideways. "Are you saying I need to diet?"

"Not at all. I'll be the one on a diet after the twins are born."

Rounding a curve, Ken said, "Twins. It's still hard to fathom. How are you feeling today? Any morning sickness, babe?"

"Always morning sickness. Every darn day, unfortunately. Since I'm nearing my third trimester, the doctor thinks it'll subside. Fingers crossed."

Ken crossed his fingers in the air for solidarity. "I wish I could throw up for you." Chuckling, he said, "Not really, but I hate that you have to go through that."

Rubbing her growing baby bump, she said, "It'll be worth it." When they pulled into the driveway, everyone rushed outside to greet them.

"Mama Suzy. Welcome!" Fernando opened her car door, eased her onto the driveway, and kissed both cheeks.

"Hi, Mom." Jon held baby Violet in one arm and reached for Suzy with the other. Vanessa began carrying the dishes. "I'll put the food inside."

Once the food and condiments were placed on the counter or in the fridge, Fernando beckoned them into the shady backyard. "How do you like the new grill my husband bought?"

"Very nice." Ken examined it as though he had never seen a grill before. The guys gathered around the grill as if it were one of a kind, Suzy and Vanessa sat in lawn chairs, and baby Violet held a rattler while perched on a quilt.

"I can't believe how well Violet gets around. They grow so fast."

Vanessa stared at her baby. "You should see her do the Army crawl. It's hilarious." As if on cue, Violet crawled off the quilt and onto the grass. Both women chuckled and raced toward her.

Enjoying the shade of a mature oak tree, Suzy settled back into a lawn chair. In the daylight, Vanessa's freckles were more prominent than ever. Studying Vanessa's auburn hair and porcelain skin, Suzy peered at the mirror image on Vanessa's lap and wondered if her twins would inherit her fair skin and red locks or Ken's brown hair. "Thanks for the impromptu invitation. You really brightened our day."

Her son, Jon, stared at his shoes. Suzy glanced up in time to see his jaw clench as Fernando flipped burgers. Something was off. Her mother's intuition kicked in. "Guys, is everything okay? Is this an impromptu visit or something else? Why am I getting a weird vibe?"

"Let's eat first, Mom." Jon avoided her gaze.

Suzy's face fell. "I knew it. What's going on?"

Holding the spatula in mid-air, Fernando said, "Sorry, Mama Suzy, but we're going to Europe."

"Who is?" Suzy asked.

Fernando pointed the spatula one by one toward Jon, Vanessa, and baby Violet. "All of us."

"All of you?" Suzy's eyebrows shot up. "What? When? For how long?"

"I knew you'd hate the idea." Jon glanced at his husband. "I wanted to ease into this."

"Pshaw. It's better to rip the bandage off." Fernando slung his arm across Suzy's shoulders. "We'll have Skype and can send photos back and forth. Besides, Mama Suzy, we'll be back in no time. No longer than a few months."

"*Months?*"

Fernando flipped another burger and added cheese slices on top. "You'll be so busy with the twins you'll never miss us."

Eyes filling with tears, Suzy said, "I know Mama Gia wants to be a part of Violet's life but the timing is"—she sniffed—"crummy."

"Sorry, Mom. Mama Gia and Fernando's brothers, Luigi, Frankie, and Vinny, are dying to see the baby. I know it isn't perfect timing, but she won't stop pestering us."

Fernando shot Jon a look.

"Well, she won't." Jon threw both hands in the air. "You know your mom texts daily and insists on constant photos of Violet."

Shrugging, Fernando sighed. "Can you blame her for wanting to see her bambina?"

Crossing the yard, Ken embraced his wife. "We were looking forward to being empty nesters." He chuckled. "At least for a few months, we will be."

Vanessa handed baby Violet to Suzy. "You can take her home for a couple of nights if you want. We'd all love a good night's sleep." Her comment broke the ice.

Reaching for the baby, Suzy said, "Everyone's leaving us, Ken."

"We'll be fine. I can change a diaper."

"Plural. There will be two babies needing diaper changes in a few months."

Winking, Ken said, "Surely you're not afraid of something that'll weigh less than ten pounds."

"I'm very afraid," Suzy quipped. "It has been a long time since I changed Jon's diaper."

"*Mom.*"

Fernando put the steaming cheeseburgers on a platter. "Let's discuss Jon's diapers after we eat."

They ate mostly in silence after the wet-blanket news. Soon, Violet squirmed, squealed, and decided to have a good, ear-piercing cry.

Suzy bounced the baby and kissed her cheek. "That's how I feel, Violet."

Fernando rushed to the piano and played "Twinkle Twinkle Little Star." Almost immediately, Violet cooed.

"My man has the touch." Jon wrapped his arm around Fernando's waist. Vanessa tweaked Violet's nose and kissed her tummy. "She loves the piano almost as much as Crystal Lake. We took a day trip to watch the boats and jet skis. The guys bought Violet a pink hat so big it looked like an umbrella perched on her head. "She'll never get a tan with that thing."

"We have to protect her skin," Fernando said, "It's brand new and simply perfect." He kissed the baby's pudgy, pink arm. "We're going to miss this charming house, you Mama Suzy, and Ken, but everything will be here when we return."

Jon's frown indicated he wasn't as pleased as his husband about going abroad. "The timing isn't the best. We just unpacked our last box. I finally got my clothes in order."

"Tsk, tsk. Don't be so rigid, Jon," Fernando said.

Suzy studied Vanessa. "I'm surprised you aren't staying here with Violet."

"Mom, that's the whole point. Like we said, Mama Gia wants to see her granddaughter."

Fernando chuckled. "I can't wait to watch Luigi change a dirty diaper. I hope it's an extra messy one."

Jon rolled his eyes. "I don't. He'll probably rub my face in it. Your brothers are nuts."

Fernando elbowed him playfully. "They're Italian and boisterous. You're used to being an only child. Being around them will be good for you. It'll be good for all of us."

"Except me." Suzy couldn't help herself. "I'm sorry, guys. I know Mama Gia wants to be part of Violet's life too. I shouldn't be selfish. It'll be hard but we'll manage."

Chapter 25

After taking two Advil for a splitting headache, Hope reached for the newspaper article about Montana. She had kept it in her top drawer for months, still unable to process the best way to handle the delicate situation. Being a counselor, she knew she was professionally equipped to wade through the relationship puzzle pieces, but on a personal basis, it was a different matter entirely. *Should I leave this alone or go to Nashville to see my thought-dead mother? Should I be the one to tell her that her husband is in love with another woman? In fact, by the way, your husband just got married.* Putting her head in her hands, Hope groaned. Eyes welling with tears, she stared at the worn newspaper article. *I thought you died in the train accident. I thought you both died. This is an impossible situation.*

As she stared at the photo of Montana, Hope's mind wandered. Her adopted mom was a hippie like her dad. She was a petite, blond woman and raised her—actually, Hope did the raising. Her parents were deadbeats, plain and simple. They rarely held down a job for more than a week, were constantly stoned or drunk, and expected her to pay their bills. Hope shuddered, finally admitting the awful truth she had tried to bury along with them. Staring at the photo, Hope could see Montana was clearly alive. *I wonder if her memory is intact. She at least remembers how to make those beloved macramé plant hangers, so maybe she'll remember her husband and me.*

Hope glanced out the window as students from a gym class jogged by. *I should join them, but my weight is the least of my worries right now. How will I handle this?* Everyone at Hilltop knows Larry as Mac, the janitor. Still uncertain why he chose that blasted name but trying to go along with it in front of the students, Hope was mystified that he couldn't remember a darn thing following the accident.

Peering back at the photo of the only mother she knew who now lay in a nursing home, Hope studied the meager surroundings. Montana was under the covers surrounded by her colorful creations. A sad thought crossed her mind. *I wonder if she has all of her limbs.* Montana had always worn short shorts with a tee from her favorite rock concert, which included many bands, but KISS was near the top of the list. She had always dressed like a teen, and much to Hope's chagrin, looked like one. Growing up, Hope always questioned why she was the only chunky person in the family with unruly brown, frizzy hair while both of her parents were lean with silky, if not greasy, blonde hair. After the accident, she found out the truth from her biological dad. Paul had the same short, round body and large brown, doe eyes she inherited. Hope chuckled. *Thanks, Dad.*

Hope laid the newspaper on top of her stacks of student files. She had read the article so many times, the paper was dog-eared and soft. After tossing and turning about Larry and Willow's wedding, she knew she and Larry had to have a face-to-face meeting with Montana—and fast. She had to convince him to go to Nashville with her.

Closing her office door, she rushed up the Hilltop stairs, checked every bathroom, and raced down several hallways as fast as her legs would allow. Eventually, Hope discovered the janitor polishing a floor in the gym with a huge round, rotating brush. Thrusting the newspaper in front of Larry-Mac one more time, Hope decided to beg. "Larry, er, Mac, this is important. Will you turn that thing off?"

He fiddled with the off switch while simultaneously giving her a puzzled glance.

"Thank you." Tapping the paper, Hope said, "Please read this article, study the photograph, and think long and hard before you answer."

Hope held her breath as Larry-Mac reached for the paper. She studied his lined, weathered face for a reaction. Any reaction.

"Nice plant hangers. I've seen one in your office."

Shaking her head, Hope persevered. "Think hard. Do you remember this woman?"

Larry-Mac shook his head. "Nope. Don't know her." He grinned a crooked smile and held up his left hand which sported a thin, silver band. "Guess who got married over the weekend?"

"I know. Willow told me." Hope managed a smile. "Congratulations. Listen, I know the timing is weird but you and I need to take a road trip right away."

"A road trip? Why?" Staring hard at the newspaper, Larry lowered his voice. "You're sure bein' mysterious, ma'am. This is a fairly new job. I don't know if I can get off work. I can't afford to lose my work, plus, remember, I'm kinda on my honeymoon. The old lady and I can't afford anything besides our stay at that silly Crescent Hotel that's supposed to be haunted, but I thought I'd attempt to cook dinner or somethin' for my wife this week. Maybe give her a backrub."

Cringing at being called 'ma'am' from the man who raised her and hearing him refer to Willow as his old lady, not to mention the backrub, Hope held up both hands. "Please don't say any more."

"Suit yourself." Larry-Mac raked his fingers through his long, greasy hair.

"Hear me out." Swallowing, Hope continued, "There's someone you need to see."

"Who?" he asked as three basketball players bounced a ball at the opposite end of the gym.

Hope raised her voice over the commotion. "This person is very important to you."

"It's the woman in the picture, ain't it?" He leaned against his cart.

Hope perked up. "Yes. Remember her now?"

"Nope."

Chapter 26

Two days after her disastrous and absolutely, positively last ridiculous online date, Cheri perched in front of her laptop and Googled the cowboy.

Unable to get her mind off the country boy, even though he wasn't her type. At. All. Still, there was something about him. He had definitely caught her attention. I *want* to get to know him better. I *need* to get to know him better. *I'm done with trolling the Internet for dates.* Laser focused, Cheri Googled every Cole she could find along with terms like "country," "cowboy," "farming" and "Missouri."

After several minutes, a Facebook account appeared for a Cole Cash. *That's ironic. If he only knew about my pile of cash.* Chuckling at the surname, she squinted at the photo. *That's him.* Her stomach lurched. *He's so cute.* Staring at his Facebook profile photo, Cheri's heart raced.

Scrolling through his photos, everything looked like something out of *Country Life,* if there were such a thing. She smiled at the images of green and yellow John Deere tractors, hundreds of round bales of hay, cows, horses, acres of land, dogs, oak and maple trees, and his ancient blue Chevy truck. Feeling like a voyeur, she couldn't stop staring at every photo.

Hands shaking, she decided to send Cole a note before she lost her nerve. Clicking on 'Message,' she simply typed: *Hi! Remember the stranger who kissed you? I'd like to see you again.* ~Cheri

She had long ago set up a pseudo Facebook account

using only her first name—sort of like Cher or Madonna—avoiding her surname, Van Buren, because she was well aware that would attract people for all the wrong reasons. Biting a manicured nail, she stared at the tiny box waiting for a response. Soon the gray dots began to move. *He's online. And actually responding.* She spun around full circle in her desk chair like a kid. Squeezing her eyes tight, she was afraid to read his reply. Finally, she forced herself to peer at the screen.

Yeah, of course, I remember you. You're a little hard to forget. :) Want to meet later today? I'm headin' to town in a couple of hours.

Cheri's stomach did a backflip. She absolutely wanted to meet him. Holding back from typing an immediate "yes" since she didn't want to appear desperate, she decided to get a drink of water but only made it halfway to the kitchen before rushing back to the keyboard.

Sure. How about four o'clock at Coconuts?

It's a date. See you soon.

"Woohoo!" Cheri cheered and did a fist pump. *Why am I so excited about this cowboy? Probably because he's unlike anyone I've ever known.* Retreating to her closet, she scanned her designer clothes. *Somehow I don't think a Versace dress is in order.* Choosing skinny white jeans, a leopard print tank, and red stilettos, she laid the clothes on a chair beside her bed and returned to her laptop. *Maybe a bit more cowboy research . . .*

~ ~ ~

Cheri left her grandmother's home in Branson nearly an hour early, allowing more than enough time to get to Coconuts. She didn't want to be late and also didn't want Cole to see her red Mercedes. Parking across the street, she stepped inside the familiar island-themed restaurant. She glanced around the bar and decided on a corner booth toward the back. Gus approached.

"Hi, Gus. I'll take a cabernet." *Maybe that'll take the edge off.*

Gus returned with her wine. "Meeting anyone?"

She nodded.

"Want menus?"

"Sure." Cheri wanted the server to leave so she could down a few sips of the wine and relax before Cole arrived. Just as her glass was poised mid-air, Cole appeared in the doorway. She studied his slender, yet muscular frame. Wearing his familiar brown cowboy boots, tight jeans, an oval belt buckle, and a navy button-down shirt with the sleeves rolled up, he made her pulse quicken. *Hot damn. He's gorgeous.*

She watched as Cole scanned the room, obviously looking for her. When he spotted her in the corner, he sauntered over.

God, he has a sexy walk. I have a feeling Alex would approve.

Cole tipped his tan cowboy hat. "Howdy."

"Hi."

Sliding into a chair smelling of outdoor spice, Cole motioned for Gus. "Beer, please. Whatever's on tap."

When he grinned, Cheri noticed his dimples. *He looks sort of like a younger, country Brad Pitt.*

Leaning forward, he pointed to her drink. "Looks like someone already started." He grinned. "Good to see you again."

She could barely speak. "Same." As another patron entered the bar and light streamed inside, Cheri studied Cole's face. Sporting a day's worth of light brown stubble, his bewitching smile and dimples would melt a car bumper. Feeling like a schoolgirl on the first day, she was at a loss for words. No man had ever had that effect on her.

Gus appeared with Cole's beer. "Anything else?"

Cheri peered at Cole. "I'm not hungry yet, are you?"

He grinned. "Nope. Got all night."

Cheri wondered if her friends would show up at Coconuts and half hoped they wouldn't.

Cole's eyes met hers. "I'm glad you found me on Facebook. I'd been cursin' myself for not giving you my number earlier. You're quite the private eye."

"Most New Yorkers are." She beamed.

Nodding, he said, "So."

"So." Cheri's childhood insecurities kicked in. She felt her cheeks flush.

The cowboy tipped his hat. "Let's start over." He extended his rough, calloused hand. "I'm Cole Cash."

Cheri broke into a wide grin and half hid behind her drink. "Cheri." If he noticed she didn't offer her last name, he didn't react. After hanging his cowboy hat on the back of one of the empty chairs, Cole took a sip of foamy beer.

Glancing at his rough hands, Cheri said, "By the way, you need some lotion."

Cole's face twisted. "Huh?"

"When you shook my hand, I noticed how dry yours were."

The cowboy studied his rough hands and absentmindedly rubbed them. "Country boys don't wear lotion. I'd be laughed off the farm if I smelled like lavender. The animals would probably run for the hills."

Cheri eyed him over the top of her wineglass. "Tell me about living in the country. What do you grow on your farm?"

His eyes twinkled. Cows."

"You grow cows?"

Cole guffawed. "No, I raise them."

Cheri's cocktail had kicked in on her empty stomach.

She felt a little woozy and teetered on her high-backed bar stool.

Cole reached for her. "Whoa. You're actin' like a newborn calf."

Cheri giggled. "Please don't compare me to a cow ever again." Studying Cole's western attire, she said, "I'm not well versed in cowboy lingo. . . Are you a real cowboy?"

Chuckling, Cole asked, "Are you askin' because I wear a cowboy hat?"

"And boots." She pointed toward his dusty, brown footwear. "Don't forget the boots."

"I guess you could call me a cowboy, but I'm more of a country boy at heart. I don't ride in the rodeo or anything like that. I live a simple life on a farm and have animals, that's all. You probably can't understand that being from New York and all."

"Well, look who's here." A tall, thin cowboy punched Cole in the shoulder. "I never thought I'd see the day when Cole Cash would be inside Coconuts."

Cole eyed the man. "I could say the same about you, Wyatt. What are you two doin' here?"

"Passin' through town after a cattle auction. Never been here before. A cold brew sounded good."

A stocky cowboy spoke up. "We're goin' to another cattle auction tomorrow. Feel free to join us. We're leavin' real early in the mornin'."

The lanky man tipped his hat in Cheri's direction. "Sorry, ma'am. Where are my manners? I'm Wyatt. I believe we met on the square several days ago."

"Yes, I remember. It was after I landed in Crystal City. Nice to see you again, but please don't call me 'ma'am.' We're probably the same age." Cheri wasn't happy about the unwanted intrusion on their first real date.

The lanky man stiffened. "Our mamas would thump

us over the head if we weren't courteous. Ain't that right, Cole?"

Nodding, Cole said, "You got that right."

Cheri decided she shouldn't alienate Cole's friends. "Manners are nice."

"Speaking of, where are mine?" Cole stood. "Bo, this is Cheri."

The stocky, overall-wearing man extended his meaty hand. "I've never seen you around here before. My guess is you're from out of state. Am I right?"

"New York," Cheri said, ready for them to leave.

"Guys, I might see you at the auction tomorrow. I was goin' to put fence up in my back pasture. I'll let you know."

Wyatt and Bo exchanged glances. "I think we're bein' dismissed." Cole's stocky friend checked his watch. "We probably should be goin'." He tipped his hat in Cheri's direction. "Nice meetin' you. If you decide to go to the auction, meet us at five in the morning to load the cattle."

After the men left, Cheri said, "I can't say I've ever heard of a cattle auction. I didn't even know they sold cows." She giggled. "I guess they're like buying shoes."

"Not really. It's usually not much of a money maker unless you get a prime bull and a cow that'll hopefully birth several calves over time." Studying Cheri's blank face, Cole asked, "Want to go with me and see what it's all about?"

"Not really. Sorry. But I'd love to see your ranch sometime."

Cole brightened. "It's more of a farm than a ranch. I'd be happy to show it to you if you're into large stretches of land and blue skies."

"That sounds divine. In New York City, I rarely notice the sky and there aren't many trees, nor grass, unless you go to Central Park. It's picturesque and serene here."

"That it is." Sipping his beer, Cole said, "I've seen pictures of the Empire State Building and Statue of Liberty.

I'm not really a city guy." Before I forget—" He fished out a simple black and white business card that was slightly smudged. A picture of a cow was on the front beside his name, Soggy Bottoms, phone number, and address. "Here's my number so we don't lose touch again."

Staring at his card, Cheri asked, "Soggy Bottoms?"

"My farm floods. It was the best name I could come up with."

"That's funny. Not the flooding but the name. I love it."

"Glad you approve. How long you here for?"

Cheri pondered his question. She wasn't sure herself. "I'm not on a tight schedule. I'll be here for a few weeks." *Unless Fifth Avenue Catering implodes at the hands of Julio.* She plunked his card in her designer bag.

After he watched her hang her purse on the back of her chair, Cole asked, "I don't suppose you want to give me your number?"

Shrugging, Cheri said, "I'll call you."

His eyes crinkled. "A woman in charge. I like that.

Gus reappeared and asked if they wanted refills. Cheri shook her head. "I'll take some strong, black coffee."

"Same," Cole said. "And maybe another beer since the lady isn't in a hurry." Staring at her, Cole said, "Drivin' here, I was wrackin' my brain tryin' to think of somethin' a city girl might like to do. Somethin' you've probably never done before."

Cheri rested her head on her chin. "You've got my attention. What do you have in mind?"

He grinned, showing his dimples. "How about a hot date of rock skippin' or a hillbilly pool party?" Wiggling his eyebrows, he asked, "Ever done either of those?"

As Gus plunked down steaming cups of java, Cheri said, "Not even close, but I'll try either one."

Cole winked. "It's a date."

Cheri's heart skipped a beat. She couldn't wait to see the cowboy again. "Which one will we do first?"

Cole sipped his coffee. "I think I'll surprise you."

"What else do you do for fun around here?"

Cole laughed. "You'll probably think it's corny, but I love old barns and country roads. I could spend a day in an old barn, sittin' on a bale of hay, chewin' on a piece of straw, and thinkin' about the history of the place." He paused. "I like thinkin' about the memories and hard times my ancestors had. I bet you've never done that in the big city."

Giggling, she said, "I've never been in a barn, nor sat on a hay bale."

"We must correct that." Cole reached for her hand. "I'd be happy to introduce you to a slower way of life. What day is good?"

After dealing with the issues at Fifth Avenue Catering—something she wasn't about to mention since it would blow her cover—Cheri said, "Any day is good." Oblivious to every other patron in the bar, Cheri couldn't tear her eyes away from Cole's tight Wrangler jeans and oval belt buckle. Chuckling to herself, she tried to imagine Sebastian wearing them. Nope. Not a chance.

Cole reached for a menu. "I'm starvin.' You hungry?"

Chapter 27

Mystified, and annoyed by Larry's lack of recall, Hope's mind went into overdrive. *Maybe I shouldn't tell him everything beforehand. Maybe if he sees Montana in person the shock of hearing her voice will jog his memory. Maybe, just maybe, everything will come flooding back.*

"Will you meet me in my office later this afternoon?" Hope's eyes pleaded with his. "Please."

Larry-Mac shrugged. "Okay. Gotta mop a floor in the men's restrooms. Those boys can't seem to hit the stool." He chuckled. "I think they're havin' pissin' contests."

Hope laughed. "That might be TMI. Take your time. I don't have any students for another hour."

While she waited for Larry-Mac to take a break, Hope trekked to the teachers' lounge for some wretched coffee. On the way, she spotted the skinny, long-haired janitor from behind squirting glass cleaner on a trophy case. *He never worked this hard when he was my dad. Not even close.*

Watching him in action made her heart both sink and swell, seemingly at the same time. She couldn't explain her feelings, even to herself. The fact that Larry still didn't seem to remember her, the train accident, and most of all his wife, Montana lying in a nursing home, made the potential marriage situation with Willow awkward and prickly at best, not to mention illegal at worst. No high school counseling course had prepared Hope to handle this dilemma. *I'm going to forge ahead. Whatever happens, happens.*

After glugging some black-tar coffee, Hope stepped through the shiny, polished hallway, thanks to the janitor's hard work. Forcing a smile, she greeted students as they rushed to class. Between "hellos," "great play" and clanging lockers, she traipsed back to her office. Staring at student file folders, she pushed them to the edge of her desk and turned to her computer but it was useless. She couldn't concentrate until Larry-Mac agreed to go with her.

While doodling on a yellow legal pad, her road trip strategy became clearer. Sipping the last of her now-cold coffee, Hope made a decision. *Maybe the shock of seeing Montana will spark his memory.* Chewing on her bottom lip, her thoughts swirled. *First, I have to coax Larry into going on this trip with me.*

~ ~ ~

A tentative knock on her door jolted Hope into the present.

"Am I in trouble, Miss Truman?" the janitor joked.

"Not at all." Hope's heart sank every time Larry-Mac didn't recognize her. "Please call me Hope. You make me feel so old referring to me by my last name. Besides, only students get into trouble with me, not faculty nor staff." She grinned in an attempt to relax him. "This'll be painless, I promise."

"Sorry, Miss, uh, Hope," he mumbled. "You've got my curiosity up, ma'am."

"Please don't call me 'ma'am' either." Hope grinned as she motioned to a chair in front of her desk. "Have a seat."

"Sounds serious." Larry's face turned solemn. "I hope I'm doin' a good job. I love it at Hilltop. I sure would hate to lose my—"

"It's nothing like that. You're doing a great job here. Not only do you keep the school clean and maintained, the students love you. I've never seen so many kids give a peace sign or say 'cool, man' these days." Attempting to project an upbeat attitude, Hope continued. "Actually, I'd like to get to know you better. Remember the road trip I mentioned earlier?"

His brow's furrowed. "I've been thinkin' about that. If we go, I'd really like for Willow to come since we're newlyweds and all."

Hope definitely didn't want Willow along when they first set eyes on Montana. It was going to be a shock for both Larry-Mac and Montana. Willow would complicate matters beyond comprehension. Clasping her hands together, she spoke calmly. "I really think it should just be the two of us. See, um, I plan to see an old friend from long ago. And this, er, friend, well, I truly believe the two of you have a long-term connection."

"A connection?" The janitor's brows knitted. "What's his name?"

"Montana." Hope held her breath as she waited to see if there was any recollection on Larry's face. Anything at all.

After staring blankly ahead, he simply said, "Interesting name. He must like mountains or westerns."

"Actually, he is a *she*." Hope held her breath as Larry shifted in his seat.

Diverting his eyes, Larry-Mac appeared uncomfortable but still nothing seemed to register. "I've already got a woman. Willow's my old lady."

"Yes, I know." She paused. "Please hear me out."

Drumming his fingers on her desk, Larry-Mac glanced at his Timex watch. "I'm not sure if this is a good idea. I need to think about it." He pushed off the arms of the chair and began to stand. "I've gotta get back to work."

Hope talked fast. "I'll smooth everything over with Willow. You can send her photos as we drive. It'll almost be as though she's with us."

Crossing his arms, Larry asked, "When are you thinkin'? And where?"

"Nashville. This weekend."

Larry-Mac's eyebrows shot up. "Nashville. Ain't never been that far south. That's pretty far away."

Hope threw in the offer of a good Italian meal—her treat. "Think of it as a mini-vacation." She forced a smile. "Maybe you'll find a place to take Willow in the future."

Running his fingers through his hair, he said, "Willow and I were goin' to the movies this weekend, plus I do laundry on Saturdays. I don't know."

"You won't be sorry." *Actually, we both might be sorry but I can't think about that.* Hope paused. "It'll be a weekend road trip. I think it's about a six-hour drive to Nashville. After our meeting with—your friend—maybe we can hit Blake Shelton's honky-tonk that night."

The janitor shrugged. "Sounds kinda fun. If Willow don't mind."

After several more questions, Larry finally agreed.

Hope jumped up from her desk and awkwardly shook his hand before he could change his mind. "Great. Thank you. Let's meet at Hilltop's parking lot early Saturday morning, say 6 o'clock. I'll find Willow and tell her."

"Tell her what you want, but I'm discussin' this with my wife."

Groaning inwardly, Hope said, "I understand."

Chapter 28

Rolling up the newspaper article, Hope rushed toward Willow's classroom. Waving from the hallway, she eventually got the art teacher's attention and motioned for her to come outside. Not mincing any words, Hope relayed the conversation she had had with Larry-Mac.

Willow had a poker face as she glanced into her classroom and back to Hope.

Shifting from foot to foot, Hope said, "Listen, I know I was harsh earlier. I want what's best for both of you, but if Larry is who I think he is, then, he's still married to Montana which means your marriage isn't legal."

Willow sucked in her breath. "I can't believe this." Swallowing hard, she asked, "Are-Are you sure it's her?"

Hope squeezed Willow's arm and softened her tone. "As sure as I can be without setting eyes on the woman and hearing her voice." Hope watched as Willow's eyes rimmed with tears. "I know how hard this must be. I realize you just got married but will you promise you won't tell Larry-Mac who she is? I want to see if his long-term memory will return. I don't want his thoughts jumbled any more than they already are before we get to the nursing home. Do you understand what I'm asking? I honestly think this will be better for everyone. I kept hoping his memory would be intact by now. We've got to see if this will work."

Crossing her arms, Willow leaned against the wall. "I don't know. We both talked about the importance of honesty before we got married. I don't feel good about this."

"I know it's a lot to ask." Hope chewed on her lip. "Look. I'm a high school counselor, not a psychologist, but I truly think if his memory returns organically and he isn't rushed or frustrated about jumbled scenarios, maybe just maybe everything will come flooding back. Surely you want that too."

Willow peeked back inside her classroom where her students busied themselves with drawing a lion's head with a massive mane. Hope peered inside and noticed an enlarged lion's head on the chalkboard but it was upside down.

"Why is your drawing upside down?"

"It tricks the mind. Students aren't overwhelmed by thinking they can't draw the intricate details of the lion's mane. I do this art exercise every year. The students start slowly at the bottom, work freestyle, and *voila*—"

Nodding frantically, Hope said, "That's exactly my point about seeing things differently to trick the mind. Does this mean you'll agree to Larry's going on the trip with me? It'll be one quick overnight. I'll pay for his room, of course."

"I don't know. I love Mac and he loves me. Why would I want to do anything to potentially mess that up?"

Bristling, Hope forced herself to remain calm. "Because he's still married to the woman who raised me and she's sitting in a damn nursing home, that's why. Montana doesn't have any idea Larry is alive. His name is Larry, by the way, but I'll call him Larry or Mac or Larry-Mac, whatever you and he prefer." Her face flushed. "I know this is crummy timing but—"

A tear rolled down Willow's cheek. "Mac wouldn't do this to me intentionally. I know him."

Hope sighed. "I know 'Mac' wouldn't, but Larry would. Let me bottom line this. Larry and Montana adopted me. They were hippie losers. I thought they both died a couple of years ago. After last year's tornado, my best friends saw Larry-Mac on television and they agree it's him."

"This is un-freaking believable." Willow swatted her long, prematurely gray braid over her shoulder.

Hope reached for her colleague's arm. "I know. I've been living with this nightmare for nearly two years."

Shaking, Hope glanced back toward the students, and lowered her voice. "Whether you like it or not, Larry and I are going to find Montana. She's his wife and deserves to know he's alive. This needs to happen sooner rather than later. He's already agreed to go Saturday morning."

Blood drained from Willow's face. "Mac and I don't keep secrets from one another. Our relationship is built on trust."

"And pot, likely." Hope immediately apologized. "I'm sorry. That was a cheap shot."

"Indeed it was." Willow stared at her tiny diamond ring with a now-matching wedding band. "How can I keep this colossal piece of news from him? That his real name isn't Mac? That he was married to Montana, and she's apparently alive." The art teacher glanced at her now-restless students and whispered, "I don't want to be married to a married man."

"You can't be. It isn't legal."

Willow distractedly twirled her braid. "What a hot mess. Assuming you're right, I'll promise to keep quiet about what you've told me on *one* condition."

"Name it."

"That you'll stay in touch by text. I want to know how the trip is going. I want to know how Mac's doing. I want to know where you are in Nashville and whether he recognizes Mon—" Willow's voice broke.

Hope bobbed her head. "Thank you. I'll text you twice a day."

Willow held up a finger. "Oh, and you've also got to promise that you'll accept me as your-your—"

"My mom?" Hope's eyebrows shot up. "That'll be a little more difficult."

Nodding, Willow said, "Fair enough. How about as your friend?"

"Done." Hope hugged Willow and ran to her office to rearrange her schedule.

She texted her friends: I NEED YOUR ADVICE. PLEASE SAY YOU'LL MEET ME AT COCONUTS AT 6, OKAY?

After Alex responded affirmatively, Suzy replied that she was on her way with her husband in tow. Cheri didn't answer. Glad at least two friends could meet, Hope jotted down a short packing list.

Chapter 29

Alex had barely left her office all day. Overwhelmed with marketing projects, she decided to work overtime. Hannah had called in sick again, more likely an escapade with Sean, which Alex couldn't prove and knew her intern would deny.

Traipsing across the darkened lobby, she waved goodbye to the two drive-thru tellers, stepped into the bank parking lot, and froze.

Standing next to an all-too-familiar purple jeep in the desolate lot was none other than Tony's nasty ex-wife. Grimacing, Alex said, "What the hell are you doing here, Nikki?"

"Well, well. I thought you were gonna have a sleepover at the fucking bank. Aren't you the model employee working long hours?" Nikki's raspy voice cut through the early evening air.

Attempting to appear more confident than she felt, Alex quipped, "Forget where you lived?"

A cigarette dangled from Nikki's lips. Sneering, Tony's ex asked, "Are you always such a bitch?" She blew smoke in Alex's direction.

"Bitches bring out the bitch in me, I guess." Fishing through her purse, Alex was furious she couldn't find her car keys. "Why don't you run along?" Motioning with one hand, Alex said, "The bank's closed, obviously. Besides, you're not a customer." *Thank God.*

Nikki spat on the ground. "I ain't going nowhere."

What a piece of work. "I forgot something. I've got to go back inside. Entertain yourself for all I care." Alex raced up the sidewalk, punched in the back door code, and stormed inside. Heart thudding, for once, she wished her hateful intern were there.

Tearing her desk apart, Alex eventually found her car keys on the floor behind her office chair. Before going back outside to confront Miss Charming, she texted Tony.

WHY IS YOUR BITCH EX AT MY BANK?

Sliding the phone into her purse before he had a chance to respond, Alex groaned inwardly at the thought of another encounter with Nikki. When she stepped outside, the barracuda unfortunately stood in the same spot, daring Alex with her black eyes.

Alex decided to preempt the questioning. "No, I don't know where Tony is, and I haven't seen your precious son in ages." Unlocking the door to her Mustang, she put one foot inside her car.

Nikki grabbed her arm. "Don't you dare touch me," Alex hissed. "We have security cameras everywhere." She pointed toward the two-story brick bank. "Back the fuck off."

Loosening her grip, Nikki took one step back, and glanced toward the building. Narrowing her eyes, she asked, "Why is Sean sniffing around here?" Lip curled, she continued. "Are you banging him as well as Tony, you whore?" Spit flew out of her mouth. "So help me God if you are—"

For some odd reason, Alex felt protective of Hannah who, she worried, was likely sleeping with Sean. Knowing her intern could never handle this bitch, Alex squared her jaw and answered in a silly singsong voice, "I don't know what you're talking about. I've never seen Sean here. And, by the way, he'd be the last man on earth I'd bang, as you so eloquently put it."

"Liar."

Ignoring the comment, Alex rolled up her window, locked the door, and sped off. *What a shit show this relationship is. And why the hell am I protecting Hannah? I need a drink.*

Chapter 30

After hearing Jon and Fernando's news, Suzy suggested they go to Coconuts. "I know I can't drink but I can pretend." As Ken parked, she noticed a dusty old blue pickup with mud-covered tires. *Hmm. That's different.*

As they stepped into the darkened bar, Suzy spotted none other than her gorgeous New Yorker friend sitting with a cowboy. Cocking an eyebrow, her mouth fell open as she observed Cheri who was obviously hanging on his every country word. Chuckling at how mismatched—yet cute—they were, Suzy felt like a lurker but couldn't turn away. "Let's get a table." She pointed to one a few tables over.

Suzy had never seen the socialite dress so casually. Admiring Cheri's skin-tight white jeans and leopard print tank, she noticed the cowboy wore faded blue jeans, a well-fitting navy button-down, and brown cowboy boots. *He's as hot as any romance cover model, and Cheri's on fire.* Turning to Ken, she said, "They do say opposites attract, but I never would have paired these two. I wonder if he knows she's a Van Buren."

Shrugging, Ken stared in Suzy's direction. "Who's the cowboy?"

Suzy grinned. "Cheri mentioned she met a cowboy at the airport. This must be him."

"Interesting." Ken glanced at a menu. Chuckling, he asked, "What do you pair with people watching?"

"Anything you want. I'm having a non-alcoholic cocktail." Suzy rubbed her burgeoning baby bump. "I'll have wine once these two are born." As the door to Coconuts opened, light streamed inside. Suzy turned. "Look who else is here."

~ ~ ~

Oblivious to being watched, Cheri waved Gus over to order food but stiffened as a shadow crossed her table.

"Well, well. Who do we have here?" Alex placed her hands on Cheri's shoulders while simultaneously beaming at Cole. "What's this? Business or pleasure?"

Cheri crossed her legs as she and Cole exchanged looks. Turning toward Alex, he asked, "Are you always this direct?"

Hope appeared at the table. "Yes, she is. I'm glad you're back, Cheri." After giving the New Yorker a hug, she turned to Cole and extended her hand.

After introductions, Cheri noticed Cole glanced at his watch. *I don't want him to leave.* She did her best to dismiss her girlfriends in the nicest way she knew how. "Great to see you. I'll join you girls, um, later. Maybe."

"We can join you right here. There's plenty of room." Alex planted herself at the high-top table.

Cole chuckled. "Are you sure she isn't the New Yorker? She's straightforward." Standing, he said, "Let me get you ladies a chair."

Alex pointed toward Cheri's red heels. "Nice. I wish I could afford designer shoes."

"These old things?" Cheri pursed her lips and Alex seemed to get the message. Making a mental note to buy plain tennis shoes at Target, she turned to Cole in an attempt to change the subject. "Where's Suzy?"

"Did I hear my name?" Suzy give Cheri a quick hug as she and Ken joined the group.

"We're gonna need a bigger table." Cole hopped up and pushed another table beside theirs. "Looks like you have as many friends as I do, New York."

Nodding, Cheri said, "I'll introduce you."

After the exchanges, Cole rubbed his chin in an obvious attempt to keep up with their banter. Gus brought two bowls of truffle popcorn, chips, and salsa. "On the house," the server said.

"Thanks, Gus." Alex fished in her purse for anti-bacterial gel. "Anybody want some?"

After everyone shook their heads, Cole turned to Alex. "You'd never make it on the farm." He glanced at his boots. "I probably have cow manure on them."

Wrinkling her nose, Alex said, "And here you are with a Van—"

Cheri cut in. "I'd love to see your farm, Cole. It sounds serene after the hustle and bustle of city life." Swiveling in Alex's direction, she furrowed her brows. Alex noticed her friend coyly slid her Rolex from the top of her wrist to the bottom. As the two friends made eye contact, Alex winked.

Grasping the undertones, Alex studied the unlikely couple. Turning to Cole, she said, "Got any friends? Any cute cowboy friends?"

He nodded. "Sure, I have several."

"Why don't you bring them here the next time you come?" Alex asked.

"Cowboys at Coconuts. That's a novel idea." Cole's eyes twinkled. "Actually, two of my friends, Wyatt and Bo, were here earlier which surprised me as much as it probably would you." Glancing at his watch, he turned toward Cheri. "I think I'll pass on the cattle auction tomorrow. I need to cut hay in the mornin'. I have an hour's drive. I'd better run." He hopped off his bar stool and hovered behind Cheri's chair. "How about walkin' me out?"

She sprang off her seat. "I thought you'd never ask."

Chapter 31

Mouths agape, the women never took their eyes off Cheri and Cole's backsides as they stepped across Coconuts and out the door.

Alex turned toward her friends. "Looks like our city girl has a crush on a cowboy."

"I think you're right," Suzy said.

Hope shook her head. "Why does this happen to everyone but me? She's only been in town for a year and already has a date."

Suzy patted her arm. "Give it time, hon."

Alex wiped her mouth. "Who needs men?"

"Hey." Ken winked. "I'm still here, remember?"

"Sorry, Ken. You don't count," Alex said.

Throwing both hands up, Ken said, "I'm not sure that's much better." He excused himself and went to the restroom.

After several minutes, Suzy glanced toward the front door. "I wonder what they're doing outside. Do you think Cheri and Cole are dating?"

Reaching for a handful of popcorn, Hope said, "Talk about opposites. I wonder if he knows she's a Van Buren?"

"Nah." Alex shook her head. "Didn't you hear Cheri cut me off when I mentioned her designer shoes and started to say her last name? I have a feeling it's a huge secret. I can't wait to hear how this went down."

Suzy nodded. "We should honor her wish of anonymity."

Hope reached for another handful of popcorn and chased it with a sip of margarita. "Yep, it's her job to tell him."

Alex stared toward the front entrance but couldn't see

the cowboy. "He's cute."

"That's my cue to leave." Ken kissed his wife. "If one of your friends will take you home, I'll be on my way. I don't want to discuss the cute cowboy."

Secretly happy for girlfriend time, Suzy squeezed Ken's arm. "Thanks, babe. See you in an hour or two."

After Ken left, Suzy requested hot green tea. After it arrived, she said, "This is such a boring drink. I really miss merlot." Resting her arm on her belly, she said, "But it'll be worth it to have two bouncing babies."

Shaking her head, Alex said, "I still can't believe you're having twins. Sheesh. I'd be ready to put a gun to my—" Likely noticing Hope's glare, she stopped herself. "Of course, you'll juggle those screaming kids like a pro."

"Alex." Hope widened her eyes. "Not helpful."

Reaching for the popcorn, Alex said, "You know me. I tell it like it is." Placing her arm on Suzy's, she chuckled. "I'm sure Hope will be more than helpful in the babysitting arena."

Suzy winked. "Your name is on my babysitting sheet too, my dear."

Shaking her head, Alex said, "Honestly, you don't want me near babies. I'd rather help you with your wedding business. Fair trade-off?"

Reaching for a sweater in her purse, Suzy said, "We'll see. I don't have any brides lined up but if I get another mother of the bride like that pretentious Mrs. Biltmore, she's all yours."

"Mrs. Bitchmore, you mean?" Alex said. "I could handle someone like her. I'd enjoy that."

Hope slapped her forehead with her palm. "I remember her. Didn't she have a stroke and become, um, nice?"

Nodding, Suzy said, "She sure did. Too bad she isn't on Facebook. I'd like to catch up with her."

"She owns the Biltmore Country Club across town,"

Alex said. "We could always have lunch there."

Suzy chuckled. "I don't want to catch up with her that badly." Glancing toward the front entrance, she said, "Cheri's taking her sweet time with that cowboy."

"So would I," both Alex and Hope said. Alex doubled over laughing. "Change of subject. What's going on with you, Hope? Why the text earlier? Not that I'm complaining."

Rubbing her forehead, Hope said, "I do have excitement, I suppose. But it's unwanted."

Alex and Suzy both leaned forward. "And?"

Hope took a sip of margarita for fortitude. "Get ready. This is a shocker. I'm pretending to be upbeat, but I'm a total and complete wreck. Willow and Larry-Mac, my thought-dead adopted dad, got married in Eureka Springs. I read a newspaper article months ago about a woman, who looks just like Montana, also known as Larry's wife, who is apparently alive in a nursing home."

After a few gasps, Alex's eyebrows shot up. "You don't even live in Utah."

"Huh?" Suzy asked.

"Polygamy. If Larry is indeed Larry, and Montana is alive, then he has committed polygamy."

Hope's eyes filled with tears. "Afraid so. I've met with my dad about this and—"

"He's an attorney, right?" Suzy asked. Hope nodded. "What does he suggest?"

Taking a deep breath, Hope said, "He believes, like I do, that I must get Larry to Nashville to see his wife." She steepled her fingers. "Maybe seeing Montana will jog his memory. Then we can deal with the legality of his marriage to Willow. I want to leave for Nashville as soon as possible."

"What a mess." Alex held up her fingers. "So, girls, let's see. What are we dealing with this time?" She ticked each item off on her fingers. "Morning sickness, a hateful intern who is probably dating my boyfriend's married brother, and the whopper of them all, Hope's adopted dad got married, but his first wife is still alive." Sipping her wine, she asked, "Does that about sum it up?"

"Don't forget the cowboy. I wonder if Cheri is coming back inside." Suzy and Hope both giggled. Alex grinned. "Yeah, I admit. I'm most intrigued about the cowboy. I figured Cheri was hobnobbing with Elton John again or maybe Keith Urban. But here she is with a real live cowboy."

"Change of subject." Suzy frowned. "One girl at the OB/GYN thought I was waiting for my daughter. She thought I was *the grandma*."

Elbowing Suzy, Alex said, "Newsflash: You are a grandma."

Suzy threw up both hands. "You're impossible."

"Well, you are." Alex sipped her chardonnay. "But you're a young, sexy grandma. There's that."

"Thanks, I think." Suzy glanced toward the entrance. "Something tells me Cheri isn't coming back inside."

"Can you blame her?" Alex asked.

Chapter 32

Still furious about Nikki's confrontation in the bank parking lot, Alex couldn't wait to interrogate her intern the following morning. Crossing the lobby, she made idle chitchat with lenders, got coffee, and waited for Hannah to arrive.

Before her intern had a chance to sit down, Alex stood with both hands on her hips. "Close the door."

Hannah's eyebrows shot up. "Are you firing me?"

If only. "Listen, Hannah, you don't have any idea who you're dealing with. Nikki is a mean, nasty, horrible woman. I'm almost afraid of her, and I'm not afraid of anyone. Don't mess with her husband. She'll tear your head off."

Hannah played dumb. "Who's Nikki?"

"Cut the bullshit. I know you're having an affair with Sean. FYI, he's married to Nikki, Tony's ex. She's a royal bitch and that's being kind." Crossing her legs, Alex said, "I'm pretty sure I've mentioned this before. Do you get the message?"

Hannah rolled her eyes. "Shouldn't we be discussing bank business? What's on the agenda today, boss?"

Clenching her jaw, Alex was half upset that she had defended her intern to Nikki in the parking lot. *So this is how we're playing it.* "Fine. Don't say I didn't warn you."

As she swiveled toward her computer, Alex saw a worried look cross Hannah's face. *I knew it.* Glancing at her project calendar, she said, "We have the Home Builders' Association trade show coming up soon. Why don't you create new flyers or brochures featuring our construction loan and real estate loan officers? Take the lenders' photos and get a statement from them about how they love helping Show-Me Bank customers fulfill their dreams. Brightening, she added, "Better yet, get some testimonials from customers saying how seamless the process was. You know the spiel."

"On it." Hannah reached for her trusty iPad giving Alex full view of her massive cleavage. Internally shaking her head, Alex couldn't believe her boss—Hannah's dad—was so dense about his daughter's transformation. *Sure, you went to the beach for vacation last year and came back as Dolly.*

Tapping on her desk calendar with a pen, Alex said, "You'll want to set up a schedule for the trade show, otherwise, you and I will be working all damn weekend. I'd suggest four-hour time slots. That way, no one's weekend will be totally destroyed." Raising her eyebrows, she added, "Except yours, of course. I want you there every day."

Hannah crossed her legs. "Are you going to be there every day?"

"Probably not. I've done this for years. It's your turn."

Chapter 33

Suzy exited The Coffee Drip after meeting with a reluctant bride who was obviously interviewing every wedding planner in Crystal City. After seemingly the thirtieth question by the bride before Suzy had finished her first cup of decaf coffee, she excused herself and left without saying good-bye. In the past, she'd never be that unprofessional. Once inside her car, she leaned against the headrest. *I'm hormonal enough. I don't have time for an indecisive bride. She can choose another wedding planner.* Patting her stomach, she thought, *These babies don't need the added stress.*

Driving on autopilot, Suzy turned on a soothing jazz station, shopped at a baby store where she bought matching baby boy and girl outfits, and eventually made her way home. After parking in the garage, she found Ken sitting in front of the television, half watching a ballgame, and half staring into space.

"Hi, hon." She set her purse on the floor by the kitchen. When he didn't answer, she asked, "You okay?"

Grunting, Ken said, "I'll tell you after dinner. I'm starving. What can I help you with?"

"By the look on your face, I'd say fix yourself a scotch. I'd love wine, but you know."

Ken crossed the room, nuzzled her neck, and simultaneously rubbed her growing baby bump. After he made a stiff drink, Suzy rinsed brussels sprouts in a colander and wondered why her husband was stressed. Reaching for a cutting board, Ken said, "I'll chop."

Working in tandem, Ken cut the greens in half, spread them on a baking sheet, and drizzled the vegetables with olive oil, salt, and pepper. She winked at him. "I've trained you well."

Patting her behind, he said, "That you have."

Stirring the blackened seasoning, Suzy rubbed it on the tilapia, sprayed the pan so it wouldn't stick, and placed the fish in the oven. Handing Ken a lemon to slice, she said, "You're really quiet. I know we've been dealing with a lot lately with the news of the twins, Jon and Fernando's new marriage, and baby Violet."

Kissing his cheek, she said, "Everything will calm down soon, hon. We'll find our new normal, as contrived as that sounds." Noticing her husband's mouth remained set in a grim line, she ran through a list of possibilities. Work? His health? Izzy? Ken was never in a bad mood.

After a few minutes, Suzy pulled the tilapia out of the oven and let it rest while she sprinkled parmesan cheese and toasted pine nuts on the brussels sprouts. "Want any bread?"

Ken shook his head as he carried plates to the table. Izzy appeared from her bedroom, unsmiling, which wasn't unusual. As typical, her cellphone was glued to her hand.

"Will you get the forks and napkins, Izzy?" Suzy asked.

Without a word, the teen grabbed a handful of silverware, threw napkins in the middle of the table, plopped in a chair, and returned to her phone.

Suzy decided not to mention their no-tech rule during meals since everyone appeared to be on edge. Dining around their round breakfast table, the threesome passed food silently, as if a favorite pet had just died.

Except for forks clacking, a cloak of graveness filled the room. Unable to stand it a second longer, Suzy asked, "What's wrong?" Her eyes bulged as a thought of despair crossed her mind. "Oh, my God. Is baby Violet okay?"

"Baby's fine," Ken said, his voice wooden.

"Thank goodness." She let out a long sigh of relief. "Then what is it? Will one of you please tell me? School issues, Iz? Did you get a bad grade? If so, your dad or I can help you with homework, or we can find a tutor." Taking a big bite of blackened tilapia, Suzy held her fork in mid-air as she glanced from Ken to Izzy and back again. "Well?"

"It's not school—exactly." Izzy picked at her food. She pushed her phone to the side, even though Suzy had noticed it lit up several times during dinner indicating incoming texts.

"Alrighty then. Since no one wants to talk. Change of subject. Izzy, have you planned our family activity for next week?"

Ken shifted in his chair with a half grunt, half groan.

Izzy stared at her half-eaten plate. "There may not be any more family activities."

Happy they had finally found a way to bond with various family outings, Suzy was puzzled by Izzy's response. She studied her stepdaughter's unreadable face. "I thought you enjoyed our adventures." Suzy ticked off activities on her fingers. "Let's see. We've gone bowling, to the movies, shopping, skating where you laughed a little too hard after I fell, and to a painting class where you showed definite artistic potential but Ken had little." Thinking her tiny joke would lighten the somber mood, but didn't, Suzy continued, voice rising. "Why in the world would we stop our fun excursions? We're all enjoying them." Glancing at Ken who stared at his almost-empty plate, sans one brussels sprout, she asked, "Will someone tell me what's going on?"

Slamming her napkin on the table, Izzy said, "You tell her, Dad." She stormed off to her teen hut, otherwise known as the bedroom of doom.

Wincing as she studied her husband's solemn face, Suzy said, "I wish I could have wine. I have a feeling I could use some."

"I definitely need another drink." Ken headed toward their makeshift bar near the kitchen and poured himself a second, healthy scotch.

Once she spotted the too-full amber cocktail, Suzy's eyebrows shot up. "This must be serious."

"It is." Ken gestured toward the couch. "Let's get comfortable. I'll help you clean up later."

Chapter 34

Thrilled Cole had called, Cheri hummed and paced while she waited for him to arrive. Still a tad confused about her attraction to him, all that mattered was that she couldn't wait to see him. *I never thought I'd date a cowboy. These sweet, innocent guys are a refreshing change from the Wall Street types I've dated in the past.*

As the doorbell rang, Cheri made herself schlep toward the foyer when she actually wanted to race like an Olympian. *I've got to at least appear as though I'm not in a white-hot heat.* After standing behind the front door a few seconds longer than necessary, she swung it open. "Hi, cowboy."

"Hi, New York. It's great to see you. I have something fun planned for today."

"Is that right?" Butterflies danced in Cheri's stomach.

Leaning against the doorjamb, he said, "Wanna go to a pool party?"

"A pool party?" Glancing at the blue sky, she said, "Sure. Sounds fun."

Rubbing the side of his face, Cole chuckled.

"What's so funny?"

"You'll see soon enough. It'll be unlike any pool party you've ever attended." Cole winked. "Guaranteed."

"Really? I've seen some crazy things in New York. You'd be hard pressed to top some of the stuff I've seen in the Village."

His eyes twinkled. "Trust me on this one."

"I'll take that challenge." Peering at her hot-pink

toenails, Cheri was glad she had gotten a recent mani-pedi. "Where's the party?"

"In my friend's backyard. Got a bathin' suit? I'll wait out here."

After disappearing inside her closet, she grabbed a black bikini. After cramming the swimsuit inside a tote, she changed into denim shorts, a black tee, and joined him on the porch. "Let's go."

"I hope you're ready for this." Reaching for her hand, Cole led her to his Chevy truck, started the ignition, and turned to a country station. As they drove away, they listened to "Sangria" by Blake Shelton. Turning to Cheri, Cole said, "I'd like to taste sangria on your lips."

Licking her lips absentmindedly, she felt her cheeks flush. "We can arrange that, if your friend has any."

"Sangria?" Cole laughed. "Doubtful, but he'll have beer, beer, and more beer."

She wrinkled her nose. "I'm not really a beer person."

"Got you covered." Cole turned into the nearest convenience store. "What kind of wine do you want?"

"Surprise me."

As Cole walked inside the store, he glanced back at Cheri who was transfixed on his backside. *Geeze. He caught me staring.* Returning with a large plastic bag, he placed it in the back seat.

Reaching in the back, Cheri peeked inside and found a chilled chardonnay, a pinot noir, and a cabernet. "This is either going to be a week-long pool party or someone has to help me drink these."

"Don't worry. You'll have plenty of help." He reached across the seat and put his rough hand on her leg.

She placed her hand over his. "I see someone forgot to use lotion again."

"Cowboys, country boys, and farm guys don't do lotion, remember?"

She laughed. "You're a nice guy, you know that? You have a nice swagger too." She grinned as he shifted in his seat. "Are you blushing? You *are* blushing. Your neck is pink."

Cole grinned. "I'm not accustomed to discussin' my swagger."

Leaning her head against the seat and enjoying the breeze in her hair, she couldn't wipe the silly grin off her face.

Why do I have so much fun with this country boy? When am I going back to my real life in New York? She glanced at an oblivious Cole who stared ahead at the road. He simply enjoyed the scenery without an outward care in the world.

I need to learn how to relax. Cheri took a deep breath. Cole gave her hand a squeeze. "Tell me more about this pool party."

Chapter 35

While Cole drove, Cheri glanced out the window. She had seen more countryside in the past hour than she had in her entire life. They passed field after field dotted with cattle or horses. Some cows slept under the trees while others waded waist deep in ponds or grazed on grass.

While studying the livestock, Cheri rolled the window down, stuck her head outside, and inhaled. "I love this country air. No pollution."

"As long as you don't mind the occasional odor from a pig farm."

"I'll pass." Relaxing as the wind blew through her long, blond hair, Cheri stuck her arm out the window. The sun warmed her. "I could use a tan. Think I can get one before the pool party?"

Cole gave her a sideways grin. "Worth a try."

Noticing farm houses and barns acres apart, Cheri said, "I'm surprised someone has a pool around here. I mainly see farmland, horses, and cows." As if to punctuate her comment, a cow mooed.

"Guess she agrees with you." Cole gave Cheri a mischievous smile. "There's definitely a pool at this house. In fact, it's the coolest, most creative pool you've ever laid eyes on. I guarantee it."

"That's quite a guarantee." Squeezing his free hand, she said, "I can't wait."

Cole studied Cheri's hands and chuckled. "New nail polish?"

"Yep. Pink camo. What do you think?"

He winked. "They're almost as beautiful as you."

Curling her fingers, she said, "You hate them. I can tell." She tugged on one edge to tear it off. "They're stick-on nails. I saw them at Walgreens, of all places." She muttered, "I guess I'm trying too hard to fit in."

Cole put his hand over hers. "Leave them alone. They're cool, but don't try to fit in. Don't change. I like you the way you are."

He likes me. Cheri turned back toward the lush green hills as Cole rounded curves. Several roller-coaster hills later, they turned right. "We're almost there."

As they drove across several round, steel rails spaced a few inches apart, Cole explained it was a cattle guard to keep cows from getting out of the pasture and onto the road. He turned down a short dirt road and pulled up to an old farm house. A screened-in porch covered the front. A tire swing hung from a tree limb and a red hummingbird feeder adorned another tree. Wind chimes jingled in the background. The house had wide white siding, gray shutters, and a gray roof. Two miniature Shetland ponies grazed in a fenced-in area in front of a weathered red barn sorely in need of a paint job.

Cheri didn't see a soul, nor a pool. "What a cute farmhouse, but where's the swimming pool?"

"You'll see." Hopping out, Cole hooked his arm through hers and led her toward the backyard.

While at the side of the quaint house, Cheri heard boisterous cheers, whoops, and hollers. After they crossed the expansive yard filled with mature trees and overgrown shrubs, her eyes widened.

Motioning with his hand, Cole said, "There it is."

Hay bales were stacked several bundles high and deep. The straw bundles were arranged in an enormous rectangle. A massive blue plastic tarp was spread across the middle and draped over the hay bales with plenty of rope securing it. Three long garden hoses continually squirted water into the makeshift pool, which was nearly filled to the brim. Cheri's hand flew over her mouth. "That's hilarious."

Winking, Cole said, "I'm guessin' this is your first hillbilly swimming pool."

"You'd be correct. I already love it." Glancing at the colorful paper lanterns hanging from a nearby clothesline, Cheri fished her cell out of her tote bag. Angling the phone to take several photos, she said, "I've got to show this pool to my girlfriends. They'll never believe it."

Reaching for her hand, Cole led her toward the rowdy group, already splashing in the ice-cold water, most with beers in hand. Cupping his mouth with one hand he yelled, "Hey, everybody. Give a warm howdy to Miss Cheri."

She heard more whoops as someone said, "Howdy, Miss Cheri." Another person yelled, "Grab a beer and jump in."

She spotted a galvanized silver tub overflowing with ice, Budweiser, Coors, and Heineken.

Cole followed her stare. "Want me to get the wine out of the truck?"

Tugging on Cole's arm, she said, "No, I'll drink beer. I want to fit—" She paused. "The wine will wait."

"But you prefer wine. They only have beer."

A stocky, shirtless man wearing overalls lumbered over. "On the contrary, Cole. You, sir, are mistaken. We do have wine. My dandelion wine is the best thing to ever touch your lips." He eyed Cheri. "Well, almost the best thing."

"Dandelion wine?" Cheri grinned. "I bet that has a cute label."

"No label, ma'am." Lifting his straw cowboy hat, the man promptly placed it back on his prematurely balding head. "It's moonshine. Best in these here parts if I say so myself."

Cheri peered at Cole. "Isn't moonshine illegal?"

"Not illegal to make it but against the law to sell it," Cole said.

Moonshine Man filled a small plastic cup for her. "Try it."

Taking a small sip, she puckered. "Wow. That's strong."

The man laughed. "And?"

Cheri lied. "It's good. Thanks."

After the man left, Cole turned to her. "You can toss it behind a shrub. I've had his moonshine before. That stuff tastes like crap."

She laughed so hard she snorted. "I like you more every day."

"Ditto. Do you have a swimsuit underneath your clothes?"

She patted her tote. "I have a black bikini."

Cole snapped his fingers. "Just my luck. I was hoping you'd have to go in wearing your clothes—or naked."

Cheri's eyes bulged as Cole unbuttoned his plaid shirt and threw it across a bush covered with blue Hydrangeas. "Is that what you're doing?"

She couldn't take her eyes off his chiseled abs and toned arms. "Um, I can't exactly fling my shirt across a bush."

"We're all friends here," he teased.

"Not gonna happen."

Slowly unzipping his tight, faded jeans, Cole stepped out of them and let them fall onto the grass.

Cheri pretended to shade her eyes but peeked between her fingers. He sported red, white, and blue patriotic swim trunks. Playfully punching him, she said, "You're a nut."

Cole grabbed her hand. "Last one in is a—"

A raspy female voice said, "Hi, Cole. Long time no see."

Chapter 36

After settling on the sofa with chamomile tea in hand, Suzy kissed Ken gently on the mouth. Rubbing his stiff shoulders, she whispered, "You can tell me anything unless it's that you're leaving me." She gave a half smile. "FYI. That would require a stronger drink than tea. Just so you know."

Unclenching his jaw, he managed a small smile. "It's not about us, babe. I love you. It's about Izzy." Taking a healthy sip of scotch, Ken added, "Actually, it's more about Izzy's mother."

Suzy had never met Izzy's elusive mother and wondered if she were in town. Ready for calm in her life, she bristled at the thought of dealing with Ken's ex while hormonal with twins. She spoke more confidently than she felt. "Go on."

Raking his fingers through his hair, Ken blurted out, "Izzy's mother and her young, boy toy boyfriend want Izzy to move to Hollywood."

Stiffening, Suzy said, "That's about the last thing I expected you to say." Setting her tea on the coffee table, she turned toward her husband. "Why?"

"Exactly." Shrugging, Ken asked, "Why and why now? Who knows?"

Suzy studied her husband. "What does Izzy think?"

He stared at the blank television. "Given the fact that she's the odd teen out in her group of friends since Nelly moved to Arkansas and the fact that boys in her class haven't yet noticed her, I think she's seriously considering it." He shrugged. "I mean, what teen wouldn't want to live in La-La Land?"

Staring into her husband's sad eyes, Suzy felt several emotions. Some she couldn't—or wouldn't—admit to Ken like the fact she'd dearly love time for the two of them before the babies arrived. Her heart swelled at the thought of actual alone time for a few months with his often-bratty, sullen daughter out of the house. Since they had gotten married after his whirlwind proposal at their high school reunion, they hadn't had much alone time as a couple.

Leaning against her husband's shoulder, Suzy could almost feel his nervous, worried energy. The rational side of her kicked in. "California probably isn't the greatest place to raise a teenager. I'm sure you're worried, hon. I'm bewildered and shocked, to say the least."

"You think you're shocked. I haven't even met Pretty Boy Toy. Why would I send my daughter to live with a complete stranger?"

"What's his name?"

Rolling his eyes, Ken said, "What else? Brody."

"That sounds about right." She locked eyes with her husband. "You know you've never mentioned your ex. Not once. I don't even know her name."

"I haven't? Surely Izzy has told you."

Shaking her head, Suzy said, "Nope. She's like a spirit that I can't see. What's her name?"

"Destiny."

Suppressing a giggle, Suzy said, "You married a woman named Destiny?"

Throwing up his hands, Ken said, "She's a free spirit with long, flowing hair who always wore sundresses and ankle bracelets. I guess I was attracted to her Type-B nature and flattered she liked a straight-laced, responsible guy like me."

Trying to picture the couple, Suzy said, "And now you're married to a slightly buttoned-up wedding planner."

Ken tipped up her chin and kissed her. "And I love her."

As Suzy reached for her tea, she took a deep breath. "Like it or not, Izzy's mother has rights too."

"Thanks for your support." Ken stood and paced.

Easing off the couch, Suzy wrapped her arms around her husband. "Hey, I'm on your side. When is this supposed to happen?"

Rubbing his chin, Ken said, "That's the thing. They want her to move there in a few weeks."

Suzy's mouth fell open. "Before the end of the school year? What's the rush?"

Ken shrugged. "Beats me. I think it will be catastrophic if she begins school mid-semester. Who knows if the teachers in California and Missouri are on the same page? Don't some states do SAT testing while others do ACT? Hell if I know." Shaking his head, he circled the room. "Who knows if all of her credits will transfer?"

"I can ask Hope. She'll know about that stuff. She works at a high school."

"Actually, grades and classes are the least of my worries." Making his way to the kitchen, he opened and closed a cabinet door but returned to the couch empty-handed. Lowering his voice, he said, "Why now? It doesn't make any sense."

Suppressing any glee about having the house to themselves, Suzy said, "I'll support any decision you make." Yawning, she said, "Why don't you finish your drink and try to relax? I'll clean the dishes." Donning pink plastic gloves, she squirted dish soap into the sink. Her phone on the counter beeped indicating a text from Jon. Glancing at the screen, her heart melted when she saw a new photo of a smiling Violet Grace. *My beautiful redheaded granddaughter.* Suzy smiled when she noticed two teeth emerging on Violet's bottom gum line. *Jon always seems to know when I need him.*

Chapter 37

Turning toward the husky female voice, Cheri narrowed her eyes when she recognized the gorgeous woman she almost beat at pool. Never taking her eyes off Cheri, Jade put the kickstand down on her motorcycle, removed her helmet, and shook her mane of shiny, black hair.

Soon transfixed on Cole, Jade asked, "How ya been, honey? Long time no see." She shot Cheri a glance. "Not since our infamous pool game where I won."

"I wouldn't call that a win," Cheri muttered. Cole stood guard by the swimming pool as if he wanted to avoid a cat fight on one hand but wanted to intervene on the other.

Breaking the tense silence, one of the ball cap-wearing guys held a beer in one hand and splashed Cole with the other. "Are you waitin' for it to warm up, pansy?"

Jade eyed Cole from his head to his toes and back again. "I see you haven't lost your figure, honey." She plucked a cigarette out of her black leather pants, never taking her eyes off him. "Anybody got a light?"

Three of the men standing around the galvanized beer tub ran to her side. All had lighters flicked.

"Settle down, boys. I only need one." Jade threw her head back and laughed.

Cheri narrowed her eyes. *Why does this woman always appear and ruin my dates with Cole?* She noticed Cole avoided eye contact with both of them.

Motorcycle woman shrugged off her cropped leather jacket, exposing a corset-style, low-cut black leather vest. Her voluptuous, tanned breasts spilled over the top. She unzipped and shimmied out of her black leather pants in slow motion, obviously ready to give the guys a show. Beneath her long pants was a tiny red bikini. She draped her clothes across her bike with an excruciating deliberateness. It was as if the party had stopped. Hell, it was as if the earth had stopped rotating. All eyes were on Cole's ex-girlfriend, and she reveled in it.

Ignoring Jade's antics, who left Cole standing with his mouth agape, Cheri climbed into the pool, clothes be damned. She wasn't about to leave the area and change now. Shivering, she said, "Brr."

"Ain't you ever been in a backyard pool before, city slicker?" one of the beer drinkers asked.

"Her name is Cheri," Cole said.

So he can speak. Cheri did her best to ignore the stares.

Motorcycle woman sauntered over, stood too close to Cole, and blew smoke in Cheri's direction.

Bristling, Cheri wasn't about to take the bait. Determined to ignore Jade, she locked eyes with Cole. "Getting in?"

He eased one leg in and then the other. "Shit. It's cold."

"Pussy," the moonshine guy yelled. Others laughed while motorcycle woman blew smoke rings in Cole's face.

"Trust me. Cole is no pussy," Jade said.

Cheri caught the attention of Moonshine Man. "Got any more of that dandelion wine?"

One of the guys hopped out and returned with a large, red plastic cup filled to the brim with the nasty moonshine. Cheri didn't care. She needed it.

Cole eyed her as she drank half the concoction in one gulp. "Whoa. That stuff is stronger than normal wine. Better slow down."

Motorcycle woman threw her head back and laughed. "That shit's not strong. Where's my whiskey, boys?"

A skinny guy with a hairless chest wearing only red suspenders and knee-length shorts splashed everyone as he jumped out, in an obvious attempt to be the first to get Jade's drink. "Coming right up."

Narrowing her eyes, Cheri shook her head. "Are you helpless? Can't you get it yourself, Jaaaade?"

Cole's eyes widened. He whispered, "You don't want her as an enemy."

Narrowing her eyes, Cheri said, "If I can handle New Yorkers, I can handle *Jade*."

Motorcycle woman took a long drag of her cigarette. The ashes grew and dangled precariously over the pool. Blowing out a puff, Jade cupped her mouth, and yelled, "Having fun with our country boys, New York?"

Cheri splashed water on her legs. "As a matter of fact, yes."

Jade flipped her jet-black hair over her shoulder as if it were an annoying fly. "Why don't you go back to the east coast? Why are you in our neck of the woods?"

Stepping out of the water, Cole said, "I think it's time for you to shut your pie hole, Jade."

"You used to like my pie hole."

Cheri couldn't stand this woman. Maybe she could drown her in the hillbilly pool. Nah. There were too many witnesses. It was obvious Jade still had the hots for Cole.

Jade spat on the ground. "You're not wanted around here. I think New York is calling."

Turning to Cole, Cheri said, "Let's come back when the black widow isn't here."

He climbed out. "Sure. Anybody got a towel?"

Jade cackled as she winked at Cole. "See you later, babe."

Bristling, Cheri reached for his hand. They walked in silence toward his truck. Once inside, she said, "Your former girlfriend is a piece of work."

Cole turned to her and nodded. "But you held your own, New York. Well done." Running his hand through his wet hair, he said, "Sorry she spoiled the fun. I would have been more forceful but that would have egged her on. I know how to handle Jade. Best to ignore her. What did you think of the redneck pool?"

"I loved it." Cheri studied her photos. "I can't wait to show my friends. But that moonshine? Hard pass."

Chapter 38

Toward the end of the school day, Hope decided she needed a pep talk from her friends before her road trip with Larry. She texted Suzy and Alex who both agreed to meet.

Arriving at Coconuts first, she ordered a margarita. Palms already sweaty, she blew on them before her friends arrived. One by one, Suzy and Alex appeared. "Thanks for meeting me on such short notice. I need some support before I go to Nashville. I've convinced Larry to go with me to see Montana. I'm a nervous wreck."

Suzy reached for Hope's hand. "You're doing the right thing."

Alex shook her head. "I can't believe Willow and Montana are sister wives, and they don't even know it. You may land a TV gig, Hope." When she noticed her friend's mouth was set in a grim line, Alex said, "Sorry, I'm just trying to lighten you up."

"This is a huge problem." Suzy lowered her voice. "It's illegal, as we've discussed."

Hope chewed on a lime slice. "I'm perfectly aware of that. You should have seen me trying to convince Larry to go."

"I'm amazed he agreed since he doesn't even remember you, right?" Alex hung her purse on a hook under the table.

Hope nodded. "Not even a little bit."

"What a damn shame," Alex said, as she waved Gus over.

"When are you leaving?" Suzy asked as she blew on the hot green tea Gus had placed in front of her.

Alex stuck out her tongue at Suzy's tea. "Since I'm not

pregnant, bring me my usual, Gus." The happy-go-lucky server said, "Coming right up."

They made idle chitchat about work. When Hope finished her margarita, she ordered a Diet Coke. "I need to be clearheaded. Where was I?"

Gripping both hands around the zebra print mug, Suzy said, "You were about to tell us when you're leaving. Chuckling, she said, "And they say pregnant women are forgetful."

"We're leaving on Saturday. I'm going home to pack after we eat." After Gus brought the soda, Hope held out her hands. "I'm shaking. I don't know how this road trip will work out. It could be a disaster."

Suzy reached for Hope's hand. "This may be exactly what Larry needs to get his memory back."

"That's what I was thinking." Alex stared at Hope. "Maybe the utter shock of being with you on a long drive, plus seeing his first wife, will jog something deep within the recesses of his brain."

"I hope so. Sometimes calling him Mac and sometimes Larry is driving *me* a little crazy. It really hurts when he calls me 'Miss Truman' or 'Ma'am.'" Hope threw up both hands. "Can you imagine? The man raised me."

Snickering, Alex said, "Actually, you kind of raised them."

Suzy nudged Alex with her elbow. "Not helpful right now. What can we do to help?"

"You're doing it. I needed to see both of you before I left." Her eyes filled with tears. "Your friendship gives me strength." Hope sniffled. "I can always count on you two. I've got to get this over with. Sorry to cut the evening short." She waved Gus over. "I need to pay, Gus."

He tore a ticket out of his pad and placed it on the table. Alex grabbed it. "This is on me. You've got enough to deal with. Go pack."

Alex and Suzy hopped up for a group hug. "Text us if you get a chance," Alex said.

"Yes, we'd love updates," Suzy added.

"I'll try. Forgive me if I forget. I'm going to be slightly preoccupied." Hope placed her purse strap over her shoulder and took a deep breath. "As hard as this will be, I'm really looking forward to one-on-one time with my adopted dad. Paul has been great about this. I forgot to tell you Paul showed me grainy pictures of Larry and Montana. They were at a gas station. He sat on a curb, likely drinking liquor for his pain. From the blurry photo, it appeared that a trucker placed Montana in the cab of his semi."

Suzy gasped and Alex's eyes widened.

Shrugging, Hope said, "It looks like they separated for whatever reason."

"You're kidding?" Alex's mouth fell open. "So this really could be Montana in Nashville?"

"Yep. It appears so. Wish me luck."

Suzy teared up. "That's the spirit, hon."

"Travel safely. Good luck," Alex shouted as Hope exited Coconuts.

Chapter 39

As she drove home from Coconuts, Hope's heart thrashed. *Tomorrow, we drive to Nashville.* Rain pounded on the hood of her car, which only darkened her mood. Turning the windshield wipers to high, her thoughts skittered from bad to worse. *I have to take this gamble. I can't stand knowing Montana is lying in a nursing home unaware her husband is alive or possibly wondering why I'm not trying to find her. I wonder if she has good care, if she still has both of her pretty legs, or has any memory of me.*

Gripping the wheel so hard her knuckles turned white, Hope focused on the road as she planned what to pack. *What a gargantuan mess I've allowed by letting this charade continue.*

~ ~ ~

Before the sun rose, Hope sprang out of bed, brushed her teeth, and threw on mismatched clothes but didn't care. At this point, if her shoes coordinated, it would be a miracle.

Pacing as she awaited Larry's arrival, she had changed the meeting location to her house so he wouldn't need to leave his car unattended in the Hilltop parking lot. She knew Willow might meet them at Hilltop but feared Larry would want her to go with them. This way, she surmised he'd likely come alone.

She had packed toiletries in a disposable Wal-Mart bag adding blue plaid pajamas, socks, a phone charger, change of underwear, and another shirt since they'd have to spend one night. As she plunked the plastic bag by her front door she smiled imagining what type of designer bag, likely Chanel, Cheri would use for a trip.

Already on her third cup of coffee, Hope's nerves were shot. Her thoughts swirled like a pinwheel as she wondered for the thousandth time whether she was making a huge mistake. Forcing the memory of the only mother she ever knew might have an adverse effect on Larry—or no affect at all. *What if Montana remembers Larry but doesn't remember me? Then what? That would cause even more confusion in this precarious situation.* She threw up her arms. *It's too late now.*

When the doorbell rang, she jumped and spilled coffee on her fake-tiled, vinyl foyer. Swinging the door open wide, Hope forced a confident smile. "Morning."

"Mornin'." Larry stood on the porch with one hand in his jeans pocket. His free hand held a dented silver thermos.

"Come in." Hope glanced behind him, half expecting to see Willow.

After hesitating a second, he entered her nondescript house but stood planted in her tiny foyer. "Ready, Miss-Hope?" He glanced at his worn, brown watch. "We've got a mighty long drive ahead."

"Yeah, I'm ready." Hope pointed to her plastic bag by the door. "I was going to offer you coffee but it looks like—"

He held his thermos in the air. "Brought my own. Willow saw to that."

"Nice of her. Um, let me go to the restroom one more time. Are you hungry?"

Shaking his head, Larry said, "Coffee and a cigarette are my usual breakfast."

Hope turned away as she scrunched her nose. She had hated his smoking growing up. Now it would fill her vehicle unless she set ground rules up front. *How can I ask him not to smoke since he has the shock of the decade coming? Alex wouldn't have any problem telling him, but I can't. I'll deal with it.* She forced herself to sound cheery. "Be right back."

On the way back from the bathroom, Hope spotted her phone on the kitchen counter. "I can't believe I almost forgot that. We'll definitely want pictures."

Shifting from one foot to another, Larry said, "I don't have a Smartphone. Can't afford one." He plucked a flip-phone out of his pocket and chuckled. "My dumb phone works just fine."

Hope patted his arm. "I'm sure it does. I'll email you the photos or print them out. Let's go."

After they climbed inside her Honda, she fiddled with the radio. "What would you like to hear?"

For the first time, he appeared to relax. "Rock 'n roll, of course."

Hope scrolled through the radio. "Here's a station with sixties and seventies rock music."

"Now, you're talkin'." Soon, Larry bopped his head and drummed his index fingers on the dash to "Glory Days" by Bruce Springsteen.

"You always did love music. We both did. That's one thing we had in com—"

"Huh?" Larry's puzzled face indicated his memory was still that—a memory.

Hope's heart sank. "Nothing. Do you and Willow share a love for the same music?"

His dull, sad eyes twinkled. "We love *all* of the same things. I'm so lucky to have found her late in life. Willow is going to be the perfect—"

Interrupting him, Hope asked, "Did you hear about that shark in the news? It bit a beachgoer, but she's going to survive." She would discuss any topic—even UFOs—if they could avoid the topic of Willow while traveling to see Montana. Staring at the road, she cursed herself for the deception but owed it to her mother. After three hours, there was little discussion thanks to the loud music. As "Rockin' Down the Highway" by the Doobie Brothers played, Hope pulled into a highway rest area. "I want to double check my directions to that nice restaurant I mentioned at school. She stared at her phone. "It's on the outskirts of Nashville. Do you like Italian food?"

"Who doesn't?" He stared at the road. "But I'm a little short on cash."

Hope cringed. Her parents never had two dimes to rub together. She had provided their food, beer, and paid their bills most of her adult years. That's why they had had a fateful knockdown, drag-out fight before the infamous train accident. "Remember, I promised dinner as my treat."

"Very kind of you, Miss Tru— I mean Hope." Reaching for a cigarette and lighter, Larry hopped out of the car. "A smoke break sounds good." He thumped the top of the car to the beat of "Barracuda" by Heart.

Bopping her head to the beat, Hope studied a Google map. "This restaurant looks easy to find. Let me know when you're ready to get back on the road."

Chapter 40

What the hell? Alex felt her pulse race when she spotted Nikki in a Show-Me Bank teller line. Reaching for the phone, she immediately called Tony.

Answering with his usual all-business voice, Tony said, "Lt. Montgomery."

"It's me. No need to be so fucking formal. By the way, your ex is stalking me."

"I'm in the middle of a multi-state case, Alex. I can't talk."

"That's it? You're not going to do anything about her?"

Alex heard her cop boyfriend mumble something about it being a free country, saying Nikki could bank wherever she wanted, and repeated he was busy. Incredulous, she yelled into the phone, "You're freaking kidding me. That's all you're going to say?"

Tony muttered something about the chief being within earshot and to deal with it.

Deal with it? "She's your ex. Keep her away from me." Shaking her head, she hung up on him. Glancing at Hannah who had stopped working to eavesdrop, Alex said, "Tony has shown his true colors. He always has excuses for his precious Nikki. I'm done. I need a change. I've got to figure out my life." Crossing her arms, Alex brightened. "I think I'll take a vacation."

Hannah puffed out her chest. "Go ahead, boss. You know I've got your back." Alex knew Hannah would like nothing more than to get her hands on her computer files and snoop through every drawer. The thought almost made her reconsider. Almost.

Holding a handful of cash, Nikki poked her head inside. "Don't you have a fancy pants setup? Bet you think you're really somethin' with your corner office and nice clothes. I know what Tony likes and it isn't this." Turning toward Hannah, Nikki said, "I hope you don't have a boyfriend. If you do, she might sleep with him."

"Get out of my office and stay away from me." Alex knew her boss was likely watching so she couldn't slam the door in Nikki's face. Instead, she gently closed it. Crossing her arms, she leaned against the door. "That, my dear, is Sean's not-so-sweet wife. See why I told you to stay away from him?"

Hannah didn't say a word. Alex waited until Nikki left the bank. Before she lost her nerve, she rushed across the lobby, and knocked on the bank president's door. "Have a minute?"

"Always." Jim gestured toward a chair. "What's up?"

"I know we normally ask for approval months in advance, but something has come up. I'd like to go on a vacation. Soon."

The bank president nodded. "I'd say the timing is good. We're between meetings and the annual board meeting is weeks away. Are you ready for the HBA Home Show?"

Clasping her hands in her lap, Alex said, "Hannah is working on handouts and planning the trade show schedule as we speak."

"Good. I'm sure she can handle anything while you're away."

Alex did her best not to grimace. Daddy's daughter could do no wrong. "So, is my vacation approved?"

"Sure. When are you leaving?" Jim glanced at a calendar with a pen in hand.

"In two days if I can get plane tickets to—wherever." Alex stunned herself when a destination popped into her mind. She couldn't wait to plan the surprise trip.

"You are in a hurry. I'll pencil you out of the office for next week unless I hear differently," the bank president said.

Standing, Alex shook his hand. "Thanks, Jim. I really need this."

Racing back to her office, Alex told Hannah to take an early lunch, checked airline fares, and booked a ticket. Leaning back, she smiled more than she had in weeks.

Once Hannah returned from lunch, Alex said, "We need to discuss my board report. I've done the bulk of the work, but I want you to proof the entire report, update customer account stats, work on the lender profile page, and include updated bank photos.

Crossing her legs, Hannah said, "What are *you* going to do?"

"Really? You're asking me that?" Alex narrowed her eyes. "I've finalized the marketing budget, came up with new campaign ideas for next year, and am half finished with the community relations report. You can see where I left off; I want you to finish it. Email me with any questions."

Hannah's eyebrows shot up. "That's a lot of work in one week." Leaning forward with her enormous cleavage showing, she asked, "Where are you going on vacation?"

None of your damn business. Alex's chair creaked as she shifted in her seat. "I'm still working out the details." She patted her budget. "Back to my board presentation. This is very important. It's the only time I meet with the entire board." Pausing, she added, "It's once a year, Hannah. I'll have to give it soon after I return from vacation. The report has to be perfect.*"*

Her intern shrugged. "No problem. I prepare presentations all of the time in my higher education classes."

"Good. Then it should be a piece of cake. I'll need twenty-five copies. Design an attractive cover with our logo and include the date. Here's the order for the contents." Alex handed Hannah a list that included the annual report, marketing campaign ideas, community relations report, a listing of the previous year's press releases, and the marketing budget. You've got all week to work on this, and I've already done two-thirds of it. Understand?"

Hannah rolled her eyes. "I know how to prepare a report and put everything in order. I'm not a kid."

Letting out a long breath she didn't realize she had been holding, Alex said, "Glad to hear it. I want to enjoy my vacation. I haven't been on anything except a staycation for nearly two years. I'm long overdue for some fun." Staring at the files on her desk, she said, "If I think of anything else, I'll put a sticky note on my computer."

Alex's boss, Jim, patted the door frame with his hand. "Have a great trip, Alex. We'll miss you but I'm sure Hannah has everything under control."

Hannah beamed. "I sure do, Daddy. Marketing will be in my perfectly capable hands."

Alex wanted to puke and again fought the urge to ask her boss how he liked his daughter's huge implants. "Thanks, Jim. I'm excited."

Shoving a hand in his pocket, he asked, "Where are you going?"

"I'm keeping it a secret." Alex grinned. "Only the airline and I know."

"Mystery lady." He nodded. "I see you don't want us to bother you about bank business. Understood. We all need a break from time to time." The bank president said good-bye and stepped across the lobby.

Still openly curious, Hannah asked, "Are you going to a beach? I have a cute bikini I could loan you." She fixated on Alex's almost-C cups. "Never mind. It wouldn't fit, plus with your OCD, I'm sure you wouldn't want a used bathing suit."

You've got that right. "I'm not going to a beach."

Hannah shrugged. "Why are you being so secretive?"

Alex wasn't sure she'd tell her closest friends she was going to New York City. Hope was in Nashville and she trusted Suzy with her life but didn't trust her cop boyfriend to somehow interrogate the information right out of them.

Grinning to herself, she decided this would be an *Eat, Drink, Chill* experience. After she saved important computer files, she plucked her phone from her black and white striped Tommy Hilfiger bag and texted Suzy and Cheri: *Goodbye Meeting at Coconuts in 30 minutes?*

The women responded with "Goodbye? What?" and "On my way."

Chapter 41

After two more hours on the road, Hope parked in the lot of the restaurant as "Bad Company" by Bad Company blared from the radio.

Larry hummed as Hope unbuckled her seatbelt, hesitant about turning the radio off since he seemed to really enjoy the music. "Hungry? Let's check it out."

Studying the nice cars in the lot, he said, "Looks fancy. Mind if I have another smoke first?"

"Suit yourself. I'll go inside and get a table." After hearing Hope was travel weary, the hostess placed Hope near a tiny, charming fireplace. The ambiance would have been perfect for a date. In this case, it was wasted on her but still appreciated.

When Larry came inside the darkened restaurant, he squinted until he spotted Hope waving. As he sat down, he smelled like a smokestack but at least he was being considerate about his bad habit and mostly waiting until they stopped and he could smoke outside.

Scanning the menu, he said, "These eats are expensive."

"Remember, I told you the meal's on me." Hope peered at him over the menu. "Besides, I can afford to splurge twice a year." She laughed at her own joke. "Seriously, this might be a once-in-a-lifetime trip."

Raising his eyebrows, Larry said, "If you say so. You've sure got my curiosity up." His face turned solemn. "I hope Willow don't mind. She's a wonderful per—"

Hope held up her hand. "Let's talk about something else. We're in the country music capital. Do you like country?"

Larry shrugged. "I 'spose I like a few country singers. Johnny Cash was cool. He sang at prisons, you know."

Hope nodded. "I did know that. He was about as cool as it gets." Endeavoring to keep the conversation away from Willow, she asked, "Do you like any current country singers or bands?"

He hesitated before saying, "Blake Shelton's pretty good. I like Keith Urban too and that guy who sings the beachy-type songs is groovy." He perked up. "But the Stones, KISS, Zeppelin, and Lynyrd Skynyrd are more my speed." He frowned as he continued studying the menu.

"I love all music—country, rock, blues, gospel, pop, you name it."

"Uh-huh. Whatever floats your boat," Larry said.

Switching gears, Hope said, "Let's order and get back on the road. What sounds good?"

After what seemed like an eternity for Larry to decide, they both ordered lasagna and house salads. The server brought sodas, scrumptious homemade bread, and placed black linen napkins in their laps.

Larry chuckled. "I ain't used to this royal treatment."

Grinning, Hope said, "Me neither. Let's enjoy it."

They ate mostly in silence except for oohing and ahhing about the mouth-watering food and occasionally requesting drink refills. Hope tried to put the upcoming situation out of her mind so she could enjoy her meal, but her stomach churned at the thought of Larry's reaction upon seeing Montana. After the server cleared the plates, she ordered coffee to go for both of them.

"That was a mighty fine meal. Thank you. Mind if I have another cigarette before we hit the road?"

"Go ahead. I'll go to the restroom again." After she washed her hands, sweat broke out on Hope's neck while she checked directions to the nursing home. *We're less than thirty minutes away. God help me.* She remembered about promising to update Willow and sent a quick text saying they were in Nashville and had enjoyed a nice meal. Hope purposely kept the message short and retreated outside.

After Larry finished his cigarette, Hope pulled onto I-24. Soon the striking Nashville skyline appeared. Pointing, Hope said, "Those buildings are beautiful. Really stunning. I want some photos." Reaching into her bag, she handed her Android to Larry. "Click on the camera icon and the big round button at the bottom." She squealed. "Hurry. Look. That building looks like Batman."

He fumbled with her phone, dropped it on the seat, angled it in several positions, and eventually, snapped a few photos. "Just in time." Larry glanced behind his seat and watched as the skyline disappeared. "I've never been to Nashville. It's right pretty."

"Too bad we don't have time to go to the Grand Ole Opry."

"Maybe I'll bring Willow here someday. She'd love that Italian restaurant and we could probably find a campground nearby. We can't afford no hotel right now." He stared out the window. "Someday maybe."

Hope grunted, the only response she could muster. Nervous anticipation, dread, and excitement combined to make her heart thrash in her chest. *I hope this isn't a huge mistake. I feel like I'm playing God here, but Larry and Montana need to know they both survived. I can't allow him to carry on with a marriage to Willow and pretend his other life never happened.*

Chapter 42

Sipping a chardonnay at Coconuts to both celebrate and calm her nerves, Alex sat at their favorite high-top in anticipation of her upcoming vacation. Once Suzy and Cheri arrived, she blurted out, "I've made a spontaneous decision, girls."

"What?" Suzy hung her sweater on the back of her chair, Cheri leaned forward in anticipation, and Gus took their orders.

Circling the rim of her wineglass, Alex said, "I've decided I need alone time, as in a week's vacation."

Suzy's forehead creased. "Alone? What fun would that be? You'll be in a hotel alone, travel alone, sightsee alone, eat alone—"

"How many times can you say *alone*?" Laughing, Alex said, "I have traveled alone, silly. Remember my job? Conferences? Bankers I trained in other towns?"

Dipping a chip in salsa, Suzy shrugged. "Still, I wouldn't like it, but that's me and you're definitely not me."

Alex studied her friends' faces. "Maybe, just maybe, if I have time to assess my relationship—or lack of—with Tony, my job, and Hannah the Horrible, I can reevaluate my life." Crossing her legs, she asked, "What do you think?"

"I say go for it." Suzy raised her Shirley Temple. "I love my husband, life, and job, but once you're married or have kids, you're tied down for years. Do it now while you can."

Cheri raised her Cosmo and clanked it with Alex's

wineglass. "I love the idea. Exactly how adventuresome are you thinking?"

Giggling, Alex said, "This won't be an *Eat, Pray, Love* trip to India. I'm not that adventuresome. It'll be more like *Eat, Drink, Chill.*"

"Ooh. I like that. Are you going to the mountains, beach, or a big city?" Suzy studied her friend. "Or I suppose you could start driving and see where you end up."

Shaking her head, Alex said, "All good ideas, but I'm not telling."

Suzy's eyebrows shot up. "You should tell someone. Promise you'll at least stay in touch."

"Of course." As if on cue, Alex's cell phone vibrated. She glanced at the screen. "Be right back."

Cheri and Suzy exchanged looks. When Alex was out of earshot, Suzy said, "She's usually an open book. Alex is becoming a secretive woman."

While in the restroom, Alex sent Cheri a text and asked her to meet one-on-one the following morning.

Once Alex returned, she picked up a menu. "Anyone hungry?"

Both women said they had already eaten. Turning toward Cheri, Alex said, "How's the cowboy?"

Chuckling, Cheri said, "You'll never believe where we went yesterday. Never in a million years."

After several guesses, Cheri regaled them with stories about the hillbilly pool party and drinking moonshine. Both Suzy and Alex doubled over laughing.

"I needed that," Suzy said. Winking, she added, "Maybe I could tell Ken how we should add a pool in our backyard."

"That's hilarious. I've never heard of a hillbilly pool party. Invite us next time." Alex finished her wine. "I'm definitely adding that to my bucket list."

Suzy's belly touched the table when she stood. "I've got to run. When will you leave?"

Rubbing her hands together, Alex said, "In two days."

Suzy stopped in her tracks. "You don't waste any time."

Winking, she said, "Nope. Never have."

Chapter 43

Hope's heart nearly thrashed out of her chest as they got closer to the nursing home. At a stop light, she turned toward him. "I have a question for you."

Larry's eyebrows shot up. "Shoot."

"Do you have any family?" He paused for far too long. Eyes dull and sad, he held her stare for a few seconds and glanced away. "Family?" He rubbed his chin stubble. "Honestly, I don't remember much about my life. Wish I did but I don't." He reached into his pocket and pulled a few tattered photos from his threadbare wallet. "I'm guessin' this is my family. I wish I knew who they were."

Almost afraid to look, Hope leaned across the seat and stared at the dog-eared photo before the light turned green. Her heart skipped a beat when she spotted her plump, adolescent image bookended by her skinny hippie parents. Larry wore wrinkled jeans, a navy tee shirt sporting a guitar, and sandals. A barefoot Montana was dressed in her usual short, frayed denim shorts and a black tank top with a tie-dye peace sign in the middle. As usual, Hope's frizzy hair was unruly, but she wore a big smile and held her mother's hand.

Blinking through tears and praying the light wouldn't turn green, Hope smiled as she remembered her sleeveless white top with the scalloped edge and bright yellow shorts. The trio didn't go together appearance wise, but they *were* her parents. The only parents she had ever known until recently. They had been a family, albeit a non-traditional family, but a family all the same. Hope swallowed past a lump in her throat.

Larry studied the photo as the light turned green. "Wonder who this cute little girl is? She has the prettiest big, brown eyes. Reminds me of two chocolate kisses."

Unable to continue driving through her tears, Hope took the first exit and pulled into a Cracker Barrel parking lot. She wanted to weep, hug him, and tell Larry everything. Every. Single. Thing. Tears trailed down her cheeks.

Obviously noticing Hope's tear-stained face, Larry asked, "What's wrong, Miss Hope? Why ya cryin'?" After parking, she took several breaths to calm herself and locked eyes with him. Words wouldn't come. All she could do was stare at her hippie dad.

Peering back at the photo, deep wrinkles formed on Larry's forehead as if he were concentrating for a difficult test. A small sound escaped. Glancing back at Hope, he said, "Wait a minute. You have the same brown doe eyes and curly, brown hair." He waved the photo in the air. "This little girl is you, ain't it?"

Hope bobbed her head as tears streamed down her cheeks. "Yes, yes. It's me." Placing her hand over Larry's, between sobs, she said, "Listen closely. You raised me. You and Montana raised me. I'm your daughter."

He leaned back against the headrest and shifted in his seat. Cars came and went in the parking lot. Unknowing patrons entered the restaurant during Larry's momentous breakthrough. Staring out the window obviously trying to digest the shocking news, he asked, "I did? I raised you?"

Hope's curls bounced as she nodded. "You sure did. From when I was a baby to adulthood." She wanted to reach across the car and hug him but they never had that type of relationship to begin with. Knowing he put this puzzle piece together was more than enough for now.

Shaking his head, Larry said, "I don't know how I could forget raising you. From when you were little, you say?"

"Yes. You adopted me when I was a baby from an attorney named Paul Taylor. His wife—my biological mom—died shortly after giving birth." Hope began crying again. "I never knew her."

Studying the photo with intense scrutiny, Larry said, "Wish I remembered you—and us—together. Sorry."

Hope reached for a tissue and dabbed her eyes. "No need to be sorry. You were in a horrible train accident. I thought you and Montana were both dead." Blowing her nose loudly, she said, "I'm just glad you're alive. Really glad. The fact that you both survived is unbelievable, really. The authorities assured me no one—" Another loud sob escaped. "We all thought you and Montana were both killed. We had a funeral for you. That's how I connected with my biological dad."

He shook his head again. "That's really somethin'. I don't remember Montana. I don't remember much from the past."

"We're going to see Montana. That's the reason for this trip."

"It is?" His eyebrows shot up.

Hope nodded. "Yes. Maybe your memories will come back once you see your wife."

Gingerly placing the photo back in his wallet, he said, "Like I said, I don't remember her."

"Hopefully, you will after you see her." Hope dabbed her eyes again, put the car into gear, and fished sunglasses out of her purse. Driving out of the lot into the blinding sun, she peered at Larry over her sunglasses. "You're still legally married to Montana, you know."

His response was: "Mind if I smoke. I need a smoke."

"Go ahead. If I smoked, I'd need a cigarette too. I know this is a shock. I've had quite a while to get used to it."

Taking a long drag, Larry said, "I may be married to Montana but Willow's my old lady now."

Ignoring the 'old lady' remark, Hope continued. "Yes, I know. But polygamy is illegal. We have to fix this. Actually, you and Willow have to handle the matter. Hopefully, Paul can help us wade through this."

He blew a smoke ring. "Paul who?"

His memory loss was almost too much to bear. "Paul Taylor. I just told you he's my biological father. You used to work for him. Both of you did, apparently, before I was born."

"Don't 'member him neither."

Nobody said this would be easy. "As I mentioned he's an attorney." Hope had never been so confused and rocked to her core in her life.

Staring ahead stony faced, Larry said, "This is as confusin' as all get out."

Blinking through tears, Hope pressed on the gas pedal as she attempted to focus on the congested traffic. She couldn't imagine what lie ahead or how it would all unfold. She'd figure it out when they got to the nursing home.

Chapter 44

After she returned from Coconuts, Alex received a text from Tony saying he was playing mini golf with little Joey. *I bet his darling ex, Nikki, is in tow.* Scrolling through her phone, she impulsively found the contact information for Cheri's limo driver and emailed Gage about her vacation plans. Before hitting send, she stared at the screen for far too long, but eventually pressed the button.

Awaiting Gage's response, Alex paced, made a turkey sandwich, and downed a Diet Coke. She forced herself to ignore her cellphone for at least thirty minutes since she didn't want to appear like an eager teenager hoping to be asked to the prom. Stepping outside, she watered her red geraniums, sat in a lawn chair, and flipped through a magazine, but it was no use. Flinging the magazine on an outdoor table, she stepped back inside and stared at her cellphone. *I've got to know if he answered.* Her eyebrows shot up when she saw his email.

Great to hear from you, Alex! How have you been? I've been stuck in New York working, as usual. I miss you and the Coconuts gang. Gage

Alex typed so fast her fingers could barely keep up. For some reason, she spilled her guts to this guy. Maybe because Gage was far away. Maybe because it was via email. Maybe because she felt comfortable with him. Maybe, just maybe, she was done with Tony.

After a surprisingly long exchange where she complained about her disastrous relationship with the cop, discussed the antics of Tony's hateful ex, and a few notable comments about Hannah, Gage's response was simple, welcome, and caught her completely off guard.

It sounds like you need a vacation. Have you ever been to New York?

Alex crossed her legs beneath her, smiled to herself, and responded: *No, I haven't been to Manhattan. I already booked a flight, and double, triple, quadruple yes, I damn well need a vacation. :)*

Gage's response was immediate. *Fantastic! I can't believe you're coming to New York. I bet Cheri will let you stay in her apartment.*

Alex's mouth fell open as she texted back: *Really? You think so?*

Her mind raced. *If my accommodations are covered, I won't go into debt with the airfare, meals, and my inevitable shopping.* Heart pounding with excitement, she stared at the screen awaiting Gage's response.

I don't know why not. Her apartment's sitting empty. Want me to ask her?

She didn't want to take advantage of her wealthy friend. Before losing her nerve, she typed: *I'm afraid Cheri will feel obligated. I want this to be a fun, low-key visit.*

Staring at her screen with more glee than she had felt in forever, Gage said: *Hey, low-key limo driver at your service. I've gotta run and pick up a celeb. Just let me know the dates.*

He's going to be surprised. She typed quickly. *I'll be there in two days.*

Seriously? I'll clear my schedule. I can't wait to see you!

Alex couldn't stop smiling. *I'm going to the Big Apple. I've been so busy I didn't realize how much I missed Gage.* Pacing, she chewed on a nail. *I've got to figure out my life.*

Chapter 45

Heart pounding almost out of her chest, Hope parked in the nursing home parking lot, removed her seatbelt, and took a deep breath. Turning toward Larry, she said, "This is it. This is where Montana lives."

Staring straight ahead, he asked, "Do ya think I should wait in the car?"

Hope's eyes widened. "Absolutely not. We drove all day for this moment."

Slowly unbuckling his seatbelt, Larry muttered, "Okay, but like I said, Willow's my old lady now."

Feeling her anger rise, Hope did her best to channel Alex. More curtly than she intended, Hope said, "If this woman is Montana, you're still married to her. We're both going inside."

As they crossed the crowded lot, they spoke to a few residents sitting in wheelchairs on the sidewalk or on nearby benches, obviously enjoying the fresh air. Many eagerly attempted chitchat, likely lonely, while others were obviously in their own worlds, heads down, taking in the sunshine.

Before she lost her nerve, Hope opened the double doors, strode past a trophy case filled with photos of residents at themed parties wearing everything from cowboy hats to leis, and glanced at the half-empty cafeteria. On the wall, Hope noticed a bulletin board filled with a month's worth of activities. Standing in front of the board, she read the daily and weekly plans. She wanted to learn what Montana had been doing while separated from them for nearly two years. Events included everything from board games to live entertainment. "At least they offered activities."

Barely noticing the bulletin board, Larry nodded.

As she approached the nurses' station decorated in childlike, cardboard letters saying, "Welcome," Hope tugged on Larry's sleeve. "Let's get someone to help us."

One tech stared transfixed at a computer and the other was on his cellphone. Hope cleared her throat. "Hello. We could use some help." She paused until one of them glanced up. "We're here to see Montana Truman."

The two techs exchanged glances. The young man in front of the monitor spoke first. "And you are?"

"Hope Truman."

"I see." He again looked at his colleague. "We don't have a Montana Truman." As he turned back toward his screen, Hope extracted the newspaper article and thrust it in his face. Pointing, she said, "This woman. I believe this is Montana."

"I recognize her, but that's not her name. She hasn't had any visitors at all. As in never. Are you related?"

Tamping down her anger, Hope attempted calmness. "I'm her daughter."

The guy who previously stared at his phone became interested. Raising his eyebrows, he asked, "You are?"

"Yes, yes, I am." She pointed toward Larry. "And this is her husband."

Both nurses gawked at them, then at one another. One raised his finger, picked up a phone, and spoke in hushed tones. Hope pushed her frizzy hair out of her eyes. Sweat broke out on the back of her neck. "Look, we've driven six hours to get here. Can we please see her?"

One of them turned away and muttered, "I don't think there's any rush."

"What do you mean?" Hope asked.

"Nothing," the man said.

Grateful she had brought an overnight bag, she bristled when an unsmiling, thin woman, with severe jet black hair approached them. The woman held out her hand. "I'm Nurse Helga. I understand you're here to see one of our residents."

Hope nodded in affirmation.

The stern nurse studied her from head to toe. "And you are?"

"I'm her daughter." She held up the magazine article and pointed toward Larry. "And this is her husband."

The nurse crossed her arms. "Interesting. She's never had visitors before. Why now?"

Losing her patience, Hope pointed with her head. "That's because we thought she died in the same train accident he was in." Lowering her voice, she asked, "May we please see her?"

Mouth set in a straight line, the nurse said, "You're too late."

Larry finally spoke up. "As in it's after closin' hours?"

The nurse shook her head.

"As in what?" Hope asked.

Chapter 46

The stern head nurse studied Hope and Larry for several seconds. "I'm sorry to be the one to tell you this but the woman in the picture killed herself two days ago."

As one resident wailed in the background, another called for help. Hope gasped. "What? How?"

The nurse waved to a man in a motorized wheelchair. Turning back, she crossed her arms and said flatly, "With one of her plant hangers."

Hope felt the blood drain from her face. Head spinning, she gripped the counter. "Oh, my God." She reached for Larry's arm. "We're too—" Her voice cracked. "—late."

Showing no emotion nor compassion, Nurse Helga said, "It happens. She'd been more depressed and bored than usual lately. Too bad she didn't know about you two. It might have made a—"

Larry clucked his tongue. "That's a damn shame." He turned toward Hope. "Guess we should hit the road. It'll be dark in a few hours."

Staring dumbfounded at Larry, Hope realized he had memory loss. Still, it was difficult to fathom that he didn't remember his dead wife. New tears flooded her eyes. *I can't go through the shock, grief, and remorse again. I can't.*

Taking a deep breath, Hope endeavored to pull herself together. A loud sob escaped. "I want to go in her room. I'd like to see if there's anything we could remove and take as a remembrance."

Obviously growing impatient and lacking one ounce of compassion, the nurse sighed. "As I said earlier, she never listed any family members. Never once talked about anyone. Never discussed *either* of you." She crossed her arms again. "She was all alone as far as we knew."

Wiping her nose with her sleeve, Hope wished her friends were there to comfort her, and she wished Alex were in tow. She'd be able to handle this woman. Swallowing a lump in her throat, she sniffled. "I can't bury her twice. I don't think I can bear the sadness."

The nurse almost smiled. "You won't have to. She was cremated and buried in the cemetery across the street. We take quick action when there's no family."

Hope angrily swiped at the tears running down her cheeks, mad at herself more than anyone. "Dammit. She does have family. *Did* have family." *I should have driven here immediately after I saw that newspaper article.* She rubbed her forehead as an empty pit in her stomach grew.

The nurse glanced at the clerks and motioned toward Hope and Larry. "Follow me to my office."

Soon they were seated in a tiny stark office stacked with patient charts, one almost-dead fern, and two half-filled coffee mugs. There wasn't a photo, nor a cheery wall hanging in sight.

Once the nurse got situated behind her desk, she pushed a button to hold her calls. Tightlipped, she crossed her arms as she scrutinized Larry and Hope.

No one said a word during this apparent cat-and-mouse game which continued for far too long. Normally beyond patient, Hope's insides churned. Larry-Mac seemed content to watch a gray and orange Monarch butterfly that landed on the outer windowsill.

Eventually, the head nurse broke the silence. Her voice rose as she narrowed her eyes. "Come clean. Who are you two? Some scammers who want her belongings? Honestly, I'm sick of money-hungry family members. We take care of our lonely residents only to have so-called families swoop in after they're gone."

Hope popped out of her chair as if she were on a spring. Slamming her fist on the desk so hard, several files fell to the floor. "How *dare* you insinuate anything of the sort. I'm Montana's adopted daughter and this-this is her husband."

"Adopted daughter?" The nurse raised her eyebrows. "Convenient."

"Go to hell," Hope said.

Expressionless, the nurse said, "I'll let that go. This time." She cleared her throat. "Besides, there aren't any belongings. We stripped her room. There's no money either if you were after that."

Hope held the nurse's glare. "And I'll let that go but don't ever say it again."

Staring at Hope, Nurse Helga said, "You can't go in the room. Another resident's moving in tomorrow morning. Her room has already been cleaned and sterilized."

Glaring at the detestable woman, Hope said, "I hope to God you weren't Montana's nurse. If you were, that might explain her depression."

"Well, I never." The nurse clucked. Tapping her watch, she said, "We're done here. You both need to leave."

"*Please*." Hope forced herself to soften her voice. "Can I take one quick look around her room? I promise I'm her daughter."

When the nurse fell silent, Hope sat back down and nudged Larry with her elbow. "Dad-Larry, show her the photo."

He plucked the dog-eared picture from his wallet and slid the worn family photo across the nurse's desk.

The nurse glanced at the photo and peered from Hope to Larry and back again. Her tone changed. "I'll admit this man looks like you, and the woman appears to be a younger Gypsy."

"Who's Gypsy?" Hope and Larry asked in unison.

"That's what we called her. She didn't remember her name. She came in here off the street nearly two years ago looking like a truck had run over her."

"Actually, it was a train," Hope said.

Eyebrows raised, the nurse said, "People rarely survive train accidents."

Hope leaned forward. "I know at least two people who have survived one." Pointing toward the photo, she repeated, "We'd be forever grateful if you'd let us see her room. We drove all the way from Crystal City."

Larry nodded in agreement. "Six long hours on the road."

The nurse handed Larry the picture. "You have five minutes."

Chapter 47

Without a word to the nurse, Hope bolted from her office and raced down the hallway, dodged residents with walkers and wheelchairs. "Which room?" she shouted.

"Two more doors down on the left," someone replied.

Flinging the door to Montana's room open, Hope stepped inside. Larry was close behind, as was the charming nurse.

Once in the room, they scanned the place Montana had likely lived for nearly two years. The bed had been stripped and a ratty recliner sat in front of a tiny, ancient television. A narrow, silver shelf above the porcelain sink was bare. Hope stared at the shelf and imagined Montana had placed a hairbrush, toothpaste, hairbands, and possibly lotion on the ledge.

Standing in the middle of the room, the nurse said, "I told you there wasn't anything in here. As I said, visiting hours are almost over. The room has already been cleaned, so if you'll—"

Hope approached the burgundy recliner in front of the television. She could still see the indentation of Montana's head and gasped. Gathering strength she never knew she had, she traced the backrest and arms. Staring at Larry, she said, "Mom sat here. Right here for God knows how long wondering why no one visited her." She plopped down in the chair and sobbed.

Larry actually teared up. "You obviously loved her. Wish I could remember Montana, but I don't."

"The last time I spoke to her, I was so angry. It haunts

me." Hope wiped a tear away with her thumb. "The three of us had such a huge fight."

"I don't 'member that either," Larry said.

Hope managed a small smile. "I'm glad."

Leaning back in the chair, she imagined Montana sitting there and watching God knows what on television. Or reading. Maybe she read. Impulsively reaching into the side pockets, Hope felt something hard. With her right hand, she pulled out a handheld ornate, silver mirror. The glass was cracked and the finish tarnished, but it was beautiful. Sucking in her breath, Hope said, "This is stunning."

"That old thing." The nurse grunted. "She stared at herself all the time and dropped it more times than I can remember."

Hope carefully traced the shattered glass. "Maybe she was trying to remember who she was. Maybe she didn't recognize the face that stared back at her. Who knows but I'm thrilled to find one of her possessions."

"You want that? Take it, but you really need to leave."

Hope hugged the mirror close. "Thank you. At least I have something of hers." Reaching back inside the side pocket of the recliner she found a balled-up tye-dye tee. Squealing like a child on Christmas, Hope said, "This is her shirt. I want this too."

"It's yours." The nurse tapped her watch. "Time to go."

Glancing toward a blue planter hanging on the door, Hope's face fell. "That's not the one she used to—"

"Of course not. The police have the other one but the case is closed since there was no suspicion of foul play." Studying the planter, the nurse asked, "Want that, too? I think she made one for every resident and nurse in their favorite color." She stared at her white tennis shoes and mumbled in a low voice, "She never offered me one."

That comment made Hope smile for the first time all day. Carefully removing the crocheted planter off the door hook, Hope placed it, along with the colorful tee, in her purse. Hugging the silver mirror to her chest, she glanced at a very quiet Larry. "I guess we should go."

Turning toward Nurse Sunshine, Hope asked, "Where is the cemetery?"

"Across the street. Her plot is near the redbud tree along the gravel drive, right after you go inside the arched entrance. Now skedaddle." Nurse Helga peeked at her watch. "I'm off soon." She actually softened her voice. "Sorry for your loss."

Hope reached for Larry's arm. "Let's go to the cemetery."

Chapter 48

Before Hope and Larry exited the nursing home, someone tugged on Hope's arm. "Excuse me. I couldn't help overhearing your conversation earlier. I have some information about the woman who died."

Eyebrows shooting up, Hope said, "You do? Please tell us anything you can think of."

The kind, elderly nurse led them to a bench outside. The sky was filled with streaks of orange, yellow, and pink hues—some of Montana's favorite colors—as the sun began to set.

Glancing behind her to make sure the double doors had closed, the nurse sat near them. "Apparently, Gypsy was taken to a hospital after the accident a few years ago. Medical reports indicated she had a fractured pelvis, broken leg, broken arm, and internal bleeding. A trucker likely in trouble with the law picked her up and drove her there according to the physician's notes. Apparently, they determined she was drunk and stoned.

According to the report, she had been bleeding profusely. The man who picked her up apparently carried her into the hospital to get help, but as soon as they wheeled her away on a gurney, he disappeared. The trucker had the foresight to scrawl a message saying he found her in bad shape at a gas station and shoved the note in her pocket. After she received emergency care and was admitted to the hospital for a few weeks, no one came to check on her. She was in and out of consciousness. Once she stabilized, she ended up here since we accept Medicaid.

"That's unbelievably sad." Hope shook her head and stared at her shoes. "She died all alone. If we had only known."

The nurse patted Hope's hand. "I wish we had known too. Gypsy didn't remember who she was. She didn't have any ID on her. She was agitated most days. The only thing that calmed her was making those macramé plant hangers.

Instinctively, Hope reached for the one she had taken out of Montana's room. "Go on."

"We never knew she had a husband, nor a daughter. She told me she wanted a fresh start as soon as she healed." Shaking her head, the nurse continued. "She didn't have the capacity to live on her own. Besides her failing health, she didn't have any money."

"Didn't you question her?" Hope asked. "Ask where she was from?"

"Sure. We asked her numerous times, almost daily. It's not unusual for many of our residents to lose their memories. We finally stopped asking after months." Shrugging, the nurse said, "Gypsy concocted a story that she had been hit by a car while walking and said the driver drove away from the scene."

Hope threw her hands in the air. "I appreciate knowing this background, but didn't you notice the television and newspaper reports about the train wreck?"

"Sure, it was all over the news, but that was in another state. No one put the information together, most likely since it was a couple who had been killed. We never dreamed Gypsy was Montana—"

"Truman. Her last name is—was—Truman," Hope said, as she edged forward on the bench and studied Larry's blank face.

Running her fingers through her hair, Hope asked, "Can you tell us anything else?"

The nurse stared upward as if for an answer. "We did the best we could to keep her comfortable. She kept to herself, didn't speak, and dearly loved making those plant holders. We gave her a white board to communicate. I remember she dotted her I's with hearts."

"That's her, all right." Hope sniffled. "Anything else you can remember?"

The kind nurse smiled. "Gypsy filled her days by watching soap operas and dearly loved music. She would write down requested sixties songs when we had live entertainment."

Hope brightened and elbowed Larry. "You both love the same music." He nodded but remained quiet.

"At least I can picture her days now," Hope said. "I'm glad you took care of her instead of that mean nurse."

The kind nurse smiled. "No comment. Gypsy's favorite day of the week was Pretty Nails Monday. She absolutely loved getting her nails done and always chose crazy blues, greens, and purples."

Smiling, Hope said, "I bet she loved that. Montana had always been too poor for such a luxury." She stared at her own bare nails. "I think I'll get a manicure with a crazy color in her honor." Hugging the nurse, Hope said, "You don't have any idea how helpful you've been. This will help my"—she glanced at Larry—"*our* grief process immensely since we've already lost her once before. At least we have renewed memories of how she lived."

The nurse patted her hand. "Remember the happy times, dear."

Standing, Hope hugged the nurse. After she stepped back inside, she jangled the car keys. "Ready to go to the cemetery?"

"You promised something about a honky-tonk," Larry said.

I give up. Maybe it's better that he doesn't remember this sad chapter. Montana loved music, so maybe she would want us to celebrate her life. "Okay, okay. We're going to pay our respects first. Then, I'll take you. A promise is a promise."

Chapter 49

Driving in a shroud of strange silence since Hope was sad, yet relieved she had some closure, but Larry seemed stumped. Crossing the busy highway, Hope drove through the arched entrance for all of three minutes before she found Montana's plot. The tiny marker on the grave simply read GYPSY.

"We need to pay our respects." They both climbed out of her Honda and stood before the grave. Bending down, Hope kissed the blue macramé planter Montana had crocheted and wrapped it several times around the marker. She tied a knot so the wind wouldn't blow it away. "Bye, Mom. *Again.*" Her voice cracked. "I can't believe I've lost you twice. I'm sorry we didn't know you were here." Her voice wobbled. "Every time I look in your beautiful, cracked mirror, I'll think of you. I promise you'll never be forgotten."

Larry bent down and patted the marker. "See ya, Old Lady."

Still crouching, Hope stopped mid-stand. "Do you remember her now?"

Rubbing his chin, Larry said, "That plant hanger rings a bell." He shrugged. "But that's about all. Sorry. I know you'd like for me to remember more, but I don't."

"It's okay." Hope wiped her nose with the back of her hand. "Want to say a prayer?"

Glancing at the sky, Larry said, "I'm usually private about that but Montana, whoever you are, I hope you rest in peace."

"Amen. Rest in peace, Mom." Her voice broke. "We love you and miss you." Eyes welling with tears again, she sniffled and reached for Larry's arm. "Let's go. It's getting dark." She fished in her purse for car keys. "We can always get that marker corrected with her proper name. I'll talk to Paul."

"Who's Paul?" Larry asked.

"My biological dad, remember?"

Larry's brows knitted, looking more puzzled than ever. "I thought you said I was your dad?"

Hope threw up her hands. "Get in the car and I'll explain it again on the way to the honky-tonk." Far too tired and sad to go to a bar, she knew she had to hold up her end of the bargain and take Larry. *The timing is beyond weird, but I can surely manage an hour since he gave up his weekend to come on this trip.*

Easing onto the highway, she said, "I told you earlier, but maybe you forgot with all of the commotion and long drive. Paul Taylor is an attorney and my biological dad. You and Montana worked for him. You both adopted and raised me. I discovered all of these details after Montana's funeral. Her *first* funeral." She waved her hand. "That's enough for today." She noticed the golden arches on an exit sign and pulled into McDonald's. "I need some coffee to get through the rest of this night. Want a small or large?"

"I don't have a lot of bread on me," Larry said.

"It's on me." *Some things never change.* For once, she was happy to have the memory of his sad sack life and familiar sixties language. "I hear your phone ringing."

As she pulled up to the drive-thru window and eagerly accepted two large, hot coffees, Larry retrieved his cell out of his pocket.

Raising his eyebrows, he chuckled. "Willow's called me ten times. I guess she misses me. I think that woman really does love—" He studied Hope. "Sorry. This is awkward now."

"You can say that again. Awkward definitely describes this circumstance." Hope sipped her java as she contemplated her new and different life. Her new normal as everyone says. She forced confidence she didn't really feel. "We'll get through this. Willow's a great person. I'll need time to get used to the thought of you two being married."

"Next week okay?" Larry winked at her. "Just kiddin'. Sorta. Which honky-tonk are we goin' to?"

"Wherever I can find a parking space." Hope turned on her blinker to change lanes. "I Googled them. There are several country bars. Blake Shelton's place has good reviews."

"Let's go." Larry shifted in his seat and finally smiled. "I could use a beer."

Chugging her coffee, Hope nodded. "After all this, a margarita would hit the spot."

Chapter 50

Unable to wait until the following day, Alex called Cheri. "Are you still in town or already in Branson?"

Answering on the third ring, she said, "I'm here. I stopped at that new kitchen store."

Relieved, Alex said, "Good. I'm about to bust. Will you come by my house tonight? I have to tell someone where I'm going on vacation."

"Sure, mystery woman. What's your address?"

Once the New Yorker arrived, Alex offered a fruit and cheese plate, and they settled in the living room. "Thanks for coming over." Popping a grape in her mouth, Alex crossed her legs on the couch. "Guess what? I'm going to New York City for my vacation! I've never been there. I can't wait. I'm also going to see Gage."

Slightly dumbstruck, Cheri said, "That's fantastic."

Putting a finger to her lips, Alex said, "This is hush, hush. Don't say a word to anyone else. I trust Suzy and Hope with my life, but they might discuss it at Coconuts by accident, the cop would hear—guaranteed—and I'd be busted. He doesn't know you, so he won't approach you. But he would interrogate my girlfriends. I'll tell them everything once I'm back."

"It sounds like you already have your answer as far as the cop is concerned, but sure, whatever you say." Cheri grinned. "Besides, a little bird gave me a heads up on the way over."

Alex's eyes widened. "Gage? We just emailed."

Nodding, Cheri fished in her purse until she retrieved a house key. "Stay at my place in Manhattan."

Resisting snatching the key out of Cheri's hand, Alex swallowed. "I couldn't. Is this the penthouse apartment you've told us about? The all-white one? I'd be afraid I'd spill something."

Cheri forced the key into Alex's hand. "I insist—and no worries. Your secret is safe with me." Winking, she said, "I had hoped Gage would catch a good woman's eye."

Alex cocked her head. "Let's don't get ahead of ourselves. He promised to show me around Manhattan, that's all. I'm too much of a mess to do anything else. It wouldn't be fair to him." Shrugging, she said, "Gage and I have emailed and texted a couple of times over the past year. Casually, you know. Between my hateful intern, the cop, and his bitchy ex's antics, I'm not sure how much more I can take."

"I don't blame you. Life's too short. You need to find happiness." Cheri nodded. "Gage is a good guy. Have fun in the Big Apple." Pausing, she said, "By the way, my maid, Pearl, is on vacation so you'll have total privacy. And my doorman is incredible. He'll help with anything you need."

After hugging and thanking Cheri profusely, Alex made a long to-do list.

Chapter 51

As Hope examined billboards and exits, her thoughts spun about losing Montana twice. The last thing she was in the mood for was live music and drinking, but she had promised. Handing her phone to Larry, she said, "Google directions to Blake Shelton's bar in Nashville."

After fumbling with the letters on the phone, Larry said, "It says to turn on the next exit, but I'm not a huge country music fan."

"I am." Hope's voice was sharper than she intended. "I like rock music too. I remember reading Kid Rock has a bar here too. Maybe the two bars are close by."

Adjusting the radio, Larry nodded. "Somethin' for both of us."

Eventually Hope found an open space after driving up and down Broadway Street four times. She parallel parked and said, "Let's walk. I need to stretch my legs."

Throngs of women dressed in short denim skirts and wearing cowboy boots occupied the sidewalks. Live music blared from every storefront. If this didn't improve her mood, nothing would. They went to Kid Rock's bar first where the music was deafening. There wasn't a seat in the place, let alone two together. Pointing with her head, Hope said, "I saw Ole Red across the street. Maybe we'll have better luck there."

"As long as they have food and beer, it's fine by me." Larry kept pace with her. "I don't want to get separated and have to hitch a ride home."

"Good point."

They crossed the street and entered the two-story brick building. The face of a bloodhound on a red sign welcomed them. The honky-tonk was packed. A band of five young men played on the stage. A giant photo of Blake Shelton filled a screen in the background. Luckily, two women seated near the dance floor reached for their purses and stood.

Like a vulture, Hope made her way to their table. "Are you leaving? Sorry to rush you but we've had a long drive and an eventful day."

One woman gathered a to-go box, and the other smiled. "The table's all yours."

"Thank you." Hope waved Larry over, and they sat down. A server wiped the table and set menus in front of them. Plucking a pad out of her pocket, she poised her pen above the paper. "What'll it be, folks?"

"Beer for me," Larry said.

"I'll take a margarita and some water."

The young server plunked her pad inside her shorts. "Are you gonna eat?"

"Yes," Larry and Hope both said in unison.

"Give us a minute. This is our first time here," Hope said.

After they decided on pimento cheese dip, a Blue Tick burger and Kiss My Ass Quesadilla which fit Hope's mood, she sipped her margarita, studied the party crowd, and tried to relax. After all, she rarely got out of Crystal City. Even though this was an emotional journey for the record books, she told herself to have a little fun. Still sad and shocked about Montana, she was happy Larry had had a small breakthrough. *At least he realized who I am, even if he doesn't have a single memory of raising me.* She made a mental note to see if he'd try therapy to try and get his memory back. Hypnosis. Anything. But for now she was mentally and physically exhausted, and two hours of fun sounded like paradise. Everyone else seemed to manage it. Maybe it was her turn.

When Larry stepped outside for a cigarette, a stocky man wearing overalls and a cowboy hat approached her. Tipping his hat, the stranger said, "Howdy, ma'am."

Hope studied him. Men didn't usually approach her. Unsure how to react, she said, "Howdy. Everyone is so polite here. I should send some of my students for training."

"Are you a teacher?" the man asked.

"No, a high school counselor."

He chewed on his bottom lip. "I'm not very good at this." Then, the man extended his meaty arm. "My name's Tucker."

"Hope."

"Beautiful name."

Not accustomed to compliments from the other sex, Hope felt pink creep up her neck. "Thanks."

Shifting from boot to boot, Tucker asked, "Are you with that man? The older guy? I don't want to butt in."

Hope giggled. "No, he's my dad. Well, make that the dad who adopted me and doesn't remember me."

The cowboy's eyebrows furrowed. "Huh?"

"It's a long story." Waving both hands in the air, Hope said, "I'm here to have fun. Mind if we don't get into all that?"

Grinning, Tucker said, "Fun's my middle name." He extended his hand. "Care to dance?"

Hope's mouth went dry. *Oh, my God. What's going on?* "Um, sorry. I don't dance."

Cocking his head, the cowboy asked, "You don't or won't?"

Hope patted an empty chair at the table. "To be perfectly honest, I don't know how."

As the server set platters of steaming food on the table, Hope glanced out a large window. Happily, Larry was still outside.

The larger man filled the seat and eyed her French fries. Scooting the dish toward him, she said, "Eat one. I'm much better at eating than dancing."

He rubbed his belly. "I'm pretty good at both."

Laughing, Hope felt her shoulders relax for the first time in forever. *I like this guy. Why does he have to live in Nashville?*

As Tucker devoured a fistful of fries, he waved the server over. "Another round, please. I'll take a beer too." He glanced at Hope. "If you don't mind my bargin' in, that is."

Mind? After the emotional upheaval of the past two years, Hope needed another drink like she needed air. "I don't mind at all. Just one more, though. I have to drive to a hotel later."

"Driving is also my middle name."

Hope reached for another fry and dipped it in the same ketchup the man had used. She noticed he was careful not to double dip and knew Alex would be pleased. "You drive a lot?"

"Five days a week. I'm an over-the-road trucker." Taking a sip of foamy beer the server had placed in front of him, he said, "The way I look at it I get paid to see the countryside."

"That sounds divine. I like to drive too." Hope plunked a lime into her fresh margarita. "I'm a little afraid of airplanes."

"Never been in one."

"Is your base out of Nashville? It's beautiful here, by the way. I love the skyline. The music and energy of this city are exciting."

"It's always a nice stop. I'm here on an overnight and thought I'd enjoy some music. I work for Prime Trucking near Crystal City."

Hope's mouth fell open. For some reason unknown to her, her heart fluttered from her chest to her toes. "Crystal City? That's where I live."

Tucker's face lit up. "No joke? I wonder why I've never see you. I'm in town most weekends."

Just as Hope was eager to fill him in on her girlfriends and Coconuts, Larry plopped down in a chair. The cowboy extended his hand. "I'm Tucker. I bought you another beer to thank you for raising such a beautiful, sweet daughter."

Larry took a big swig. "Thank ya. Much appreciated. My name's Mac. I don't know if Miss Tru— Hope told you, but I don't remember much after the accident."

Hope interjected. "We aren't discussing that. We're here for entertainment and a break from . . . everything."

Shrugging, Larry took a healthy swig. "Did she tell you about my old lady? Willow and I are newlyweds."

The cowboy held his beer in the air and tapped Larry's. "Congratulations."

Hope swallowed and avoided Larry's gaze. She wanted a lighter conversation and turned back to the trucker. "Do you have any family?"

"Nah. I'm an only child and my parents passed, but I meet nice people everywhere I go." His face brightened. "Like you."

Hope wasn't used to having a man pay attention to her. Having gorgeous girlfriends like Suzy, Alex, and Cheri who always stole the show was a challenge. She loved her friends but got a little tired of always being the overweight, frumpy one, not that she'd ever complain to them. They loved her and she loved them. Her students adored her, she had a roof over her head, and a good job. But this was different. A man noticing her felt nice. Really nice. Hope wasn't quite sure how to handle the attention.

The cowboy ate another fry and stood. "I should be goin'. I don't want to intrude."

Larry bopped his head to the music. "Nice meetin' ya."

Hope didn't want Tucker to leave and surprised herself with newfound confidence. "Wait. About that dance."

Chapter 52

On the drive back to Branson in deep thought about Alex and Gage hooking up in New York, Cheri's phone trilled. She didn't bother glancing at the screen. "Mom?"

Chuckling, the cowboy said, "It's Cole."

"Sorry. My mom usually calls about this time of day."

"Your mom? You haven't mentioned her. What's her name?"

After she paused for an awkward silence, Cole changed the subject. "Have you ever been to a drive-in?"

Cheri smiled into the phone. "A movie?"

"Yup."

"No, but it sounds fun."

"Are you free tomorrow night?"

"No."

"Too bad." Cole's voice dropped.

"I'm not free because I'm going to the drive-in with you."

He laughed. "Good. The drive-in is in Aurora. Do you want me to pick you up in Branson?"

Cheri's mind raced. "I have to go to Crystal City for a quick cater—" She caught herself. "For a quick meeting with someone. Want to meet at Coconuts?"

"Yep. See you at six. I'll be sure to wash the mud off my boots. After all this rain, the mud is knee-deep to a grasshopper."

Giggling, Cheri said, "I've never heard that phrase. We haven't had much rain in Branson, just clouds."

He continued. "It has poured here, but the cows don't seem to mind. Remember the name of my farm?"

Switching to her other ear as she drove, Cheri asked, "Remind me."

"Soggy Bottoms. Pretty classy, right? And it's livin' up to its name."

Smiling so hard, her face hurt, Cheri said, "I love the way you talk."

"Thanks, New York. You're not so bad either. See you tomorrow."

I wonder if this relationship has a chance. After she parked in her garage, Cheri went straight to her closet. *What should I should wear to a drive-in?*

Jittery about the upcoming date, Cheri decided to call her mother who picked up on the first ring. "Hi, Mom. How's Paris?"

"Darling, it's divine. I miss you. I'm so happy you and Julio came here last spring."

Hearing her mother blowing smoke, Cheri decided not to mention it. "How's Daddy?"

"Same-o." Victoria's voice seemed flat. "You know your dad. Always working."

Hearing ice clink, Cheri wondered if her mother was day drinking again. Picturing her parents' opulent stateside and European homes, her mind wandered to the country photos of tractors, cows, and hay bales she found on Cole's Facebook page. *I'm dying to tell Mom about him. She'd almost literally croak if she knew I was interested in someone who drove a tractor, plus she still thinks I'm engaged to Sebastian, even if he is in Dubai and we never talk.* Unable to keep the surprise, she blurted out, "I met a nice guy. He has a farm and cows. He's sort of a cowboy."

Victoria was silent for far too long. Cheri heard her blow more smoke as ice from her drink clinked. Her mother's tone changed. "I know your fiancé has been in the Middle East for far too long. Sebastian will surely be home in a year. Then we can focus on your wedding."

Bristling at the thought, Cheri didn't respond.

Victoria's voice had an edge. "I think that country air is getting to you, darling. You belong in a big city." Obviously tiring of the conversation and unwilling to consider Cheri's feelings, she said, "I've got to run. I have a date at Gigi's Couture. She ordered a new case of my favorite Bordeaux."

Cheri knew it was no use to try and convince her socialite mother that a relationship with a country boy might work—and that she had never, ever been in love with Sebastian. Mad at herself for falling to peer pressure and accepting his ring to begin with—and for not breaking up the engagement from afar—Cheri forced herself to sound cheery. "Have fun shopping, Mom. Tell that adorable designer, Gigi, I said hello."

After the line went dead, Cheri tamped down the urge to call her mother back and say, "It's not the country air that's getting to me. It's a country boy."

Chapter 53

Taking Hope's hand, the cowboy beamed. "That's more like it." As Tucker lead her toward the small dance floor, Hope's stomach flip flopped. Breaking into a sweat, she tried to tell herself the onlookers sitting on barstools weren't paying any attention.

As other dancers crowded around, Hope's entire body shook. Whispering in his ear, she said, "I've never danced before. I might pass out or step on your toes."

Grinning, he said, "You can't hurt my big feet. I've got you." Tucker took her in his strong arms, placed one hand on the small of her back, and led her to the far end of the dance floor as the band played "When You Say Nothing At All" by Alison Krauss. "Change of plans. I was going to teach you to two-step but this song calls for a slow dance. How does that sound?"

"Easier. It sounds much easier." Hope placed two shaky hands on Tucker's shoulders and kept enough space between them that another person could have joined in. As they swayed to the music, she relaxed and moved a little closer. Tucker did the same. By the time the song ended, her head rested on his shoulder and their bodies were touching.

When the music stopped, Hope dropped her arms and stepped back. "Sorry if I was in your space."

"I'm not." Winking, Tucker said, "You can be in my space any time you like."

He's flirting with me. A man is flirting with me. The swirly feelings in Hope's stomach were new to her. She had had butterflies from nerves, but this was different. A good different. The stirring excited her. For once, she felt like an adult. An adult woman with needs. Something she had squelched for over two decades was bubbling to the top, and she loved it.

After they approached the table, Tucker pulled out her chair. Yawning and stretching, Larry said, "It's gettin' right late. Mind if we leave. Been a long day."

Hope's face fell. Exhausted as well, she had renewed energy from a certain cowboy. "We'll leave soon. Why don't you go over to the gift shop and pick something out for yourself."

"Good idea." Larry hopped up and began to browse souvenir items behind the cash register. Turning to Hope, Tucker asked, "Mind if I call you sometime?"

Mind? Feeling her face flush, Hope reached inside her bag, fumbled around, and finally wrote on the back of a cocktail napkin. "I'd like that." Scribbling her phone number, she said, "Here's my cellphone number. Or you can reach me at Hilltop High School. *What am I doing? I gave the guy my number and we just met. He'll think I'm desperate. I guess I am.*

Studying her number, Tucker smiled. "We sure didn't have pretty counselors like you when I was in school."

Hope fluffed her frizzy hair. "Thanks. You're sweet."

"Like I said, I'm on the road all week but home most weekends. When I'm back in Crystal City, I'll give you a call. Maybe we can have dinner and catch a movie."

Doing her best impression of a non-eager, lonely woman who hadn't dated since her teens, Hope said, "That would be nice."

Folding the napkin, Tucker stuffed it deep inside his pocket.

Larry returned to the table holding an Ole Red ball cap and a woman's tee. "I sure would like to take my old lady a gift, but I'm a little low on cash."

Sick of the all-too-familiar lines, Hope reached for her purse but Tucker beat her to it. Thrusting two twenties toward Larry, he said, "The souvenirs are on me." He glanced at Hope. "Meeting this charming woman made my day."

"You don't have to do that." Hope extracted her wallet.

The cowboy waved his hand in front of her billfold. "You can buy me a soda the next time we get together."

Heart skipping a beat, she said, "Deal. It was lovely meeting you."

Tucker stood and offered his hand. "Until next time." Hope watched as he crossed the room and stepped outside. Waving through the big glass window, he disappeared. *I'll probably never hear from him again but that was exactly what I needed after this sad day.*

Hope approached the casher while Larry paid for his souvenirs and watched him pocket the change. *Naturally. He hasn't changed that much.* Yawning, she said, "Let's find our hotel. I thought we could stay at a Holiday Inn Express or a Hampton Inn. Maybe we can use your AARP card and get a discount."

Chapter 54

Awakening early, Alex couldn't wait to fly to New York. Deciding to stock up on toiletries, her car, as if on autopilot, drove to T.J. Maxx instead. After two hours, her cart was piled so high anyone would think she didn't own a stitch of clothing.

After she shoved her bags in the trunk, she got a quick mani-pedi, and sped home. Checking her mailbox, she cursed herself for not stopping the mail. *It'll be fine for a few days.*

Stepping onto her front porch to water her ferns, she spotted a pile of boxes on her doorstep from Amazon containing shoes and yet more clothes she had ordered at the last minute. *I don't have time to try all of this on. OCD is such a curse sometimes.*

She wolfed down a quick turkey and pepper jack cheese sandwich, veggie chips, and a Diet Coke. Feeling strange for not telling Tony nor her friends, she occupied her mind by staring at her bulging walk-in closet. Throwing every black top she owned on the bed, since Cheri had told her New Yorkers love to wear black, and she wanted to fit in. Adding two pairs of discounted skinny designer jeans, two short skirts, one turquoise and black maxi skirt, a denim dress with a wide leather belt, an elegant red dress, white, lacy top, leopard print tunic, three different jackets, and more black tops. Crossing her arms, she examined her heaping bed. *That should do it. Everyone in New York is so fashionable. I can't take my bank suits.*

Alex made a mental note to shop on Fifth Avenue—or was it Sixth—and had planned to leave space in her luggage for new clothes. After two hours of packing and repacking, she added a variety of silver and gold jewelry and put her shoes in individual plastic bags so the filthy, nasty soles wouldn't touch her outfits. *I don't want someone else's bathroom urine on my clothes.* Chuckling, she imagined how Hope would throw clothes and shoes together in a jumbled mess, urine and dirty soles be damned. Hell, Suzy probably would too.

Jittery about not telling anyone except Cheri and Gage her whereabouts, she unzipped her suitcase and rearranged it yet again, deciding she was the Worst. Packer. Ever.

Rechecking her list, Alex added her phone charger, favorite perfume, makeup, and hair products. She stared at the bulging suitcase. *I've got to stop or I won't be able to fit in a pair of socks. I hope I can sleep.*

Chapter 55

Cheri tried to watch a reality television show on the Food Network but was too nervous about seeing Cole to concentrate. Instead, she ran on a treadmill in the guest bedroom. After thirty minutes, she showered and wondered what to wear to a drive-in.

What are we going to talk about? There wasn't much time to talk at the pool party. Her childhood shyness kicked in. *I can't talk about being a Van Buren. I get the feeling he wouldn't date me if he knew.*

Dressed in white jeans, red wedge shoes and a floral red and white top, Cheri left Branson early so she could hide her Mercedes toward the back of Coconuts. Stepping inside, she recognized many of the regular Happy Hour patrons. Thankfully, they didn't recognize her, or at least not her real persona. Choosing a high-top table near the back of the room, Cole arrived five minutes later looking more handsome than ever in tight jeans, a black tee, and new, non-muddy boots.

Beaming when he spotted her, he placed his cowboy hat on the back of a chair. Hopping onto a bar stool, he said, "I'm glad you didn't start drinkin' without me."

Gus walked toward them. "What are you two having?"

"What beverage accompanies a drive-in movie?" Cheri asked.

"Definitely beer. It goes well with popcorn," the server said. "In fact, I'll bring some of our infamous truffle popcorn to get you in the mood."

Cole chuckled. "I'm already in the mood."

Cheri raised her eyebrows. *The cowboy is in rare form tonight.*

When the beer arrived, Cole grinned so big his dimples showed. I hope you like horror flicks."

Face contorted, Cheri said, "Uh, not really."

He laughed. "They're good for snugglin'."

"And hiding my eyes. I'll never sleep tonight if I watch a scary movie."

"And that would be bad?" He smiled devilishly. "Seriously, if you'd rather stay here, that's fine with me. We can always catch a movie another time."

Sipping her beer, she said, "I'd love to go. I've never been to a drive-in theater. I'll be brave, or hide my eyes."

~ ~ ~

After leaving Coconuts, Cole drove thirty miles and eventually pulled up to an antiquated, obviously popular drive-in movie theater. The gravel parking lot was filled with pickups. A tiny concession stand was off to one end. Parking toward the back, Cole turned the ignition off and placed his arm across the seat.

"Welcome to your first drive-in movie. This is real high-society."

"I love it." Cheri held his gaze. "I hope we celebrate a lot of firsts together."

"Me too. Want anything to eat? A hotdog or burger?"

Rubbing her flat belly, Cheri said, "I'm still full from that truffle popcorn."

"I'll get a couple of sodas. Be right back."

While he crossed the lot to the concession stand, Cheri's mind raced at the thought of being in the truck with Cole for two hours. Just the two of them with other vehicles only a few feet away. She decided to embrace the new, exciting experience.

When he returned, Cole handed Cheri a soda through the window, climbed inside, and placed the speaker on the window's edge. Turning a small, round knob, the volume increased. "Loud enough? Too loud?"

The movie previews blared. "Maybe turn it down a notch." Studying the ancient speaker, she asked, "How old is that thing?"

"It should probably be in the Smithsonian but it works." He shifted in his seat and took Cheri's face in his hands. "I've missed you. My farm chores keep gettin' in the way."

"I've missed you too. I'm glad you asked me out." Something about this cowboy calmed her. As Cheri sank into Cole, he stroked her hair and face. Tingling all over, she turned her mouth toward his and they kissed like two teens who had just discovered French kissing. Leaning back to catch his breath, Cole peered at the screen. "Looks like we missed the openin' scene."

Kissing his neck, she made her way toward his mouth. "What's your point?"

After several minutes, the windows steamed over. When someone knocked on the window, Cheri jumped. Cole glanced toward the noise.

"Hey, mister." The insistent knocker waited all of two seconds before pounding on the window again. Raising his voice, he called, "MISTER."

Cole wiped Cheri's lipstick off his lips with the back of his hand and rolled down the window. When he peeked outside, he spotted a young boy, likely six or seven.

"What can I do for you, little fella?"

"My ball rolled under your car. I can't reach it. Will you help me?"

Straightening his shirt, Cole said, "Sure, buddy. Give me a second."

Giggling, Cheri hopped out the passenger side. "I see it.

It's under the wheel." Reaching, she retrieved the red ball. "Here you go."

"Thanks." The boy toddled off.

Cheri turned to Cole. "He's so cute."

Cole followed the youngster with his gaze. "Sure is. Do you like kids?"

Squirming, Cheri said, "Uh, I like other people's. I'm not in any hurry to—"

"Me neither." Cole slid closer and tilted her face toward his. "Now where were we?"

Chapter 56

After sleeping fitfully, Alex downed a large mug of coffee and slid her fully charged phone into her gigantic red purse. *Today's the day. New York, here I come.*

Still feeling guilty about not telling her closest friends her vacation plans, she had rehearsed every what-if situation over and over. She couldn't chance Suzy mentioning her visit to Ken and having Izzy overhear. Likewise, Hope might tell a colleague and a student could overhear. It was too risky. Tony was a cop. He'd pick up on the tiniest detail. Besides, she had already emailed her itinerary to Gage. This was a done deal.

After loading her bags in the trunk of her Mustang, Alex checked her watch and broke out in a sweat. *Shit. Shit. Shit. Why do I do this to myself? My flight leaves in ninety minutes.*

Driving at warp speed, she breathed a sigh of relief as she followed the airport signs to the parking lot. Orange cones blocked off short-term parking where she had planned to park since she was running late. As Alex drove into the long-term lot, every single space was full.

Fuming, she drove up and down nearly every aisle, finally finding an empty space at the back. Sweating bullets, she heaved her bags onto the pavement, locked the door, and raced toward the airport.

When she reached the counter, Alex hurled her suitcase onto the weight stand and handed the ticket agent her driver's license. The employee checked her watch. "You're three minutes past the cut-off time. Sorry."

Alex's mouth fell open. "It's because you're freaking short-term parking lot was blocked off. By the way, long term is totally effing full." Deciding to stretch the truth, she said, "I'm sure I lost fifteen minutes trying to find a damn space."

The young employee shrugged. "Sorry." She glanced behind Alex. "Next."

Alex thumped her massive purse on top of the counter. "Look. I've dealt with so much shit the past few years—more years than you've been working—and I'm treating myself to a getaway. I can't miss that plane." She locked eyes with the employee. Something crossed over the woman's face—first condescendence, then possibly pity.

Sighing, the uniformed clerk glanced once more at her watch.

Sensing her change in mood, Alex softened her tone. "*Please.*"

"Oh, all right." Glancing at the scale, she said, "Forty-eight pounds. That'll be thirty dollars."

Fishing inside her bag, Alex said, "Any way to upgrade to first class? I could use a drink."

The employee's eyebrows shot up. "It's nine in the morning."

Undeterred, Alex asked, "Is first class available?"

"All full." The airline clerk placed the tape indicating the destination on the bag, slung it on the belt, radioed ahead and told them she had a straggler bag for United Flight 666, and extended her hand for Alex's credit card."

"Did you say Flight 666? I'd never book a flight with that number." Alex studied the boarding pass the agent had given her. "I thought it was number 5552."

"That airplane had a mechanical." Clearly tired of Alex, the agent exaggeratedly leaned around her and yelled, "*Next.*"

Gripping her boarding pass, Alex reached for her carry-on. The attendant patted the counter. "Don't forget your baggage claim ticket. We rarely lose bags"—she fake coughed—"but, you know, just in case."

Stuffing the claim ticket in her pocket, Alex rushed toward security, pulling her carryon behind her. *Flight 666? You've got to be kidding me.*

Breathing a sigh of relief after making it through security without seeing any of Tony's cop friends who occasionally patrolled the airport, Alex found her gate, propped her feet on top of her carryon, and tried to relax.

After the ticket agent called her group, Alex got in line and boarded. Shoving her bag in the cabin overhead, she plucked a magazine out of her purse and exhaled. *Let the adventure begin.*

Chapter 57

After a tumultuous flight on a tiny, connecting plane the size of a prehistoric, flying bird, Alex still squished between two enormous men who thought every arm rest was theirs, couldn't disembark fast enough. She had practically held her breath the entire time because of the airborne germs and had decided in advance that she wouldn't use the disgusting restroom.

Upon landing she said a little prayer of thanks after the scary flight number. Gathering her purse and carryon, she entered the airport, checked the monitors, and glanced at her watch. *I've got to remember to move the time ahead one hour for Eastern Standard Time when I arrive, otherwise, I'll be later than usual.* Chuckling to herself, she considered the possibilities ahead. *Should I wander through the Big Apple, explore, shop, dine, and think about my relationship with Tony before seeing Gage?* Mind flitting from one option to another, she passed a Starbucks, ordered a venti skinny vanilla latte, a bag of almonds, and headed toward her gate. *I'm not about to miss this flight.*

Balancing her coffee, purse, and carry-on, she found a seat near a charging station and plugged in her phone. *I want a full charge in case I get lost.* Finally relaxing, Alex sipped her coffee and tore into the bag of almonds. Checking her email, she breathed a sigh of relief that Hannah hadn't contacted her. *I hope she has my board report ready to go the minute I return.* Staring at her cellphone, Alex wanted to text Suzy and Hope but decided to keep it a mystery.

A booming voice made her jump as agents began calling groups to board. In Group 4, Alex dumped her coffee cup in the recycle bin and stood in line near the gate. In fact, it seemed as though every passenger stood in line at the same time. A huge bottleneck occurred. Finally, two groups were called, but not hers. Alex noticed airline employees at the counter were whispering, checking the monitor, and glancing at the remaining passengers. *What the hell?*

After what seemed like forever, an older employee said, "We'll be calling four passengers to remain behind. The aircraft is over the weight limit."

Alex's stomach churned. *They had better not call my name.* The lingering passengers fidgeted and gawked at one another as the woman grabbed a microphone. She called out Mike Hunter, Scotty Stephens, Jackie Easterly, and Alexandra Mitchell. "Will the four of you approach the counter? The rest of the passengers may continue boarding."

"Oh, my God," Alex said to no one. "No. Just no." Glancing from the relieved passengers who happily handed over their boarding passes to the stern woman behind the counter, part of her wanted to bolt for the plane. But she knew TSA didn't joke around, and she wasn't in the mood to go to jail. *All I want is to go to New York City on a big ass adventure. Why are there roadblocks literally everywhere?*

The older employee reached for Alex's boarding pass. "We'll rebook you on a flight tomorrow morning."

Gripping the ticket so hard, she punched a hole through the paper. "No. I paid for the flight like everyone else. Let me on this plane."

"Sorry, ma'am. We're overweight."

Alex leaned forward and hissed, "What the hell do you mean overweight?"

The woman spoke slowly as if Alex were addled. "The plane weighs too much. We have several international passengers on this flight who have a great deal of luggage.

Luggage is heavy. It's unfortunate but we can't take any chances, as I'm sure you understand." Clicking on the keyboard, she said, "Let me see what flights are available—"

Stiffening, Alex said, "No, I *don't* understand. Besides, if this is all about weight, I'm not overweight. By the looks of some of the passen—" She stopped herself. Counting to five, she said, "I've had some complicated-as-hell years. Sorry about my French. Nothing earth shattering but an extremely annoying relationship mainly due to my boyfriend's crazy ex. I'm sure you have more worthy people with bigger problems, but—" To Alex's dismay, her eyes filled with tears. "This trip is a gift to myself. I've never done anything like this. Please let me board."

Glancing at the passenger list, the clerk murmured something about her spiteful ex-husband's first wife. Handing Alex her boarding pass, she told her to board then called another unfortunate passenger to stay behind.

Chapter 58

Finally rushing on the plane with every other passenger seated, a woman across the aisle glared at Alex. "I'm only late because they held me up." *Not that it's any of your business.*

Gratefully buckling her seatbelt, she observed the flight attendant demonstrate how to perform the oxygen . . . "In the event of an—"

Peering out the window, Alex stopped listening as the plane ascended. Tops of trees disappeared into a patchwork of countryside. *I'm ordering a chardonnay. I'm on vacation. I don't care what time it is.*

Seated in the back of the plane near the disgusting restroom, Alex wasn't about to complain. Not. At. All. She was bound for the Big Apple. That's all that mattered. Thrilled no one was seated next to her but feeling a bit sorry for whomever got left behind, Alex fished a book out of her purse. She also reached for earplugs since two toddlers were a row ahead and already squabbling and wailing. Their young mom handed them baggies filled with Cheerios and gold fish crackers.

Pushing the ear plugs in as far as they'd go, Alex felt her shoulders relax. *I haven't had time to read a book in months. This will be a treat.* She remembered buying the novel on Amazon, but for the life of her, couldn't remember the plot. As she cracked open *The Marriage Lie,* she scanned the praise for the novel and couldn't wait to dive in. After a few pages, she grimaced and slammed the book shut. *The damn plot is about a plane crash. Oh, my freaking God. Who wants to read about a plane crash while on a plane?* Shoving the book back into her purse, she glanced out the window, but curiosity got the better of her. Reading quickly, she wondered whether the husband was on the Orlando or Seattle flight and how in the world could he be on both? Her heart raced but she couldn't put the damn thing down.

When a flight attendant asked if she wanted anything, Alex nearly jumped out of her seat. "Yeah, thanks. A chardonnay and a Diet Coke."

The attendant rolled her eyes, likely since she had to retreat to the front of the plane for the wine. As passengers lined up for the restroom, the flight attendant turned sideways to pass them. Wading through the long line, she eventually brought the wine, and asked Alex for cash.

Raising the tray, Alex placed the Diet Coke between her legs and plucked out a five. After paying for the wine, the stewardess said, "Have a nice flight."

"It's been great so far," Alex deadpanned. She held her book in the air. "As long as the pilot keeps us airborne, I'll be happy." While she read and sipped her wine, a long line of passengers, who apparently didn't bother to go to the restroom before takeoff, made their way to the toilet. The last one left behind a scent that made Alex's toes curl. Coughing, she tore off pieces of her napkin and stuffed them in her nose.

Another passenger who looked like a typical gym rat tried his best to make eyes with her as his Sponge Bob-type body took up the entire aisle. She had zero interest in the musclebound guy. Tony and Gage were more than enough to juggle. Using the book as a cover, she held it in front of her face and took deep whiffs until the obnoxious smell dissipated.

As the landing gear strained, she peered out the window. The skies had turned an ominous, inky black. Lightning slashed through the heavens. *Oh, no. Please get us down safely and I'll*—she tried to think of a bargaining chip—*I'll be nicer to Hannah. Thank you, God. Amen.*

Alex tightened her seatbelt as the plane hit one bumpy air pocket after another. Placing both hands on the seat in front of her, she rested her head against the blue vinyl, germs be damned. *This flight can't end like the book.*

Chapter 59

The next morning's drive back from Nashville was mostly silent, sans rock music. A lot of rock music. The trip had been bittersweet, shocking, and incredible all rolled into one. Deciding she had previously grieved enough for Montana, Hope forced herself to focus on the present and her future.

Larry turned the dial to a satellite rock station and bopped his head to "Born to be Wild" by Steppenwolf. Peering at her hippie dad over her sunglasses, Hope thought, *That song title about covers it.*

Lost in a dreamy state as she recounted the slow dance with the cowboy as Larry fake drummed on the dashboard, Hope wanted to blurt out the encounter to everyone, especially her girlfriends, but had decided not to tell them, at least not for a while. If she never heard from Tucker again, she didn't want to be embarrassed. For now, being singled out by him and asked to dance were enough. Tucker reminded her of her comfiest sweatshirt. *I hope I see him again. If not, I want to remain in this afterglow for as long as I can.*

After a Starbucks stop since she and Larry were both fading, Hope said, "Just one more hour."

"I'm ready to get home to my old lady." Larry cracked the window. "Mind if I smoke? It's been a long weekend."

"Go ahead." Hope knew she could endure anything for another hour. They passed several tiny towns that didn't offer much more than a stop sign and a gas station. Rundown houses and population signs boasting a hundred or less people were the norm. Trees dotted the rolling, green hills as miles of curvy highway stretched before them.

"Turn the Page" by Bob Seger played as she pulled into her driveway. "That song's appropriate. Maybe we should turn the page. What do you think?"

Sitting up straighter, Larry said, "Look who's here."

Not surprisingly, Picasso was parked in front of her house. Willow had the windows open and was half asleep in her artsy VW Microbus that her art students had painted last spring. Once he spotted Willow, Larry jumped out before Hope had fully stopped. Running toward his second bride, Hope had bittersweet feelings as they embraced.

Gathering her plastic bag of belongings, she crossed the grass, and said hello to her colleague.

"How did it go, Mac? Did you see her? I want to know everything." Willow stared from Larry-Mac to Hope. Placing his bony arm around her shoulders, he said, "I've missed you."

"Let Larry, er, Mac fill you in. I'm wiped out." Halfway toward her front door, Hope turned. "Thanks for going with me to Nashville. We'll sort everything out eventually."

As Larry-Mac and Willow gawked at her, Hope waved goodbye, and unlocked her front door. Once inside, she leaned against the door and made herself a promise not to cry. She had shed enough tears over this situation. As her thoughts turned toward Tucker, she got happy goosebumps. But just as quickly, her heart plummeted. *Why didn't I ask him for his number? I'm so inept at dating.*

Chapter 60

When they eventually landed after extreme turbulence, nerves shattered, Alex shakily retrieved her carry-on and made her way down the aisle behind absurdly slow passengers. Once at the front, she thanked the young, female pilot who looked as though she should be a freshman in college, ponytail and all. "Great job on landing this beast. I don't get scared easily, but that storm was a bitch." Covering her mouth, she said, "Sorry for cursing. I'm a little shook up."

The young woman smiled and shook Alex's hand. "My pleasure, ma'am. Enjoy your stay."

Nodding, Alex made her way to baggage claim. *If my luggage made it, I'm golden.* As she descended an escalator among throngs of people from every ethnicity, she grinned when she heard a variety of languages. "I'm not in Crystal City anymore." Staring at illuminated signs containing arrival information and multiple carousels in two directions filled with luggage going around and around, she squinted as she tried to make sense of the boards. Then she spotted him.

To her surprise, her heart hammered. More handsome than ever, Cheri's limo driver held a white, cardboard sign with her name in big, bold letters. Dressed in dark jeans and a crisp, light blue shirt rolled up to his elbows, as their eyes met, Gage winked at her. Alex's pulse rate kicked up several notches. Barely able to contain herself from running into his arms, she couldn't stop smiling as she made her way toward him. *I made the right decision coming here.*

Careful not to stampede a squalling tot who sat in the middle of a packed area, Alex nonchalantly reached for the distressed mom's diaper bag and backpack as though she had zero fear of kid germs. While keeping one eye on Gage and wondering when it would be acceptable to use antibacterial gel, a desire she hadn't felt in far too long fluttered from her belly to her toes and settled somewhere in between. *I really shouldn't jump Gage's bones right here, right now. Not in front of the squealing kid at least.*

Even though they hadn't spent much time one on one over the past year, she had never been able to get Gage out of her mind. He hadn't wanted to trample on another man's relationship, even though said relationship was rocky on a good day. But here Gage stood in all his handsomeness, holding a sign for her and grinning like a toddler holding a triple scoop ice cream cone.

Chapter 61

Pulling her red carry-on, Alex grinned from ear to ear as her heels clacked across the floor. "Is that sign for me?"

"Who else?" Gage reached for her carry-on. "Welcome to New York."

Feeling like a tween, she pointed to the sign. "Nice touch." Unfamiliar bashfulness overcame her. "It's great to see you."

"Likewise." Gage gave her a playful elbow. "I thought I'd never see the day." Glancing toward the multiple carousels, he asked, "Do you have a checked bag?"

"Are you kidding? I would have brought three, but I'm pretending to be low maintenance."

"I'm not touching that. What color are your bags?"

Pointing toward her carryon, Alex said, "Red like this one. I bought matching bags at T.J. Maxx before I left Crystal City. I got a great bargain."

"Bargain hunters are good in my book." Approaching the carousel, Gage scanned the many colors, sizes, and shapes of luggage from duffel bags to dog carriers to guitar cases. Seemingly every bag was black.

Wide-eyed, Alex studied multiple screens listing a gazillion flight arrivals to determine which carousel her luggage would be on. Fumbling with her phone to find her flight number, she dropped her favorite tube of lipstick which promptly rolled under a cart and got squished. Wincing, she fumbled her cellphone before it landed on the floor too.

"Need some help?" he asked.

"Yes." Nervous laughter escaped. "My friends may think I'm all big city because I'm pretty good at faking it. I've only flown one other time and that was to a tiny airport in Burbank." Waving toward the multiple screens and carousels, she said, "In Burbank, there was only one carousel. It was impossible to make a mistake."

Gage reached for her carryon. "LaGuardia is a little bigger than that. You flew out of Chicago, right?"

"Yes."

"I see four flights from Chicago. Do you remember the flight number?"

Alex held her phone in the air and scrolled. "It's buried among my emails somewhere."

Gage reached for her hand. "We'll get our exercise. Your bags are either on carousel 3, 5, 6, or 8."

Alex noticed a mass of travelers appeared calm as they chatted and strolled out the door with their luggage intact. "Why am I the only nervous person who over packs?"

Waving his hand, Gage said, "Those people probably travel often. We'll find your bags."

"I hate feeling out of control like this. I'm always in con—"

"I know you are." Gage winked. "Now you're on my turf." Gage studied the bags rotating on the carousel. "I don't see any red luggage. Let's go to the next one."

Alex's eyes bulged. "What if someone took them?"

"I highly doubt that. No one would know whether you weighed one hundred pounds or four hundred—or whether you were male or female. Why would anyone chance it?"

"That makes sense." Alex's eyes darted around the room. "I think I see one of my bags." She pointed with her head. "On number 5."

Glancing in the direction she indicated, he asked, "Is it the red bag with the leopard print tag? That looks like you."

"Am I that obvious? Yeah, that's it." While Gage retrieved her bag, Alex scrolled through her email to see if there were any emergencies at the bank. When she didn't see a message from Hannah nor her boss, she relaxed. *Now I only have to worry about Hannah snooping through my desk.*

Once Gage secured both bags, he placed her carryon on top and motioned toward the door. "Nice job on picking a bright color." After Gage extended the handles, he motioned toward the glass doors. "Ready to see the Big Apple?"

Alex's stomach did flip flops. "Lead the way."

"Hungry?"

"I'm starving." Alex said.

As they exited the airport, Gage said, "I thought I'd give you a quick tour of Manhattan before we have a nice dinner. Sound good?" She nodded as Gage held the outer door open. "I'm really glad you're here."

Feeling more confident than she felt, Alex said, "What do the kids say? This will be epic."

Chapter 62

As Alex and Gage stepped outside the terminal past swarms of passengers, Alex took in the chaotic hubbub. "New York is electric. I can already tell it's very different from Crystal City."

Laughing, Gage said, "We're still at the airport."

She shrugged. "But I can tell."

Across the street, travelers stood in multiple, long lines for hotel shuttles. Along the sidewalk, another line formed for a string of cabs. Alex noticed there was a queue and a man in charge who told people which cab was next.

Pointing, Gage said, "We're going over here."

Following his finger, Alex noted several black, shiny limos. Her mouth fell open. "You brought your limo for me?"

"Of course." As they approached the stretch vehicle, Gage pushed a button on his key fob and loaded her luggage.

Alex reached for the doorknob.

"Wait." His eyes twinkled. "I'll do that."

"Seriously? I'm not a real passenger or some celebrity. I'm definitely not a socialite like Cheri. I'd feel silly."

With a flourish, Gage opened the back door. "No need to feel anything but special. This is my welcome-to-New York gift."

Beaming, Alex said, "I'm going to feel like a princess. Wait until I tell Suzy and Hope." Sliding her hand across the cool, tan leather, she said, "It even has that new limo smell."

"Glad you approve." Pointing toward a bottle of chilled white wine and a silver tray containing various cheeses and chocolate-dipped strawberries, Gage said, "For you, madam."

"If you ever call me that again, I'll punch you." Winking, she said, "But thanks. I'm starving." Alex reached for the wine.

"I know you're a businesswoman and used to being in control, but let me pour."

Alex patted the seat. "Only if you join me."

He eyed the impatient limo drivers behind him. "I've got to get moving and open up this spot. I'll have a drink later at dinner. I can't risk losing my license, but go ahead." Reaching into a tiny refrigerator, Gage retrieved a chilled wineglass and filled it expertly without spilling a drop. "Cheers."

Reaching for the wineglass, Alex said, "I'll have one glass to calm my nerves. We'll celebrate over dinner. Where are we going first?"

"Wherever you want. We can go to Rock Center, Radio City Music Hall, Central Park, the Empire State Building, Times Square, or Ground Zero if you're up for that."

Sipping her wine, Alex was glad there wasn't a barrier between them. That all sounds good, but I don't want anything depressing on my first day."

"I agree." Gage eased into traffic, "Let's go somewhere fun tonight. How about Rockefeller Center where they have the ice skating rink? I'll show you where they air the *Today show.*"

"I'd love that. Didn't you tell me you met Cheri at the skating rink when she was being accosted by paparazzi?"

Nodding, Gage said, "Good memory. I guess I owe my job to those jerks."

As she stared out the window, Alex noticed row after row of yellow cabs. People honked incessantly but it didn't appear to be akin to road rage, more like impatience and everyday life. "I've never seen so many taxis in my life."

"Uber and Lyft are definitely cutting into their business, but I predict the cabbies will always be here." At the light he turned around. "Having fun?"

Alex felt her cheeks flush as Gage caught her reapplying lipstick. Shoving the tube inside her bag, she nodded. "Great fun." Mouth agape, she again plastered her face against the window. "The skyscrapers are incredible. I can't believe how many people are on the sidewalks." As Gage eased into Manhattan, she studied the crowd. "Cheri was right. Everyone wears black."

Gage winked. "Including me."

Like a child seeing everything for the first time, Alex asked, "Do you mind if we drop off my luggage first?"

"Great timing. Cheri's penthouse is nearby."

Studying the interior of the limo which could easily hold several people, Alex leaned forward. "How much longer?"

He glanced toward the bumper-to-bumper cars. "About fifteen minutes, give or take, depending on traffic."

Alex groaned. "I'm not sure I can wait that long."

"Huh?"

At the next light, Alex bounded out of the limo. Horns blared and passersby stared. She reached for the door handle and jumped inside as a shocked, wide-eyed Gage's mouth fell open. "What are you doing?"

"It's lonely back there." Buckling her seatbelt, Alex turned toward him and smiled.

Gage shook his head. "You're something."

Shrugging, Alex said, "I wanted a front seat view."

Chapter 63

Gage parked the limo in the adjoining lot to Cheri's apartment, retrieved the bags from the trunk, and rolled them toward the glass enclosure. After tipping Cheri's doorman to deliver the luggage to Cheri's penthouse, Gage reached for Alex's hand. "Since you're a first timer, you've got to experience Times Square. Let's walk like tourists."

"I am a tourist."

Staring openmouthed at the massive, provocative billboards with scantily clad women and sexy men, Alex pointed. "You wouldn't see these in the Bible Belt. This is one sexy city. I love it."

Chuckling, Gage said, "I barely notice them anymore. I'm glad you're here."

After walking for seemingly miles, Alex, who was anything but a wimp but hadn't worn sensible walking shoes, asked Gage if they could get the limo. While he drove, she took photos of the Chrysler Building, Empire State Building, and Radio City Music Hall. "These will make great Instagram and Facebook posts but I'll have to wait to post them until I return."

"Why?"

"Uh, this is sort of a mystery trip." Not wanting to mention Tony, Alex said, "I don't want the bank to know where I am."

Nodding, Gage said, "Understood."

Both famished, they decided to make their way toward Rockefeller Center for a late dinner. Gage requested a table near a window overlooking the skating rink. After gorging on pasta, salad, and wine, Alex stifled a yawn. He winked. "Bored?"

"Hardly. I was up way too late packing, and much too early to catch my flight. It's been a long travel day."

"You're probably beat." Gage got the server's attention, paid the bill, and they made their way toward Cheri's penthouse.

Dreading how to handle the goodbye, Alex squeezed Gage's hand. "Thanks for everything. You were so great to pick me up—with my name on a sign no less—provide a limo, and show me the sites." Rubbing her belly, she said, "And that dinner was fantastic. I can't wait to see what's in store for tomorrow."

Glad he took the hint not to follow her up to Cheri's penthouse, Alex's mind raced. *I wonder if Tony has figured out I've left town.* Scolding herself for thinking of the cop after all Gage had done, she hugged Gage and kissed his cheek. "Until tomorrow."

After he left, Alex could still smell the lingering scent of his cologne and wondered why she liked it so much.

Chapter 64

Waking up in Cheri's lush penthouse apartment, Alex felt like royalty. Padding from room to room, she was in complete awe. *I wouldn't know how to live like this, but I'll give it the good old college try.* Imagining the life of a socialite was both exhilarating and exhausting. *It sounds amazing, but I like my privacy too much.* Chuckling to herself, she knew she'd be on every magazine cover telling a photographer to shove it.

Wondering what Gage had in store for the day, Alex grabbed her purse, cellphone, and took the elevator downstairs.

Cheri's smiling doorman greeted her. "Good morning, Miss Mitchell. May I assist you with anything?"

Staring out the gold-trimmed, glass-paneled front door and already astonished by the hurried crowd on the sidewalk, Alex said, "Yes, as a matter of fact. Do you know where I can find a limo?"

Knitting his eyebrows, the doorman's face turned solemn. "Weren't you satisfied with Gage's services?"

Alex controlled her giggles—and her gutter mind. They hadn't even kissed, but she knew what the doorman meant. "Actually, the limo is *for* Gage. I want to surprise him."

Stroking his chin, the doorman said, "Ah, I think I see." He reached for a phone and said, "There are several services available. Want me to choose for you?"

"Yes, please. I'm going to take a quick stroll first."

~ ~ ~

Stepping outside, Alex grinned when she noticed dog walkers everywhere. The sidewalks bustled with tourists, many of whom blocked traffic by taking photos of the massive, provocative billboards and skyline. Mostly dressed in black were businessmen and businesswomen all seemingly in a huge rush to get to their respective offices. Casually dressed, young women—likely nannies—pushed strollers. A few unique characters dressed in costume, each seemingly trying to outdo the other.

Alex strolled past a busy diner below the Wellington Hotel on 55th and 7th. *I love the energy here. Love hearing the different languages. Even the honking cabs don't annoy me. Maybe I could live here.* She laughed to herself. *Nah. I couldn't live without my friends and Coconuts. Maybe I can convince Gage to move.*

After a quick stroll and more photos of the cityscape, Alex texted Gage and asked for his address. He replied with a string of question marks.

She responded: *Don't ask.*

After he gave her his address, she returned to the lobby of Cheri's apartment. The cheerful doorman gestured toward a white limo and opened the door for Alex. After climbing inside, she gave the driver Gage's address. Leaning back, her heart raced at the thought of seeing his reaction.

As the driver wove in and out of traffic, he glanced at a small screen to the left of his steering wheel showing a maze of streets.

"Do you know how much longer it'll take?" Fishing in her purse, she popped in a breath mint for good measure.

"One more turn, and we'll be there."

Her stomach flip flopped. *I can't wait to see Gage's reaction.* As the driver parked in the driveway of a narrow, two-story brownstone, Alex peeked out the window. Every house in Gage's neighborhood looked the same. Row after row of narrow, two-story brick homes. Unlike Crystal City, these houses appeared to be inches apart with tiny lawns, a few steep stairs leading to the front door, and identical floorplans.

As Gage opened his front door, locked it, and bounded down the stairs, he stopped in his tracks, mouth open, when he spotted the limo. Wearing dark jeans, a crisp, white shirt, and dark sunglasses atop his head, Alex thought he had never looked sexier.

Telling the driver to stay seated, she opened her door and stepped onto the driveway.

Gage pointed toward the stretch vehicle. "What's this?"

Winking, she said, "A limo."

Cocking his head, he roared. "Someone's a comedienne. I meant, "Why is it here? My limo is—"

Alex leaned against the immaculate stretch vehicle. "I decided it's about time someone drove *you* around. And, if you don't mind, I'm going to tag along."

Gage opened his mouth and closed it without uttering a word. He stared from the limo to Alex and back again. "I'm speechless. No one has ever done anything like this for me."

Alex grinned. "Until now."

Crossing his lawn, Gage said, "I thought this was *your* big trip. Why am I getting the special treatment?"

"Because you're a gentleman, that's why." Alex kissed Gage's cheek. "And you deserve it."

The driver's voice boomed through his open window. "Do you two need a chauffeur or what?"

Simultaneously, Alex and Gage said, "Yes."

The driver stepped outside and opened the back door. "Where to?"

Gage settled in beside Alex. Even though there was room for many more people, they sat touching. "Just drive." He buckled his seatbelt. "I'm really gonna enjoy this."

"Want any music?" the driver asked.

"Yes," both answered.

The driver left them alone except for occasionally pointing out tourist sites.

Gage glanced around the limo. "I see it's well stocked. "Want some wine?"

"It's a little early, but hey, I'm on vacation. Plus, I never turn down wine." Alex reached for a bowl of exotic olives and popped one into Gage's mouth. Already feeling relaxed after two swallows of chardonnay, she said, "I have a question."

Gage's arm brushed up against hers. "I'm all ears."

Half leaning into Gage, she asked, "Have you ever made out in a limo?"

"I think I'm about to." Gage curled his arm across her shoulders, caressed her cheek, and gave Alex a quick kiss. When she returned the kiss, he pulled her closer, stroked her long, blond hair, and nibbled on her bottom lip.

Alex thought she might have a heart attack. Breathing in and out in an attempt to steady herself—partially from the wine but mostly from Gage—she said, "Whoa."

Concern filled his face. "Feeling okay?"

"Never better." Alex returned Gage's kiss which became more and more probing. When they both came up for air, he said, "Now I've definitely made out in a limo."

Alex giggled. "I'm checking this off my bucket list too."

Gage kissed her again but stopped abruptly. Rubbing the top of his short-cropped hair, he said, "I shouldn't have done that." Staring into her green eyes, he said, "Should I have done that? Are you still with the cop?"

Blowing out a long whistle, Alex said, "Way to kill a moment." She hesitated, staring at her lap. "I-I suppose we're still together. It's complicated, but yes, as messy as it is and as awful as it is most days, we're still dating." Teary-eyed, she turned toward Gage and placed her hand over his. "You're a great guy. A *really* great guy."

"I feel a *but* coming on." Placing a finger to her lips, he said, "Don't talk. It's okay. I get it. I'd be pissed if we were together and he hit on you. Like you said, it's complicated. Still, the limo was a great surprise, and the kiss was even better."

"Thanks for understanding." Alex hated that Tony had already nearly ruined their perfect day from afar.

Tapping on the glass between them and the chauffer, Gage waited for the window to lower. "Take us to Go Zen in the Village."

"What's Go Zen?" Alex asked, glad for a distraction.

Gage squeezed her hand. "It's a cool, fairly new eclectic restaurant. Actually, it's vegetarian but you'll never miss the meat. Cheri's favorite restaurant was Gobo, which closed. The chefs from Gobo and Zen Palate joined forces to open this place. Up for it?"

Nodding, Alex said, "Sure. I can eat anything as long as you're there." She immediately regretted sounding so cheesy. Leaning back, her mind raced. *Maybe I should just end it with Tony from here. Send him a chicken shit text and get it over with so I can see if Gage and I have a chance.* Her stomach churned. *I can't do that to him after all we've been through. I owe Tony an in-person breakup. Shit.*

Chapter 65

Annoyed Alex hadn't returned his calls nor texts, Tony jumped at the chance to watch Joey since Sean was undercover and Nikki was God knows where. Rounding the familiar corner to Joey's school, Tony parked in a back alley behind the playground along with a string of other parents. Craning his neck, he eventually spotted his son-turned-nephew running alongside a mass of children. Stepping outside his car, Tony whistled and waved until he got Joey's attention.

Backpack flopping up and down as he ran, Joey bounded toward him. Opening the door, Tony said, "Hey, buddy. How was school?"

"Fine."

"How about your ball team? Having fun?"

"Yep."

Annoyed by Joey's one-word answers, Tony reminded him to buckle his seatbelt, told him his mother was busy, and attempted to find an activity. "Want to go bowling?"

Brightening, the young boy said, "Yeah."

~ ~ ~

Once inside the loud bowling alley, they went to the counter to get bowling shoes. After the clerk found their sizes, they headed to an alley at the far end. Joey laced his shoes and said, "Now what?"

"Pick out a ball."

Taking an agonizingly long time to choose a ball, Joey eventually returned to the lane. Tony studied his nephew who he had raised as a son. "New hairdo, I see. How does it stick up like that?"

Shrugging, Joey said, "Gorilla glue from Wal-Mart. Want to touch it?"

Tony patted the spiky, stiff hair. "Yeah, little man. You've definitely got a mohawk going on."

"Do you like it?" Joey asked.

"If you do."

Joey cocked his head. "That's not an answer."

"You're right. I hate it."

A smile crossed Joey's lips. "Good. I didn't think you would."

"Getting mouthy, I see. Are you taking after Uncle Sean?"

Joey's face reddened. "He's my dad, remember?" Storming off, he took his ball, stood at the end of the lane, and promptly rolled it into the gutter.

Damn Sean. Damn Nikki. My boy isn't the same. This is going to be a long game. Selecting his bowling ball, Tony rolled strike after strike. Joey hit mostly gutter balls but jumped up and down when he knocked three pins down.

"Great job, little guy. I'd rub the top of your head if it wouldn't cut me."

Absentmindedly touching a spike, Joey said, "I like it. Let's play again."

Starving, Tony said, "Another time. We can get a pizza then I'm taking you home."

"Okay." Joey unlaced his shoes as Tony put the balls away. "There's a new pizza place next door." After they devoured a pepperoni and sausage pizza, Tony drove him home. "It's getting late. Do you have any homework?"

Nodding, Joey said, "Spelling words and a few math problems."

"Need any help?" Not the best speller, Tony half hoped he'd say no.

"Nah. Mom will help me."

Rounding the corner to Nikki's house, he spotted her purple jeep in the driveway. "Looks like your mom decided to come home. You're in luck with that homework." Hugging Joey, Tony didn't bother going to the door. He watched until he ran inside and drove away. *I think I'll surprise Alex. I'm in the mood for the Tony and Alex Show.*

Driving to Alex's house on autopilot, Tony was surprised to see the lights weren't on. Checking his watch, he grumbled, "She never goes to bed this early."

Stepping onto her porch, he knocked. Nothing. Tony knocked louder, but there was still no answer. *Dammit. She must be with her girlfriends at Coconuts.* Glancing around her porch, he noticed her mailbox was stuffed with mail and magazines. *Where the hell is she?*

I'm going to Coconuts. Within minutes, he arrived, eager to buy her a drink to get her in the mood for their favorite pastime. But Alex's white Mustang wasn't in the parking lot, nor were her friends' cars.

Isn't this the perfect damn day?

Chapter 66

After the limo driver dropped them off in front of Go Zen, an eclectic, modern restaurant with an open floor plan where patrons could watch the chefs cook, Alex relaxed. Determined to enjoy her limited time with Gage, she did her utmost to put Tony out of her mind—at least while she was on the East Coast. *God knows he'd do the same given the chance.* Her jaw clenched at the thought of his ex and his hateful brother. *Why wouldn't I want to get out of that fresh hell? Why shouldn't I have a little fun? I'm single. We aren't engaged.*

"Someone's in deep thought." Gage nudged Alex with his elbow. "What do you think about this place?"

"I think it's cool. I also think I need a chardonnay." She took a deep breath. "Pronto."

Gage slipped the hostess a twenty. They were seated immediately at a corner table. A server dressed in all black brought menus, water, a pot of oolong tea, and asked if they'd like to hear the specials.

"I'd like some chardonnay first, please." Alex studied the weighty menu. "These dishes sound amazing." Glancing around the room, she noted all ages and ethnicities. Many ate at long, community tables.

"I love New York. It's so different from back home."

"Where's home?" the server asked.

"Missouri."

He grinned. "Flyover state."

"Hey, it's beautiful with mountains and lakes. We have

nice places too." Alex felt herself bristle. "You should come visit."

"I'm teasing you. My parents are from St. Louis." The server did a little fist bump. "Go, Cards."

"Love the Cards." Alex gave him her best half-pleading, half-flirty look. "About our cocktails . . ."

Gage ordered a beer and the server scampered off. "Be right back, Missouri."

Opening his menu, Gage pointed toward several items. "Everything's delicious. You can't go wrong."

Closing her menu, Alex said, "Usually I like to be in charge, but for tonight, order for me."

Chuckling, Gage said, "Oh, you've been in charge all day by surprising me with the limo. Nice touch." Reaching for her hand, he said, "That meant a lot."

As soon as the server returned with their adult beverages, Alex took a healthy swig of wine.

Gage's eyebrows shot up. "Take your time. We've got all evening, and you can order more."

Shrugging, Alex said, "I'm trying to relax." She studied the chefs. "Has Cheri ever been to, what's it called, Go Zen?"

Gage peered over his menu. "She suggested it since half of the chefs are from Gobo. Anytime she gets requests for vegetarian entrees at one of her events, she and I come here. She said it gives her inspiration."

"She's so cool. I never thought I'd know a gorgeous socialite and actually like her. I'm a little picky if you hadn't noticed."

"She thinks the world of you, Suzy, and Hope. You've really helped her acclimate to Crystal City."

"Do you think she'll move to Branson full time?" Alex asked.

"Nah. Her heart's in Manhattan, but she enjoys the change of scenery. Temporarily, that is." The server reappeared and Gage placed their orders. Within minutes, the table was crowded with several small plates: pumpkin soup, mushroom fries, avocado salad, sesame seitan, lettuce wraps, and pesto linguine.

Alex's mouth watered. "This is the end of my diet. Everything looks and smells amazing."

Sliding several platters toward her, Gage said, "Wait until you taste it."

She sampled some of every dish. "I wish we had Go Zen in Crystal City. This is incredible." After several minutes of eating in silence, Alex studied Gage while she ate. Thoughts of Tony threatened to dampen her mood. They both got a second cocktail refill and Alex scraped the last bit of food off her plate. "That's one of the best meals I've ever had. Thanks for suggesting this place."

The server returned. "Save room for dessert."

Rubbing her belly, Alex said, "I couldn't possibly."

Grinning, Gage said, "You've got to try one bite of the Death by Chocolate Cake."

"Oh, my God. I shouldn't."

The server watched the interplay. "And?"

Shifting in her chair, Alex said, "I can probably manage a bite or two."

After dessert was served among oohing and ahhing, Alex crossed her arms. "Amazing. Simply amazing. I'm satiated. What do you want to do next?"

Gage polished off his beer. "I thought we could walk off this food with a stroll through Chinatown."

"Perfect."

Chapter 67

After they left the restaurant, Gage asked the limo driver to wait another hour. The evening air had turned chilly. Alex shivered, and Gage placed his arm across her shoulders. Relieved she had a reason to cuddle and not feel guilty about it, she snuggled against his warm body. "Thanks for the incredible meal."

He winked. "Thanks for the incredible company."

As they strolled the lively streets of Chinatown, Alex noticed pigs and ducks hanging by their feet from street vendor stands. Peering inside a booth with chocolate confections, Alex said, "I can't resist chocolate." As she reached for one, Gage whispered, "Those are chocolate-dipped ants and crickets."

"Gross." Alex stepped back as if a swarm of bees had landed.

Gage chuckled. "Don't knock it until you've tried it. Want one?" He winked. "They have a nice crunch."

Wrinkling her nose, Alex said, "Hard pass." She noticed several Asian vendors sold a large variety of food while tourists curiously peered inside the unique booths and sampled their creations. Even though she was full, the delicious smells made her mouth water.

As they ambled past the street vendors, Alex studied several New Yorkers who made bold statements with diverse clothing—or little clothing—and random painted bodies. One was spray-painted green with a pointy headpiece and holding a torch, obviously mirroring the Statue of Liberty. A few people played a guitar or bongo drums on the sidewalk for tips.

As a gorgeous young woman stepped toward them with two friends on either side, Alex couldn't tear her eyes from the cover-model-ready female. Peering closer, she gasped. Mouth open, she glanced at Gage who was staring in the same direction. "Is she naked under that open coat? Like, totally naked?"

Without missing a beat, Gage chuckled. "Yup. That's nothing."

Alex had to force herself to keep from gawking at the sexy woman. "I can't get over how different it is here." Staring down at her clothes, which were stylish in Crystal City, she frowned. "I feel so boring and average here."

"You're anything but." Gage reached for her hand. "Want to go to Broadway? It's too late to get tickets for tonight, but we can see some fun shops and the former Ed Sullivan and David Letterman Theater. You'll get some great photos there."

~ ~ ~

After the limo driver drove them to Broadway, they rushed out of the limo while a line of cars honked behind them. Gage told him when to pick them up. As they approached the old Ed Sullivan Theater, Alex marveled at the intricate gold doors and the infamous marquee. "Imagine how many celebrities have crossed through that door. It blows my mind."

After taking several photos, Gage asked if she were going to post them on social media. Almost forgetting, she paused with her finger over the *send* key. "I think I'll wait."

"It's not because of the bank. It's due to the cop, right?"

Shrugging, Alex said, "I mean, I could post them. I really don't think he'd hop on a plane." Voice lowering, she said, "I'd never hear the end of it, plus I don't want Hannah to know where I am, nor some idiot burglar."

Nodding, he said, "That makes sense."

Tugging on the gold door handle to the infamous, old TV show theater, she said, "I wish it were unlocked. I'd love to go inside."

Stepping aside for another tourist to take photos, Gage said, "I've never been inside either. I think Cheri catered a couple of events here years ago when David Letterman had his show." He pointed toward a rectangular billboard. "He had an ad on that billboard stating he was #2 in late night television. I always thought that was hilarious."

Alex laughed. "That's funny."

As they crossed the street, billboards highlighting several popular Broadway and off-Broadway shows filled every available space. One billboard high atop an ancient building caught Alex's eye. "Eww. That's gross."

Gage followed her gaze. "What?"

Pointing toward the ad featuring a giant bug, the copy read: WE HAVE BEDBUGS and gave an 800 number to call. Alex rubbed her arms. "My skin is crawling just thinking about that." Her OCD anxieties kicked up a notch. She couldn't stop staring at the enormous bug. Fixated on the creature, she always did her best to keep her disorder at bay. Counting was easy to hide because she did that silently. Five, eight, and thirteen were her favorite numbers. Of course, her knot-tying paper straw ritual hadn't been an issue since there didn't appear to be one straw in New York City, at least not anywhere they had frequented. Forcing herself away from the giant bedbug, she shivered. "That's going to give me nightmares."

Gage suppressed an obvious laugh. "No worries. That alert is referring to certain hotels, I'm sure. I can guarantee Cheri's apartment doesn't have bed bugs. Her maid, Pearl, is meticulous."

"Good. Let's change the subject." As they started down the sidewalk, Alex said, "Look. There's a Hershey's store. Maybe they'll have samples. I could use a chocolate fix."

His eyebrows shot up. "After that Death by Chocolate cake?"

"Is there a better way to go?" Grinning, Alex said, "I'm kidding, but a girl can never have too much chocolate." Half pulling Gage down the sidewalk, once inside, she inhaled. "Oh, my God. The whole store smells like chocolate. We need a store like this in Crystal City. Hope would go nuts. We'd have to move our get-togethers from Coconuts." After spotting a three-tier dripping chocolate fountain in the corner, her mouth curved into a smile. "Is this what heaven looks like?"

"Pretty close, I imagine." Gage studied the liquid chocolate and licked his lips. "What do you want to do after this?"

Yawning, she replied, "I think jetlag is catching up with me."

"Say no more. We still have a couple of days, right?"

"Oh, yeah. I'm enjoying my *Eat, Drink, Chill* trip." Reaching for Gage's hand, Alex said, "And I'm loving every minute." *I'm confused as hell about my love life but appreciating every second of this adventure.*

Chapter 68

After crying all morning, Suzy blew her nose. "I don't know what's wrong with me."

Ken poured a second cup of coffee. "Babe, I'm sure it's the pregnancy. Can I get you anything?"

Face puffy, Suzy said, "Not unless you can carry these babies for a few months. I'm sick of being nauseous."

Setting his coffee on the counter, Ken said, "I wish I could." He grinned. "Not really, but you know what I mean. It'll be over in a few months." Turning toward both chirping phones charging near the toaster, he brightened and held up his cell. "This will cheer you up. Jon wants us to meet them for breakfast. Are you up to it?"

"As in today?" Suzy asked.

Glancing back at the screen, Ken said, "Yep." He held her phone in the air. "You've got the same text."

Already crossing the living room to change, Suzy said, "Respond that we're on our way. Is baby Violet going to be there? It has been too long since I've held her."

"I believe the whole gang will be there." Ken responded affirmatively using both thumbs.

~ ~ ~

As they climbed into the car, Suzy struggled with her seatbelt. "These babies are getting bigger." Giggling, she said, "I've got to loosen the strap."

"Protect that precious cargo, sweetie." Ken eased onto the highway and took the first exit sign for IHOP. "I'm starving. I'm glad Jon and Fernando suggested breakfast."

When they entered the busy lobby, Fernando held a cooing baby Violet high in the air. Jon studied a menu near the hostess stand, and Vanessa ran to hug Suzy. "You're glowing, Suzy." The freckle-faced young mother patted Suzy's baby bump. "Just a few more months. I can't wait to see the twins. Have you thought of names?"

Ken and Suzy exchanged glances. He shook his head. "We haven't decided." Suzy reached for Vanessa's hand. "I remember when you were pregnant last year. You, Jon, and Fernando chose the perfect name for Violet Grace. We're struggling with names for the twins."

Wrapping his arm around his mom's waist, Jon said, "It'll come to you. Thanks for joining us last minute."

Handing baby Violet to Suzy, Fernando kissed both of Suzy's cheeks. "I'm sure you want to hold your granddaughter, Mama Suzy."

After they were seated and ordered, Suzy played Patty Cake with Violet who was dressed in her usual lavender at Fernando's insistence. Within minutes, the server brought coffee, juice, hot tea, and platters of pancakes, bacon, biscuits, and eggs.

Suzy set Violet in a high chair and cleaned the tray with anti-bacterial wipes. Tearing off tiny pieces of food, she placed it on the baby tray. Giggling, Suzy said, "She eats it faster than I can get it to her."

Everyone chuckled. Fernando said, "Some days Violet out eats my husband."

"Thanks for inviting us. I love spontaneous get-togethers." Suzy's eyes filled with tears. "I was having a bad morning, hormonal, I guess. This is just what I needed."

Jon and Fernando exchanged glances. Vanessa stared at her food. Picking up on their non-verbal actions, Suzy said, "What's going on? I get the feeling this isn't an impromptu breakfast."

Jon opened his mouth and closed it. Fernando squared his shoulders. "Mama Suzy, there wasn't a good time to do this."

"To do what?" Suzy asked, eyes already filling with tears.

Fernando reached for his mother-in-law's hand. "We're leaving for Italy after breakfast."

Suzy stopped with a bite of multi-grain pancake in mid-air. "You're leaving now? Today?"

"Sorry, Mom." Wincing, Jon said, "Fernando, Vanessa, and I discussed how to handle this. I know this seems abrupt, but you've been distraught lately, so we thought this might be best."

"What do you Americans say?" Fernando waved his coffee cup in the air. "Rip the Band-Aid off?"

Leaning against Ken's shoulder, Suzy said, "I know your mother wants to be part of Violet's life. I can't be a selfish grandmother, but this stinks." Wiping away a stray tear, she said, "We're going to the airport with you."

Jon shook his head. "No, that'll make it harder. Let's say goodbye here."

Sniffling, Suzy reached for baby Violet. "You've got to send me pictures every week. We must live chat too." Kissing the baby's cheeks, she said, "I want to watch her grow."

"Done," Jon said. "I love you, Mom. We'll be back in a few months."

Fernando attempted to lighten the mood. "No worries about the live chats and photos. My mama will see to it, otherwise she'll thump our heads." Vanessa rubbed Suzy's arm. "Sorry, Suzy. I'm going to miss you too." She brightened, "But I'm really excited about my first plane ride and seeing another country."

"We'll manage." Ken reached for the check. "Breakfast is on me. Have a safe trip across the pond. Please stay in touch."

After tearful farewells in the parking lot and many more kisses and hugs, Suzy and Ken wrapped their arms around one another as they waved goodbye. When the car was out of sight, Suzy squeezed her husband's hand. "I wish I could drink."

Chapter 69

Cheri had already spoken to two clients and checked in with Fifth Avenue Catering. Her new pastry chef, a female, seemed to get along with Julio and had promised to email several new quiche recipes for a socialite's upcoming wedding brunch reception—one with bacon, one kosher, and another vegetarian. Cheri responded, "Make sure you also have fresh fruit, chocolate hearts with the couple's initials, several pitchers of mimosas, and it will go smoothly."

She signed off, changed clothes yet again, and paced while waiting for Cole. *I wonder what exactly Cole meant by camping when he called?* Glancing at the clock, timely as always, the doorbell rang at noon. Cheri opened the huge, rather squeaky, front door. "Hi."

Examining the doorjamb, he said, "You need some WD40 for that."

"Some what?" she asked.

"I'll fix it later." He extended a red rose he had plucked off a bush along Cheri's driveway. "For the prettiest girl this side of the Mississippi."

"That's sweet. Thanks." Smelling the rose, she motioned for him to come inside.

Cole studied her four-inch heels, yellow sundress, and a gazillion silver bangle bracelets encircling her tiny wrist.

Biting his lip in an obvious attempt to hide his laughter, Cole said, "Hey, New York, we're going campin'. Sure you want to wear that?"

Cheri peered down at her clothes. "What's wrong with what I'm wearing? It's a simple dress."

He pointed. "Those heels will get stuck in the dirt."

Cheri stared at her leopard print stilettos. "Oh, I didn't think about that. I don't want to ruin these. I just bought them."

Motioning toward her bare legs, he added, "And your legs will be covered with mosquito bites or chiggers."

"What's a chigger?"

Cole shook his head "You don't want to find out. I have bug spray."

Cheri's face fell. "I'm not sure what you have planned for today. My idea of camping out is a rundown Holiday Inn that doesn't offer breakfast. I've never gone camping in the country."

"You'll never know if you like it until you try it." Leaning against the doorframe, Cole said, "Why don't you change into jeans, tennis shoes, and a tee shirt? Got any of that? You'll be more comfortable. I'll wait here."

Cheri mentally assessed the designer clothes in her wardrobe. She knew she had a black Calvin Klein tee . . . somewhere. And some black and silver Coach tennis shoes. She plunked her enormous orange Kate Spade bag on the porch. "Will you watch this while I change?"

"Sure but nobody's here to steal it but me." After she disappeared, Cole watched a little boy precariously pedal a bike across the street. He wanted to help the little guy but didn't want to leave Cheri's purse unattended.

Cheri's cell phone was perched on top of her bag. When it rang, Cole resisted the temptation to look at the caller ID—until it rang incessantly for a third time in a row. No longer able to resist, he took a peek. CALLER UNKNOWN appeared on the screen. *Interesting.* But he decided not to ask any questions.

Cheri reappeared with two bottles of chilled water and thrust one toward him.

"Thanks." Cole looked at her appreciatively. She had donned a black tee, jeans that fit like paint, and stylish tennis shoes. This time, she wore zero jewelry except for huge silver hoop earrings. He also noticed she had pulled her long hair into a playful, high ponytail.

"Much better. You'll want a jacket."

"It's seventy-five degrees."

He shrugged. "It gets cold at night."

"I didn't know we'd be out that long."

Cole's eyebrows shot up. "Is that too late, New York?"

"Not at all." Cheri ran back inside and reappeared with a khaki jacket with a leopard print lining.

Before they drove off, Cole plucked another flower and tucked it behind her ear. "Now you're ready."

"You're sweet. Where exactly are we going?"

"You'll see." Cole turned up the radio and sang along to "Done" by The Band Perry.

"You have a nice voice." She noticed a pinkish hue work its way up from his neck to his ears. "Are you blushing?"

"Heck no." Cole stopped singing.

"Please don't stop. I rarely hear country music in New York. It's a treat."

Gripping the wheel with his calloused hands, Cole increased the volume and turned onto a narrow, country road. "I hope you don't get car sick. It's a curvy drive. If you feel woozy, look straight ahead and crack the window. It'll help."

"Good to know." Cheri stared out the windshield. "I'd hate to puke in your truck."

He chuckled. "You and me both."

As Cole drove, they got behind a giant green John Deere tractor pulling a trailer loaded with massive round bales of hay. "Darn. This will slow us down quite a bit."

Frowning, Cheri said, "Oh, no."

Cole defended the driver. "A man's gotta work. Have you ever watched someone bale hay? What am I asking? Of course you haven't."

"Nope. I've also never seen such a huge tractor either, let alone those gigantic hay bales. We don't have tractors snaking around Manhattan." She giggled. "This would cause a nasty traffic jam. I can just hear the taxi horns now."

As if on request, "International Harvester" by Craig Morgan came on the air. "Do you think the radio heard us talking about that tractor?" Laughing, Cheri said, "Cute song."

Twenty minutes and several songs later, they finally passed the tractor. Cole turned down what looked like a deserted, rocky road. A cloud of dust followed them. He eventually pulled up to a wooded area.

Cheri shivered. "It's a good thing I trust you. This is desolate."

Rubbing his chin, Cole said, "Gosh, I hadn't thought about that." He held his key near the ignition. "If this makes you nervous, we can leave."

Cheri held her hand in the air. "The thing is I do trust you. I really do. I just won't mention this adventure to my parents."

"Are they protective?"

Cheri threw her head back. "Is there a stronger word than *protective*?"

"They should be protective of a gorgeous young woman like you. I bet you have good parents."

Cheri decided not to mention the fact she had a nanny and chef as a kid and rarely saw her globetrotting parents while growing up—or now, for that matter.

Cole parked. "Hop out. I'll gather our gear."

She raised her eyebrows. "Gear?"

"Yep. Campin' requires a lot of gear." Cole reached into the back, grabbed a duffel bag, and a blue tent that was rolled up like a patio umbrella. He handed a wooden picnic basket to Cheri.

Her mouth fell open. "You brought food?"

"Yep." He winked. "Even remembered the wine."

"I'm impressed."

"Let's go." Cole motioned with his head. "There's an openin' over yonder."

Cheri lugged the wicker basket. "Thank goodness you told me to change. I'd hate to do this in heels, although I walk all over New York City in them."

Nodding, Cole trudged forward, obviously on a mission.

Pointing to an opening in the woods, he said, "There's a clearin' over there, plus a spring. Perfect for a picnic."

Stopping short, Cheri asked, "In the woods? Are there any animals?"

"Only snakes, the occasional bear, skunks, rabbits, squirrels, opossums, and maybe a coyote or a mountain lion."

Cheri stopped in her tracks. "Please tell me you're joking."

Shifting his gear, Cole said, "Black bears are pretty rare around here. Coyotes come out mainly at night but aren't interested in us."

"And mountain lions?"

"Also rare. Likely, all we'll see are squirrels and birds. Maybe a snake."

"Snake?!" Cheri discovered newfound interest in the grass.

Linking his arm through hers, Cole said, "Don't worry. You're with me."

Chapter 70

Stepping through a clearing where a beautiful lush, green patch of soft grass appeared surrounded by towering trees, Cheri felt like she was in the fairytale "Snow White," minus the Seven Dwarves.

Spreading out a blanket, Cole pointed. "You can set the picnic basket on one corner to hold it down while I pitch our tent." He unfolded the canvas and removed stakes and a hammer out of the duffel bag.

"Can I help?"

"Sure. Grab that end and pull on the canvas. I need to put stakes in all four corners." When Cole was satisfied with the positioning, he drove the stakes in the ground. Within minutes, a small tent featuring a screen door emerged. He zipped it closed. "That'll keep the bugs out."

"Good." Rubbing her arm, she asked, "Now what are we going to do?"

"We're going to enjoy nature. Get down to basics."

Cheri studied the serene, albeit isolated, area. Growing up in Manhattan, she hadn't seen many trees and grass except for Central Park. Staring at him, she asked, "Such as?"

Grinning, Cole ticked off his fingers. "Lots of choices. We can skip rocks, drink wine, take a nap, hike, tip cows or—"

"Let's have a glass of wine and then you can teach me how to skip rocks." She paused. "Wait. Did you say 'tip cows'?"

Chuckling, Cole said, "Country joke. Maybe. Some say it's real; others say cow tippin' is fiction." He winked as he unscrewed the cork while motioning with his head. "You'll find two very expensive, plastic wineglasses in the picnic basket."

Cheri opened the two-handled wicker basket covered with a red and white checkered cloth. Inside were two blocks of cheddar cheese, pepper jack cheese, Ritz crackers, a cluster of red grapes, and strawberries. "Nice." She peered at Cole. "I'd say you're housebroken."

"I try. Only the best for New York." He reached for the wine bottle as she held the empty glasses. "What shall we toast?"

"Country boys." Cheri grinned. "Let's toast country boys."

Winking, Cole said, "I'd rather toast city girls."

"Let's do both," she said, and they did. After they drank their glass of chardonnay, Cole leaned back on his elbows, crossed his boots, and stared at the vast blue sky. "I could spend all afternoon lookin' at clouds, but I bet this bores you to tears."

"Not at all." She leaned back, mirroring his posture. "I've never really paid attention to clouds." After pointing toward a cloud shaped like a puppy, she said, "Believe it or not, I'm enjoying the slower pace. The countryside's beautiful. I haven't paid much attention to nature and animals before. I like it. I'm kind of surprised myself." Crossing her ankles, she continued staring at the sky. "Don't get me wrong. New York is an amazing, energetic, diverse city but I could get used to this peace and serenity. I hate being chased by—" Cheri stopped herself yet again.

"Chased by what? Purse snatchers? I heard there's a lot of violence in New York."

Ignoring his question, she weighed her words. "It's much better than it was years ago. You should visit sometime."

Cole looked at his dusty boots and worn jeans. "I'd fit right in, I bet."

"No one would notice a thing, trust me. Well, maybe your slight twang."

"I don't have a twang."

"Right." Cheri held out her glass for more wine. "Just half a glass. Then, let's go skip rocks, whatever that is."

After finishing the wine, they closed the picnic basket, and Cole reached for her hand. "The spring is over yonder."

Cheri chuckled. "I like the way you talk. Sometimes it's almost a foreign language."

"Sometimes you talk too much." Cole kissed her cheek, catching the side of her mouth.

She squeezed his hand. "That was nice, cowboy." She tugged on his arm. "How far are we going?"

He pointed. "Just over the hill." They continued to walk hand in hand until they reached the edge of a small body of water.

Cheri peered at the spring. "I can see my reflection. The water's crystal clear."

"We used to drink it as kids." Cole squatted down and dipped his fingers in the water.

Cheri followed suit. "It's cold. Really cold."

"Springs are refreshing. Many come from caves. We have several thousand caves in Missouri."

"Really? Have you explored any?"

"Sure. I've spelunked a few times. We'll have to do that someday."

"Maybe." She grimaced. "Aren't there bats?"

He heehawed. "Only the ones who want to drink your blood."

Her eyebrows shot up.

"I'm joking. Bats keep to themselves unless you disturb them."

"I don't think I want to find out."

Leaning over, Cole cupped his hands and drank the cool water.

"Is it safe to drink?"

"You never know if there's a dead cow or another animal on the other end of the water but I've drank out of springs my whole life."

"Dead animals?" She wrinkled her nose. "I'll pass."

While squatting, Cole sorted through the tan gravel along the creek bed beside the spring. After examining several rocks, he selected a flat, smooth rock slightly larger than a half dollar. "Watch." Holding the rock between his index finger and thumb, he threw it sideways, flat side down, across the water. The rock skipped across the top of the water, leap frogging three times before sinking to the bottom.

"That's so cool." Hands on her knees, Cheri said, "I want to try."

"Look for a flat rock."

Cheri searched and searched until she found an oval-shaped rock about two inches long. She held it in the air. "Will this work?"

"It should. Give it a try."

Throwing the rock into the water, it sank immediately. Her shoulders dropped.

Cole chuckled. "It takes practice. Here, let me show you." He sorted the rocks and found two more good stones. Bending down behind Cheri, he took her arm and placed the rock between her finger and thumb. Holding her hand sideways, he pulled it back. "Before you throw it, make sure the flat side is down. Then toss it across the water from the side."

She tried, but again, her rock sank straight to the bottom. Cheri frowned. "I can't do it."

"Keep tryin'." Cole skimmed a few more rocks that skipped across the top of the water three to five times each.

"I'm determined to do this." After searching through the stones, Cheri lined up several good, flat rocks and took aim.

One after another plummeted downward. Finally, her last rock skipped across the crystal water twice.

Jumping up and down, she shouted, "I did it. I did it."

"Nice job, New York."

Cole stood and stretched. "Before it gets dark, want to search for Indian arrowheads?"

Cheri's eyes widened. "There are Indians around here?"

Laughing, he said, "We have descendants of several tribes in this area, mostly Cherokee, Creek, and a few others. There aren't Indians running around in a headdress or anything but they're very proud of their tribes and ancestors, as they should be."

"When you said arrowheads, I pictured bare-chested Indians with bows and arrows."

"Have you seen a lot of John Wayne movies?" Cole chuckled. "Arrowhead huntin' is one of my hobbies. I've found several." Cole explained the different shapes and sizes of arrowheads and how some were used for weapons, others as tools, and some were used for preparing food. "They vary but most are small, maybe one-half to one inch long. They come in all shapes and sizes. Many are broken. It's a real prize when you find one that's still intact." Cole scrolled through several photos on his phone. "Here are some I've found."

Studying each photo with care, Cheri said, "I feel like I've stepped back in time."

"Let's hunt for some." Pointing toward a clearing, Cole said, "I've found a few over here." Cheri followed him. Bent over, they studied the ground in silence for what seemed like an eternity.

As something poked out of the dirt, Cheri bent down and dug it out. She held a broken arrowhead in the air. "Is this one?"

"Yup. Good job. That was fast. Dang. I haven't seen one."

"Beginner's luck." Cheri beamed. "I have to admit I haven't paid much attention to nature when I jog in Central Park. I usually have music blasting in my ears and don't notice much."

"There's not a lot to do here so I notice the little things."

"It's a big change from my life but a nice one."

"Think you could get used to it?" Cole asked.

Cheri stared into Cole's cornflower blue eyes and decided to be honest. "I'm not sure. I think I'd miss the city and all it offers." She noticed his face cloud and grabbed his hand.

"Let's look for more arrowheads. Ready, set, go!" She took off as Cole chased after her.

Panting to catch up, he said, "You must jog often in New York. You're fast."

"As often as I can get to the park. I have to make an effort to find the time and—"

"Shh." Cole covered her mouth with his. It was a soft kiss that was too short by anyone's standards. "You talk too much."

Cheri leaned into him. "You know I'm a mess, don't you?"

"A hot mess." His eyes crinkled.

She jabbed him in the sides. "I'm not that bad. But I'm not a country girl. I don't think you could ever convert me either."

"I'll take that as a challenge." Cole grinned so wide, his dimples showed. "Let's suspend the arrowhead huntin'. I'm starvin', and you haven't had my famous Hobos."

"Your famous what?"

Cole smiled. "Hobos. I need to get somethin' out of the truck first."

Chapter 71

As they walked toward Cole's blue pickup, Cheri asked, "What's a hobo?" Her face fell. "We have plenty of those in New York City, sadly."

"Not that kind of hobo. You'll see." Reaching for a plastic Wal-Mart bag from the back seat, he handed it to Cheri as he grabbed a white and blue Rubbermaid cooler. "I'll carry the cooler if you carry the bag. There's a small table cloth in there. Follow me. I have a secret dining table in the woods."

Cheri chuckled about dining in the woods. *If my celebrity clientele could see me now.* She carried the Wal-Mart bag while Cole heaved the cooler onto his shoulder.

"What's in there? I can tell it's heavy."

"Do you always ask so many questions?"

"Maybe I missed my calling as a reporter." Reaching for his hand, Cheri said, "This is quite an adventure. I love it."

Cole squeezed her hand with his free one while he steadied the cooler on his shoulder. Pointing with his head, he said, "It's up yonder." Walking hand in hand, they approached another clearing near a babbling brook. Cole set the cooler on the ground and extended both arms to the side. "What do you think?"

Cheri glanced around. "Where are the restrooms? The sound of the running spring water makes me want to pee."

Cole howled. "That's one of the downsides to nature. You'll have to squat behind a tree."

Cheri's face fell. "You're joking, right?"

He shook his head. "Dead serious."

"I'm almost afraid to ask about toilet paper."

"I figured a city girl like you might not appreciate usin' a leaf so I brought a roll. It's in the bag."

Cheri glanced from side to side.

"No one's lookin' except for squirrels. Don't worry."

"Um, okay. Don't look."

Cole pointed in the opposite direction. "I'll look for wood to build a fire while you do your business."

Cheri took a tentative step and stopped. "Promise you won't watch."

"Cross my heart." Cole made an exaggerated 'X' across his upper chest before walking away. "I'll be too busy gatherin' limbs."

As Cole sauntered off, Cheri watched his trim backside. His tight Levis hugged his toned legs. His tee highlighted his muscles and tan. He didn't have an ounce of fat on him and had just enough muscles to look sexy but not overdone.

Waiting until he was out of sight, Cheri gripped the roll of toilet paper and scouted for a discrete area. After spotting three trees close together, she squatted and heard a twig snap.

"I said, I didn't want you to—" Yanking her pants up, she realized the intruder was a squirrel that scampered by and ran up a tree. Cheri watched until his bushy tail was out of sight, uncomfortable having even a squirrel watch her relieve herself.

After she finished, she wondered what to do with the small amount of toilet paper she had used. Deciding to bury it under leaves, she assumed it would disintegrate in time. Stepping back toward the clearing, she noticed Cole had already stacked and crisscrossed several tree limbs in a growing pile.

"By the look of that huge heap, I assume we're going to be here a while."

"Hopefully. We have a tent, remember." Grinning, he asked, "Hungry?"

"Starving. First I need some antibacterial gel since there aren't sinks and soap around here."

Cole grinned. "Good plan."

Cheri dug through her expensive, cavernous purse. "This stupid bag needs pockets. Everything falls to the middle." After several minutes, she plucked a tiny green aloe antibacterial bottle out of the corner and squirted a large amount on her hands. "There. Alex would be proud. I almost feel human."

"You definitely look human. Actually, you're about the most perfect human species I've ever seen."

Cheri felt herself blush.

"Not used to compliments, New York?"

"Not meaningful ones, cowboy." Rubbing her belly, she asked, "How long will the hobos take?"

"Not long, but eat some cheese and crackers while I start the fire. They'll cook twenty minutes or so."

Cheri beamed her movie star-like smile. "You brought cheese?"

"Yep. By the way, you could make a guy lose his mind with that gorgeous smile of yours."

"No more compliments tonight. I'm cutting you off."

"Compliments make you uncomfortable, don't they? Okay, I'll criticize you if you insist." Grinning a wicked grin, he said, "You're a wretched city slicker who doesn't have enough sense to wear jeans and comfortable shoes to the woods."

Placing her hands on her hips, Cheri said, "Hey."

Cole gave her a devilish smile. "I thought you didn't want any more compliments."

She cocked her head. "That doesn't mean I want insults."

Reaching for her hand, he said, "You know I'm teasin'. At least I hope you know. Let's go back to the spring while we wait for the fire to get hot."

Bending down, Cheri and Cole splashed their hands in the refreshing, cool stream. "See, there's sort of a sink here." Cole chuckled, cupped his hand, and took a sip, wiping the excess liquid from his chin. "Aren't you thirsty?"

Wincing, Cheri said, "I'm thinking about those dead animals that might be on the other end, plus I don't want to pee behind a tree again. One tree per day is my limit."

"Have it your way. Remember, I brought other liquid libations." After skipping a few more rocks, he stood. "Let's check on the fire."

Walking hand in hand toward their special spot, flickering yellow and orange flames greeted them. The fire seemed to dance like a jazz troupe atop the burning wood. Cole reached into his duffel bag and pulled out a navy quilt covered in interlocking circles made from various fabrics and colors. "My late grandmother made this quilt." He hugged it to his chest. "I keep it in my truck so she's always with me. I have a red one on my bed."

"That's sweet." Holding the thick fabric, Cheri studied the pattern and intricate hand stitching. "It's handmade? That's unbelievable. What an incredible keepsake." Turning away so Cole couldn't see the tears in her eyes, Cheri's heart plummeted while she thought about her parents. The Van Burens weren't that close. They were *pretend* close. That is, they faked their chumminess in front of the paparazzi. Rather than big hugs, they mainly air kissed or blew kisses. "I love yous" were said but weren't exactly heartfelt. They didn't have anything like this family heirloom to pass down to future generations except for a few of her sweet Nana's belongings.

Cheri's mind drifted. She had always longed for a close-knit family that ate around a big dining room table every Sunday. Instead, she ate meals in five-star restaurants usually after a limo ride or chartered flight. The Van Burens were meant to be seen and heard but not exactly felt. They weren't big on emotions, rather big on impressing others. Her family was always dressed to the nines—just in case a photographer captured their image. *At least we always look good in the society pages.*

Cole broke the silence as he spread the quilt on the grass. "Someone's deep in thought."

Eyes glistening, Cheri said, "I'm taking it all in. I've done so many simple, yet incredibly moving things today. Stuff I've never considered before. Activities I've never even heard of." Spreading her arms wide, she said, "Look what I would have missed if we hadn't met." Taking Cole's hand, she said, "Thank you."

"Aw, shucks. My pleasure. It wasn't the most excitin' day. Nothing like New York, I'm sure, but—"

She put a finger to his lips. "Shh." After kissing him, she said, "It's a perfect day."

"And it's not over." Brushing his hand along her cheek, he said, "Far from it."

Cheri touched his calloused fingers. "I'm famished, though."

"Thought so." Cole opened the hinged basket, found a baggy containing the fruit, and popped a strawberry in her mouth. "Maybe this will stave off your starvation. I thought we'd have another glass of wine before dinner."

She chewed the fruit. "Delicious." Cheri chuckled. "Wine in the woods. That sounds like a country song."

"As a matter of fact, it does. Country boys can be classy, too, you know." He rummaged for the wine opener and got the chilled chardonnay from the cooler. "We still have half. Don't worry. I brought a second bottle along with the cheese and strawberries. I figured you were used to all the trimmin's."

If he only knew about my caviar and champagne brunches. Groaning inwardly, Cheri wondered if she'd ever be able to tell this sweet, good-natured cowboy she was a Van Buren. *I don't want to lose him.*

"Penny for your thoughts."

"I'm happy, that's all." Staring at a hawk swirling in the sky, Cheri said, "I don't think I've ever been this relaxed." Sipping the wine Cole had handed her, she steadied herself, realizing she hadn't eaten much all day except for the strawberry and a little cheese. She felt a luscious warm feeling from her stomach to her toes.

Leaning against Cole, she said, "I like the country. I like *you*. Thanks for—" Her voice wobbled. "Thanks for everything." Motioning across the food and wine spread out on his grandmother's quilt, she added, "I like country boys."

"I think the wine is loosenin' you up. You can stop thankin' me." His eyes crinkled. "And . . . the feelin's mutual. I like you too."

Cole refilled her wine and popped open a Bud for himself.

Peering at him over her plastic wineglass, Cheri asked, "What are we going to do after we eat and drink? It'll be dark in a few hours."

Winking, he said, "I can think of a couple things."

She giggled as she leaned back on her elbows. "I can't get over how big the sky is here. In Manhattan, skyscrapers block most of the horizon. In the country it seems to go on forever." Pointing toward the sky, she said, "The sun is setting. It's gorgeous."

Streaked with yellow, orange, and pink hues, the early sky was dotted with billowy, white clouds as the sun shone through tree limbs, making shadowy designs on the ground. Setting her glass on the grass, Cheri said, "This serenity is better than any yoga class. I'm already more Zen than I've ever been. If there was somethin' to do around this small town, I could almost get used to this."

"What do you mean something to do?" Cole asked. "There are tons of things to do."

"Such as?"

"Campfires."

"And?"

"Star gazin'."

Cole shifted on the grass. "Let's see. Hoedowns and county fairs."

"Intriguing." She chuckled. "Anything else?"

"Sure. Rodeos, truck pulls, I could go on and on. You'll have to hang around a while and find out." He clinked her plastic glass with his beer can. "Here's to campin' with a beautiful woman."

"And a handsome guy."

"Right."

"It's true." Finishing her drink, she felt a little woozy. "Maybe we should eat or I might get drunk."

He winked. "And that would be bad?"

"Very." She flashed a smile.

"Slave driver." Cole crumpled his empty can and threw it into a plastic trash bag. Rubbing his hands together, he said, "Prepare yourself for a gourmet campin' meal."

"I can't wait. I get tired of cooking all the time."

Cole jumped on her comment. "You cook?"

"You could say that." *Crap. I don't want him to know about Fifth Avenue Catering. My cover will be blown.*

Raising his eyebrows, he said, "Good to know. Maybe *you* should make the hobos."

Cheri laughed. "Good try. Another time. I enjoy cooking. It relaxes me."

Cole grinned. "I can't wait for you to show me just how much it relaxes you. I'll gladly be your guinea pig."

"Deal."

Opening the cooler, Cole pulled out a package of ground beef, potatoes, and carrots. He dug through his duffel bag for aluminum foil and tore off two big sheets. Spreading the foil across the top of the cooler, he used a pocketknife to slice the veggies and formed beef patties in the sexiest way Cheri had ever seen.

Her mouth watered while she watched him work. "Can I do anything?"

"Nope. My treat." Cole placed the vegetables on top of the burgers, sprinkled the food with salt and pepper, and folded the two tin pouches into a tent shape. Throwing the tin packages onto the edge of the fire, he wiped his hands on his jeans. "Now we wait."

"What did you call this dish again?"

"Hobos."

She nodded. "I get it. Vagrants make them because they don't require pots and pans."

"Probably. I never really thought about it. Want a refill?"

Cheri wanted to keep her wits about her in the woods. "Maybe I should wait."

"Sip it slowly." Cole poured wine for Cheri and fished another beer out of the cooler. They sipped their drinks in silence as the yellow and orange flames popped and crackled.

Transfixed on the outdoor fire, Cheri said, "This is cozy. I love the smell. I think I like camping. So far." Sitting cross-legged on the quilt, her knee touched Cole's leg. A chill ran up her spine, and she shivered.

"Are you cold?" Cole unbuttoned his shirt, apparently to give it to her.

Cheri stared at his tanned six-pack. Feeling the urge to kiss his bare chest, she resisted as a spark landed near her foot. Jerking back, she said, "That was close."

As Cole struggled with a button, Cheri fixated on his body. "You don't have to do that, but thanks for the offer. I brought a jacket, plus, the fire is warm."

He re-buttoned his shirt and poked the foil hobos with

a long stick. Turning them over, he moved them away from the direct flame. "Dinner's almost ready."

"Good. Let me help."

Motioning toward the duffel bag, he said, "You can set out our fancy paper plates. I brought only the best for you. They're even sectioned off so our food doesn't touch. I don't like food that touches."

Cheri put her hands on her hips. "That could be a problem."

"Why?"

"I like to layer my food when I cook, sometimes placing the protein at a nice slant for appearances, and—"

He raised his eyebrows. "Layer it?"

"I usually put a starch on the bottom, meat in the middle, vegetables or fruit on top, depending on the dish, with a nice sauce drizzled over everything—or maybe a schmear underneath."

"Sounds fancy." Cole grinned. "I sure wouldn't turn it down."

Grinning thinking about the national food awards she had won while attending culinary school, Cheri decided she had probably said more than enough. She wanted to keep her chef background a secret, at least for now. She couldn't chance his Googling her. "Are the plates in the bag?"

"Yep. Right beside the upscale plastic forks and knives."

As she reached inside the enormous bag, her thoughts wandered to her mother. *I can just see my mother, Victoria Van Buren, in the woods eating on paper plates with plastic cutlery. She would be aghast. But she doesn't know what she's missing.*

Digging through the duffel bag, Cheri discovered a folded red and white checkered tablecloth, plastic ware, paper plates, and white napkins. "This bag is like a bottomless pit. You thought of everything."

Using two long, skinny branches like giant chop sticks, Cole pulled the steaming aluminum pouches off the fire. After they were cool to the touch, he placed the packets at the end of a rickety, wooden picnic table.

Cheri spread the checkered tablecloth on the opposite end. "I may be a city girl but I don't think tables just appear in the woods. Did you put this table here?"

"Yep. Years ago."

I wonder how many other girls he has brought here. Why do I care? He's here with me now.

Opening a hobo packet, Cole emptied it onto a paper plate. "Careful, it's hot." Holding several napkins, he grabbed a burnt edge of foil and emptied the second hobo onto another plate. "Want your food separated?"

"I'll have it layered. It smells great, by the way."

"I forgot something."

Cheri's mouth watered as she stared at her searing plate of food. Inhaling the rustic scent of wood, burger, and vegetables, she said, "This smells scrumptious."

Reaching into the cooler, Cole plunked a bottle of catsup on the table. "There. Dinner is served. Care for a refill?"

"I'll stick with the water I brought." Opening both water bottles, she placed one in front of Cole.

He frowned. "Hobos are best paired with wine and beer."

"You even know culinary lingo. I'm impressed. Are they best paired with a nice white or red?"

"I suppose I should have brought red wine for red meat but you seem like a white wine kind of girl."

"Really? And white wine girls are—"

Reaching across the table, he kissed the top of her hand. "Beautiful. White wine girls are beautiful."

"I'm never having red wine again." Cheri stabbed her food with her fork. After she blew on the sizzling creation, she took a huge bite, groaned happily, and rubbed her belly. "This is fabulous. Really, really good."

"Pretty basic, but thanks."

"The flavors meld together and taste like . . . like . . . what's the word?"

"Campfire," Cole said.

Grinning, Cheri nodded. "Campfire. That's it."

Chapter 72

Taking another huge bite of her hobo, Cheri said, "I see I need to start cooking outdoors more often." Thoughts swirling with new menu ideas for Fifth Avenue Catering, she said, "At the very least I need to get a grill."

"You don't have a grill? A grill is a necessity in the Ozarks."

"I'll work on that." Devouring her meal like a hungry wolf, the thought of spending more time with Cole was dizzying, exciting, and . . . puzzling. *Cole isn't my type. An online dating site would never pair us together. Neither would my mother, for that matter.* The image of Cole sauntering over and climbing into her father's impeccable limo wearing dusty cowboy boots and a matching well-worn hat made her laugh out loud.

"What's so funny?"

She smiled mischievously. "Nothing."

He raised one eyebrow. "Not sure I believe you."

Consuming every last bite, Cheri stood and stretched. "I'm cleaning up. I assume there's a roll of trash bags in that bottomless bag of yours."

Chuckling, Cole said, "There might be one or two."

"You're great with details. I could use you at my—" Stopping herself yet again, Cheri tossed trash in the bags and refolded the tablecloth. Wrapping her arms around Cole's neck, she said, "This was a fantastic idea and great day."

Leaning down, he kissed her and lingered. She didn't resist. Snuggling closer, she rested her head against his chest.

Nuzzling her neck, he said, "You smell like sunshine. In fact, you are a ray of sunshine. I never thought city girls were—"

"Shh." Pulling him down on the quilt, she kissed Cole. After a probing make-out session that would make the queen of romance novels, Nora Roberts, blush, they untangled themselves, rested on their elbows, and observed the darkening sky. "It's so quiet, peaceful, and calming here." Glancing from side to side, she said, "I'm not sure I want to be here after dark, though."

A crackle made them both stiffen. One twig snapped and then another. Hairs raised on the back of Cheri's neck. Stiffening, she whispered, "What's that noise? Could it be a bear?"

Perfectly relaxed, Cole put his arm around her. "Some black bears have been spotted in Arkansas but are pretty scarce in Missouri. It's more likely a raccoon or skunk. Maybe just a squirrel. I don't think we have to worry."

Cheri's heart hammered as the footsteps got louder. Voice low, she said, "It's getting closer. Do you have a weapon?"

"Yeah." He frowned. "But it's in my truck."

Cheri's eyes widened. "Maybe you should run and get it." Pausing, she said, "But I don't want to be left alone."

"I have a pocketknife on me. It could be a deer or turkey. We're on their turf. Don't worry. They won't bother us."

Cheri could almost feel her heart stop as heavy footsteps approached the clearing. "That is not a small animal. It's getting closer. Someone, or something, is out there." Gripping Cole's arm, she snuggled closer and asked, "What should we do?"

Cole put a finger to his lips indicating she should stop talking. She noticed his jaw clenched as he reached into his jeans and retrieved a small pocketknife. Both of them stiffened as a towering image emerged.

Cheri put her hand over her mouth to stifle a scream.

Chapter 73

Padding around Cheri's ultra-modern apartment, Alex thought, *A kid would destroy this place.* Stepping from room to room, she hoped there weren't hidden cameras. She wasn't exactly snooping but was curious about the socialite. *Maybe Tony's cop genes have rubbed off on me.*

At the top of her list was admiring Cheri's massive closet. It contained enough outfits to clothe a female army. Every label was from a designer—some she recognized but most she didn't. Tempted to try everything on, Alex knew she didn't dare. Plus she was taller than Cheri and at least one size larger. Between the rows of shoes and purses, a gleaming jewelry armoire caught her eye. "Jewels." *I think I need coffee before I snoop through those.*

Alex peered at the ceiling, still wondering about surveillance. *Surely Cheri wouldn't have watchful eyes in her closet. Still . . .* As she contemplated her next move, Alex headed toward the gleaming kitchen.

For an apartment, the kitchen was huge, which made sense for a caterer. Admiring the light gray cabinets and white quartz countertop with ribbons of a darker gray, Alex spotted a Keurig coffee maker and plunked a pod inside. Fishing through cabinets for a mug, she found gorgeous China and white mugs, naturally. *She must love white.*

While the coffee brewed, her mind skittered to Tony. *I feel like I'm cheating on him, but I'm also torn about Gage. I'm not calling Tony. I deserve this getaway. Besides, he'd probably somehow trace my call and be on the next plane.* After the coffee brewed, she sipped the java and attempted to push thoughts of her mostly intolerable relationship out of her mind. Glancing out the window, hurried businesspeople and tourists rushed along sidewalks, seemingly ten people deep in every direction. *You'd think it was Christmas Eve. I love the energy, but our slower Midwestern mojo is fine by me. I wonder if Gage would be bored in Crystal City. I wonder what Tony would think of Manhattan. What does it matter? I have to figure out what I want.*

Already brewing a second cup, Alex devoured a blueberry muffin and banana she had bought at a deli across the street. There seemed to be a deli, florist, or camera shop on every corner. *At home there's a church on every corner.* Both New York City and Crystal City could use some variety.

Rinsing off her plate, she placed it in the dishwasher. After reheating her coffee in the microwave, Alex retreated to Cheri's closet where she decided she could live a long and happy life.

In awe of her expensive clothes and accessories, plus a three-paneled mirror on one end like freaking Saks, Alex was almost giddy when she spotted bottle after bottle of expensive perfumes lined up on a glass shelf.

Spritzing both wrists, forearms, behind her knees, and her belly, she wrinkled her nose. *I must smell like a brothel.* Once again, her eyes landed on the armoire. *I'm going in.*

After fishing through a massive amount of silver, gold, turquoise, pearls, and diamonds, Alex felt like a kid playing dress up. Eventually tiring of the activity—and feeling somewhat guilty—Alex reached for the door to close the jewelry cabinet, but a blue Tiffany's box pushed to a far corner caught her eye. She held the box for a few seconds before putting it back untouched. *I shouldn't open that. It looks like a gift.* But the jewelry box seemed to double dare her.

Unable to resist, Alex opened the signature blue box. Her mouth fell open. The biggest diamond engagement ring she had ever seen was inside. *This is a massive, no joke engagement ring.* I don't understand. *Cheri's engaged? Was engaged? Why didn't she tell us? I've got to tell Suzy and Hope. Shit. I can't tell anyone. They'll scold me for snooping.*

Alex glanced behind her, even though no one else was around. Temptation got to her and she shoved the ring onto her finger. Admiring the gigantic diamond from every angle, she couldn't believe her eyes. *I'll never have a ring like this. I wonder who gave it to her. I wonder if Gage knows. I can't breathe a word to him either. Crap.*

Letting out a low whistle, she browsed Cheri's massive closet. *I don't dare try any of these gorgeous clothes on.* I've spied enough. Staring again at the ceiling, she peered back at her diamond ring-bearing hand. *I've got to take it off before I lose it.*

Removing the ring, Alex did her best to remember exactly where the box had been in the armoire. After placing it on the left side, then the right, she settled on somewhere in-between and scolded herself for invading her friend's space, especially after Cheri had generously offered to let her stay in her apartment.

I guess Miss New York has a few secrets of her own.

Chapter 74

Shivering from fear, Cheri moved closer to Cole and linked her arm through his. A taller than average, extremely slender man emerged. His image in the shadowy reflection of the fire made him appear enormous and monster-like.

"Well, well," the man said in a shrill voice that didn't fit his physique.

Cheri's eyes widened. Clapping her hand over her mouth, she muttered, "Oh. My. God."

Cole jumped to his feet still clutching his pocketknife. "Who are you?"

"None of your damn business, cowboy. I see Cheri's been a little busy while I was working in Dubai the past two years."

Poker-faced and as cool as a glass of sweet tea, Cole asked, "Mind tellin' me what's goin' on?"

Crossing his arms, the towering man approached. "I could ask you the same thing."

Standing beside Cole, Cheri's mouth went dry. "I can't believe this." Holding onto his arm, she felt his biceps flex in anticipation of whatever was about to happen.

"Exactly what do you plan to do, cowboy? Stab me with your tiny knife?" The tall man laughed for far too long. "Cheri, have you lost your ever-loving fucking mind?"

Cole turned toward Cheri. Her face had become ghostly white.

Narrowing her eyes, Cheri said, "What the hell are you doing here, Sebastian? You scared me to death. Ever heard of a freaking phone?"

The man poised his cell in mid-air. "I could ask you the same thing. I've tried calling you many times since I returned to the States. Apparently, they've never heard of cell towers in Hicksville."

Staring from the man to Cheri and back again, Cole said, "I take it you know this guy."

A forlorn Cheri nodded slowly. Finally finding words, she said, "This is—"

"Experiencing memory loss, Cheri?" The tall man bellowed in a screechy voice. "I'm Sebastian. Sebastian Pierce, also known as Cheri's long-lost fiancé." Crossing his arms, he glared at Cole. "But enough about me. Who the hell are you?"

Cheri never took her eyes off Cole's brooding face and avoided Sebastian's angry glare. *I wonder how long it'll take him to notice I'm not wearing my engagement ring. I've got to come clean to both of them.*

Voice rising even higher, Sebastian shifted his hands to his hips. "Have you lost your senses? Why are you out here in the fucking woods? My God, you belong in the city not—" Sebastian waved his hand with a showman-like flair. "Definitely not here." He added, "Anywhere but here."

Suddenly finding the ground intensely intriguing, Cheri stole a quick glance toward Cole's crestfallen face.

Forehead creased into deep lines, he turned to her. "Is this true? Are you engaged?" Cole reached for her bare left hand. "I don't see a ring."

"Good point, cowboy. Where is that five-carat diamond I bought you?"

Cole's eyebrows shot up. "Five carats?"

Glancing absentmindedly at her ring finger, Cheri's voice was barely a whisper. "It's in my closet."

Sebastian scowled. "This isn't funny. I know I'm a bit of a workaholic and haven't been available the past several months—okay two years—but you could have talked to me. They have phones in the Middle East." His voice rose another notch. "You *should* have talked to me."

"You're right." Eyes filled with tears, Cheri felt immense shame for not having the courage to break up with Sebastian, telling her parents, girlfriends, and especially, sweet Cole. "I should have talked to you. I should have had the courage to break up. You were so far away. I thought it could wait until you returned." Her voice wobbled. "Don't worry. The ring is in a safe place. I'll get it back to you."

Cheri couldn't meet Sebastian's eyes, nor Cole's. In her mind, she had already called their engagement off. She just hadn't bothered to tell anyone. Knowing she'd disappoint her high-society parents, Sebastian's wealthy bloodline, and all of New York City, she had put off the weighty decision until it stared her in the face. Since Sebastian had been working in Dubai, it had been easier to simply push the engagement to the deepest recesses of her mind. *Now I'm caught in my own web of deceit.*

Cheri's mind blurred with her escapades since arriving in Crystal City. *I've betrayed Sebastian, Cole, my girlfriends, and my parents. I went on ridiculous Internet dates to see if there were any good men available. Now I've found a great guy and ruined any possibility of a relationship before it barely started.* Her mouth went dry. *I don't want to marry Sebastian, plain and simple. I never did. I hate myself for being such a chicken.*

Snapping back to attention, she forced herself to face Sebastian. "How did you find me—us?"

"Easy. Ever heard of a private investigator? Your dad uses one all of the time." Grinning a wicked smile, Sebastian said, "Besides, your life is fairly routine, my dear. Finding you wasn't that difficult." Pointing toward Cole's truck, he added, "And that decrepit thing sticks out like a flashing billboard."

Cheri narrowed her eyes. "Nice of you to have me followed."

Shrugging, Sebastian said, "Nice of you to go out on your fiancé."

She exhaled. "We need to talk."

"That's a start." Sebastian's steely gaze unnerved her. "You owe me an explanation. We're getting on a plane to New York tomorrow. You can explain this madness then."

Cheri shook her head. "I'm not going back to New York with you."

Reaching into his pocket, Sebastian waved documents in the air. "I've already booked our flight. First class, of course, since I couldn't charter a private plane in this godforsaken place." Glancing at his now-dirty shoes, he wrinkled his nose. "I just bought these Italian loafers. They're fucking ruined." Crossing his arms, he said, "I need a Bloody Mary pronto." Scanning their camping site with darting eyes, he obviously noticed the empty wine bottle and Cole's crushed beer can sticking out of the trash. "I see Happy Hour is all the rage in the woods."

Cole visibly cringed. Ignoring Sebastian, he faced Cheri. "Didn't you think the fact you were engaged might have come in handy? I'm not that kind of man." Quietly, Cole folded the quilt and dusted off his jeans. He extended his hand to Sebastian. "Look, I'd never move in on another man's girl. That's not cool. If you're engaged, forget I exist." Gathering up small pieces of foil, he slammed them inside the plastic bag.

Cheri reached to pick up a fork that had fallen out. Cole shook his head. "No need. I've got this. Looks like you've got your own unfinished business to clean up." After pulling the stakes out of the tent, he rolled the canvas into a ball and placed it near the picnic basket. Opening two bottles of water, he doused the fire, picked up his camping equipment, and headed toward his ancient pickup. As the driver's door creaked open, Cole turned. Locking eyes with Cheri, he said, "I knew you were too good to be true." Climbing inside, he sped off before Cheri could utter a word.

Chapter 75

Sebastian stepped toward Cheri. "Good riddance to that hick."

"He's not a hick. He's a nice guy." Tears rolled down her cheeks. "A really nice guy."

"Whatever. You don't belong here." Gesturing like a game show host, Sebastian said, "Look at you. Imagine the tabloid headlines if someone snuck a photo of you looking like this?" He pointed toward her casual clothes and tennis shoes. "Cheri Van Buren doesn't belong in the woods. You're a wealthy woman and a business owner. You need to act like it. Your parents would be mortified if they saw you right now."

It was as though every creature in the woods stood still as they observed Cheri's mortal mistake. Leaves appeared to stop blowing and the stream must have changed direction. Cheri swiped at her tear-stained cheeks. *Dammit. I deserve this treatment, but Cole doesn't. I owe Sebastian an explanation. Hopefully, after I reason with him, he'll leave.*

Nice enough for a mind-numbing workaholic, Sebastian wasn't for her, especially now that she was falling for Cole. Besides the boredom factor, there was absolutely no chemistry between them, never had been. Knowing full well she already had more feelings for Cole than she ever had for Sebastian, Cheri felt her stomach plummet to her feet. The fact that her parents loved Sebastian didn't help. Most likely they loved his pedigree. *I'll never hear the end of this.*

Reaching for her hand, Sebastian said, "Let's go." But Cheri shoved her hands in her jeans and didn't move.

"Do you plan to stay here with this hick? He already drove away, you know."

"Don't be a jerk." Forcing back more tears, she narrowed her eyes. "Stop calling him a hick. Cole's a good, decent man. A hard-working man. In fact, I've made several friends here. *Real* friends."

Raising his eyebrows, Sebastian scoffed. "Friends out here in Snoozeville? You must be kidding." Studying her up and down, he asked, "Are you going through the change early or something?"

Fuming, Cheri realized she was afoot deep in the woods, so she weighed her words. "Is it so implausible that I like it here?"

"Yes." Sebastian reached for her arm. "Let's find a nice restaurant, if that's possible in this dinky town." Studying the woods and clearing, he said, "Surely people eat around here." Softening his voice, Sebastian said, "Please. We're engaged."

Cheri's heart sank. *Sebastian ruined our perfect day, but he's right. I'm engaged. We're engaged.* As if to encourage her, rays reached between the arms of the trees, almost pulling her. Willing her. "You're right." *Let's get this over with.* "What are you driving?"

Motioning with his head toward a field, Sebastian said, "A Jeep. I rented a Jeep, if you can believe that. It's over there, I think. I got a little turned around in this cow-crap-filled field." Holding his nose, he added, "Let's go." He reached again for Cheri's hand, but she kept both hands in her pockets.

With a wooden tone, he said, "I don't know what your problem is. You never acted like this in New York."

After walking seemingly in circles for what seemed like miles, they finally found his rented green Jeep. Reluctantly climbing in, Cheri's mind raced about how to end the engagement—and quickly—and mainly how to repair the damage with Cole. Much more concerned about the latter, she chewed on a lacquered hot pink nail as they drove in silence along the hilly, pot-holed road.

When a tractor got in front of them going less than half the speed limit, Sebastian slammed his fist on the dash. "Dammit." He blared the horn.

"That's not nice. A man's got to work."

Clenching his jaw, Sebastian said, "Now you're defending farmers. Who are you and where is Cheri Van Buren? You should be shopping in Europe with your mom."

He has no idea how I've changed the past year. Deciding to change the subject, Cheri said, "There's a little diner in town, but I'm not hungry. We already ate hobos."

"Ho-what?"

"Hobos."

Snorting, Sebastian shook his head. "I can't believe your cultured upbringing is gone in one fell swoop after meeting a cowboy in Hicks—"

"Stop calling it that." Sick of his insults, Cheri turned the radio on. Country music blared. "This is a good song."

Sebastian glanced at Cheri as if she had grown a second head. "You like that twangy crap? Since when?"

"Since now." Defiantly, Cheri turned up the volume. Closing her eyes, she rehearsed their upcoming conversation in her head, even though she knew Sebastian wouldn't take the breakup lightly. She decided she would rip off the breakup news like the last piece of paper in a notepad since it was way past time to end this relationship.

After several curvy, hilly roads, Cheri pointed toward a tiny brick diner. Sebastian pulled into the lot and parked among several pickup trucks in a dirt lot. A dust cloud formed around them. Waving his hands as though he had never seen dust, Sebastian muttered about the countryside as Cheri marched inside.

White, lacy curtains covered the windowpane windows and a hitching post for cowboys to tie up horse reins was on one end of the parking lot. A horse whinnied as they approached the front door.

"What is this? Fucking Bonanza?" Sebastian shook his head. "I feel like I'm on another planet."

"I think it's charming and relaxing." Cheri reached for the door. As they stepped inside, an overly friendly, almost downright nosy, waitress greeted them. She asked where they were from and said she hadn't seen them around "these parts."

Ignoring her, Sebastian strode past the miniscule hostess stand crowded with a cash register. He plopped down at a table. Cheri smiled at the woman and followed Sebastian.

"Okay, seat yourselves." Still chatting, the waitress handed them greasy menus. The place smelled of burnt coffee, fried food, and had mismatched wooden chairs.

Sebastian wrinkled his nose. "High society."

Sighing, Cheri said, "Stop putting everything down. I like it here."

"Are you off your meds?" He asked.

Ignoring him, she picked up a rolled paper napkin.

Holding a pad, the server turned to Cheri. "Whatcha drinkin', honey?"

"A Bloody Mary. Pronto," Sebastian said.

The server pursed her lips. "Sir, we don't serve alcohol." Plucking a pencil from behind her ear, she poised her tiny pad in mid-air. "We have sweet tea, coffee, and Pepsi products."

"I'll have coffee," Cheri said.

"What do you mean you don't serve alcohol? I've never heard of such a thing." Snorting, Sebastian said, "This is going to be a long, damn night. I'll try the sweet tea, whatever that is."

The server cocked her head. "It's tea and it's sweet." She shuffled away to get their drinks.

Sebastian reached across the table with both hands, but Cheri kept hers in her lap.

"Stop playing games, Cheri. Cut it out. You obviously have cold feet." Peering around the half-empty restaurant, he said, "We can delay the wedding another year if that's the problem. I have to go back to Dubai for another hotel project for six to eight months anyway. They want me to design two more hotels." Softening his voice, he said, "I've heard a lot of brides get cold feet. I don't blame you for that."

Swallowing, she said, "It's not cold feet."

His voice rose. "Then, what is it?"

"You . . . Me . . . Us."

The server reappeared with Cheri's coffee and Sebastian's sweet tea. Plucking a straw out of her apron pocket, she placed it on the table.

Grunting, Sebastian said, "I don't need a straw. I guess you haven't gotten that memo in Hicks—"

"*Sebastian*. Stop it."

Undaunted, the waitress held her pad in position. "Ready to order?"

"I'll try a slice of pecan pie," Cheri said.

Sebastian scanned the sparse menu, front and back. "BLT."

"Want chips or fries with that?"

He glanced at the server. "I don't suppose you have sautéed vegetables or sweet potato fries?"

"No, sir." She stared at their menu board. "We have fried okra if you don't like regular fries."

"I don't have enough Tums for anything fried. How about coleslaw?"

"Comin' right up."

Cheri heard her shout the order to the cook while simultaneously cutting the pecan pie. Yelling across the room, the waitress asked her, "Honey, want ice cream or whipped toppin' on your pie?"

"Neither, ma'am. Just the pie."

Sebastian raised his eyebrows. "Ma'am?"

"Everyone's polite here. You should try it sometime."

Within minutes, their food arrived. Cheri picked at her crust while Sebastian wolfed down his sandwich and slaw.

Toying with a large pecan, Cheri worked up newfound courage. "That stunt you pulled today was not cool."

Sebastian smirked. "Still mad I interrupted your 'date?'" He made air quotes.

Glancing around the diner, Cheri lowered her voice. "I think it'll be better for both of us if I get to the bottom line." Taking a deep breath, she blurted out, "We're not right for each other, Sebastian. I've known for some time, maybe even from the start, which was unfair to you, I realize. I take total blame for that." Licking her dry lips, she continued, "I should have had the courage to tell you before you left for Dubai, but I didn't. My parents were elated about our engagement; yours were overjoyed. All of New York City appeared to be cheering us on." Pausing until she knew she had his full attention, she spoke directly. "I'm breaking off our engagement. I broke it off in my mind nearly two years ago. I just didn't bother telling you, anyone else, nor myself, for that matter."

Eyes like slits, he asked, "Ever heard of a fucking phone, Cheri?"

"Exactly." Cheri nodded. "The fact that you're such a workaholic, and we never even talked except for a quick text every few months proves my point. I know I should have told you much sooner, but I didn't want to break it off over the phone. Sebastian, I'll be blunt. You're not the man for me." *There I said it. Finally.* Cheri felt immediate relief.

Face clouding and voice rising, he asked, "And a silly cowboy *is* the man for you?"

Swallowing, Cheri said, "I don't know who the right man is, but it's not you. Sorry." Her voice wobbled. "I didn't want to hurt you. I certainly didn't want you to find out like this."

Jaw clenched, a vein appeared in his forehead. "Exactly *when* did you become unhappy with our relationship?"

Cheri took the last bite of pie, chewing slowly as she endeavored to think of a good response. "Honestly, I'm not sure. I tried to make myself have feelings for you."

Sebastian visibly winced.

Studying his thin face, she waited until the intrusive, friendly waitress refilled her coffee before continuing. "I've been unhappy for a long time. At first, I wondered if it was just a thing I'd come out of. I thought being away from the city might clear my mind, but it had the opposite effect. Since I've gotten away and met new friends, new life has been breathed into me. A life I love."

He scowled. "New life? Really? By the hick and his tongue, I presume?"

Throwing up both hands, Cheri said, "Will you stop it?"

Sneering, Sebastian took a bite of his sandwich. Crossing his arms, he said "You've been drinking too much country Kool-Aid. Do you think the cowboy could afford a diamond ring that isn't from Wal-Mart?"

Mouth in a straight line, she said, "That's mean. I just met the guy. Besides, it isn't about the size of the diamond."

"Tell that to your mother. You're a Van Buren. You can't lower yourself to this-this—" He waved his hand. "Whatever the hell this ridiculous flyover place is." Shoving his empty plate aside, he wiped his mouth, and tossed the scrunched napkin on the table. "Once you get on that plane tomorrow, see your penthouse apartment, and let me put that gorgeous diamond back on your finger, you'll come around."

Cheri shook her head. "Did you hear a word I said?"

Chapter 76

As the last patron left the diner and the server swept the floor, Cheri's stomach churned. *I'm getting exactly what I deserve. I should have broken the engagement off much sooner. Now I'm paying for it by losing Cole.* Her eyes filled with tears.

Sebastian laid the plane tickets on the table. "Unless you have a ride home or want to walk, what, forty miles to Branson, I think you're going back to New York with me."

"I can call a cab." She scanned the almost-empty diner. "Maybe they have Uber drivers."

Sebastian laughed so loud he snorted. "In your dreams. Not a lot of conveniences here, are there?"

"I'm not going back to New York. I have unfinished business here."

Scoffing, he said, "Unfinished business certainly didn't keep you from leaving Manhattan."

Crossing her arms, Cheri's voice rose. "I said I'm staying here."

Sebastian peered left to right, as if it mattered in the desolate diner, and said, "I didn't want to tell you this. It was supposed to be a huge surprise but—"

Cheri's face fell. "What?"

"When your parents found out I was back in the States, they flew back from Europe to throw you—us—a surprise pre-wedding gala. Victoria has everything planned down to the last detail. You know how your mother is." Lips curving into a smile, he said, "She's been working hard on this event from Europe. Victoria chose the venue and has already invited three hundred of their closest friends." Tapping the tickets on the table, Sebastian said, "Your mother has orchestrated a lavish menu and ordered the finest wines and champagne. She has a florist making extravagant centerpieces the size of a VW, and here's the kicker, she hired Justin Timberlake to perform."

Cheri's mouth flew open. "No." She put her head in her hands and moaned. "No. Please, God. No."

Undaunted, Sebastian continued. A wicked, winning smile twitched the sides of his mouth. "That's not all. Your mom has already alerted prominent media on the Q-T, of course." Clucking his tongue, he made sure the server wasn't within earshot. His eyes held Cheri's. "Get this. *People Magazine* said they'll cover the event after your parents promised them the scoop." Sebastian knew he had already won. "So you see, Cheri, you must go back with me. Besides, you're not made for small-town living." Wrinkling his nose, he gestured around the diner to accentuate his point.

Rubbing her temples, Cheri felt an enormous headache bearing down. "I-I can't believe this. No wonder I haven't heard from Mom much lately. She's likely been overwhelmed planning this party behind my back. I hate surprises. She *knows* I hate surprises." Mouth dry, she asked, "Are you sure Daddy's going to be there?"

"But of course." Sebastian beamed. "So it's settled. You're coming back with me, right?"

Cheri's mind raced from one bad scenario to another. *I can't believe this.* She fixated on a crumb.

Sebastian waited five seconds before saying, "Earth to Cheri."

Shaking her head, she said, "I can't. I've got to stop dragging out the inevitable."

His tone changed. "Are you honestly going to disappoint your parents? *Embarrass* your parents? The society pages will have a heyday with this. Think about your family name.

Are you going to humiliate the Van Burens? Are you going to destroy their legacy in one fell swoop?"

He knew her soft spot. She couldn't let her parents down. "Dammit."

Sebastian reached across the table and softened his tone. "Listen to me. We'll work through this. You'll love me again. You did once, right?"

Dammit to hell, she finally had the chance to break it off with Sebastian face to face, and now her freaking parents were in the mix.

"When was the last time you saw your parents?"

A tear snaked down her cheek. He knew that would get to her.

"Well, how long has it been?" he asked.

"I saw Mom briefly last spring in Paris, but Dad? Forever. It has been forever," she whispered.

"I'll take that as a 'yes.'"

Voice wobbling, she splayed both hands on the table. "Okay. Okay. I'll go back with you."

"Good girl. I thought you might."

Chapter 77

After thinking about her perfect day with Cole and having to go to New York with Sebastian, Cheri felt nauseous. *I know I'm making one of the biggest mistakes of my life.* Her mind wandered. *But my parents, Mom's planning, and the press. Oh, God.*

While Sebastian rambled and drove, she turned her phone back on. Eyes widening, Cheri counted ten texts from her head chef at Fifth Avenue Catering in New York. Scrolling quickly, her mouth went dry as she read the last text from Chef O'Leary which simply read: I QUIT.

Crap. I've got to check on my business. That's another reason to go with Sebastian. Dammit.

~ ~ ~

After arriving at her Branson home, Cheri found her house key. "Good night, Sebastian. There are plenty of hotels in Branson."

His mouth fell open. "What are you talking about? We're engaged. We haven't seen each other in two years."

Shaking her head, Cheri put both hands on her hips. "You aren't sleeping here. I'll see you in the morning. Remember, I'm only going back for my parents and to check on my business. I want to make sure you're clear about that." She gave Sebastian a steely gaze, closed the door in his face, and leaned against it. *It's about time I cleared up this fiasco. Surely my happiness is more important to Mom and Dad than our family name. If it's not, too bad.*

Chapter 78

While Gage worked, Alex decided to take a train to Ground Zero. Studying the subway map, she bought a Metro card, and hopped on, hoping she wouldn't be lost forever in Manhattan. Holding on to a rail while passengers stood, read, or stared at their phones in the hot train, she gazed out the tiny windows as the train raced past.

Once she exited, she joined step with the masses and immediately recognized the sobering memorial. Taking time to study the heartfelt condolences including handmade quilts, cards, teddy bears, and photos from every state and country, she visited the museum. Purchasing a single white rose at a gift shop, Alex's eyes filled with tears as she stepped back outside, knelt down with the flower, and wrote a note: *You'll never be forgotten.*

Alex said a silent prayer for the victims and first responders then put her arm around a young girl who was overcome by the weight of the monument. After an hour, she had to leave. *I'm glad I paid my respects, but I've got to end my trip on a happier note.*

Traipsing through the crowd, she braved several intersections where passersby taunted traffic lights and were barely missed by rushing cars. Googling the location of Bloomingdales, she decided she could walk fifteen more blocks. *I've never walked so much in my life. New Yorkers seem to do this daily.*

Eventually, her feet hurt and she hailed a cab. Once inside the shopping mecca, she was spritzed with perfume and overcome by the enormous amount of people and merchandise. As she strolled the designer purse section, then jewelry, she was enticed to the makeup counter by an aggressive woman wearing leopard print from head to toe.

The makeup artist told Alex to sit atop a furry stool. Glancing at the scene, Alex noticed every makeup artist was dressed the same, music blared, and there seemed to be some sort of competition to makeover the patrons as quickly as possible. Leaving the "free" makeup session thirty minutes later, with much darker, thicker eyebrows than normal, plus two hundred dollars of makeup she didn't need, Alex hoped Gage would be ready to meet soon.

As she took an escalator to the second floor, her phone vibrated. She smiled when she saw a text from Gage asking her to meet for lunch at Sardi's. His second message included the restaurant's address. Texting back, she responded she was on her way.

Hailing a cab, Alex felt like a real New Yorker when she gave the driver directions. "Sardi's, please. It's in the Theater District on 44th—"

Cutting her off, the cabbie said, "I know where it is. Been around forever."

Fine. Settling into the seat with her purse and shopping bag in her lap—since Gage had told her stories about people leaving purses, phones, and wallets behind in cabs—butterflies filled her stomach. *Why am I always excited to meet Gage and dread seeing Tony? I need to listen to my intuition.*

Once the driver stopped across the street, she paid him, and hopped out. Stepping inside the popular dining spot, she marveled at the caricatures of celebrities adorning the dark walls.

She glanced around the crowded room and spotted Gage at a table for two. Smiling, he waved her over. "I see someone went shopping."

"After going to Ground Zero, I decided to do something lighter." Holding the shopping bag in the air, Alex said, "This contains expensive makeup I didn't need."

"Nice eyebrows."

"Haha." Alex glanced up as a server wearing a dark red jacket, white shirt, and black bow tie greeted them. He filled their water glasses and handed them menus. "Can I interest you in our lunch specials?"

After hearing about the items, they decided on the Sardi's Special Appetizer for Two including bruschetta, asparagus rolled in smoked salmon, roasted bell peppers, and grilled shrimp.

"It's a good thing I walk my legs off here. Otherwise, I'd gain twenty pounds on this trip."

"You could use a few pounds." The server brought sodas and their food arrived quickly. Between bites, Gage told her about the wannabe influencer who had hired him to drive her around Manhattan all morning, insisting he take photos of her holding various products in front of iconic sites for her Instagram page.

Groaning, Alex said, "What a weird job that must be. Not yours, the influencer. This place is so different from the Midwest. Fun but crazy different." Glancing around the room, she pointed out her favorite caricatures. "Those are so cool. Look, there's Lucille Ball, Humphrey Bogart, and Cate Blanchett." Swiveling her head, she added, "And Tom Hanks, Carol Burnett, and Hugh Jackman."

Eyes twinkling, Gage said, "Are you going to name them all?"

Alex studied yet another wall and pointed. "There's Elizabeth Taylor and Farrah Fawcett. Oh, Tony Danza and Morgan Freeman." Turning back to Gage, she said, "Okay, I'll stop, but this is exciting."

After they polished off their meal, Gage leaned back.

"I have an idea." He paid the bill, reached for her hand, and ushered her outside.

As she stood by his limo, Alex asked, "Where are we going?"

"Central Park. You can't come to New York without seeing Central Park."

"Great. I'm sitting in the front." After Gage worked his way through monumental congestion, he parked in his private, hideaway spot and led her to a tree-lined, grassy area.

Alex's pronounced eyebrows shot up. "This is the first green grass I've seen since coming to New York."

"I thought you might like it." Gage pointed toward a bench.

They sat on the bench, legs touching, as people jogged past, rode skateboards, or relaxed on blankets. Music from teens seated nearby filled the air.

After nearly an hour of people watching, Alex shifted on the bench. "Do you remember I'm going home early tomorrow?"

He nodded. "Unfortunately, yes. I wish you could stay longer."

"Me too, but if I do, I might be out of a job. Hannah would like nothing more than to see her name on my office door."

Brushing a stray golden hair off her face, Gage said, "I understand. We've all gotta work. I'll take you to the airport tomorrow."

"No, you've done enough. I'm taking a car service. The bellman at Cheri's place has already scheduled it."

Gage's face fell. "So this is goodbye?"

Placing her hand over his, Alex said, "For now. You've been great. I've had an amazing time. Thank you for everything."

Wincing, he said, "That sounds formal."

Staring into his sad eyes, Alex said, "Sorry. I guess I'm getting back into bank mode already. I have a big presentation to give in a few days. I love New York and especially enjoyed spending time with you."

Nodding, he asked, "But not enough fun to break up with the cop, right?" Offering his phone with a half-smile, Gage said, "Now would be a good time."

Her eyes filled with tears. "I don't know. I'm confused." Alex faced Gage on the bench and placed both hands on his shoulders. Eyes glistening, she said, "I want to be honest with you. I wish breaking up with Tony were that easy. As impossible as our relationship is, we go back a few years. I just . . . I'm not . . . I don't know."

"You're not ready," Gage said.

Leaning over, Alex picked at a blade of grass. "Some days I'm more than ready, trust me."

Taking a deep breath with hurt written all over his face, Gage said, "But you're saying I shouldn't put my life on hold—or should I?"

Alex couldn't believe Gage was willing to wait. She paused before answering, her thoughts more muddled than ever. *I can't ask him to wait.* Swallowing hard, she said, "You should live your life however you choose until I get my head straight."

Gage nodded slowly. Exchanging niceties for the rest of the afternoon, they strolled around Central Park, but her indecision and fear had ruined her perfect trip.

Chapter 79

With almost no sleep due to second-guessing her conversation with Gage and wondering if she should have broken up with Tony from afar, Alex managed to strip the silky sheets and remake the bed in Cheri's lush bedroom, complete with a white fur on the foot of the bed. Surprising herself, she had packed her belongings—all before five in the morning.

After one last walk-through to make sure she hadn't left anything behind, Alex took the elevator to the lobby. As the doorman had promised, a car service was parked out front. Peering up and down the busy, traffic-jammed street, Alex half hoped Gage would surprise her with one last goodbye but understood why he didn't show. After one more glimpse down the sidewalk hoping for a sign of him, she shook the doorman's hand, tipped him, and thanked him for his help during her trip.

Stepping toward the outer door, Alex nearly ran into a handsome fifty-something man and a giggling dark-haired beauty. Alex noticed the doorman practically fell over himself as he assisted the couple with their luggage. She overheard the woman say, *"Bonjour. Merci, Monsieur."*

Sighing inwardly, Alex thought, *If I had a sexy accent, I might feel better about my crappy love life. Now I see how Hope feels on the daily.*

After the driver loaded her luggage and expertly wove through traffic to LaGuardia Airport, Alex scanned several emails from the bank. Frowning about the upcoming board meeting presentation, she fired off an email to Hannah reminding her to prepare twenty-five identical reports for the Show-Me Bank board meeting. Once she reminded her intern yet again of the contents she wanted to cover—and the order—she realized they had arrived at LaGuardia. She paid the driver, checked her bag, and found her gate. Spotting a coffee shop near the gate, she bought a skinny vanilla latte and settled into a seat.

Once her group was called to board, Alex placed her carryon in an overhead bin and tried to read a magazine but couldn't concentrate. Scrunched between two loud, chatty passengers, she couldn't wait to land. She glared at a teen who continually kicked the back of her seat, had never been happier to hear the landing gear go down, albeit sad to leave Gage and New York City.

Beyond tired, she debated whether to drive to the bank or see if her girlfriends could meet at Coconuts. The thought of collapsing at home moved up to priority one as she trudged through the Crystal City Airport. Staring at the carousel luggage in a daze, Alex turned on her cell and frowned while reading several angry texts from Tony.

WHERE THE HELL HAVE YOU BEEN?
ALEX, JESUS.
CALL ME BACK!!
DAMMIT.
CALL ME NOW. I NEED YOU.
I'M NOT KIDDING.

Gee. Welcome back. So much for the chill part of my vacation. Almost regretting her decision to tell Gage she wasn't ready to break up with the cop, Alex resisted responding to Tony's irate texts. *Why should I get stressed immediately upon my return? He can wait.*

Retrieving her luggage, she pulled it across the parking lot and tried to remember where she had parked. *Oh, yeah. The freaking back forty.* Once she found her Mustang, she plunked her bags in her trunk, and rolled down the windows to let the heat escape. Before she had backed out, her phone rang. Since it was Tony, she let it go to voicemail. He called a second time and then a third in rapid succession. "*What?*" she hissed.

"Where the hell have you been, and why haven't you called me back?" Tony sounded livid, yet somehow different.

Alex paused, trying to decide how to answer. "I've been on a much-needed retreat. Hello to you too."

"A bank retreat?" Pausing, he said, "It doesn't matter." His voice rose a notch. "Alex, I need you. *Right. Now.*"

"Tony, stop with the vague cop crap. I'm not one of your criminals. Just tell me what's up. I'm exhausted and want to go home. I've been up longer than the sun." Exhaling, she said, "And welcome home to me."

Her thoughts drifted to the amazing trip and a lingering hug from Gage at Central Park whose eyes—and lips— still haunted her. Alex knew she had been vague about her relationship, leaned toward breaking it off with Tony, but couldn't do it from New York. Even for her, that would be cold, plus she didn't want to make any promises to Gage until the breakup was a done deal. She and Tony had a lot of baggage with both good and disastrous memories.

Welcome back to the real world. Dammit. I totally unplugged for days and now this.

Voice booming, Tony said, "Hannah said you were on a mystery vacation. What the fuck?" Before she could respond, his voice softened. "Alex, I need you."

"Horny?" Alex deadpanned.

Tony paused for far too long. "It's-It's nothing like that." His voice faltered.

She thought she heard a slight sob. "Tony, what is it? Is something wrong?" Alex heard a faint, rare sniffle from her cop boyfriend, making her chest tighten. She pressed her phone to her ear. "Oh, my God. Is Joey okay?"

"He's fine."

"Then what is it?" Placing the phone on speaker and onto the passenger seat, she eased onto the road, her stomach balling into knots. Gritting her teeth, she said, "Let me guess. Your precious Nikki needs you?"

She heard another sniffle, but Tony attempted to cover it with a cough. Gripping the wheel, Alex said, "Tell me already. You're scaring me. Dammit, Tony. Where are you?"

A faint, "I'm at Walgreens," was all he offered.

Alex pushed on the gas pedal. "Shit. A robbery?"

"I wish." Tony cleared his throat. "It's Mrs. Mcgillicuddy."

Smiling into the phone, Alex said, "I remember your mentioning her. Isn't she the sweet old lady who shoplifts?"

Tony's voice lightened a beat. "The one and only."

"What did she steal this time? Wait. Let me guess. She pocketed green nail polish, pink hair dye, or a greeting card? Or maybe socks or—"

"She's dead." Tony's voice was flat.

Alex's heart plunged. Even though she had never met the woman, she knew Tony had always come to her rescue, paid for her shoplifting, and often said Mrs. Mcgillicuddyvreminded him of his late grandmother. Lowering her voice, she said, "I'm sorry. You must be crushed, Tony. How and where did this happen?"

"It happened right here inside Walgreens." He paused. "I'm still at the store writing my report."

"How did she . . . die?"

Tony bellowed as if he wanted all of the customers at the store to hear. "Some new hire—a stupid, show-off punk—obviously didn't get the memo to call me for Mrs. Mcgillicuddy's shoplifting antics. The little prick practically accosted the old woman and scared her to death." Tony's voice broke. "Because of him, she had a fucking heart attack according to the first responders."

"Oh, no." Alex shook her head, even though he couldn't see her. "That's horrible. I can't believe the poor woman died at Walgreens, her favorite store."

A long, loud sigh escaped Tony's lips. "Not of her own volition. Not in my opinion, anyway."

Passing every car on the road, Alex said, "I'm on my way. Is it the Walgreens on Campbell or Republic Road?"

Tony said, "Campbell," and hung up.

At the next light, Alex did a U-turn. As furious as she got with her boyfriend and as much as she hated his ridiculous family baggage, she knew he had a soft spot for this old woman and had bailed her out more times than Alex could remember. Tears filled her eyes. *I'm on my way, Tony. What a way to end a vacation—and a life.*

Chapter 80

Before pulling into the chaotic scene in the Walgreens lot, Alex noticed Tony's police car, an ambulance, fire truck, and orange traffic cones preventing onlookers from entering the scene. Travel-weary, she persevered and texted him. *Can I come inside? I'm in the parking lot.*

After what seemed like an eternity, Tony responded. *Not yet. I'm interrogating the little bastard.*

Leaning against the headrest, Alex waited. And waited. Her thoughts flitted to Gage for a moment but she squelched them. *Tony needs me. I'll have to figure out my life later.*

Eventually, two paramedics wheeled out a gurney with the poor woman under a covered sheet. The responders didn't bother with lights or sirens since Mrs. Mcgillicuddy was obviously already dead. Alex made a cross sign over her chest, even though she wasn't Catholic, nor overly religious. Craning her neck, she searched for Tony as employees and a few customers exited the store.

Once the ambulance and firetruck drove off and a worker removed the traffic cones, she bolted inside. Traipsing through several empty aisles, Alex eventually spotted Tony sitting in a chair by the pharmacy. Head down, he feverishly filled out paperwork. A pimply, red-faced kid stood beside him. From the splotches on the kid's face, Alex discerned he was the culprit and had been crying. A lot. She noticed the young employee wasn't in handcuffs but Tony obviously wasn't letting the guy out of his sight.

Employees stole glances and whispered behind the counter. A few remaining customers stared but most gave the officer—her boyfriend—a wide berth. Once again, Alex wished Tony weren't a cop. Sure, she loved a man in uniform—and fully admitted the allure she'd had her entire adult life for uniform-wearing men—but instances like this brought his unique position home. Being a positive person, she didn't like being surrounded by negativity. Tony dealt in that world daily.

Evidently feeling her presence, Tony, grim-faced, glanced in her direction but didn't say a word. She mouthed, "Hi," but he simply returned to his paperwork. Knowing she shouldn't interrupt, Alex felt antsy and wondered how long the report would take. Guilt overcame her. A woman had just died. A woman who Tony thought highly of and took it upon himself to rescue, albeit for minor theft, many times over the years.

As Alex trudged through the aisles pretending to shop, she spotted a humongous black purse on the floor. She chuckled remembering how Tony often said Mrs. Magilicutty had carried a purse as big as a raccoon. No one seemed interested in the bag. Alex kept her eye on it but didn't want to touch it, not because of the germs for once, but because it likely belonged to the dead woman.

She approached Tony but didn't want anyone to know he was her boyfriend. "Sorry to interrupt, er, Lt. Montgomery, but—" She pointed. "—is that the deceased woman's purse?"

Glancing toward the floor where Alex indicated, Tony said, "I suppose it is since no one else has claimed it. I haven't gotten that far." He narrowed his eyes and fixated on the young teen whose chin quivered. "Feeling bad about scaring the old woman to death now, son? Literally to fucking death?"

While staring at his dirty tennis shoes, Alex noticed the young man's ears turned fire-engine red as he avoided the officer's gaze.

Tony turned back to Alex. "Why don't you pick up the purse and bring it over here? Maybe we can find out if Mrs. Magilicutty has any family members I can contact."

Nodding, Alex strode toward the purse and immediately thought about all of the germs on the bottom of the bag but forced herself to grab the handle. She shuddered as she plunked it beside Tony. "Should I go through it?"

"Yeah. See if you can find contact info while I deal with this punk."

Reaching for the handle as the teen boy's chin quivered again, Alex said, "I'll go through it in my car." *There's no way I'm going to sit in the germ-laden pharmacy chairs. I could catch some hideous disease.*

"Fine. I'll be done soon." He glanced at the kid. "Maybe."

When she stepped outside, she moved her car to a shady area, laid tissues on the passenger seat, and placed Mrs. Magilicutty's purse on top. Taking a deep breath, she sorted the usual pens, compact, lipstick, a glasses case, wallet, keys, and antibacterial gel—which she helped herself to. Keeping the wallet and cell phone out to search for family member clues, she began placing the items back inside when a yellowed, crumpled piece of paper caught her eye. The page was at the bottom of the bag. *This has been in here a while.*

Carefully unfolding the worn, wrinkled paper, Alex noticed it was written on an attorney's letterhead. A navy, raised logo was emblazoned at the top: SULLIVAN, AGEE & FREEMAN. After skimming past the legal jargon, she flipped over to the second page. Scanning the final two paragraphs, she gasped. "No way."

Chapter 81

Rubbing her throbbing temples, Alex thought about Mrs. Magilicutty's untimely death, Tony's grief, and the immature kid at Walgreens who had likely caused her heart attack. Her confusion about Gage had to be put on the back burner. Way back.

Hands trembling, she smoothed the crease in the paper and studied the recap of the will. Apparently, the old woman was rich. *Very* rich. Alex absentmindedly chewed on her bottom lip as she reread the will a second time. Not only was Mrs. Magilicutty wealthy, she had left everything to Tony! There didn't appear to be any heirs. Lt. Tony Montgomery was listed as her sole beneficiary. Drawing in her breath, Alex stared out the window. Everyone and everything blurred. *He'll never believable this. Never.* Her stomach churned as she waited for Tony to exit the store.

Alex jumped when Tony eventually appeared at her car. Motioning for her to unlock the door, she moved the woman's purse, tissues and all, to the back seat. Once inside, he slammed his fist on the dashboard. "Damn that punk. What an asshole. She was a good woman."

"I'm sure she was. But try not to take it out on my car. I kind of like my Mustang."

Only focused on one thing, Tony continued. "That little bastard killed her. She was a poor old woman who couldn't afford little pleasures." Blowing out his breath, Tony shook his head. "The little prick was trying to be a big shot. Now she's dead."

"I'm sorry, Tony. I know you thought highly of her. This is unbelievably sad." Alex rubbed his arm. "What can I do?"

His voice caught, which was a first. Tony always kept his emotions intact unless it had to do with little Joey. Rubbing the back of his neck, he stared ahead. "I really liked her. Don't ask me why other than the fact that she reminded me of my grandmother. The managers knew to call me every time she shoplifted, which was usually weekly." A chuckle escaped. "She simply enjoyed items like ridiculous purple lipstick." His jaw tightened. "The employees all knew I'd pay for her purchases. That damn new kid—"

Alex placed her hand over his clenched fist. "It's tragic. What are you going to do about the kid?"

Shrugging, Tony said, "I can't very well arrest him for spooking someone. She was old so I can't prove he caused the heart attack. I just wanted to put the fear of God in that asswipe. Maybe he'll think twice before he picks on the elderly." Leaning against the headrest, Tony said, "Let's get out of here. I could use a beer."

"Say no more." Alex pulled out of the lot and headed to Coconuts. *He's too upset to comprehend the will. I'll wait until he calms down.*

Chapter 82

After Gus brought their drinks, Alex reached for Tony's hand. "I'm sorry this happened, but there's more you should know."

"More?" Confusion crossed his already miserable face.

"A lot more." Sipping a chardonnay, she ordered chips and salsa. "Drink part of your beer first."

"I have a feeling I'm not going to like this." Taking a big gulp, Tony licked foam off his top lip. "Does this have something to do with your finding-yourself trip?" His frown lines became deeper as he slumped back in his chair. "Are you breaking up with me?"

"Not today." She grinned as he roared. "Made you laugh at least." *If he only knew how close I came.*

Tony's lips curved into a half-smile as he bit into a chip and chased it with a swig of beer. "At least that's one good thing about today. Where did you go anyway?"

"Not important. Let's focus on today's events." Alex weighed her options as she dunked a chip in the salsa. *I can drag this out and wait for him to calm down or be my blunt self.* She decided on the direct angle and glanced behind them. The tables surrounding them were empty. Leaning forward, Alex lowered her voice. "You aren't going to believe what I'm about to tell you."

"Shit. Why all the drama? I've had enough for one day." He gulped half his beer. "Spit it out."

"I guess I'll jump right in and—"

"Get to the bottom line." Tony drained his beer and waved his empty glass in the air.

Gus nodded and promptly brought another. When the server was out of earshot, Tony said, "I'm off-duty now and need booze. Stop pussyfooting around, Alex. Just fucking tell me."

Alex raised her eyebrows. "Okay. Listen closely. Mrs. Magilicutty was rich—very rich—from what I read in her will."

Brows knitting, he asked, "How do you know she had a will?"

"I found her purse at Walgreens, remember? As I searched through it, I discovered a crumpled document buried at the bottom." She winced. "Sorry, bad choice of words. Anyway, it had obviously been there a while."

"Who keeps a will in their purse?" Tony polished off three more chips as he studied Alex.

Shrugging, Alex said, "Apparently, Mrs. Magilicutty does. Or did."

Leaning back, Tony said, "Is that your big news?"

"Partially." Holding his gaze, she swallowed before saying, "Mrs. Magilicutty left everything to you." Alex swiveled on her bar stool and met Tony's dumbfounded gaze as the information sank in.

Tony's face turned ashen, barely detectable in the darkened bar, but still obvious to Alex. Running his fingers through his hair, he dragged out his response. "What did you say?"

Alex cocked her head. "You're not hard of hearing, lieutenant."

Tony shook his head. "I don't want her money. Money ruins people." He ticked off his fingers. "Four things that cause people to commit crimes are drugs, power, sex, and—"

"Money. You've told me this a gazillion times. See, I listen." Studying him, she said, "I never thought you, we'd, have this conundrum. It's bizarre, isn't it?"

He shook his head. "I don't understand why Mrs. Magilicutty shoplifted if she was rich. It doesn't make any sense."

"Probably for the thrill." Alex managed a small smile. "Or maybe she had a crush on you and knew that was the only way she'd get to see you."

Actually grinning for the first time all day, Tony said, "I hadn't thought about that possibility."

"Back to her will. What are you going to do about the money?"

Whistling, Tony said, "Do you know how much shit I'll catch from the other cops if they find out?"

Alex shrugged. "Who cares?"

"I do." Brushing chip crumbs off his leg, he said, "I can hear it now. They'll try to borrow cash or rib me and ask when I'm getting a Ferrari." He stared at a slow-moving ceiling fan and a rowdy group of college kids, obviously pondering the magnitude of his new-found wealth. Placing both hands on the table, he said, "It isn't worth the harassment."

Finishing her wine, Alex motioned to Gus. "Want more food?"

He shook his head. "I can't eat after all this."

Laughing, Alex pointed to the almost-empty bowl. "You polished off those chips." When Gus appeared, Alex ordered coffee for both of them and a slice of coconut pie to share. "We can figure this out together—if you want my help."

He nodded. "Bankers and money go together, don't they?"

"That we do." After she put creamer in her coffee, she peered into the brown concoction as if for an answer. Within seconds, she brightened. "I've got it. I know what you can do."

"What?"

Chapter 83

After meeting with a potential bride at The Coffee Drip who received an unfortunate breakup text during their consultation, Suzy tried to console the distressed bride-to-be to no avail. Weeping loudly, Suzy rubbed the young woman's arm and spoke in soft tones. Doing her best to soothe the heartbroken woman, she asked if she'd rather go outside.

"No! My life's ruined." The almost-bride-to-be wailed, moaned, and slammed her fists on the table. Every coffee shop patron turned toward them. Wincing, Suzy said she could relate since she had been through something similar with a previous fiancé years ago—different but still heart wrenching—and it all worked out for the better.

Sniffling, the woman whimpered, "You have?"

"Yes, and thank goodness I didn't marry that man." Calming down slightly, Suzy took her cue. "Hon, I have a doctor's appointment. Can I make a call for you? To your mom, maybe?"

Head still on the table and plucking every napkin out of the dispenser to blow her nose, the almost-bride handed her phone to Suzy. "Her number's under 'Mom.'" Suzy scrolled through the contact numbers, dialed, and handed the phone to the girl. Glad she had a reason to leave, she whispered good-bye, and drove across town for her appointment. *What a nightmare that wedding would have been.*

~ ~ ~

Sitting in the waiting room for an appointment with her obstetrician, Suzy again compared herself to many of the young, twenty-something, if that, moms. Covered in tattoos and piercings, she held herself back from giving them advice and wondered if Alex would be able to do the same. *Doubtful.*

A baby wailed in the corner. *I should take advantage of my peace and quiet while I still have it.* Scrolling through her Weddings by Suzanne Facebook page, Suzy gave an update to potential brides, commented on her tagged photos, and thanked them for referrals.

Her phone pinged. Feeling a huge sigh of relief when she realized the boys, Vanessa, and the baby had landed safely in Europe, Suzy scrolled through new photos of baby Violet. Jon had sent photos of the baby at the airport, on the plane, in a car seat, and one with a smiling Mama Gia holding the precious bundle. Fernando's brothers, Luigi, Vinny, and Frankie, photobombed the shot and held rabbit ears behind each other's head. *I can almost see Jon rolling his eyes. Maybe being around Fernando's crazy brothers will loosen him up a bit.*

Chuckling as if Fernando's Italian brothers had heard her, the next photo sent from Fernando's phone showed Luigi giving Jon a noogie. *He's going to hate that, but I'm sure it's a rite of passage in this crazy family. At least he'll enjoy fantastic food. Fernando's mother knows how to cook. She proved that at the guys' wedding last spring.*

Texting back saying she missed them already but was glad they had landed safely, Suzy asked the guys to keep the pictures coming. Staring at each photo again, she felt one kick and then another. Placing her hand on her lower belly, she took a selfie of her belly, and said: *The twins said hello. They just kicked for the first time. I love you, son. You'll have a brother and sister in a few months. Mom*

Chapter 84

Staring at Tony over her zebra print coffee cup, Alex's mind swirled with potential ideas for the use of the money. One idea rose to the top. "Why don't you set up a trust fund for Joey's college?"

He brightened. "That's a good idea. But how?"

"Easy. Show-Me Bank has a trust department. I'll schedule a meeting for you."

"Slow down on setting up an appointment. I want to think about this. Weigh my options. Decide if I even want the dough."

"Want it?" Alex's eyebrows shot up. "Why the hell wouldn't you? Obviously, Mrs. Mcgillicuddy wanted you to have it."

Tony ran his fingers through his hair. "You haven't even told me the amount. If it's huge like you said, then it's too much for one boy's college."

Grinning, Alex said, "I could help out by making a helluva dent at T.J. Maxx. Maybe I'll even buy the whole damn store."

Spewing his coffee, Tony said, "It's that much?"

Absentmindedly stirring her coffee, Alex tried to comprehend the will and fact that Tony's the beneficiary. "Even though I work at a bank and am surrounded by cash, I'm not used to considering how to blow through massive amounts of money."

"How massive?" He leaned forward. "Tell me."

"Three mil, Tony. Three. Million. Dollars." Alex spoke slowly and deliberately as if she were talking to a two-year-old.

"Holy shit." Shaking his head, he muttered, "That's a far cry from a cop's lousy salary." Tony let out another slow whistle. "Damn. Why, Mrs. M, why?" He rubbed his forehead as if trying to understand the reasoning behind his beloved elderly shoplifter. "I've got to handle this the right way. I don't want to blow through it. I want to be responsible and make Mrs. M proud." His eyes widened. "I think I've got it. I'm pretty excited about this." Reaching for Alex's hand, he said, "Let's go."

Holding a bite of pie in mid-air, Alex said, "Wait. What is it?"

"Later." He ate one more mouthful, fished out forty dollars, and left it on the table for Gus. "My treat. Let's go to your house and watch the Alex and Tony show."

"You're impossible. Don't you ever get tired of that show?"

"Never."

~ ~ ~

Alex drove Tony back to Walgreens so he could get his car. After both pulled up in front of her house and stepped inside, she wrapped her arms around Tony's neck. "I know this has been a rough day. I'm freaking exhausted after all of the travel, but I'm sorry about that sweet old lady. I know she meant a lot to you."

The normally jaded cop's eyes glistened with tears. Turning his head, obviously trying to hide his rare, softer side, Tony said, "Yeah, rough day." Rubbing his jaw, he said, "I'm having second thoughts."

"About the will?"

He grinned. "No. About being the usual Greek God you've come to expect."

"Same here. About being a goddess, I mean."

Tony pulled her close. "Sometimes you frustrate the hell

out of me and other times you're the best. Most days, you're pretty special."

"Ditto, I think. At least occasionally." Alex reached for the remote. "We can see the Tony and Alex show any time. Let's watch a real movie and veg."

Moving toward the couch, they chose a Clint Eastwood action flick, and were silent for two hours, both likely lost in their thoughts. When the movie ended, Tony yawned, and stood. "I'm going home. I'm spent. I need a good night's sleep. This has been one helluva—"

"No explanation necessary. I get it. I've got to get back in work mode anyway." Opening the front door, Alex stopped short, reclosing the door. "You didn't tell me your other idea for spending the money."

Clearing his throat, Tony began to speak but his voice faltered. "I-I want to establish a Fallen Officer's Fund for the Crystal City Police Department. It'll mean the world to the CCPD."

Tears snaked down Alex's cheeks. "That's perfect, Tony. Absolutely perfect."

Without another word, he nodded and stepped outside.

Alex watched as her cop boyfriend drove off. *This is the Tony I fell for. Why can't you be like this all of the time?* Remembering the good times with the cop and wondering if they would ever outweigh the bad, her mind switched to her recent, enjoyable memories with Gage. *Why did this happen when I was ready to make a break? Ready for a fresh start with a sweet limo driver.* Eyes welling with tears, she stared at her unpacked luggage. *I give up on the boyfriend front.*

Chapter 85

Trying to keep her mind off the good and bad times in Nashville, Hope filled her days with back-to-back student appointments. At the top of her to-do list, was avoiding Larry and Willow. *I want them to be happy but I'm not ready to accept them as a married couple.* Though she did agree to contact her attorney dad, Paul Taylor, to file the proper paperwork regarding Montana's death and how to handle the legality of Larry and Willow's marriage. Paul assured her he'd take care of everything.

As students chattered in the hallway and lockers clanged, Hope stared out the window counting the hours until the final bell rang. Knowing she had to get out of her funk, she drummed her fingers on her desk and tried to give herself a pep talk but it didn't work. The cowboy in Nashville was all she could think about. *I'm not the least bit surprised Tucker hasn't called. That probably isn't even his real name.* Glancing at her calendar, she tried to remember when Alex was returning. *I need a girlfriend fix. I wish she'd hurry back. Maybe hearing about her fabulous trip—wherever she went—will cheer me up.*

~ ~ ~

Cuddling on the couch, Suzy and Ken watched the western, 3:10 to Yuma. Unable to tear her eyes away, Suzy reached for the gigantic bowl of popcorn between them. "Why don't we watch more westerns? This is a great movie."

"I could watch a western twice a week," Ken said, as

he placed his arm around his wife's shoulder. "I've enjoyed seeing more of you since Alex and Hope have been away."

"Same here, honey, but I miss them terribly." Glancing at the date on her phone, she said, "Hope should be back from Nashville, and Alex returns today, I think. I'm sure Happy Hour at Coconuts will be in order soon. I can't wait to hear about their trips."

Nuzzling his wife's neck, Ken said, "In that case, we're watching another western movie tomorrow night." Winking, he said, "I might even wear my chaps."

"You have chaps? Well, now."

Chapter 86

The following afternoon, Hope texted Alex and Suzy and asked them to meet at Coconuts, even though it was a Sunday. She needed to see her best friends after losing Montana a second time.

After both agreed, Hope drove straight to Coconuts, arrived first, and hopped onto her favorite bar stool.

Cleaning a table nearby, Gus said, "You guys don't usually come in on Sundays. This day's usually for the sports crowd."

Shrugging, Hope said, "Unusual situation."

"Does that mean you still want a margarita or something different?"

Hooking her purse beneath the table, Hope said, "The usual, Gus. Thanks."

Alex and Suzy arrived together and embraced Hope in a group hug. Alex asked, "How was the trip with Larry?"

"How was your mystery trip, Alex?" Suzy asked. "We have a lot to talk about."

"Yes, we do." Waving to get Gus's attention, Alex ordered a chardonnay and a virgin strawberry daiquiri for Suzy. "Let Hope go first." Lowering her voice, she said, "I'm dying to know. Did you see Montana? Did Larry remember her?"

Suzy chimed in. "I worried about you the entire time you were in Nashville. I know this had to be awkward at best."

"Awkward doesn't begin to touch it." Hope splayed her hands on the table. "Bottom line: Larry's in love with Willow and they got married, as you know." Exhaling, she added, "Larry doesn't remember Montana, and . . . she's dead."

Both Suzy and Alex gasped and shouted questions, "What?" "Dead? How?"

Tracing the edge of the table, Hope's eyes reddened. Shuddering, she said, "She hanged herself."

"Oh, my God." Alex's mouth fell open. "How awful. I'm sorry. How?"

Suzy held up both hands. "Do we really need to know?"

"Yes," Alex said, always interested in every detail.

Hope leaned forward, grim-faced. "You're never going to believe this. Montana killed herself using one of her plant hangers."

"Damn," Alex said.

"That's horrible. So sorry, hon." Suzy reached for Hope's hand.

Rubbing her temples, Hope said, "Listen, I'm mourning her all over again, but I refuse to go through the dreadful depression I experienced the first time around. I can't grieve twice. I can't have another funeral. Mentally, I can't take it. I've got to move on. Larry is happy. Willow is happy. *I* should be happy."

"That's the spirit," Alex said. "It sounds contrite, but I'm sure Montana would want you to get on with your life."

Nodding, Suzy said, "I agree. Give it time. Have you talked to Willow?"

"Only a quick wave when we got home. She was parked in front of my house. I'm sure she was worried sick while we were in Nashville. It's too soon for a deep discussion." She managed a smile. "When Larry saw her van, Picasso, he practically galloped into her arms like a scene from a Hallmark movie featuring older hippies." Sipping her margarita and reaching for peanuts Gus had placed in front of them, Hope said, "I believe they're truly in love. I've got to figure out how to deal with them as a husband and wife."

"You'll find a way, hon," Suzy said.

Brightening, Hope said, "There *was* a small breakthrough. On the trip, Larry produced an old family photo he kept in his wallet. It showed Larry, Montana, and me. After a few minutes of staring at the picture, he realized the pudgy, little girl was me." She chuckled. "Same big, brown eyes and frizzy hair that I have now, only standing between two tall, lanky blondes."

"Wow." Alex leaned forward. "That's not a small breakthrough. It's major."

"Definitely major," Suzy said. "Maybe his full memory will return."

"Maybe. Maybe not." Hope shrugged. "I'm not sure if it was part of his memory returning or if he reasoned it was me since I insisted he go on the trip. Either way, I'm glad he has the photo and plan to get a copy of it to frame."

"Maybe this is the start you two needed." Alex sipped her chardonnay. "Did you have any time for fun?"

Suzy nodded, adding, "I hope you did. Nashville is a cool city."

Plunking a lime slice into her cocktail, Hope stalled. She wasn't ready to talk about the man she met and their special dance. Besides, he might never call. She didn't want to be embarrassed. Normally, she told Suzy and Alex absolutely everything. But this one time she decided to keep a secret. Forcing an undetectable gaze, she said, "There wasn't much time for pleasure. It was a long drive and emotionally draining."

"Understandable." Alex squeezed Hope's arm. "We should all go there sometime. I hear they have some fun honky-tonks. Who knows? Maybe one of us would meet a cowboy."

"Wouldn't that be something?" Hope grinned inwardly.

Chapter 87

"About your mystery trip, Alex—" Suzy covered her mouth and nearly hurled after Gus strode past with a huge platter of fried calamari. Continuing to hold her hand over her mouth, she said, "This is the longest pregnancy ever."

Scrunching her nose, Alex reached for her phone. "While I was sitting on the tarmac, I Googled morning sickness remedies. "I'm going to buy you a sea band bracelet. I read the reviews and some women said it helped. It can't hurt to try, right?"

Resting her head in her hands, Suzy said, "I'll try anything. You wouldn't believe my newest craving. It's pepperoni pizza, chocolate ice cream, and milk. I can't get enough of it." Winking, she said, "Poor Ken has to make midnight runs to the grocery store."

"Eww," Alex said as she raised her chardonnay in the air. "That sounds gross."

Getting Gus's attention, Suzy ordered milk. "I can't get enough of it."

After the server returned with a cold glass of milk, Alex nearly gagged. "That smell. Get it away from me."

Suzy threw up her hands. "Who doesn't like milk?"

Wrinkling her nose, Alex said, "Me."

"Pregnancy cravings trump your sensitive tummy, Alex." Fixated on her friend, Hope said, "Enough suspense. Where did you go on your *Eat, Drink, Chill* trip?"

Fidgeting on her bar stool at the thought of sweet Gage meshed with her newfound knowledge about Tony, Mrs. Magilicutty, and the will, Alex wasn't ready to tell all but knew she owed them an explanation. "You'll never believe where I went."

Both Hope and Suzy swiveled toward her.

Deciding to blurt it out, she said, "I went to New York City, stayed in Cheri's penthouse apartment, and saw Gage." Dusting her hands in satisfaction, Alex said, "Then I came home to Tony who was in an emergency situation."

"Oh, my God. Why did you keep this from us?" Hope asked.

Suzy leaned forward with a slight milk moustache. "So Gage didn't convince you to leave the cop?"

"Please wipe your mouth, Suzy, or I'll puke right here. To answer your question, it's a very convoluted story."

Suzy wiped her mouth. "Okay, done. Now, tell us."

A table of sports fans dressed in red jerseys hooped and hollered, breaking the idyllic beach feel of Coconuts. Alex turned in their direction and spotted three flat-screen TVs on the wall near the bar. "Since when does Coconuts have televisions?"

Within earshot and holding a platter of foamy beers in chilled pilsner glasses, Gus shrugged with his free shoulder. "Since we're diversifying."

"Diversifying? Coconuts is known for its chill setting," Hope said.

"Listen to you with the lingo," Suzy said.

Rolling her eyes, Hope said, "I work around kids, remember?"

Gus continued. "Apparently, our numbers were down last quarter. Management wants to attract new customers."

"Great. Just great," Alex said.

Hope and Suzy focused on Alex. "You were saying something about Gage and the cop."

Alex knew it wasn't her place to mention the crime scene, nor the will, so she said, "Gage was wonderful. He showed me all of the iconic sights. We ate at amazing restaurants, and he even picked me up in a limo." Pausing, she added, "New York City is electric. You've got to go sometime."

Hope and Suzy exchanged glances. "That's it?"

"It's enough for now. I wish I could say more. My head's spinning with confusion about both men, plus police stuff I can't talk about. It's your turn, Suzy."

Picking at a loose thread on her green sweater, Suzy said, "I suppose we all have drama. Jon and Fernando are now in Europe for an extended time with Vanessa and baby Violet. It's already killing me, but I know Fernando wants to see his family, plus Mama Gia understandably wants to be part of her granddaughter's life."

"Yeah, Mama Gia's pretty irresistible." Alex wiggled her eyebrows.

Staring from the beach mural to the rowdy sports crowd, Suzy said, "I knew Jon and Fernando's marriage, plus the addition of his high school girlfriend and baby, was an easy transition—almost too easy. Their intermingled relationships are incredible, but since Fernando's family lives in Italy, I have to share." Sighing, she said, "I love Fernando as if he were my own son and Jon is the happiest I've ever seen him."

"So what's the problem?" Alex twirled her wineglass.

"I'm fearful they'll all love Europe and want to move there." Suzy's eyes reddened. Touching her growing baby bump, she said, "I want them to be part of the twins' lives too."

"I'm sure it's hard, but you had to expect it since Jon met Fernando in Europe and his family lives there," Hope added.

"I suppose. But I'm Jon's family. And his dad, of course, when he isn't hunting, golfing or working." Blotting a tear, she said, "I already miss them." Brightening, she added, "I have new pictures of baby Violet. Want to see them?"

"No, sorry, Grandma." Waving to get Gus's attention, Alex said, "Ladies, I'm tired and have a huge board presentation this week. I've got to go. I still haven't unpacked."

Hope's eyebrows shot up. "Miss OCD hasn't unpacked? What has gotten into you, Alex?"

A limo driver, plus a nicer version of Tony I had nearly forgotten existed. I'm off my game.

Chapter 88

Forcing herself to arrive a few minutes early, Alex punched in the bank code, not thrilled to return to work. Thoughts of Gage, Mrs. Magilicutty, and the late woman's surprising will jumbled her thoughts. Chatting with Marla, an always cheery loan assistant, and Paula, a sweet New Accounts rep, who wanted to hear about her vacation, Alex told both women she had gone to the Big Apple. After answering a barrage of questions, she made her way toward her office.

As expected, Hannah was seated at her desk, feet on top. "Hiya, boss. Welcome back."

"Bet you enjoyed taking over my office the past week." Alex plunked her purse on the floor. "I'll take my desk back now."

"Hello to you too," Hannah said, as she motioned dramatically toward Alex's office chair. "I kept it warm for you. How was your trip?"

After she glanced at the mound of mail on her desk, Alex took a good look at her intern. Biting her lip to keep from laughing, Alex turned away. While she was in New York, Hannah apparently dabbled in more cosmetic surgery. She now had enormous, glossy bubble lips to match her gargantuan breasts. *What the hell are you doing to yourself?*

Forcing herself not to make a comment, or God knows, a joke, since Alex knew she'd get into trouble with human resources, she did her best deadpan expression. "I'm going upstairs for coffee. Be right back." She shot out the door before laughing out loud. Returning with a cup, she turned on her computer.

"No coffee for me?" Her intern pouted. The sight made Alex chuckle again.

"You know where the employee lounge is." Studying a horrendously long line of emails, Alex deleted junk emails and prioritized the others. While staring at the screen, she asked, "Do you have the board report ready for me to present?"

"That's it? No chitchat about your mystery vacation? Geeze. I thought some time off might mellow you. You need to learn how to relax." Hannah patted a stack of folders. "The board reports are ready."

"Good. Thanks. They're in the proper order?" Alex sipped coffee as she stared at the stack.

"Of course." Hannah grinned. "Easy peasy. I'm going to get some coffee."

Gesturing with her hand, Alex said, "Go ahead. I think I see my boyfriend coming in the front door."

Hannah turned toward the entrance, took a step, and stopped.

Watching her intern, Alex said, "You look pale. Feel okay?"

"I think I need to eat something. Be right back." Hannah never took her eyes off the parking lot as she crossed the lobby and bounded up the stairs.

~ ~ ~

As Tony approached the Show-Me Bank entrance, he stopped short when he saw his cop brother. Both had never gotten along and avoided each other like territorial alley cats.

Sean spoke first. "What are you doing here?"

"I could ask you the same." Tony pressed Mrs. Magilicutty's will underneath his arm. The last thing he wanted was for his asshole brother to find out he was suddenly rich. "I came to see my girlfriend. You?"

"None of your business," Sean said, "but I came to cash a check."

"Ever heard of a drive-thru window or direct deposit? It's convenient." Tony locked eyes with Sean, daring him, as always.

Spitting on the sidewalk, Sean asked, "Do you enjoy always being an asswipe?"

"Only around you. I learned from the best. Thanks, brother." Tony opened the front door and stepped inside. Ignoring the hellos from friendly employees, he made a beeline toward Alex. Hannah crossed the lobby in front of him. Snorting, Tony muttered, "Nice lips." Once inside Alex's office, he said, "What the hell happened to her? She looks like a carp."

Covering her mouth, Alex said, "I know. She's getting carried away with cosmetic procedures."

"Nice boobs, though."

"Nice of you to notice." Crossing her arms, Alex gave him a pretend hurt look.

Placing the manila envelope on his lap, Tony said, "You know I prefer your size. My brother's a different story. He's the big boobs guy."

"Whatever." She pointed toward the envelope. "Is that the will?"

"Yep." Already fidgeting in his chair, Tony said, "I hope this doesn't take long. I hate this legal mumbo jumbo shit."

"I'd say three mil is well worth every minute." Standing, Alex straightened the skirt of her sleek, new red suit.

Whistling, Tony said, "Speaking of, you look like a million bucks. Why don't you dress like that for me?"

"For burgers, pizza, or the Tony and Alex Show? Nah. I'll pass. Nice of you to notice, though." Motioning with her finger, she said, "Follow me. We can grab coffee on the way."

As Alex and Tony crossed the lobby, she glanced outside and spotted Hannah talking with Sean.

Tony followed her stare. "What the hell?" His eyebrows shot up. "Do they know each other?"

Hannah and Sean were standing too close for strangers. Their stance looked much too familiar for a banker and a customer. Alex thought back to the time she thought she saw them at Coconuts. It was dark inside, as usual, and the bar had been overflowing with a Happy Hour crowd. She couldn't be positive it was them but had had a niggling feeling ever since. Mind racing, she wondered whether to tell Tony. Knowing her cop boyfriend would overreact and possibly make a scene about the bank president's daughter, Alex downplayed it. Shrugging, she said, "I saw her speak to him in the teller line earlier. Maybe he forgot something and she brought it to him."

Tony eyed the couple. "Sean never forgets anything." Narrowing his eyes, he continued. "He likes big boobs and probably those big lips. I bet she could do some crazy unmentionables with those things."

"Gross. I don't want to envision my intern and your brother," Alex said, "Trust Department, remember? That's our mission. Follow me."

Chapter 89

Two hours later, Tony descended the bank stairs two at a time. All smiles, he crossed the lobby toward Alex's office. Not bothering to sit in a chair, he closed the door. "It's done. The CCPD Fallen Officer Fund has been established. I can't wait to tell the Chief." Pacing, he said, "I don't want any publicity, though. I'm not sure how I'll go about this." Midstep, his face lit up. "I also set up a college fund for Joey and kept enough to get a new car and add to my pension. We should take a nice vacation, Alex."

Feeling as though she was betraying both Tony and Gage, Alex forced enthusiasm. "Well done." She stared at the board reports and dreaded the upcoming meeting. "Were the officers helpful in the trust department?"

"They're called officers too?" Tony snorted. "That short, bald guy was a real snooze fest, but he made the process fairly painless. It took forever." Flexing his fingers, he said, "I've got a cramp in my hand from signing paperwork." Reaching for her hand, Tony's voice softened. "Seriously, thanks for helping me. I wouldn't have known where to begin. Want to celebrate tonight with a romantic dinner?"

Still clinging to memories of New York City and Gage, Alex wasn't ready to jump in the sack with Tony, nor to have a festive dinner. "Let's postpone the celebration or go to Coconuts for a quick cocktail."

"Coconuts?" Tony winked. "I can afford a steak place now. I'm not relying on a crappy cop's salary."

"You know I love Coconuts." Faking a yawn, Alex said, "Besides, I have jetlag. I wouldn't make it past eight o'clock."

Frowning, Tony said, "Are you in competition with the trust guy for the snooze fest crown? I thought you'd be more excited."

"Rain check, okay?"

Obviously confused, he shoved his hands in his pockets. "Whatever. I guess we can postpone a nice dinner—or there's always the Tony and Alex show."

For some reason, Alex felt like she was cheating on Gage. And when she was with Gage, she felt as though she were disloyal to Tony. "Tony, I can't think straight right now. I have to make a big presentation to the board this afternoon. I've got to clear my mind."

Hanging his head, Tony said, "You're a real killjoy. I'll see if little Joey wants to go to a movie or have pizza."

"That's the spirit. I'm sure Joey would love that." She still thought of little Joey as Tony's son since he was when they met—or so she thought. "Tell the little man I said hi." Tony left the bank without a goodbye and didn't bother turning around.

This was a big day for him. I know he's disappointed I didn't celebrate with him. I'm a jerk. Sighing, Alex began opening her mountain of mail.

When Hannah returned from lunch, Alex bombarded her intern with questions before she had a chance to sit down. "Exactly how do you know Sean Montgomery?"

Blushing, Hannah said, "We met when he opened an account here, remember?"

"Your pink cheeks don't lie. Are you dating a married man, Hannah?" Clearing her throat, Alex added, "Granted, he's married to a royal bitch."

Hannah jutted out her big chest. "I don't know what you're talking about."

"Right." Alex stiffened when she spotted several bank board members mingling in the lobby. "It's almost showtime."

Chapter 90

Still jetlagged, Alex gathered the folders Hannah had compiled for the annual Show-Me Bank board meeting and made her way to the conference room.

This meeting was one of her most dreaded events. Most of the members were pleasant, some slept through the meeting, but others asked pointed questions. Alex never knew what to expect and always over prepared. Constantly on her game—until now due to vacation—Alex felt uneasy about relying on Hannah to compile the data. Normally, she would have combed through it beforehand, but Tony and Sean had distracted her. She told herself it would be fine since Hannah reminded her weekly about her master's degree. Compiling a board report should be a piece of cake for the higher ed genius.

Taking a deep breath, Alex entered the conference room with her head held high, faking confidence she didn't feel. The bank president sat on one end. Mrs. Timmons, the board president, sat beside him. A few executive vice presidents and other board members were interspersed around the table.

After greetings, Alex distributed the report. While standing at the far end of the rectangular table, she presented branding campaign ideas for the upcoming year, discussed the popularity of the bank's booth at a recent trade show, reviewed the annual report, gave a community relations update, covered media relations for the past quarter, and mentioned several plans for the upcoming year. As she flipped through her copy, she stopped mid-sentence when she noticed four pages were out of order. Hoping the error was in her packet only, she continued without missing a beat.

Pursing her lips, Mrs. Timmons asked, "Where's page eight?"

"Um." Alex thumbed through her copy. "It appears that pages eight and ten are mixed up." She glanced at her boss whose brows were furrowed. Wanting to throw her intern some shade, Alex decided to take the heat since she was in charge of marketing, plus Hannah was his damn daughter. Persevering, she felt her neck get blotchy from nerves. "Let's discuss the marketing budget. We do our best to work within the constraints of a small budget, and I'm pleased to report we've accomplished a great deal this year. We've created a dozen different television commercials alone and—"

"Is this everything?" Mrs. Timmons melodramatically flipped pages from the front to the back of the report. "I don't see any budgetary totals. What are your projected expenses? How much do you plan to spend in marketing next year?"

Sneaking another glance toward her boss, Alex hoped he'd chime in since they met weekly to discuss marketing, but he let her walk the gangplank—alone. She wanted to shout that his darling daughter had screwed up the freaking report while she was on vacation.

Clearing her throat, Alex squinted at the budget. "You're right, Mrs. Timmons. I don't see line items for television, radio, and billboard advertising. I worked on my budget before my vacation and relied on—" Stopping herself, she decided to wing it. Even the older board members who normally slept through her presentation were at full attention. All eyes on her, Alex's mouth went dry. *What were the damn totals? Her mind raced. Between Gage and Tony, my mind is a freaking blank.*

Hesitating a half second, Mrs. Timmons continued peppering her with questions. Rattled, Alex felt her face get hot as every board member and bank executive swiveled toward her. Going by memory, she blurted out the totals for paid advertising. The board unanimously, and quickly, voted to approve the marketing budget for the following year.

The minute her presentation was over, Alex stepped into her office to confront Hannah, but she had already left for the day. *Probably getting another fucking massage.* Heart pounding, she opened the marketing budget file on her computer and immediately saw her error. *Dammit. I was off by fifteen thousand dollars. Now we'll have to manage with a much smaller budget. Shit.*

Furious and beyond embarrassed, Alex stomped out of the bank without saying a word to anyone. She didn't leave a note, nor update her voicemail—something the bank president was obsessive about. Too upset to call her intern for fear she'd tell Daddy's daughter where to shove it and get fired, she drove to Coconuts and ordered a chardonnay. *Who the hell cares if it isn't 5 o'clock?*

~ ~ ~

As Gus brought wine, along with chips, salsa, and a Diet Coke, Alex's anger did the opposite of subside. Usually wine relaxed her but not today. *That little bitch did this on purpose. She wanted me to fall flat on my face in front of the board. She's gunning for my job.* Before she lost her nerve, Alex picked up her cell to shoot off an email to Hannah.

I can't believe you screwed up my board report. Pages were out of order, and you forgot to include the budgetary line items. Mrs. Timmons chewed my ass out. That cranky old witch needs to retire. She's been on the board for far too long. Show-Me Bank needs some young blood.

Thanks for nothing, Hannah. I know you did this on purpose. You think since you're daddy's little girl you can get away with these stunts. I'm your boss and don't forget it.

Finger pausing over the send button, Alex swallowed. *I can't send this. What if she shows her dad? I could get fired.*

I'm a bank vice president. I've got to rise above the fiasco. By next week, it'll all be forgotten. Feeling at peace with her decision, Alex set her cell on the table, leaned over, reached for another chip, and accidentally pressed the send button. *Shit. Shit. Shit.*

Clapping her hand over her mouth, she said, "Oh, my God" to no one. As Gus refilled her soda, her phone pinged. *That was fast.*

Unable to stand it one second longer, Alex picked up her phone and rolled her eyes as she read Hannah's response:

Hi Alex! I'm confused by your email. I really like Mrs. Timmons. She's young at heart, is an incredible leader, and loves to hear every aspect of marketing. She always has Show-Me Bank's best interests at heart. Maybe you should have taken a longer vacation, boss. I don't think it did you much good. Cheers, Hannah.

That suck up. That bitch. I hate her. Wishing she could choke her intern through the tiny screen, Alex reread Hannah's reply and dropped a salsa-covered chip to the floor. Bile rose in her throat when she realized Hannah had added the bank president's email, as well as every Show-Me Bank officer and board member, and had hit *reply all*. Both of their emails went to every freaking one of them. *Oh, my God. That bitch did this on purpose too. I'll probably be fired.*

Chapter 91

Alex waved to Gus for a second glass of chardonnay.

"Are you here alone?" Gus glanced at a clock near the bar, but like every good server, didn't mention the time.

Running her fingers through her hair, she said, "Let's just say I've had a few bad weeks, as in really bad."

The friendly flip-flop-wearing server said, "I understand. In that case, the next glass is on the house."

"Thanks, Gus. That's sweet." Setting her phone down, Alex jumped as a shadow appeared across the table.

A cute cowboy wearing tight jeans and dusty boots tipped his big western hat. "Howdy."

Taken aback, she said, "Hi."

Extending his hand, the cowboy said, "I'm Cole Cash. Aren't you friends with New York?"

Alex's lips curved into a smile. *This is exactly the diversion I need.* "Do you mean Cheri?"

"Yep. Have you seen her lately?"

"No, but I've been in New York."

His eyebrows shot up. "Popular place."

"Huh?" Alex studied him as she sipped her wine.

"Nothin.' I've been hearin' a lot about New York lately. Never been there and I'm already tired of it. Thanks anyway." Nodding, he turned to walk away.

"Don't leave. You just got here. Want a beer? I could use some company."

The cowboy hesitated.

Alex patted a bar stool. "Don't worry. I won't bite."

Sitting down, Cole said, "I won't turn down a beer."

Grinning, Alex said, "I didn't say I was buying."

"Thanks. I needed a laugh." Waving Gus over, Cole ordered a Budweiser. As it arrived, Alex caught him staring at her ring finger.

Clearing his throat, he said, "I'm glad you're not married." Cole peered at a couple entwined in the corner and muttered, "I'd never move in on another man's woman."

"I'm not sure what you're talking about, but I've never been married. Probably won't be at this rate." Eyeing the cowboy, Alex asked, "Have you ever been married?"

"No, ma'am."

Her eyebrows shot up. "Ma'am?"

Cole grinned. "Habit. Cheri didn't like it when I said that either. We were having a picnic and I— Never mind. I won't bore you."

Shifting forward, Alex rested her chin on her hand. "Back up. You and Cheri went on a picnic together? I'm anything but bored. Go on."

Cole shrugged. "Doesn't matter."

Cocking her head, Alex said, "You can't start a story and not finish. Are you two dating?"

After a healthy gulp of beer, he said, "Not since I found out she's engaged."

Sucking in her breath, Alex's mouth fell open. "Engaged? Cheri's *engaged*?" She immediately thought of the massive diamond she found in Cheri's closet. "She told you this?"

"Nope. Her fiancé did."

Slack-jawed, Alex said, "I want to hear all about Cheri and her fiancé. I really wish Suzy and Hope were here. I guess Cheri isn't who we thought she was. Too bad. I really like her."

Cole took a long swig of beer. "I found out after we had a great day. I taught her how to skip rocks and search for arrowheads. We drank wine and enjoyed nature." Grinning, he said, "I even made dinner." He stared into his drink. "She's somethin' special, but . . . she isn't available."

Glancing around the darkened bar, Alex thought of how she, Suzy, and Hope had welcomed Cheri into their group. "That's a helluva shocker. I'll give you that. But none of us are perfect—especially me," Alex said. She twirled her wine stem, lost in thought. "Cheri isn't snooty at all. I think she's a good person. I'm usually a great judge of character." Pausing, she said, "Maybe there's a reason she kept the engagement a secret."

Appearing crestfallen, Cole held up his empty glass. When Gus brought another beer, Alex ordered a Diet Coke. Staring at the cowboy, she could tell he was disheartened. "She's a sweet person. Maybe there's more to this. Let's hear her out."

Placing his hat on the back of a chair, Cole asked, "What makes you think she'll come back? What does this place have to offer a New Yorker?"

"Besides us?" Alex chuckled. "Actually, she seems to love it here. After her dumb string of Internet dates, you should be a refreshing change."

"She dates strangers off the Internet too?" The cowboy stared at his boots, then shook his head. "I'm so stupid."

What is my problem? I didn't have any right to tell Cole about her past dating life. Chewing on her bottom lip, Alex said, "It wasn't my place to tell you about her private life." A nervous laugh escaped. "I don't suppose you can forget about this entire conversation." As she waited for an answer, the lazy ceiling fans did little to assuage her mood. She loved and admired her New York friend and wished she hadn't said a word. Leaning forward, Alex said, "My love life is a freaking disaster. I'm the last person on earth who should give relationship advice. Please forget everything I said."

Cole eyed her. "Actually, I'm glad you told me. Maybe it'll make it easier to move on knowing there isn't a chance in hell for the two of us. We wouldn't last as long as sidewalk ice cream in July." Shrugging, he added, "I figured she was too good to be true. I don't know how she got under my thick hide so fast."

Shuffling to his feet, Alex said, "Don't give up on her, cowboy. Like I said, maybe there's a reason."

He shrugged. "Maybe."

Alex smiled in an attempt to give him hope. "Let's hear Cheri out."

"If she ever comes back."

"She will. She loves that house in Branson. What did you guys do on your date in the woods—the PG version, that is?"

Hooting, he said, "I made hobos for her." Cole bent over and held his sides from laughing.

"I bet she loved those—whatever they are."

Cole explained how he made hobos, talked about teaching Cheri to skip rocks and hunt for arrowheads, and mentioned how Sebastian had surprised the hell out of them. Riveted, Alex didn't even blink. The room had darkened, Gus had cleaned every table, and there were only a handful of patrons remaining.

When Cole finished, he leaned back. "That's my story. Sounds like a country song, right?"

Grinning, Alex nodded. "Sort of. It sounds like she was having a lot of fun with you."

Cole studied Alex. "Do you really think a country boy like me has a chance with New York?"

"As a matter of fact, I do." Alex drained her soda. "Don't ask me how I know, but I have a good feeling about you two, especially after you told me about your day together."

Placing his hat on his head, Cole said, "For all I know, she flew back to New York with that tall, skinny guy and is married by now." He put two twenties on the table. "Nothin'

I can do 'bout that. Drinks are on me. Thanks for cheerin' me up. I have a long drive and need to bottle feed some newborn calves."

Alex studied Cole's brooding face and wanted to console him. "Maybe she's breaking the engagement off now."

Cole snorted. "Doubtful. He said he bought her a five-carat diamond." Staring at his dusty, worn boots, he mumbled, "I could never compete with that."

Feeling an impulsive need to cheer him up, Alex reached for Cole's arm. "That doesn't matter. It's not about the ring. It's about love."

"You're quite the romantic." Tipping his hat, Cole managed a smile.

"I do believe in love. There's someone for everyone, I think. I hope." Gathering her purse, she said, "Maybe I'll find it someday." After they stepped outside toward their respective cars, she shouted over her shoulder, "Don't give up, cowboy. Never give up."

Chapter 92

Dressed in a fuzzy pink robe, Suzy paced while she drank hot chamomile tea to soothe her nerves. Ken and Izzy had caught a six o'clock flight to Hollywood. Tempted to see Izzy's bedroom of doom, Suzy decided to leave that until another day.

When it was still dark outside, Izzy had rolled two bulging suitcases, a carryon, and her laptop into the hallway. Ken's eyes were red, but he held himself together in front of his daughter. Suzy had hugged her stoic stepdaughter, and said, "Please keep in touch. Let us know what's going on. Text pictures, okay?"

Izzy bobbed her head as she gave Suzy a one-armed hug.

Smoothing her stepdaughter's hair, Suzy said, "If you aren't happy in California, know you'll always have a home here."

Ken's voice wobbled. "That's right, honey. Always." He sniffled. "We love you so much." Turning so his daughter couldn't see his tears, he carried her bags to the garage, and placed them inside the SUV. When he reentered the house, he slung his arm across Izzy's shoulders. "I guess this is it. I still can't believe my baby is Hollywood bound."

They had only been gone an hour, but the house already felt eerily quiet and empty. *I can't believe she left, especially now with the twins coming. Actually, I can believe it. Izzy had told me in no uncertain terms that screaming babies in the middle of the night wasn't her idea of a good time.* Glancing out the window above the kitchen sink, Suzy decided she couldn't blame her. *At least I'll get to learn more about Ken's ex, the ghost from his past.*

~ ~ ~

After spending the night in a hotel, Ken called, sounding as though he hadn't slept. "I hate this place. Parts of the city are sad and pathetic. And the traffic must be fourteen lanes wide. It's absurd. I don't know what Destiny sees in this godforsaken state." His voice caught. "What if Izzy loves it and never wants to come home?"

"Honey, you know what you always tell me—don't borrow trouble. I'm sure she'll miss us, at least you, and be curious about the twins. Hopefully this is a phase. I have a feeling she'll want to graduate with her friends." Suzy grimaced as Ken's first photo came through. "That traffic looks dreadful."

"Gotta run, honey. I want to grab an egg sandwich before I board the plane."

"Have a safe flight, babe. I love you." Suzy hung up feeling mystified. On the one hand, she and Izzy had never gotten along well. She was glad to be rid of Izzy's stupid phone addiction which annoyed her to no end. On the other hand, she couldn't wait to have her husband to herself but did want her stepdaughter to be involved in the twins' lives. They'd be half siblings, after all. With mixed emotions, she refilled her tea. *This will be an interesting experiment and life change.*

Chapter 93

Dreading going to work after the disastrous board report and especially after the horrible email blast exchange, thanks to Hannah, Alex made sure she was on time.

Before she passed the copier machine near the back door, her boss, arms crossed, and not in a relaxed way, glared at her. "Meet me in my office."

I'm getting fired. Mind racing, Alex followed Jim into his corner office and sat in a chair. Shoulders stiff, she chewed on her bottom lip. "I guess I should start from the beginning."

Mouth in a grim line, Jim said, "Whatever you have to say right now doesn't matter. I'm disappointed in you, Alex. First, your marketing report was a disaster. Then you had the audacity to call our esteemed board president names." Throwing up his hands, he added, "If that wasn't enough, you accused my daughter of setting you up."

Always one of the bank's stellar employees who received high praise during evaluations, Alex couldn't believe her ears. "I-I—"

The bank president raised his voice. "I'm not finished. Hannah's in charge of marketing now. At least until the dust settles. We'll see how it goes."

Alex opened her mouth to defend herself but closed it. Nepotism was on the tip of her tongue but blurting that out wouldn't pay her monthly bills.

"I have a customer coming in." Her boss's tone was wooden.

Knowing it was no use to contest his decision while he

was still furious, Alex didn't utter a word. Gathering her purse, she crossed the lobby where Hannah was already seated—at her desk. *She's obviously already been told about our role reversal.*

"Morning, Alex." Crossing her feet on the edge of the desk, Hannah said, "Before we begin, I'd like some coffee."

Alex scowled at her intern but didn't say a word. She knew she couldn't quit. Not until she had several months of cash saved. As she climbed the stairs to the employee lounge, she wished she had the nerve to spit in her intern's coffee. The thought made her smile at least. *I've got to look for another job. But where will I go? Another bank? Jim would likely make me sign a non-compete clause. I really shit in my nest.*

Returning to the office where Hannah was stretched out as if she were in a recliner, Alex plunked the coffee on her desk and slumped in a chair usually reserved for customers or Hannah. "I guess you're thrilled with how this went down. You and I both know exactly what happened. Thanks for setting me up. You added those names and hit 'reply all.'"

Pursing her enormous lips, Hannah said, "I don't know what you're talking about."

Alex rolled her eyes. "Whatever. We need to work on the—"

Voice shrill, Hannah said, "*I'm* in charge now. I'll tell you what we're working on. Why don't you update the annual report?" She gave a wicked smile. "I know how much you loathe those."

"The report doesn't need to be updated for months." Alex reached for a pending file. "We need to—"

Undaunted, Hannah continued. "After that, I'd like for you to pick up some brochures at the printer."

"Why?" Alex's brows knitted. "The printer delivers."

"Pick them up anyway." Hannah turned toward her

computer. "What's your password?"

She's enjoying this role reversal way too much. I can't tell her my password is: ihatehannah123. "Um, I've forgotten. Just change it to something you'll remember for now."

Clicking the keyboard, Hannah said, "Yeah, right."

Chapter 94

Still humiliated and furious after discovering Sebastian had created the greatest illusion since Houdini to get her on a plane to New York, Cheri plucked her ring from her armoire and had her doorman hand deliver it to Sebastian on a freaking silver platter. At least that gave her satisfaction.

After three cups of coffee, she worked up the nerve to call her surprisingly not-so-shocked mother the news. Breathy, and blowing smoke, Victoria attempted to be motherly and take Cheri's side. Cheri half heard her mom's "Darling this and darling that and mentioning she noticed Cheri never spoke of her fiancé, which was *odd*." She felt relief after her mom promised to tell her always-absent father since disappointing him would be too much to endure.

Pacing her plush living room, Cheri read the note Alex had left thanking her for her hospitality. *I've got to come clean to my girlfriends—and fast—before they find out my secret.*

Stepping from room to room, a headache bore down. Still angry with Sebastian, mad at herself, and sick with worry about Cole, she peered out a window and watched the unknowing masses on the Manhattan sidewalks. All she could think about was her simple, yet perfect, day with Cole. *I've got to go back soon. After I meet with my employees at Fifth Avenue Catering, I'm hopping on the next available plane.*

~ ~ ~

Within three hours, she met with rattled employees and assured them Fifth Avenue Catering was in capable hands with Julio, even though those words didn't come easily. She wanted to coax Chef O'Leary back, but he wasn't her top priority at the moment.

After reviewing applications for a catering van driver, she met with her new, perky female pastry chef. While sampling potential updated menu items and reviewing the next month's client events, her now-sober sous chef pulled her aside to discuss his disdain for Julio. Waving his hands wildly, the chef said, "Julio has changed nearly every menu item and struts around like a peacock. He acts like he owns the place; no one likes him."

Cheri knew she had to get her head back in her business but really only wanted to deal with a certain cowboy. Promising to smooth things over, she assured the chef the company was in good hands, if only to convince herself. Too drained to go out or call Gage, she went home and ordered a pizza.

The next morning, Cheri donned a curly red Lucille Ball-like wig, a black turtleneck sweater dress, leopard print heels, and huge sunglasses. She asked her doorman to summon a car service to the airport. Fully aware she looked ridiculous while inside the airport, she didn't care. She didn't want any distractions. Paparazzi be damned. She'd outsmarted them again. Settling in the back seat of the car, she purposely cut the time close.

Once the driver dropped her off at LaGuardia, she checked in and had to lift the edge of her wig for TSA to prove she was herself since her blonde-haired I.D. didn't match. She boarded with ten minutes to spare. Buckling her seatbelt in first class, a flight attendant brought warm cashews and a chilled Bellini. Cheri nodded thanks, put in earbuds, and tried to gather her thoughts. *Will Suzy, Alex, and Hope be mad I kept my engagement from them? How will I explain this to Cole?* Mulling over the best strategy as the aircraft ascended, she decided she would tell her girlfriends first. Maybe they'll have advice about approaching Cole.

Attempting to read a novel proved futile. Her mind raced as the words blurred. It was no use. She closed the paperback and slept fitfully for two hours. The second the plane landed, Cheri texted Alex, Suzy, and Hope: *I'm back from New York. I need to tell you something important. Will you meet me at Coconuts tonight at six?*

Alex answered first in all caps: HELL YEAH. WHAT'S UP WITH YOU AND THE COWBOY?

Cheri responded: *We need to talk.*

Hope added: *Hi! I don't know what you're talking about, but I'll be there.*

Suzy responded: *See you at six.*

After she landed, Cheri hailed a cab and arrived at Coconuts by five-thirty. Her stomach churned at the thought of losing her friends. *I love these special women. I never should have kept my ridiculous engagement from them.* Her mouth went dry. *What if they hate me now?*

She stepped into the darkened bar, went straight to the restroom, and removed her wig. Cramming the curly mess into her bag, Cheri fluffed her blonde hair, and settled at their favorite table, heart pounding.

Gus approached. "What're you having?"

Cheri waited half a second before answering, "Angry Balls for two of us." The cocktail suited her mood. Surprised to see Alex arrive early for once, she patted the seat beside her. "We need to talk."

"Yes, we do." Alex slid her turquoise jacket off and placed it on the back of her chair. Her silver charm bracelet dangled as she reached for a cocktail. "Good choice." Raising the drink in the air, she said, "Thanks for letting me stay in your gorgeous apartment. I felt like a princess."

"You're welcome. Tell me about New York and Gage." Crossing her legs, Cheri said, "I've been dying to know."

Chapter 95

After the shock of the damn board report and getting demoted, Alex wanted to collapse but knew she had to tell Cheri what she had repeated to the cowboy. She waved Gus over. "I'll take coffee too. I'm drained."

As he slid a cup of steaming coffee in front of Alex, Cheri requested water. "I'm dehydrated from flying. I'll take water when you get a chance, Gus." Smiling at Alex, she said, "So, tell me everything."

Alex felt a blush creep up her neck. The afterglow of her outings with Gage would be told much differently if she hadn't dealt with Tony's trauma. She wasn't in the mood to go into details. "We had great fun. Gage is the perfect gentleman. He picked me up at the airport, had my name on a sign, and gave me limo rides. Did you have something to do with that?"

Sipping her water, Cheri said, "That was Gage's idea. He's a romantic, that guy. I know he likes you."

"The feeling's mutual." Alex sighed. Staring at a couple holding hands across the room, she said, "I thought I had made my decision as far as the cop." Something crossed her face. "I was almost ready to break up with him."

"Wow." Raising her eyebrows, Cheri said, "One trip did the trick, huh?" She paused, and even though she tried to hide it, her face fell. "It sounds like you've had a change of heart."

Shrugging, Alex said, "More like a delay, I suppose. After I returned, unbelievably crazy things happened to Tony. I can't possibly break up with him now."

Cheri studied her navy nails. "Well, it's your life. I'm sure you'll work it out however it's meant to be."

"Thanks. By the way, on my last day, I stood in the lobby chatting with the doorman as I waited for a driver. An older, handsome man with a booming East Coast accent caught my eye. He strode inside like he was on a mission. A young, beautiful brunette was plastered by his side. Your doorman seemed to know both of them. The doorman seemed flustered, grabbed my luggage, and placed it on the sidewalk. He couldn't get me out of there fast enough."

Eyes widening, Cheri asked, "Did the woman have a French accent by any chance?"

"As a matter of fact—" Alex stopped mid-sentence. "That's an insanely wild guess. How did you know?"

Cheri's eyes filled with tears. "Let's just say it's something that has nagged at me since I returned from Paris last year."

"I remember the woman was friendly and attractive. The guy was handsome but a lot older and—"

Putting her head in her hands, Cheri said, "That's likely because he's my dad."

Alex clapped a hand over her mouth. "Oh, my God. Do you think?"

Nodding, Cheri said, "I hope not, but I have a nagging suspicion. Mom said Dad has been distant the past year. A total workaholic, which isn't unusual, but it's worse than ever." Tracing a crack in the table, she said, "Dad didn't even make time for me when I was in Paris last spring." Sighing, she added, "The woman you saw might be a French fashion designer named Gigi. Mom has become fast friends with her. This will crush her. She took Gigi under her wing and introduced her to her socialite friends." Jaw tightening, Cheri said, "If this is true, look how the designer paid Mom back."

Eyebrows lifted, Alex said, "That's awful. What makes you so sure it's her?"

"Number one, Gigi must have had financing to open a startup boutique in Paris. Most beginning designers don't have the kind of money for a small business in a trendy city—let alone Paris. And Mom said their finances took a hit last year but has never mentioned it again. I wasn't too worried since they're worth millions. I assumed any financial loss was due to bad investments, but—" Cheri paused. "Maybe Dad has been financing Gigi's Couture."

"Maybe. Maybe not." Always the banker, Alex said, "She might have gotten a commercial loan. In the states, we have Small Business Administration loans. Maybe they have something akin to SBA loans in France."

Cheri shrugged. "I suppose that's possible, but there's more."

Leaning forward, Alex asked, "What?"

"I found a blue topaz heart-shaped gold earring in Mom and Dad's kitchen last spring. Mom was defiant it wasn't hers. She said she never wore lab-generated stones."

"Mostly diamonds, I assume." Alex studied her wealthy friend. "I'm sure the Van Burens have a maid. It's probably hers."

Cheri shook her head. "That was my first guess too. Mom said her maid's ears aren't pierced."

Crossing her arms, Alex said, "It could belong to anybody, right? A friend of your moms, maybe."

"I suppose but I'm going to get to the bottom of this . . ." Raising her cocktail, Cheri said, "Cheers. I'm glad you and Gage had fun at least. Let's change subjects until I know for sure."

Alex leaned forward. "Couldn't you simply ask your doorman if this person was your dad?"

"Daddy has always greased palms to get his way. I'm quite sure my doorman was paid handsomely to keep quiet—

and to keep the paparazzi away. Until I'm certain, I'll try not to worry. I'm definitely not saying anything to Mom. She already drinks too much, smokes like a chimney, and has lost weight." Sipping her cocktail, Cheri said, "Let's discuss something—anything—else. Besides, I called you girls here for a reason." Glancing at her Rolex, she said, "Hope and Suzy should be here any minute. I have some explaining to do. Actually, a lot of explaining."

Chapter 96

Right on time, Suzy and Hope stepped inside. Light filled the crowded, darkened bar. Alex and Cheri both waved. After a quick group hug, Cheri said, "Drinks and appetizers are on me, ladies. Order whatever you want."

"Are you sure?" Hope studied the menu. "Crab cakes sound good. Oh, and roasted asparagus." Frowning, she said, "I know I should eat a salad."

"Eat whatever you want," Cheri said. After everyone decided, Gus took their orders, returned at warp speed with drinks, as well as a meat, cheese, and olive platter for a hearty appetizer.

Reaching for an olive, Hope said, "This is a treat, but you don't have to pay."

Cheri bobbed her head. "Yes, I do. I'll get to the bottom line. I haven't been honest with you."

Suzy and Hope exchanged glances. Alex spoke first. "No, you haven't."

Cheri turned to the banker. "You didn't think to mention that earlier? How do you know?"

Shrugging, Alex said, "Doesn't matter. Go ahead."

Cheri splayed her manicured, blue nails across the table. "I could make this a long and winding story, but I'll get to the point with the Cliff Notes version. Cole and I were on a perfect date in the country."

Suzy's mouth flew open. "Wait. Cole? The cowboy?"

"Let her continue," Alex said.

Cheri looked downright wistful. "Yes, the cowboy. We had a dreamy date in the woods."

Hope interjected again, "*You* were in the woods?"

Alex rolled her eyes. "Will you let her finish?"

Cheri beamed, reliving the special day. "Cole taught me how to skip rocks, search for arrowheads, build a fire, and make hobos."

"My hippie parents used to make hobos." Hope studied the New Yorker. "Thanks for the nice memory. We should all go camping and make them sometime."

Alex sighed. Loudly. "Will you let her finish?"

Sipping the amber cocktail, Cheri felt her shoulders relax for the first time in days. "As I said, Cole and I had a picnic. He even brought wine, cheese, and strawberries. He was so sweet and then—"

"I'm calmer just thinking about it." Suzy patted her ever-growing belly. "Goodness knows I won't have many quiet days in a few months."

Hope rolled an ice cube in her mouth. "Sounds like a perfect day."

Crossing her arms, Alex said, "And . . .?"

Cheri rubbed her forehead. "It *was* perfect until my fiancé found us—somehow—in the woods. You'd have thought we left breadcrumbs like the fairytale. But in actuality, he hired a freaking private detective. There's no telling how long I've been followed. It gives me the creeps. Anyway—"

"Wait. Fiancé?" Suzy's eyebrows shot up.

Hope's mouth fell open. "You're engaged?"

Cheri wiggled her bare ring finger. "Was."

Alex chimed in. "So you broke it off?"

Voice quivering, Cheri said, "I haven't worn the ring in nearly two years. I knew it was wrong from the beginning." Her eyes reddened. "But I was too big a chicken to break it off or tell anyone. Sebastian, that's his name, talked me into flying back to New York with him. He said my mom had planned a huge surprise pre-wedding gala for us, my parents were flying in from Europe, and had arranged for Justin

Timberlake to perform. He knew I wouldn't miss seeing my parents. He also said *People Magazine* had the exclusive and told me I couldn't tarnish the family name and be a no-show." Putting her head in her hands, she said, "I bought it. Hook. Line. And sinker."

Hope slapped a hand on the table. "I'm sure that's exactly how my pre-wedding party would go, especially the famous performer and *People Magazine* part." She giggled. "Go on. Sorry for interrupting. It's so surreal."

"I know. My life's a tad crazy." Cheri nibbled on an olive. "I believed Sebastian since my mom loves to throw lavish parties, plus I've been homesick for my parents, especially my dad—"

Suzy sat riveted. "This is unreal."

Tapping her fingers together, Alex said, "How did this all go down with your fiancé?"

After a group of boisterous Happy Hour patrons passed, Cheri turned to all three women who had scooted forward, hanging on every word. "After we landed in Manhattan, Sebastian took me to dinner and said my parents were going to join us for dessert. I was sick to my stomach the entire time wondering how I could tell him—and them—I didn't want to go through with it. But he made my decision for me. While eating Crème Brule, Sebastian admitted he lied about the event to get me to New York. He thought he could change my mind about breaking off the engagement."

"The bastard." Alex cupped her mouth.

Noticing Suzy and Hope's shared glances, Cheri was ashamed but persevered. "Sebastian chose our favorite restaurant, requested a table in the corner, ordered lobster, and a bottle of their most expensive wine. I guess he thought once I was in familiar surroundings I'd forget all about Crystal City, Branson, the three of you, and especially the cowboy. After hemming and hawing through dessert as I fixated on the door waiting for my parents who never showed, he admitted he lied. I immediately stormed outside."

"Then what happened?" Hope scooted even closer to the table.

Wrinkling her nose, Cheri said, "It was ugly. He chased after me. We had a huge fight on the sidewalk. As I officially broke up with him and told him to go to hell for deceiving me—yes, I know that's rich since I deceived you but—" Unable to meet her friends' eyes, she said, "I saw a couple of cameras flash." A nervous laugh escaped. "I'm still waiting for our tiff to appear on the cover of some rag magazine."

"Hopefully, the cowboy doesn't read those." Alex let out a whistle. "That's some story."

"All true." Cheri fidgeted with the napkin in her lap.

Suzy studied Cheri. "I wish you would have told us about your engagement all along, but I'm glad you're telling us now."

Holding her hands out like scales, Hope said, "Your life or mine? At the moment, I'm glad mine is monotonous."

"Remember your lost and found hippie parents? Your life's not that boring, Hope." Alex turned to Cheri. "I might have decked Sebastian. Did you fly back right away after that fiasco?"

Managing a small smile, Cheri said, "The temptation was there but I do try to protect the family name. I flew back within two days." She ticked off her manicured fingernails. "I checked on Fifth Avenue Catering, tried to reassure my employees, and met with a few anxious, high-profile clients." Sipping her cocktail, she said, "Oh, I also hired a delivery driver and promised to try and rehire my main chef. It seems the employees aren't fond of Julio. He's a bit of a showboat."

"Not Julio." Alex winked. "I remember him from the Bridal Bonanza wedding cake competition last year. He's cute."

Cheri groaned. "But tough to work with, apparently."

"Well done on managing your personal life and career," Suzy said. "I know from experience it isn't easy to balance both."

Chuckling, Cheri said, "Red Bull helps."

Hope squeezed Cheri's hand. "Thanks for telling us now. Remember, you can tell us anything. That's what friends are for."

Alex waved Gus over. "I'm gonna need another drink, Gus. Maybe I should buy this round."

Cheri, Suzy, and Hope swiveled toward Alex.

"Now what?" Hope asked.

Alex gulped. "Since we're telling secrets today, I have one, too."

Chapter 97

After their drinks were refreshed, Alex had trouble meeting Cheri's eyes. When all eyes were on her, she blurted out, "There's no easy way around this. I'll come out and tell you, Cheri. When Cole came to Coconuts hoping to find you, he was so forlorn. I invited him to sit with me. He told me about your wonderful day in the woods and mentioned your hush-hush engagement. He was devastated, and so was I. I couldn't believe you had kept such a major secret from us. Girlfriends don't do that."

Rubbing her eyebrow, Alex continued. "I told him maybe you didn't know who you wanted to date. I mentioned your string of online dates. It was wrong. I shouldn't have. It came out because I was angry with you for keeping secrets, plus I felt sorry for Cole. It was childish." Wincing, Alex said, "I felt for the guy. He looked like a lost, wet puppy."

Cheri's eyes filled with tears. "He did?"

Alex nodded. "Oh, yeah. I wanted to prop him up. Again, it wasn't my business to tell him. I'm really sorry. There's more."

"More?" Taking a healthy sip of Angry Balls, Cheri said, "Do I want to hear this?"

Running her fingers through her hair, Alex said, "After you graciously let me use your gorgeous penthouse apartment, I repaid you by snooping through your closet."

Both Hope and Suzy gasped and said, "*Alex!*"

"I know. I know. I shouldn't have, but your closet is amazing. It was like a magnet pulling me. When I saw the jewelry armoire, I went in and noticed the blue Tiffany's box."

Cheri's mouth fell open. "So you already knew I was engaged?"

"I guessed. That was a stunning, over-the-top, humongous diamond, by the way." Alex paused. "I hope you'll forgive me."

"I forgive you but—" Cheri's eyes filled with tears. "Guess I can kiss the cowboy goodbye."

"Why?" Alex asked.

Cheri ticked reasons off on her fingers. "Number one: I lied to him. Number two: He met my fiancé. Number 3: He knows I'm a mess and dated several men. Number 4: He'll never trust me. Should I continue?"

Hope bit into a crab cake. "Don't give up on him. If he's truly smitten, and if you are, too—and it sounds like you are—you'll make it work." Eyes twinkling, she said, "I know I don't date, but I have all the answers. I'm a high school counselor-slash-magician."

Nodding, Suzy said, "Don't let the cowboy get away. That's my advice." She winked. "And I know a thing or two about couples."

Drumming her fingers on the table, Cheri said, "Okay. You've convinced me. Now I need to get up my nerve."

Alex put her hands on her hips. "I have a question. Why the hell were you dating guys off the Internet if you were engaged?"

"That's another ridiculous antic I'd like to take back." Tracing the rim of her glass, Cheri said, "I guess I wanted to make sure Sebastian wasn't the one. After meeting so many loser guys online, I almost decided to make my engagement work." Grinning, she said, "Then, I met a certain cowboy."

"You like him, don't you?" Suzy asked.

"A lot. He's different in the best way possible."

"What have you done together?" Alex asked.

"Danced, played pool, went to a hillbilly pool party." Brightening, she said, "Oh, and we went to a drive-in. It was my first. Our last date was our infamous campin' date. Then, Sebastian showed up and the rest is history."

"Sounds fun. Maybe I should date a cowboy." Alex winked. "You're even dropping your g's. How cute." Alex tapped her leg.

"I did?" Cheri giggled.

"Yep. And you're blushing," Suzy said.

Cheri brightened. "I don't get any respect around here, and that's the way I like it. You girls make me feel normal and not high society."

"I might trade for a day. You know, to see what the other side of the tracks is like." Hope's mind wandered to the man she met in Nashville. She wasn't ready to tell her friends about Tucker—unless he called, which didn't look likely. Forcing enthusiasm, she dipped another bite of crab cake in a dill aioli sauce and said, "Tell the cowboy soon."

"Yes, don't let the engagement news fester," Suzy said.

Eyes welling with tears, Cheri asked, "I will. I promise. Do the three of you forgive me for my secret engagement?"

"Of course," Suzy and Hope echoed.

Chewing her lip, Alex said, "I forgive you since you forgave me."

Cheri raised her glass. "Here's to girlfriends."

Alex clanked her cocktail against Cheri's glass. Sighing, the New Yorker said, "I have a feeling this conversation won't be as easy with Cole."

"We all make mistakes." Hope jumped off her bar stool. "Group hug."

Voice faltering, Cheri said, "You're the best friends I've ever had. I hope Cole is this understanding."

Chapter 98

Staring at her messy kitchen after trying out new recipes while attempting to work up her nerve to talk to Cole, Cheri was relieved to hear her phone ring. She glanced at the screen. "Hi, Mom."

"Darling, how are you after our last discussion about Sebastian?"

"I'm fine. Getting back on track. It was over a long time ago, Mom. I've said all I care to on this subject." Squinting, she asked, "What's wrong with your left eyebrow? It's drooping."

Victoria waved her hand dismissively. "I just need a tune-up, darling. Some more Botox, maybe fillers."

Unhappy her beautiful mother now had a frozen face, Cheri changed the subject. "How's Dad? Did you two ever go on a surprise vacation like we discussed last year?" Hearing glass clank, she knew her mother was drinking again and did a quick calculation of the time between Branson and Paris. It was too early for alcohol but she let it go.

"You know how your daddy is. Work. Work. Work." Victoria lit a cigarette.

Cheri let that go too. "I haven't talked to Daddy in ages. I miss him."

"Darling, I know he misses you too." Her mom's voice rose. "He did manage to get away to New York for a few days."

Cheri's stomach plummeted as she recalled the conversation she had had with Alex about the handsome, older man and young French woman. She didn't want to believe that man was her father. "Dad went to New York? Did you go?"

"No, darling." Victoria took another drag. "Your father went alone."

Staring at her mother's not easily detectable emotions, but still sad face, Cheri asked, "Why in the world didn't you go with him?"

Victoria sipped what looked like a gin & tonic. "He insisted I'd be bored to tears. Your father said he had back-to-back meetings with developers, plus a board meeting. It was a quick trip."

"Mom, you love New York. All of your friends are in New York. Your gorgeous house is there. Why didn't you insist on going?" Cheri leaned against her sink overflowing with dirty mixing bowls.

Taking a healthy gulp of her cocktail, her mother's voice became flat. "I tried. He wouldn't have it." Diverting her eyes, she said, "Tell me about your friends and that cute bar you like. What's it called? Coconuts?"

Thinking the worst but not wanting to alarm her mom, Cheri said, "My friends are great, and yes, it's called Coconuts. You should visit sometime. Suzy, Alex, and Hope want to meet you. Actually, Alex is a banker. She was in New York recently, so I let her stay in my apartment." *I'm not about to mention she might have seen my dad and Gigi until I'm positive.*

"That was nice of you, darling." Victoria seemed bored with the conversation. Glancing at her diamond Rolex, she said, "I didn't realize it was so late. I have a date at Gigi's Couture." Brightening, she said, "That reminds me. Gigi designed the most fabulous jumpsuit. It's leopard print, with a plunging neckline, and a wide, wrap-around red belt. It would look divine on you. I'll have the maid send it."

If Gigi is having an affair with my dad, that's the last thing on earth I'd wear. "I don't want it, Mom."

"What?" If her mother could move her forehead, her eyebrows would likely be raised. "You'll love the jumpsuit. It's darling. Leopard print is your favorite."

"I have enough clothes." Immediately feeling guilty for turning down what was undoubtedly a beautiful designer garment from someone she had found guilty without evidence, Cheri added, "Thanks anyway, Mom. Maybe another time."

"What has gotten into you? No woman has too many clothes, but whatever. I've got to run. Gigi wants to show me her newest fashions and said she bought a case of my favorite Bordeaux. I'm helping her plan a trunk show. It's great fun to watch her grow her business. I'm thrilled to be a tiny part of it. I'm sure she'll be a smashing success in the fashion world. I can see her as the next Valentino or Stella McCartney." Victoria paused. "She's almost the daughter who is too far away from me—except I'm not nearly old enough to be her mother, of course. She values my fashion advice. It makes me feel good. Ah, it's getting late, darling. I must go."

Cheri's mother hadn't been this animated in a long time. Glad she had a purpose, she wanted to bolster her. "I'm glad you're excited about helping Gigi, Mom. I'm sure your advice is invaluable. Bye for now. I love you."

Blowing a kiss into the phone, her mother said, "*Ciao*, darling. Much love."

Cheri stared at the darkened screen. *If that young designer is sleeping with my dad and buttering up my mom, so help me.* Pacing from the kitchen to her window overlooking Crystal Lake, she tried to calm herself. *I need more proof. I can't accuse my father of an affair based on a couple Alex saw in the lobby of my apartment.* Reaching for her purse and keys, she loaded her dishwasher and stepped into the garage. *I can't put this off any longer.*

Chapter 99

After a PTA meeting, where Hope assisted the principal and other key educators field parents' questions about a variety of hot topic issues from test scores, bullying, scholarships, school safety, sports, and fundraising for new computers, she trudged back to her office. Drained, she straightened her desk and turned off the computer. As her office phone rang, she tucked it between her ear and shoulder. Half paying attention, she flipped the calendar over to the following day to review her first student appointment.

"Hope Truman."

"Hey," a man said.

Instantly recognizing the Nashville cowboy's voice, Hope was suddenly full of energy. "Hey." She smiled into the phone.

His voice was soft. "Sorry I haven't called."

"I didn't think I'd ever hear from you again."

Hesitating, Tucker said, "I was afraid of that."

Switching ears, Hope leaned back in her squeaky chair and hoped a student wouldn't utilize her open-door policy. "Did you lose my cell number?"

Chuckling, Tucker said, "As a matter of fact, the washing machine ate it. I forgot to remove the napkin when I laundered my overalls. Your number was in shreds."

"I see." Relieved, Hope said, "I'm glad you remembered I work at Hilltop."

"Yeah, it didn't come to me right away. I've had family business and been in Alabama."

"Oh?"

His voice grew somber. "My first cousin died in a motorcycle accident. I took over a week off to be with my aunt and uncle in Alabama. He was their only son. They're understandably destroyed." Pausing, he said, "I'm not playin' games. I'm not that type. I'll give you my aunt's phone number. She'll verify I was there."

Eyes filling with unfamiliar tears, Hope almost whispered, "No need. I believe you. I'm sorry about your cousin." Forcing confidence she didn't realize she possessed, she said, "I was hoping you'd call. I've missed you."

"How 'bout dinner sometime?"

Wanting to be coy like Alex, Hope blurted out, "Yes, sure, when?"

"It'll be a couple of weeks. Since I took vacation days for the funeral, I've got a two-week, long-haul gig, but you're at the top of my list when I return."

Hope had never smiled wider. "I'll be waiting."

Chapter 100

Gripping the steering wheel of her grandmother's red Mercedes, Cheri's knuckles whitened. After deciding she would come clean to Cole, she wanted to go whole hog. At least she thought that was the saying she overheard in the pool hall at Lefty's in what seemed like forever ago.

The jetlag from her whirlwind New York trip with Sebastian, followed by a late night at Coconuts, and concern over her parents' marriage had given her a nearly blinding headache. Worried about how she would explain her then-engagement to the cowboy, she had tossed and turned the night before. *I don't have anyone to blame but me.*

As she rounded one curve after another, her mouth went dry. Several possibilities flooded her mind, none of which comforted her. *Is Cole still interested? Will he be home? Will Jade be snuggled up with him—or worse? Will Cole speak to me after Sebastian showed up in the woods?* Her stomach churned. *I can't believe I fell for Sebastian's antics. Cole is the one I care about. He's the one I-I don't know exactly how I feel, but I've never felt like this.* She slammed her fist on the steering wheel. *Why did I do this to him? To us?*

A tear slid down her cheek as she swerved to miss a turtle. Watching the turtle spin in her rearview mirror, she winced. She glanced back at the road and noticed the turtle had steadied himself. *Thank goodness. I don't need bad karma.*

Rounding another curve, followed by a steep hill, she hit a pothole and blew a tire. *Crap. I'm not changing it. I've got to get to Cole.* Slowing to a crawl—much like the turtle—the car limped along the winding country roads. A cow mooed in the distance almost in harmony with the *thump thump thump* of her flat. Cheri's mind raced. *I've probably lost Cole forever.*

After driving over several narrow, rolling hills, Cheri managed to wave back to the friendly drivers in the rare, oncoming traffic. She glanced at acres of green pasture and wildlife on either side of the road. A young girl rode a horse in a pasture. Several cows stood belly deep in a pond. Grinning, Cheri again thought about how different—and nice—the country was from the big city.

Glancing at Cole's business card, she double checked the address, and studied her GPS system. *I'm getting close.* Breaking out in a sweat as she rounded a bend toward a gravel road, she attempted to distract herself by turning on a country station. "God's Country" by Blake Shelton filled the air. *He's right. This is God's country.* An enormous field of daisies caught her eye. *Daisies are my favorite. Maybe this is a sign.*

Turning up the volume in an attempt to drown out the rhythmic, noisy flat tire, Cheri listened to the words in an attempt to calm herself. It didn't work. As she approached Cole's house, her heart raced when she spotted his blue Chevy pickup. *He's home. What will I say? What if he slams the door in my face? What if Jade's inside?*

She parked, turned the ignition off, and leaned back. Taking several deep cleansing breaths, she gathered her purse before she lost her nerve. Wobbling in heels across the crunchy gravel, she crossed the grass, and stepped onto the homey, wide front porch. A welcoming swing hung on one end. Her heart pounded. *Here goes nothing.*

Cheri raised her hand to knock on the front door but her fist froze in mid-air. *Who do I think I am barging back into his life? He thinks I left him in the woods for my fiancé, which I did.* Raking her fingers through her hair, she lost her nerve. *Why would he take me back? We're from two different worlds. This isn't fair to him.*

Eyes brimming with tears, Cheri dropped her hand to her side and tiptoed off the porch.

As the screen door creaked open, she froze mid-step.

"Thought I heard a car. Didn't expect you, though."

Feeling like a schoolgirl, Cheri relaxed when she saw Cole's warm smile. Nervously switching her purse from side to side as she lingered on the porch step, she studied his kind face. The cowboy was even more handsome than she remembered. His tight jeans fit in all the right places and his white tee showcased his deep tan. Muscles flexing as he leisurely posed with one arm on the door frame and a hand in his pocket, he was obviously enjoying her awkwardness.

"Where's what's-his-name?" Rubbing his chin, Cole said, "You know the guy." He snapped his fingers. "Now I remember. Your fiancé."

Chewing on her lip, Cheri chose her words carefully. "I deserve that. Sebastian's in New York. And . . . he's my *former* fiancé."

Shielding his eyes with his hand, Cole made an exaggerated look around the yard. "Are you sure he didn't hitch a ride? I don't want any more surprises."

Spreading her arms, Cheri said, "No one's here but me. Sebastian won't be sneaking up on us again, I promise. I broke off our engagement." She swallowed, awaiting his reaction.

"That's a good start." Cole stared at the driveway. His eyebrows shot up when he noticed her Mercedes. "Not too shabby."

Shrugging, Cheri said, "This was my nana's car." Stepping toward him, she said, "I'll be happy to start from the beginning."

He studied her face. "I don't need to hear every little detail, but the guy in the woods was a whopper."

"I'm sorry. I should have been honest with him—and with you." New tears filled her eyes. "Our date was perfect, you were perfect, and I ruined everything." She blew out her breath while the cowboy studied her. After an awkward silence, Cheri stammered, almost afraid to hear his answer. "I hope you'll forgive me. Um, are you alone?"

"Not now." Cole took two steps and wrapped his arm around her waist. "Come here, New York." Brushing Cheri's hair out of her eyes, he traced the outline of her face, tipped up her chin, and pressed his lips against hers.

Cheri's body melted into his. After a lingering kiss, she whispered. "You're not mad?"

"Not any more. We've all got baggage."

Cheri gazed into Cole's clear blue eyes. Swiping at a lone tear streaming down her cheek, she said, "I never should have gone back to New York with Sebastian. Before I came to Crystal City over a year ago, I had already decided to break off our engagement. I hadn't bothered to tell anyone—not even myself." Shifting from foot to foot, she stared at the porch swing to avoid his eager eyes. "There's more." Lowering her voice to almost a whisper, she gulped and said, "For one, you need to know my real name. I'm Cheri Van Buren." She glanced up, half winced, and forced herself to hold his gaze.

The cowboy didn't flinch at her wealthy surname. Cheri assumed he didn't read the society pages and knew she had to have that uncomfortable conversation soon but decided to tackle one major hurdle at a time. She didn't want to overwhelm him.

Winking, Cole extended his hand. "Cole Cash. Now, stop talking." Pulling Cheri closer, he covered her mouth with his. After kissing her cheeks, forehead, and neck, he said, "Are you going to stand on the porch all day or come inside?"

Cheri blew out a sigh of relief and beamed. "Let me get my suitcase."

His mouth curved into a smile. "Pretty sure of yourself, I see."

She felt a blush creep up her neck. "Not really. I don't know, I—"

Lifting Cheri with ease, Cole carried her across the threshold. "Your suitcase can wait. 'Bout time you came back, New York. Welcome home."

Also from **Soul Mate Publishing** and **Beth Carter**:

THURSDAYS AT COCONUTS
(Coconuts Series Book 1)

As the go-to wedding planner, Suzy can't find her own wedded bliss and has one shocker of a wedding day. It doesn't help that she's still pining for her high school sweetheart, the one who got away. Handling neurotic brides is the best part of Suzy's day until her son brings home a bombshell from Europe.

Alexandra, a beautiful marketer with a "touch" of OCD, falls for a bad-boy cop who's married and possibly stalking her. But he sure is sexy. Alex tries to stay at arm's length after she puts her job—and life—on the line for the officer who isn't always a gentleman.

Hope hates her name, looks, and frizzy hair. As a high school counselor, she dishes out sage advice to students, yet can't see she's enabling her deadbeat, stuck-in-the-seventies hippie parents. After tragedy strikes, she reexamines their relationship and discovers a secret that almost went to the grave.

Friends since high school, the thirty-something women meet every Thursday at Coconuts for their own form of friendapy.

Available now on Amazon: THURSDAYS AT COCONUTS

CHAOS AT COCONUTS
(Coconuts Series Book 2)

To most, Coconuts is simply a bar. But for three best friends, it's their oasis. That is, until everything comes crashing down.

Socialite Cheri Van Buren makes a splashy, paparazzi-filled visit to Coconuts. Secretly dabbling in disastrous online dating, the wealthy caterer desires normalcy away from the society pages. A few girlfriends would be nice too.

Hope's life is routine, if not dull. The most exciting part of her day is counseling students until a monster tornado heads toward Hilltop High. Now she's in shock—and not just from the devastating twister.

Alex oversees a marketing intern from hell who appears intent on stealing her job. Her relationship with her sexy cop boyfriend isn't so sexy, especially after his ex-wife stalks her.

Suzy's new marriage is challenged by her surly teen stepdaughter, a unique Halloween wedding, and her son's ever-changing nuptials. If that isn't enough, the family discovers an astonishing revelation requiring a giant leap of faith.

Will the women overcome the chaos or will it tear them apart?

Available now on Amazon: <u>CHAOS AT COCONUTS</u>

BABIES AT COCONUTS
(Coconuts Series Book 3)

A clash of cultures.
A chaotic wedding.
A surprise baby.
Just another day at Coconuts.

Coordinating the most joyous day of her son's life should be easy. After all, Suzy is a wedding planner. But a meddling future mother-in-law wasn't on the checklist. A wacky rehearsal dinner, a beach wedding, and a baby—not necessarily in that order—ensures bedlam, if not hilarity, among the two head-butting moms. The show must go on, with or without the wedding party.

Hope is adept at counseling students but has given up on dieting and having sleek hair. She has even gotten used to the fact that her adopted father no longer remembers her—until a surprise engagement and a newspaper article leave her in shambles.

Sexy banker Alex conveys *totally in control* while ignoring the simmering boil of her disastrous relationship. Her marketing rival is her kryptonite, but a disastrous bank event may spell her downfall.

Socialite Cheri Van Buren seems to have the perfect life. The New Yorker deftly juggles celebrity events but is growing concerned about her jet-setting parents' strained marriage. After competing in a cake-decorating contest, another chef leaves her speechless.

More than a Happy Hour haven, Coconuts is the unknowing guardian of shared secrets, bombshell revelations, a few tears, and joy. Will the best friends ever find happiness? It doesn't look good.

Available now on Amazon: **BABIES AT COCONUTS**

SLEEPING WITH ELVIS

Pepper Langley, an unemployed preschool teacher with a fear of flying and boating, hopes a vacation to remote Key Lime Island will bolster her confidence and salvage her relationship with her rogue boyfriend. From tiny Nowhere, Arkansas, she scrimped all year to afford the lavish trip, but a deadly storm changes everything.

Gorgeous Elvis impersonator Ty Townsend flees to Key Lime Island between gigs. During this hiatus, he reevaluates his profession after twice forgetting the King's lyrics. He craves the isle's solitude—far away from social media haters—where he shares beach life with a cursing parrot. The last thing on his mind is a woman, especially one who isn't supposed to be there.

Will their secrets tear them apart or will they find happiness on the sand and stage?

Available now on Amazon: **SLEEPING WITH ELVIS**

Beth Carter

After being a bank vice president and a hospital public relations director, Beth Carter shed her suits and heels to reinvent herself at a certain mid-life age. While drinking copious amounts of coffee, she has penned: THURSDAYS AT COCONUTS, CHAOS AT COCONUTS, BABIES AT COCONUTS, COWBOYS AT COCONUTS, SLEEPING WITH ELVIS, MIRACLE ON AISLE TWO, and SANTA BABY, a novelette.

Carter is a multi-award winning author of a 2015 RONE Award, named Best Debut Author in 2015, and a 2017 & 2018 RAVEN Award runner-up for Favorite Contemporary.

The author also writes children's picture books including WHAT DO YOU WANT TO BE?, SOUR POWER, THE MISSING KEY, and SANTA'S SECRET. Additionally, her work appears in four six-word memoir collections and numerous anthologies.

Splitting her time between Missouri and Florida, Beth Carter is often found writing at Starbucks—if she isn't shopping at T.J. Maxx, boating, or watching deer in her backyard.

~ ~ ~

Connect with Beth Carter here:

Website:
http://bethcarter.com

Facebook:
https://www.facebook.com/authorbethcarter

Twitter:
https://twitter.com/bethcarter007

Amazon Author Page:
http://amazon.com/author/bethcarter

BookBub:
https://www.bookbub.com/authors/beth-carter

Beth's Book Babes – Request an invitation to this online private reader group through the author's website, www.bethcarter.com

CPSIA information can be obtained
at www.ICGtesting.com
Printed in the USA
BVHW040145260420
578531BV00014B/856